Shadow
OF A
DOUBT

Also by Tiffany Snow

Shadow
OF A
DOUBT

A TANGLED IVY NOVEL

TIFFANY
SNOW

Text copyright © 2015 Tiffany Snow

Published by Montlake Romance, Seattle

www.apub.com

Amazon, the Amazon logo, and Montlake Romance are trademarks of Amazon.com, Inc., or its affiliates.

ISBN-13: 9781477829103
ISBN-10: 1477829105

Cover design by Jason Blackburn

Library of Congress Control Number: 2014958173

Printed in the United States of America

For Leslie, whose friendship and loyalty I cherish.

PROLOGUE

He came in the dead of night.

I was accustomed to his unannounced arrivals, so when I woke to the feel of a man sliding under the sheets with me, I wasn't afraid.

He was already naked and it only took a moment for him to slip my nightgown over my head and toss it aside. He kissed me and I wrapped my arms around his neck, pressing my body against his.

His skin was warm, his body hard. His taste and touch were drugs I craved more fiercely than the most avid heroin addict.

We didn't speak. I didn't welcome him home or ask about his day. He couldn't tell me about his job even if he wanted to, though I didn't suspect that fact bothered him. It was the nature of spies to be secretive, but since I'd known only one, I supposed I wasn't an expert on the subject.

These thoughts were driven from my mind as his hands skated down my body. He shifted my legs apart, moving to lie between my spread thighs. I focused on him, memorizing the feel of him pressing against me.

The night passed in a blur of whispered sighs and moans, sweat and skin beneath tangled sheets, until the pleasure he'd wrung from me forced me into an exhausted and sated slumber.

When I woke to sunlight streaming through my window, he was gone.

CHAPTER ONE

I was hard-pressed to keep a stupid grin off my face as I got ready for work.

Devon had come last night.

It had been weeks since I'd seen him, each night going to bed hopeful, each morning waking up disappointed. My cell phone hadn't rung with a call in the middle of the night, the number blocked. Its silence mocked me.

But I hadn't been disappointed last night.

My body still tingled when I thought about what had passed in the early hours of the morning, a shiver running down my spine.

I finished running a brush though my hair—long, straight, and pure white-blonde. My makeup was minimal. Some would say I was fortunate to have been born pretty, but it had always been more of a curse than blessing to me. Though without my looks, I might never have caught Devon's eye.

Some men were attracted to lush figures, which I didn't have. Tall and on the too-skinny side of thin, I had the perfect shape to wear the designer clothes I couldn't afford that filled my closet. That shape was not one men usually drooled over.

Other men were all about the face. Devon was one of those men. He didn't seem to mind my angles and planes where there should be soft curves. He liked my face. He liked it a lot. And he'd once told me he liked the way I moved, the way I walked.

Maybe influenced by one too many runway shows, I tried to do justice to the clothes I wore. So I stood tall, shoulders back, chin up, and sashayed my ass down the street, usually in four-inch heels. It made me feel good about myself and gave me a confidence that had taken me years to acquire.

Glancing at my watch, I saw I was going to be late for work if I didn't hurry. Worcester Bank opened early and I had to be there even earlier for my job as a teller. I'd been daydreaming of last night, putting me behind schedule.

I hurried into the kitchen, then grabbed a mug and filled it with coffee. I needed a quick fix before I left. That's when I saw it.

A stack of money on the kitchen counter.

I stared in confusion for a moment, then set aside my mug and reached for the money. Next to it was a note.

For anything you might need.
-D

Absently, I counted the stack. It was about a half-inch tall and only contained hundreds. When I was through counting, I just stood in amazement.

Ten thousand dollars. Devon had left ten thousand dollars just . . . sitting on the kitchen counter.

My happiness abruptly deflated like a popped balloon. Last night had seemed special—a wonderful reunion after too many weeks apart. But now it was sordid, tainted by money left figuratively on the bedside table, as though Devon were compensating me for having sex with him. I lived in his apartment, for which he paid all the bills, but that seemed . . . different than a pile of cold, hard cash.

I didn't know what to do with the money. I couldn't leave it sitting out. Back in the bedroom, I hesitated, then put it in the top drawer of the nightstand. That was probably the most appropriate place for it anyway, I thought somewhat bitterly.

Now I was really late for work. I drove my own car although I had the keys for Devon's Porsche. He'd left them when he'd left the keys to his apartment and a directive to move out of my best friend Logan's place and into his. But driving such an expensive car made me nervous, so my old sedan was preferable.

Marcia, another teller at the bank and one of my few close friends, was pouring herself a cup of coffee in the break room by the time I hurriedly clocked in and tossed my lunch into the communal refrigerator.

"Oh, pour me a cup, too, please," I said, somewhat breathless from my dash into the building after I'd parked my car.

She obliged, pouring a second cup and eyeing me. "You look a little tired today," she said. "Everything okay?"

"Devon came last night," I said, taking the cup from her. We fell into step together as we walked to the front of the bank and to our teller booths.

"It's April and you started this . . . relationship . . . on New Year's," she said. "Six times in four months, that should make you happy." Her voice was carefully even. She didn't really "get" my relationship with Devon, but wanted to support my decisions, which was more than I could say for Logan.

"I was," I said, pausing outside my booth, "but then this morning, I saw he'd left money on the kitchen counter."

Marcia raised her eyebrows. "Money?" I nodded. She frowned. "How much?"

I glanced around before answering, then lowered my voice. "Ten thousand dollars."

Her eyes flew open wide. "Ten thousand—"

"Shh!" I glanced around again, but no one had paid attention.

"Ten thousand dollars," she said again, this time much more quietly, but no less astounded. "Are you kidding me right now?"

I shook my head. "I counted it."

"Did he talk to you about it?"

"No. He just left a note."

"And it said?" she prompted.

I pulled the scrap of paper from my pocket and handed it to her. She read it, then handed it back.

"What do you think it means?" I asked.

She shrugged. "I have no idea, but you know I don't understand how this relationship works anyway. Maybe it's just what he says. Some money in case you need it."

"But I'm already living in his apartment. He pays all the bills. Why would I need money?"

"Girl, if you think you're going to get sympathy from me because your boyfriend gave you ten grand to spend on whatever you want, you're looking in the wrong place." Her dry comment prodded a grin out of me.

We had to stop there because customers had entered the building. I was busy all day and when I did pause to eat lunch and chat with Marcia, we didn't talk about Devon or dissect the events of last night. Not that it stopped me from dwelling on it all day.

Was I making a big deal out of nothing? Ten thousand dollars was a lot of money. Maybe it was a goodbye gift? Maybe I wouldn't see him again?

The thought made my stomach clench as anxiety struck. Surely he'd tell me if he wasn't coming back? He wouldn't just leave and not say a word?

But I wasn't one-hundred-percent sure he wouldn't do just that.

I had no way of reaching him. When he called, his number was always blocked, and he didn't call that often anyway. There was no predictable pattern to it and he rarely stayed on the line for long.

Warm spring air greeted me when I stepped out of the building a little after six o'clock. I was tired. The lack of sleep last night and a long day at work had taken their toll and I couldn't wait to get home and relax.

Home.

Was that how I thought of Devon's apartment? Home?

It was the closest thing I had to a home since moving to St. Louis from Dodge City, Kansas, last summer. I'd stayed with Logan for a while, but then Devon had swept into my life and one of his conditions for *remaining* in my life was that I move out of Logan's place and into his. Since he was hardly ever home, I had the place to myself. A perk I'd gladly give up if it meant I'd get to see him more often. Six times over the past four months wasn't enough, especially when the longest visit had been only ten hours.

I unlocked and climbed into my car, tossing my purse onto the passenger seat. I pulled my door shut with a slam just as the rear door opened and a man slid into the backseat.

Alarmed, I reached for my door handle. "Hey! What're you—"

But I was cut off when he reached over the seat and took a fistful of my hair, yanking my head back. I gasped in pain, and with my next breath, I felt the cold slide of a blade against my throat.

"Hallo, luv. Been a while, eh?"

I caught sight of the man in my rearview mirror.

Clive.

He used to work with Devon, if I used the term *work* loosely. The details were sketchy. What I did know was that he'd once betrayed Devon and left him for dead, and that Clive's brand-new wife had been murdered by a poison that had also infected me. I, however, had survived.

I swallowed. "What do you want?" I asked, proud of my steady voice.

"I want Anna back, but that's never going to happen," he said, speaking of his dead wife. "So I'll settle for the next best thing."

He stopped and I thought he wanted me to ask what that was. His fingers pulled harder at my hair and tears of pain burned at the corners of my eyes. My fingernails dug into my seat as I scrambled to think what to do.

"What's that?" I managed.

"Revenge."

Ice-cold panic flooded through me. He was going to kill me. I could almost taste it.

"Anna didn't deserve to die. She was innocent," he said.

"Killing me won't bring Anna back," I said. "I'm innocent, too."

"Yes, but I don't care about you, darling. Besides, I'm not going to kill you. Not yet, anyway. I want Devon."

My mouth went dry. "I-I don't know where he is."

"Of course you don't. No one knows where Devon is unless he wants them to know. You're the bait . . . and I'm the hook. See you soon, Ivy."

Clive was up and out of my car as quickly as he'd entered, leaving me a shaky, trembling mess.

I didn't go anywhere. I just sat there, thinking furiously. Clive was back. He wanted to kill Devon and was waiting until he came back to strike. Which meant he was watching me.

No way could I just drive to Devon's apartment and lead Clive right there. That would be really dumb. But where else could I go? It wasn't like I could sit in the car in the bank's parking lot all night.

The first person I thought of was Logan, my best friend. But we'd had a falling out recently and things were still dicey. If he knew that I was in danger again because of Devon, he'd go crazy. He hated Devon as it was and this wouldn't convince him otherwise. Not that it'd be a good idea even if he could tolerate Devon. It wasn't like I wanted to lead a psychopath to Logan's door.

The same was true of the rest of my friends. No one needed to be involved in my drama, especially if it might put them in danger. So that left . . .

Picking up my cell, I scrolled through my contacts until I hit upon the one I wanted. After a moment's hesitation, I dialed the number. I wasn't sure he would pick up, but after several rings, he answered.

"Agent Lane."

"Scott," I said. "I'm sorry to bother you. It's—"

"Ivy, yeah, hey! It's good to hear from you," he interrupted.

I winced a little at the enthusiasm in his voice, wondering if this was a bad idea. Scott had wanted to go out on a date after New Year's and at first that would've been fine. But then Devon had come back into my life and I'd had to turn Scott down when he asked for that date. Not wanting to divulge Devon's presence stateside, I'd made up an excuse about not being ready to start dating again. He'd taken the rejection with good grace.

"How are you doing?" he asked.

"Um, well, not so good," I replied. "I'm having some trouble and I thought maybe you might be willing to help me."

"Trouble?" he asked, his voice turning cautious. "What's going on?"

I glanced around the parking lot, uneasy. Was Clive still out there somewhere? Watching? "Maybe I can meet you someplace?" I asked.

"Where are you?"

"I'm at work."

"Okay, there's a restaurant not far from there called Claddagh's. It's an Irish pub. Do you know it?"

I did.

"Go there. I'm only fifteen minutes away."

The pub was busy, but not too crowded, and I slid into a booth in the back to wait. The waitress came by and I ordered a glass of wine to steady my nerves.

"Ivy, it's so good to see you."

I looked up just as Scott leaned down and gave me a brief hug, then sat in the seat opposite me. The waitress returned, dropping off my wine and taking an order for a beer from him. She left and he scrutinized me, his expression shifting into a frown.

"You look a little pale," he said. "What happened?"

I took a deep breath and launched into my story, recounting the history between Devon and Clive, from how Clive had betrayed Devon and left him to die, to how Devon had tracked Clive here a few months ago, and ending with the tragic death of Clive's bride, Anna.

"Devon demanded to know who Clive was working for when he'd betrayed Devon, but it turned out he'd only done what he had to in order to protect his wife, Anna. But instead of Devon being able to help save her, she was poisoned by the virus and died . . . horribly." I shuddered, remembering how the blood had poured from her eyes and ears.

"But they destroyed that virus, right?" Scott asked, referring to the synthesized airborne pathogen a company had created with the intention of selling it to the highest bidder. It was deadly, acted much like the Ebola virus, only faster, and there was no known cure.

Except for me. The only person walking around with the vaccine flowing through her veins.

"I think so," I said. "Devon told me he'd erased all their data and that everything that had been made was gone."

Scott's eyes narrowed. "I don't like the fact that the only thing we have to go on is Devon's word that a virus with the potential to wipe out eighty percent of the world's population is no longer a threat."

I shrugged helplessly. I had no way of reassuring Scott and I wasn't about to tell him that I carried the vaccine.

He sighed, then gestured for me to continue. "Sorry for interrupting," he said. "What's going on that you're in trouble?"

"Well, I told you all of that so I could tell you how he showed up today," I said. "Clive."

"Showed up? Showed up where?"

"In my car. The backseat. He held a knife to my throat and told me he wanted revenge." Saying it made me relive it, and I took another fortifying gulp of wine.

"He held a knife to your throat?" Scott sounded pissed, his eyes narrowing. "And you say his name is Clive?" He took a notebook from his pocket and jotted down a few notes. "His wife was Anna. Any idea what happened to her body?"

"I don't know," I said, somewhat confused by the question. "I'd assume it was burned since she was infectious."

"I need to check on that, but you're probably right," he said, still writing. "Our labs will want to study the body if it hasn't been destroyed."

"I'm afraid to go home," I blurted, and Scott glanced up from his notebook. "I don't know if he knows where I live, and I don't want to lead him there if he doesn't. He said he wants to use me to get to Devon."

Scott frowned. "Why would he think using you would get to Devon? He left months ago."

This was the part I'd been dreading. I didn't speak and I felt my cheeks get warm. Scott's eyebrows lifted.

"Ivy," he said. "He *did* leave months ago, right? You haven't seen or heard from him since Paris, right?"

I couldn't look in his eyes any longer. My gaze dropped, which was answer enough for Scott. He muttered a harsh curse.

"Tell me."

I swallowed hard, then answered. "He came back. Explained to me why he'd done what he had. Told me he wanted me to move into his place."

"So he's here now?" Scott interrupted. "You didn't want to lead Clive to Devon at his apartment?"

"No," I said. "I live in his apartment, but he's rarely here. He's only been back a handful of times since New Year's."

"Since New Year's," Scott repeated, and I saw understanding dawn in his eyes. "So when you turned me down . . ."

"I'm sorry," I said. "I didn't know if the FBI would still be looking for him. I didn't want to lie to you."

"But you did," he said, bitterness in his voice.

"I didn't have a choice."

"I don't agree with that, but it's neither here nor there at this point," he said. "So Clive had the opportunity to kill you, but didn't. He wants Devon."

"Right."

"Well, just call him," Scott said with a shrug. "If you're afraid he's monitoring your cell or something, you can use mine. Warn Devon about Clive, then tell him to get his ass back here and take care of it. It's not like you need some psycho holding a knife to your throat." He dug his cell phone from his pocket and held it out to me, but I didn't take it.

"Um, I can't," I said.

"Can't what?"

"Can't call Devon."

"Why not?"

This was so awkward, I hated even having to say it. "I don't have his number," I confessed. "Or any other way to reach him."

Scott looked at me in disbelief, surprise rendering him momentarily speechless. Then he said, "You have no way to communicate with Devon? No phone number or emergency contact information?"

I shook my head.

"What if you need something?" he asked, and now I could see anger building in his eyes. "He just pops into town whenever he feels like it and leaves the same way?"

It was about a thousand times worse hearing Scott say this than Marcia. At least Marcia was a woman and didn't judge me—women the world over did stupid things for men and we all knew it. But having a man look at me like I was out of my mind to allow myself to be in a relationship like this . . . I wasn't able to keep my mortification at bay and I could feel my face burning.

"I didn't say it was a perfect relationship," I murmured, at a loss as to what else I could say.

"A perfect—are you kidding me?" Scott fumed. "You're in danger and have no way to reach him. It's not a relationship, Ivy. It's called having a fuck buddy."

I felt the blood drain from my face at the utter scorn and derision in his words.

"Excuse me." I slid out of the booth. "I shouldn't have called you."

"No, wait," Scott said, jumping to his feet and catching hold of my arm. "I'm sorry, Ivy. I don't mean to sound so harsh. Please stay."

I stared at my feet, the ground blurring as unshed tears built in my eyes.

"I'm sorry," he repeated, and he did sound contrite. "Sit down. Please."

Finally, I gave a curt nod and sat back down in the booth. Scott took his seat again, too.

"Okay, so I won't go into my thoughts on how Devon is treating you," Scott said. "Let's just solve the problem, okay?"

I looked up at him. "Sounds good."

Scott took a good look at my watery eyes and his jaw tightened, but he didn't say anything.

"So you can't go to Devon's apartment because you'll lead this Clive guy there," Scott said. "And I'm assuming you don't want to lead Clive to where you used to live either, right?"

I nodded. "Plus, Logan and I aren't exactly getting along right now," I said.

"Somehow I doubt he'd care about that if he knew you were in trouble."

I didn't argue. It was probably true, but that didn't change the fact that I wasn't going to drag Logan into it.

"So I guess I see why you called me," Scott said with an almost imperceptible sigh.

"I thought . . . since you're an FBI agent . . . you might be able to help me," I said. "I don't want Clive to climb into my car again." My throat thickened and I had to brush a hand across my eyes.

"Shh, it'll be okay," Scott said, reaching across the table and taking my hand. "Let's get some dinner and we'll figure it out, okay?"

He sounded so kind and capable, his hand reassuring on mine, and I nodded.

We had dinner—well, Scott ate. I mostly picked at a salad, his words about Devon echoing inside my head. Combined with what I knew to be Marcia's disapproval, plus Logan's, it seemed everyone thought what Devon and I had was a complete and utter joke that was entirely on me.

Scott made small talk, asking me how my job was going and things like that, which I readily answered. We steered carefully clear of talk about Devon. I saw his eyes flick appreciatively over me a couple of times and I regretted my choice in clothes for the day. I'd worn a Michael Kors dress I'd found on the clearance rack at Nordstrom that I loved, but I was afraid maybe it was sending the wrong message to Scott.

The top was tight and black with a low-cut scoop neckline, while the skirt was tan with a black trim that edged an open slit reaching from the hem at mid-calf to my upper thigh. I didn't have a lot of cleavage to display, but the black and gold belt made my waist look tiny and the dress showed a lot of leg, which I had plenty of. Paired with my gold crisscross espadrille wedges, it was a businesslike yet still sexy outfit. Clothes were my Achilles' heel and I liked dressing well, though my bank account didn't appreciate my shopping habits.

I tried to pay for dinner, but Scott insisted. He took my elbow as we walked outside. The evening was cool, but the sun was setting a little later every day, so the last rays of sunshine still lit the twilight sky.

"Why don't you come and stay with me for a few days," Scott suggested. "Until you have time to figure this out. I'll drive you to Devon's apartment for some clothes and we'll go from there."

I was taken aback, though his kindness shouldn't have surprised me. "Um, I don't know," I said. "That sounds like an awful inconvenience for you."

Scott shrugged, smiling ruefully. "I'm a sucker for a damsel in distress."

I didn't smile back. I didn't like being the said damsel, and I didn't want to have to be saved. "I'd rather just be a damsel in a normal life."

He shook his head, his expression turning grim. "That won't happen until you break it off with Devon."

I couldn't argue with that, and neither could I argue with his plan to let me stay with him for a few days. I could leave a note for Devon . . . for whenever he decided to come back.

We drove in his car and I directed him to Devon's apartment. He followed me inside the lobby, sticking quite close and gazing into the deepening shadows.

"Nice place," he observed, once we were exiting the elevator on Devon's floor.

I was unlocking the apartment when Beau poked his head out from his place across the hall.

"Hey there, Ivy," he said in his usual jovial way. "I heard two voices and thought maybe Devon had come back. I have an in for this amazing and rare merlot that I just know he'd totally love."

Beau was talking fast, but his shrewd gaze was sizing up Scott.

"Hi, Beau," I said. "No, he's not back yet. This is . . . my friend. Scott. Scott, this is Beau."

Beau stepped out, his smile friendly as he held out his hand to shake Scott's.

"Nice to meet you," Beau said. "Any friend of Ivy's is a friend of mine."

"I bet," Scott said, and I could tell by the way he said it that he'd already figured Beau out—a salesman who could sell ice to an Eskimo.

"Are you a wine guy?" Beau asked. "Because if you are, I've got—"

"I'm more of a beer kind of guy," Scott interrupted. "But thanks."

"Sure, man. No problem."

"We'll talk to you later," I said, walking into the darkened apartment. Beau waved as Scott followed me inside. I closed the door behind me and reached for the light switch. "Sorry about Beau. He's a very enthusiastic sales—"

I stopped talking.

"Holy shit," Scott breathed.

I had to agree.

It seemed Clive had already found the place . . . and completely trashed it.

The furniture was ripped apart, glass broken, the television shattered. Everything that could be destroyed had been. Red paint had been tossed over the entire apartment in drips and splatters. Against the whites and ivories of the fabric and carpet, it was garish and macabre.

"Oh my God," I breathed, taking a step forward. Scott grabbed me, yanking me to a halt.

"Don't move," he said. He was looking down at the floor in front of me. I followed his gaze. Saw nothing.

"What is it?" I asked.

He nodded toward my feet. "There's a trip wire. Do you see it? It's transparent. Difficult to spot."

I looked harder and after a few moments, I saw it. Barely two inches in front of my leg, it was a hair-thin wire that ran across the entry, but I couldn't see what the ends were attached to. Not that it mattered. I was sure whoever had done this hadn't rigged it so that balloons and confetti rained down on the one who triggered the wire.

"Now what?" I asked.

"Now we very slowly and very carefully retrace our steps out of here," Scott said. "And I'll call the bomb squad."

A bomb.

Scott kept a tight grip on my arm, carefully leading us backward and out the door to the hallway. Moments later, he was on his phone and I heard sirens in the distance. He banged on Beau's door, ordering him to take me outside and not let me out of his sight, then he began evacuating the rest of the building.

The bomb squad came, along with a lot of other official-looking people, both in uniform and out of uniform. A few of them wanted to ask me questions, and Scott helped me field those.

It was a friend's apartment. No, I didn't know where he was. No, I didn't know who would have done that, and so on.

"Hey, Lane," a man called out, heading toward us. Scott turned as he approached. "Good job spotting that," he said. "The wire was hooked to a bomb loaded with shrapnel. Guaranteed to kill anyone within a ten-foot radius and leave nothing but body parts behind."

A shudder went through me. I'd nearly set off that bomb. If Scott hadn't seen it . . .

"Any prints?" Scott asked, taking my hand in his and slotting our fingers together. It was reassuring and I held on much too tightly.

"Doubtful," the man said. "It was skillfully made and triggered. Whoever did that isn't dumb enough to leave prints behind. But we'll check."

"Thanks," Scott said. "Has the rest of the place been checked out?"

"Yeah. We're giving the all-clear to the other residents now."

Scott led me by the hand back up into the apartment. I hesitated at the open door.

"It's okay," he assured me. "If the guys say it's clear, then it's clear."

His obvious faith and trust in the competence of his friends helped ease my fear. We headed inside.

I wasted little time in throwing clothes that were salvageable and other necessities in a suitcase. While it may have been safe, the devastation done to the apartment and the yellow police tape that now surrounded it were unnerving. I thought about leaving Devon a note, then discarded the idea. It wasn't like he wouldn't see that something had obviously happened. He knew how to reach me, if he wanted to.

That last thought was bitter, and I realized that some of what everyone else saw in our relationship was beginning to sink in to me, too. I'd been terrorized twice today, by the same man that Devon knew was alive and who had betrayed him once before. Devon had barely spoken to me the other night, hadn't even asked how I was doing or anything about my life. We'd had sex and he'd left after leaving the money on the counter.

Speaking of which . . .

I threw that in the bottom of my suitcase, too, piling my clothes on top of it. If I was going to be playing a cat-and-mouse game with Clive, then I might need that money.

"Ready," I said, rolling my suitcase into the kitchen where Scott stood, waiting.

"Did you want to leave him a note or something?" he asked.

I tipped my chin up a notch. "No. He's a smart man. I'm sure he'll figure it out." I shrugged. "Or not. Perhaps his current fuck buddy will keep him too occupied for him to care what happens to me."

Scott's lips tipped up in an appreciative grin. "Let's go then."

Beau and his sixth sense had him popping out of his apartment again as we left.

"You okay?" he asked me in an undertone. Scott took the hint and continued down the hall, where he pressed the button for the elevator.

I nodded. "I'm fine. I'm just going to stay with Scott for a while. I have no idea when Devon is going to be back—if he'll be back."

"If I see him, want me to tell him where you are?"

Tell Devon I'd left and moved in with another man? I smiled. "Yes. Do that."

The elevator dinged and I hurried down the hall and into the waiting car next to Scott. The door slid shut.

CHAPTER TWO

Scott drove me back to my car and I followed him to his place. He lived in an older suburb about ten miles from downtown. The apartment building wasn't as new or luxurious as Devon's, but the neighborhood seemed decent. Scott took my suitcase and I followed him inside.

It was a two-story complex with four apartments on each level. We took the stairs up and went to the first door on the left. Scott unlocked it and pushed the door open, letting me precede him. When he stepped inside, he flipped on a nearby lamp.

The space immediately said "bachelor" to me, with a black leather sofa, bigger-than-appropriate television, and blank walls. But it was nice, the furniture tasteful and everything clean and picked up. There was no dirty laundry on the floor or dirty dishes lying around. No half-empty pizza boxes littered what I could see of the kitchen.

"How long have you lived here?" I asked.

"They assigned me here almost a year ago," he replied. "I have an extra bedroom I can put your things in. There's not currently a bed in there, but you can sleep in mine and I'll take the couch."

"You don't have to do that," I protested, feeling guilty. This guy had gone out of his way for me once before, and now he was doing it again. I knew he was interested in me, but I had nothing to offer him in return.

"I know I don't have to," he said, flashing me a grin. "I want to."

Our gazes caught and held. Scott was tall, even for me, and I was a tall woman at five foot nine. His shoulders were broad and well muscled, his hair and eyes both a deep chestnut. If not for Devon, Scott would have definitely caught my eye. He was a good man, an honest man, who I'd spent Christmas with walking the streets of Paris. While it had been a nightmare because of being stranded there and hunted by Devon, Scott had taken care of me and turned a horrible situation into a really nice memory.

"Thank you," I said, trying to put a lot of emphasis and meaning into those two words, because at the moment, I didn't know what I would've done without him.

"It's my pleasure," he said. "There's a bathroom in the hallway. Let me know if you need anything. I'll go make up the bed for you."

He left the room, closing the door behind him. I sighed, pushing a hand through my hair. He was right. Nothing was going to be normal in my life while Devon was still a part of it. But *was* he a part of it? *Fuck buddy.* Was that all I was to Devon? Scott was a man—he would know how men viewed these things. Maybe I'd been romanticizing the situation with Devon. He'd been the first man I'd ever had a successful and gratifying sexual relationship with. I'd been afraid that years of abuse at the hands of my stepbrother, Jace, had broken me permanently. Devon had changed all of that.

Maybe it was time to acknowledge the fact that I was nothing more than a sexual diversion, a liaison, for Devon and move on with my life.

But he wanted you to move into his apartment, my traitorous subconscious whispered. *Surely that means something.*

Well, maybe it did, but it didn't matter. It wasn't like he was around to share the apartment—or life—with me.

I dug for my toiletries and pajamas—soft pants with a matching camisole top—and headed into the bathroom. After scrubbing off my makeup, changing my clothes, and brushing out my hair, I felt more normal. Coming out of the bathroom, I spotted Scott in the living room sitting on the couch. When he saw me, he jumped to his feet.

"Can I get you something to drink? Are you hungry?" he asked. His gaze wandered over me and the Adam's apple in his throat bobbed when he swallowed.

"I'm fine," I said. It felt slightly awkward to be forced into a more intimate situation with someone that I didn't know all that well.

"I was just watching TV," he said. "Want to join me?"

"Sure."

The sofa was plenty big that I didn't have to sit right next to him, which would've been weird and uncomfortable. I was very conscious that I didn't want to lead him on in any way, though I knew he was attracted to me. I was attracted to him, too, but I already had a mucked-up relationship. I didn't need another.

We sat in companionable silence watching a Monsters of the Deep special on the Discovery Channel, though I wasn't paying much attention. After a while, I asked, "So what happens tomorrow?"

I didn't know how much attention Scott was paying either because he was quick to answer. Glancing at me, he said, "Tomorrow I'll get a report from forensics on the bomb. Maybe there were prints. Also, we'll go through some photographs, see if you can pick out Clive. If not, we'll get a sketch artist to work with you, see what we can come up with."

I breathed a little sigh of relief. He had a plan. That was good. Having a plan was good. Because I felt adrift and lost. And maybe it showed, because he reached out and took my hand again.

"You all right?" he asked.

I nodded. "Yeah. It's just . . . I have no place to call home at the moment. The man I thought was my boyfriend is nowhere to be found. And there's some psycho out there who wants to hurt me, maybe kill me, and is probably watching my every move." I shrugged. "All in all, I've had better days."

Scott's smile was sympathetic. "I know it sucks right now, but it'll be okay. You can stay here as long as you like. I'll keep you safe."

I decided to go for blunt honesty. Games weren't my thing.

"You know I can't offer you anything more," I said. "Not right now. Maybe not ever."

He shrugged. "I like you. I like being around you. More isn't necessary. I'll take what I can get."

I guessed he liked blunt honesty, too.

We hung out there like that until the end of the show. Scott kept hold of my hand, and I almost pulled away, but then thought it might get awkward and uncomfortable between us. I didn't want that, so I let it be.

"I think I'm going to go to bed," I said when the credits started to roll.

"Sure." He stood and led me into his bedroom. "Make yourself at home."

It was a nice room with a big bed. That pang of guilt struck again. "Are you sure about this?" I asked. "I could always go to a motel or something." Though the idea of being alone against whatever Clive had planned next made a chill run down my spine.

"I'm not a fragile flower," Scott said, turning down the covers on the bed. "The couch isn't exactly roughing it. Trust me."

I laughed a little at this. He did have a really nice couch.

"Okay. If you're sure."

"I am."

He smiled at me, his chocolate eyes warm, his jaw roughened

with a five-o'clock shadow. Yes, Scott was very easy on the eyes. If not for Devon . . .

"Good night," I said.

"'Night, Ivy." He softly closed the door on the way out.

I climbed into bed, the sheets soft from many washings. Scott's scent permeated the blankets and pillow, but it was comforting to me, and I fell asleep faster than I thought I would.

The buzzing of my cell phone woke me. Disoriented, I looked around the dark room, and it took a second for me to remember where I was. Then my phone buzzed again and I grabbed it off the table. Maybe it was Devon calling me.

"Hello?"

"Ivy, darling. You're having a sleepover! I take it you didn't like my extreme home makeover?"

My eyes went wide and I was fully awake. "Clive?"

"Perhaps not a dumb blonde after all," he said. "I was wondering if they'd still be picking up pieces of you scattered all over the street. I'm somewhat glad they're not. A bit more entertaining this way."

"Entertaining how?" I asked, my voice stiff.

"Gives me a bit of a challenge, playing with you whilst I await Devon's arrival."

"He's not coming," I said. "We're not in a relationship. I hardly ever see him. He may never come again."

"Oh, I can guarantee he will," Clive replied. "You see, Devon has one weakness."

"What's that?"

"A woman he allows himself to care for. And you, dear Ivy, have become that woman."

I squeezed my eyes shut, simultaneously glad to hear that maybe I meant something to Devon, and devastated that those feelings would be used against him.

"So he will come. Trust me on that."

"I don't want you to hurt Devon," I said. "Please. He was your friend—"

"Was," Clive interrupted. "But no longer."

I swallowed. "Are you going to kill me, too?"

"I was going to, but then I realized . . . you're hiding a secret, aren't you, Ivy?" His voice lowered to a whispering hiss. "And I love secrets."

The line went dead.

Staring into the darkness, I replayed the conversation in my head. There wasn't just one secret I was hiding, but two.

I glanced at my purse, where I'd hidden the pages from the journal—an encrypted recipe for the vaccine. No one besides Scott knew I had those pages, and even he didn't know what the code hid within them. I'd sent them to him for safekeeping and he'd returned them to me, but Devon thought I'd destroyed them. Even now I wondered if I should do that, but something wouldn't let me.

The next morning I was up early. I wasn't accustomed to sleeping in someone else's bed and the late night phone call from Clive had nightmares playing inside my head.

I knew what he was talking about when he said I had a secret, and it terrified me. Only one person other than Devon was still alive after knowing I'd been infected with the deadly virus . . . Clive. He alone knew that I shouldn't have survived. The fact that I was still alive meant I was immune, and immunity meant the virus could be weaponized and controlled.

Clive had worked for the same people Devon did—a British intelligence service called the Shadow—and Devon had told me if they knew I carried the vaccine to the virus in my blood, not even he could protect me from them. I wasn't supposed to know about the Shadow, but I'd been drawn into their plans and Devon had told me. There was a lot I didn't know, but what I did was enough to have me looking over my shoulder constantly.

Scott was in the kitchen by the time I'd showered and changed into black skinny jeans and a long-sleeved shirt. It was formfitting and in a thin enough material that I wore a camisole underneath. The deep rose color of the fabric went well with my fair skin and I left my hair long and straight.

"No sleeping in on a Saturday?" I asked. The smell of fresh coffee greeted me as I stepped into the sunny kitchen.

"No rest for the wicked," he replied with a grin. "Coffee?"

"Please."

He poured me a cup and I added cream and sugar from what was sitting on the counter—of course no man would have artificial sweetener—and I sat at the small, wooden table.

"Did you sleep well?" he asked.

"Yes," I lied. "Thank you." I hesitated, wondering if I should tell him about Clive, then I decided that I should. Scott was trying to protect me, after all, so it only seemed right that he should know Clive was watching and knew I was there.

"I got a phone call from Clive last night," I said.

Scott looked up sharply from where he'd been pouring his own cup of coffee. "He called you?"

I nodded. "The number was blocked, but he said he knew I was staying here."

"What else did he say?"

"Just scary threats," I hedged, not wanting to divulge any more about the virus and vaccine than I had to. The less Scott knew, the better it would be for his safety, I thought. "He hung up after just a minute or so."

"We'll head down to the station soon," Scott said. "Then we'll swing by the store and get you a new phone and number."

My instinctive dismay must've shown on my face. "What's wrong?" he asked.

Logic and sense kicked in and I shook my head. "It's nothing. Dumb."

"What?"

I shrugged. "It's just . . . I hate to get a new number, that's all." Sort of the truth, but not really.

Understanding dawned on Scott's face. "Devon won't have your new number," he said. "Is that what you're thinking?"

I nodded, chagrined. It was so pathetic. I had no way to reach Devon, but didn't want to take away the one method he had of communicating with me. I needed to quit thinking about him, but he was there constantly in the back of my mind. I'd told Devon I loved him, but now I wondered if I wasn't really in love so much as obsessed. And obsession was never a healthy thing.

"It's your decision," Scott continued. "I won't make you do something you don't want to do." But I could read his face and saw exactly what he thought of that.

"No, you're right," I said. "A new number would be best." Devon was a spy. If he wanted to call me, he'd find a way no matter how many new phone numbers I got.

"Are you hungry?" Scott asked.

"No, thanks. Just coffee." Breakfast wasn't my thing.

"Don't tell me you're one of those women who never eat," he teased.

"You've seen me eat," I protested.

"Oysters don't count."

The reminder of our Christmas dinner in Paris made me smile.

It had been a bad situation, but Scott had turned it around and made it into one of the best holidays I'd ever had. We'd had a fancy multi-course meal at a swanky restaurant, then walked to Notre Dame. I didn't know what I would have done without Scott coming to my rescue when I'd had no one else to turn to.

Scott drove us to the FBI building, where he had to get a special pass for me. Then we went into a darkened conference room where a computer and projector were set up. A second man came in. Scott introduced him as Agent Brooks, and he sat at the computer while Scott and I took chairs in front of a long table.

"Brooks is going to show some photos," Scott said. "Just let me know if you recognize any of them as Clive." He nodded to Brooks.

They showed me several photos, none of which contained anyone I recognized. It wasn't until the tenth or twelfth photo that I said, "That's him."

Scott and Brooks glanced at each other. "That's him?" Scott asked.

"Yeah." I looked at the screen, easily recognizing Clive. He was about six feet tall, with dark hair and light eyes. Not as striking as Devon, but definitely an attractive guy. He also didn't exude the same kind of danger and menace that Devon did, yet I wouldn't want to cross him. The photo had been taken at a distance with a very good lens, and his features were sharp and distinct.

Neither of the men said anything.

"Is that wrong?" I asked. "That's him. I'm sure of it."

"No, you're not wrong," Scott hastened to reassure me. "We didn't know his name was Clive, we just know what he does."

"Well, what does he do?"

The question was directed at Scott, but it was Brooks who answered.

"He used to work for MI6," he said. "Then he dropped off their radar about a year ago. We hadn't heard anything about him, thought maybe he'd been killed in action. Then intelligence came through a few weeks ago that he was stateside, had gone rogue, and had been hired as a hit man for one of the local mafia groups. We've been following him since then, but lost him a few days ago."

Well, that certainly didn't sound good.

"So what am I supposed to do?"

"There's nothing you can do," Scott replied. "I just need to keep you safe. If we're lucky, Clive will show his face and we'll be able to take him out."

"And if we're not lucky?"

Neither man replied to that, which didn't surprise me. The answer was fairly obvious.

Scott and I didn't talk much as we walked back to his desk. We sat down and I glanced at him, but he appeared deep in thought. I wondered if he was having second thoughts about helping me. Harboring someone who was being tracked by a former spy turned mafia hit man didn't sound like a real smart thing to do. But he surprised me.

"Have you ever fired a gun before?" he asked.

"Yes," I answered. "My grandpa taught me how to fire one, but it's been a while." I opened my mouth to tell him about the gun Devon had given me, but decided against it at the last second. I had no idea where that gun had come from and in my haste to leave the apartment the other night, I hadn't brought it with me.

"Good, so you wouldn't be opposed to having one on you for protection?"

I shook my head.

"Then let's go."

He drove us to a gun shop called Liquor, Guns & Ammo. When he parked, I just looked at Scott and raised an eyebrow.

"Really?"

Scott grinned. "Not a combination I'd endorse," he said, making me laugh.

It took a few minutes to fill out the paperwork and wait for the background check so I could buy a gun, but then I was cleared and we were looking at several different handguns.

"You know the basic premise," he said. "Point and squeeze the trigger." He held one of the handguns out to me, butt first. "This is a Glock G19. It's a nine millimeter, which should stop anything coming at you. How does it feel in your hand?"

It was heavy, but in a good, reassuring way. We tried a few more, but I liked that one the best. Before I could get out my credit card, he'd already given the man his.

"Scott, that's six hundred dollars," I said, horrified that he was paying for it.

He shrugged. "You can pay me back later."

That comment made me remember. I had ten thousand dollars in Scott's apartment. Yes, I could certainly pay him back.

"Let's go practice."

He took me to a firing range since the store itself didn't have one. Only a couple of other men were there and Scott requested earmuffs for both of us.

In one of the booths farthest away from the other two men, he set both guns on the shelf and adjusted the muffs so one ear was uncovered. I did the same.

He showed me how to load the cartridge into the gun and how to rack the slide. It took several times before I could do it. My hands were smaller and weaker than his and the slide was difficult to move. Finally, I got the hang of it.

"Now there's no safety on this," he said. "The safety is the trigger. It won't just fire if you drop it. You have to pull the trigger."

I nodded, trying to get used to the feel of this new weapon. The one Devon had left had been smaller and lighter.

"Don't ever point it at something you don't want to shoot," he warned.

"Got it." I prayed I'd never have to point it at anything at all.

"Okay, let me show you," he said, picking up the Glock and helping me hold it correctly. His hands were steady and capable, whereas mine felt too small and clumsy.

"Are you sure I'm going to be able to do this?" I asked.

"Absolutely," he said, moving to stand behind me. "Trust me."

Scott put his arms over mine as I held the gun up and sighted the target. His body was pressed against my back, which made me a little uncomfortable, but I tried to ignore it. He was just trying to help.

"Now just look along the barrel to your target," he said. His voice was directly in my uncovered ear. "You want to go for the torso, not the head," he continued, and I was glad he hadn't noticed the effect his touch had on me.

"Why?" I asked.

"The torso is a nice big target," he explained. "The head's too small. Even if you don't kill him, a solid hit to the torso will stop him and give you some time.

"When you're ready, just squeeze the trigger," he said. "Don't hold your breath, and don't close your eyes."

I took a deep breath, released it, and squeezed the trigger. The gun barked in my hand and a round hole erupted in the second ring of the torso.

"Nice!" Scott said, taking a step back. "Looks like you remember the important part."

I smiled at his praise. "Thanks."

"Let's do a few more," he suggested.

I sighted the gun and squeezed off several more shots. More holes appeared in the target.

"Good job," he said. "But let's try this." He stepped up behind me again and cupped my elbows, raising my arms to sight the weapon. "You pull a bit to the right. Have you noticed?" I nodded. "You can correct for that. I can show you how."

His hands were wrapped around mine, but now they loosened their grip, sliding slowly up my arms, the fabric of my sleeves caught in his fingers so his skin touched mine. My throat was suddenly dry and I swallowed. I didn't like men touching me, though I knew Scott wouldn't hurt me. Devon was the only one who could breach my defenses. But Scott was helping me and I didn't want to hurt his feelings, though every part of me itched to step away.

A moment went by as I tried to figure out what to do, but then his lips brushed my neck and I couldn't stop my involuntary response as I jerked away from him. My face heated in embarrassment at my not-so-subtle rejection.

"I-I'm sorry," I stammered. "You said compensate, right?" I quickly sighted the gun and squeezed the trigger. A hole erupted dead center in the black torso.

Scott didn't say anything, and I was too much of a coward to turn around. Instead, I ejected the chambered cartridge and fiddled with the gun.

"Ivy," Scott said. "I was out of line. I'm sorry."

My head jerked up and our gazes collided. Now I felt even worse. "It's not your fault," I said. "It's mine. You're nice, and I really like you. But I can't . . ." I shrugged helplessly, unable to put into words that I belonged to someone else. "Are you still going to help me?"

He frowned. "Of course I am. We're friends, right? And friends help friends. Even if there are no 'benefits.'"

He winked, which made me laugh a little, and the tension was broken.

Scott had me put the Glock in my purse along with a spare box of ammunition before we left. As we were driving back to his place, he said, "Hey, I'm hungry. How does Chinese sound?" I readily agreed.

A few minutes later, we pulled up to a restaurant with a sign that simply read "Chinese" and we headed inside.

"Can you order me beef and broccoli?" I asked. "I need to go to the ladies' room."

"Sure," Scott replied, stepping up to the counter.

There was a window in the ladies' room and I stared at it for a moment. I could leave, if I wanted. Scott was in danger now because of me. What if Clive came after me and Scott was hurt or even killed? How could I live with the guilt?

In the end, I was too afraid to leave. Shame made me want to cringe at my cowardice, but I couldn't make myself leave the only person who might be able to keep me safe.

Scott was waiting patiently for me when I returned, the steaming plates of Chinese food on the table where he'd sat. I slid onto the chair opposite him.

"Beef and broccoli, at your service," he teased.

"Thanks," I said, picking up a fork and taking a bite. I eyed him thoughtfully as I chewed. "Don't you have to go back to work or something?" I asked.

He grimaced a little. "Clive is someone on our radar," he said. "Finding him again would be a good thing."

Understanding dawned. "I see. So since Clive is after *me*, then I'm kind of like . . . bait."

Scott looked apologetic. "I know that sounds—"

"It's fine," I interrupted him. "I came to you, remember?"

There was an awkward silence after that, and Scott finally said, "Ivy, it's not just that Clive is important to us. It's also . . . you. It's personal . . . you're personal . . . to me. That's why I'm protecting you myself. And I would even if Clive wasn't of interest to the FBI."

"Why?"

"Why what?"

"Why would you do that?" I asked, genuinely confused. "Why put your life on the line for someone you barely know? Even for a nice guy, that's asking too much."

His eyes were warm and steady on mine. "What can I say? You bring out my chivalrous side. Not to mention that," he leaned closer, his grin widening, "it's kind of my job."

I was disappointed at the teasing rather than a serious response, but I let it go. Yes, he was an FBI agent, but even I knew they didn't take personal protection to this length. Perhaps Scott realized I was upset because the rest of the meal passed in stilted silence.

Outside, the sun was setting, the last rays blinding enough for me to slip on the set of aviator sunglasses in my purse. But we'd only taken a few steps on the sidewalk when Scott grabbed my elbow and pulled me to a halt.

"Listen to me," he said, his voice lower and a much more serious expression on his face. "You want to know why I'm doing this?"

I nodded, tipping my head back to look at him. He was so close our bodies were touching, and he still had his hand wrapped around my arm.

"The truth is, I think about you all the time, Ivy. I think about the first time I saw you, how scared you were when I told you the truth about Devon, how lost you seemed when I found you in Paris . . ." His voice trailed away as he studied me, a pained look on his face. He lifted a hand and brushed my hair back from where the breeze was stirring tendrils by my ear. "It kills me to see you unhappy and afraid. Tragic and innocent and so beautiful it hurts. I know you don't feel the same, and I don't want to pressure you. But if you need me, then I'm going to be here for you."

I was stunned at all this and stared wordlessly at him, my mouth agape. I was glad my sunglasses were still on so he couldn't see the shock that had to be showing in my eyes. Tragic? Was that how he saw me? How . . . demoralizing. I'd survived so much—my stepbrother, my stepfather, international terrorists—and because of how I looked, he'd classified me as helpless. Yet another reason my looks were more often a curse rather than a blessing.

I couldn't even begin to process how I felt about his confession, though I felt like I should say something to him as he stood there, waiting for my response.

"Scott? Is that you?"

Scott turned around at the voice coming from behind him, and I saw a woman standing several feet away. Petite and brunette, she was cute with a pixie haircut and pretty brown eyes. She was smiling, but when she saw me, her smile quickly faded.

"Oh. I-I didn't realize you were with someone," she stammered.

"Um, no, it's fine," Scott said, stepping away slightly. His hand slid down my arm to capture my fingers in his. "How are you, Jess?"

"Good. I'm good," Jess replied, her gaze dropping to our joined hands. I saw her swallow. I tried to subtly ease my hand from Scott's, but he tightened his grip.

"This is my friend, Ivy," Scott said. I moved forward to shake her hand. "Ivy, this is Jessica." He didn't provide any further information, but I wasn't stupid. She had to be an ex.

"Nice to meet you, Jessica," I said with a smile. Her answering smile was forced as her gaze took me in from my oversized sunglasses to the tips of my knee-high black suede boots. I quickly took off the glasses so I wouldn't seem rude, and her smile turned into a grimace.

"Nice to meet you, too," she said weakly. I could read the defeat on her face and it made me feel awful. She seemed sweet and was adorable, her petite stature one I envied, as was her curvy figure. She was that girl-next-door pretty that I wished I was.

There was an awkward silence. "So, how's work going?" Scott asked.

"It's fine. Same as always," she replied politely, her earlier obvious pleasure at seeing Scott now gone. "You?"

"Yeah, the same," Scott said, just as polite. I was really starting to feel out of place, not to mention embarrassed about the things Scott had been saying to me right before his ex-girlfriend had shown up.

"So how did you two meet?" she asked, and I recognized the look on her face. She wanted to know, but also didn't.

"Work," was Scott's succinct reply. "Listen, we gotta go, but it was good seeing you, Jess. Take care, okay?" He stepped forward and gave her a brief hug and I swore she paled a little. I wanted to kick Scott. Men were so clueless sometimes. I was sure he *thought* he was being nice, but I also doubted Jessica would want to smell my perfume on Scott.

Her voice was faint as we headed for Scott's car. "Yeah, bye."

I didn't say anything until we'd driven away. Jessica had watched us go, her expression resolute.

"She seemed really sweet," I said. "Your ex?"

Scott glanced at me, surprise etched on his features. "How'd you know?"

I rolled my eyes. "Seriously? I'm a woman. We always know."

"Jess and I met when I first moved here. We dated for almost a year. We broke up right after Thanksgiving."

"Why?"

He shrugged. "It was getting serious and I wasn't sure I was ready for that. Didn't want to lead her on, so I broke it off."

And had met me almost immediately after. Hello, rebound. No wonder he'd gotten so interested in me so fast.

Guilt swelled and I wanted to say something, especially after all he'd said to me before Jessica had shown up, but before I could, something slammed into us from behind.

"What the hell—?"

Scott glanced in the rearview mirror, his words cutting off. I grabbed onto the car door, twisting in my seat to look out the back. A huge pickup truck was behind us, the lights glaringly bright through the back window. The truck slammed into us again, harder this time. The car swerved wildly, then everything was spinning out of control. The world flipped upside down with the sound of rending metal and the screech of tires.

CHAPTER THREE

When the world finally stopped moving, I realized simultaneously that my head was killing me and that I was upside down.

Blinking, I tried to get my bearings. I was held in my seat by the seat belt, but the car itself had flipped. Looking over, I saw Scott was in a similar position, but still unconscious. Or dead. I gulped and prayed he wasn't dead.

It took several precious seconds for me to undo the belt, trying to brace myself against the ceiling so I wouldn't fall. After unfolding myself from the seat, I climbed through the shattered window, leaves and dirt from the ground rough against my palms. I had to get around to Scott's side and help him. Shakily, I got to my feet.

"There you are, luv. My, you do have nine lives."

I gasped, whipping around to see Clive. He smiled.

"Heard from Devon?" he asked. "He's being quite difficult, playing hard to get like this."

"What are you doing?" I asked, my voice shaking.

"I'm entertaining myself," he said. "Tell me, Ivy. Who else knows you're immune to the virus that killed Anna?"

I didn't answer, but Clive just smiled. "You like your mate?" He nodded toward the car. "How about I kill him? How would you feel about that?" Reaching inside his jacket, he pulled out a gun. "Do you think he'll bleed out faster upside down?"

"No!" I gasped. "Leave Scott alone. He doesn't have anything to do with this."

His gaze was calculating. "Then answer my question. Who else knows?"

"Devon. That's all."

"Excellent." He smiled.

"Freeze, Clive." Scott's voice startled me.

Somehow, Scott had climbed out of the car and had circled behind Clive. He was pointing a gun at Clive.

"Aren't you enterprising?" Clive said, still facing me.

"Drop your weapon," Scott ordered. "And turn around. Slowly."

"I don't think so," Clive said. "I've still got your girl here. And if you shoot me, the bullet may go right through and nick her."

Scott said nothing, his hands steady as he pointed the weapon in a two-handed grip at Clive's back.

"So here's what we'll do," Clive continued. "I'm going to walk away, and you're going to let me."

"And why would I do that?"

"Because Ivy really needs medical attention."

It was the only warning I had before the gun in his hand barked once. Time seemed to slow as I stumbled back, thrown nearly off my feet by the force of the impact. I looked down and saw blood seeping from my arm. Then the pain hit and time sped back up into chaos.

"Ivy!"

Clive ran straight at me as I stood, frozen in shock, then he sprinted past me into the darkened trees lining the road. There was a rushing sound in my ears and I saw the muzzle of Scott's gun flash once. Twice. But I heard nothing. Then the ground was rushing up to meet me and Scott was running, sliding to his knees beside me.

His mouth was moving, but I heard nothing. Then a searing pain in my arm as he pressed hard. I bit back a scream, clenching my teeth against the pain. Flashing lights appeared as an ambulance and the police arrived. An EMT ran toward us.

The next few minutes were a blur of pain and movement as they loaded me into the ambulance. I told them I could walk, but my words fell on deaf ears. A needle in my arm soon had pain medication flowing, and I drifted into a pharmaceutical-induced nap.

"She'll be all right. Just a flesh wound. Though she'll be sore and have a scar."

The words filtered through my consciousness as I pried open my eyes. I recognized the bright lights and antiseptic white walls immediately. The hospital.

Turning, I saw a nurse standing by the bed. She smiled when she saw my eyes were open. "How are you feeling?" she asked.

I didn't really know. I could tell the medication was still flowing through my veins as I felt no pain. She didn't seem to take it amiss that I didn't reply.

"Ivy."

Scott appeared on the other side of the bed.

"You're going to be okay," Scott said, resting his hand in mine. "I promise."

"How long do I have to stay?" I asked, my voice raspy and low. I swallowed on a dry throat.

"Just overnight for observation," the nurse answered. "You should be able to leave tomorrow."

"I'll stay with you," Scott said, taking my hand.

The nurse left soon after that, flicking off the fluorescent lights so only a small one remained on to provide a bit of illumination.

"What time is it?" I asked.

"About midnight," he said. "But don't worry about that. Go to sleep. Get some rest."

"Clive got away?" I persisted.

He nodded. Grim. "But we have an APB out on him. We might get lucky."

Somehow I thought Clive probably knew how to avoid being captured by law enforcement.

I was tired and my body felt heavy. Scott's hand felt good in mine, but I longed for Devon. My eyes stung and I closed them to keep the tears at bay. Would Devon know I'd gotten hurt? Would he care if he did?

"I'm so sorry about your car," I said.

"It's okay," he said. "Insurance takes care of it, plus the Agency since it was technically in the line of duty."

That was a relief. "And you're okay? Nothing injured from the accident?"

"I'm fine," he said. "Bit of a concussion, but I've had worse."

We'd nearly been killed in a car wreck. Scott had been threatened by Clive. I'd been shot. And Scott had a concussion. I was literally the angel of death.

Despite my efforts, tears slipped from my eyes to slide down my cheeks.

"Aw, it's okay, Ivy," I heard Scott murmur. "Don't cry."

His kindness was the last straw and I started sobbing in earnest. Mortified, I used my good arm to cover my eyes with my hand. The bed dipped and then I felt Scott's body next to mine.

"Shh. It's okay," he soothed.

"It's n-not ok-kay," I stammered through my tears. "You could've d-died." I didn't want to be responsible for anyone's death—least of all Scott's—but I had no idea what to do to get Clive to stop. "Why d-didn't he j-just kill me?"

Scott pulled me against his chest, careful of the bandage on my arm. He smoothed my hair and held me until I'd stopped crying. His thumb brushed at the tear tracks on my face.

"I imagine he didn't kill you because you're immune to the virus," he said. "That is what he said, right?"

I hesitated, my stomach sinking. Scott had overheard, and I didn't want to lie to him. I nodded.

"How?"

"Mr. Galler," I said. "He tricked me into being injected with the only formulated vaccine. I was poisoned with the virus along with Anna. I survived. She didn't."

"Devon knows this about you, and now so does Clive."

"Yes."

His arm tightened around me. "We need to take you into protective custody," he said grimly. "I'll call in the morning, get some agents over here to transport you."

I cringed into him. "I just want my life back."

"I want you to have your life back," he said. "And I'm going to do everything in my power to make sure that happens."

The thought of going into protective custody and more people knowing about my immunity depressed me. Add to it the fact that Devon would have no chance of finding me once that happened and I felt as though my entire world was falling apart.

 ❧

I don't know what woke me; my eyes just suddenly popped open. I was still lying next to Scott, only now I was on my back. I lay utterly still, listening intently. It was darker inside the room than it had been earlier, the only light that which filtered in through the window in the closed door.

Had there been a noise? Had a nurse come in the room? But it didn't feel like that. Something . . . wasn't right.

The hairs on the back of my neck stood up and goose bumps erupted on my skin. My whole body was stiff with tension, though I could sense Scott sleeping soundly next to me.

"Wake up, mate," a voice said. "I like for a man to look at me before I kill him."

I gasped in surprise. I knew that voice.

Devon had come.

CHAPTER FOUR

I heard a switch being flicked and light flooded the room. Devon stood by the bed, gun in hand, the hard metal of the barrel pressed against Scott's temple.

"Wake up, Sleeping Beauty," Devon said, tapping the barrel against Scott's head. "Your training is for shite and your aim even worse. So much for keeping my girl safe."

Scott was wide awake now and he slowly turned to face Devon. The barrel moved to settle at the center of his forehead.

"That's better." Devon smiled, and it sent a chill down my spine. I'd seen that smile before. Cold. Humorless. Dangerous. "Any last words, mate?"

But Scott didn't seem fazed. He looked at the gun, then at Devon. "You must be Devon Clay."

"Ladies and gents, he's smarter than he looks," Devon said.

"Devon, what are you doing?" I asked. I'd seen Devon kill before. He was very good at it.

"I've come to collect you, darling," he replied. "Be a good girl and get dressed." He extended a hand to me.

Unsure as to what to do, I didn't move, glancing uneasily between Devon and Scott.

"Be quick about it," Devon chastened me.

"Don't hurt him," I said.

"Then don't give me a reason to," he replied. His smile was gone, his expression cold and hard. "He'll be quite lucky if I don't punish his complete ineptitude, letting you get shot."

I took his hand and eased out of bed, conscious of my nakedness underneath the inadequate hospital gown, but no one spoke. I pulled on a pair of jeans and Scott's button-down shirt he'd discarded earlier. My shirt was nowhere to be seen. I wanted to get Devon out of here and away from Scott as quickly as possible.

"She's not going with you," Scott said.

"The hell she's not," Devon replied. "And may I remind you that you're not in any position to be making demands."

"You'll end up killing her," Scott insisted. "You might even be the one to do it rather than someone else. Either way, she'll end up dead. Is that what you want?"

A flicker of something crossed Devon's face, then was gone. "Predicting the future, are you? Be sure to buy a lottery ticket. You'll have better odds of being right."

I slipped on my shoes and combed my fingers through my hair. I approached Devon once I was dressed.

"Ready, darling?" Devon asked lightly, glancing at me. Reaching out, he briefly cupped my cheek, his thumb brushing my skin.

"I-I guess," I stammered. I hadn't expected him and his sudden appearance set me off balance. But even so, the frisson of excitement he always made me feel fairly crackled along my skin like a shiver of static electricity. Though he held a gun on a man, I couldn't take my eyes off him. I must be crazy to be so obsessed with a man like him.

Dressed full-out in a gray suit so dark it was nearly black, he wore a white shirt and striped tie, the knot perfectly tied in a full

Windsor. The single button on his coat was done precisely up and the crease of his pants looked like they'd just come from the dry cleaners. He had light-brown hair that could be blond in the right light, and blue eyes so light they were akin to ice. Energy and menace oozed from him, drawing me in like a moth to the flame that would ignite me.

My memory never did him justice.

"Then we're off," he said to me, though he was still looking at Scott. "And I'd take it quite personally if you were to follow or attempt to stop us, mate."

I gulped at the threat, then grabbed my purse. Devon headed for the door, gun still in hand, and held it open for me.

"Ivy, wait," Scott said, vaulting out of bed.

I paused.

"Don't go with him," he pleaded. "Stay. For your own sake."

"I can't," I said, shaking my head. "I'm as dangerous to you as he is to me."

Our gazes held for a long moment.

"I have to go," I said. "Thank you. Be safe." I hurried through the door before Scott could stop me.

We were in the elevator when Devon spoke. "I was wondering if you'd actually stay with him," he said, almost conversationally, as though he didn't care one way or the other.

"Did you want me to?" I asked stiffly. I wasn't happy about him holding a gun to Scott's head. Though my question was blunt, I doubted I'd get a straight answer. To my surprise though, I did.

"If I wanted you to stay with him, I wouldn't have come for you."

Our eyes met and it was suddenly hard to breathe.

"Let's go," he said, tucking his gun into the holster at his side and taking my hand in his.

I was tall, but Devon still loomed over me by several inches. He led me out into the darkness to the street where his Porsche was parked. After opening the passenger door and letting me settle inside, he got behind the wheel.

"How did you know I was here?" I asked as he pulled out and headed down the street. Devon never drove the speed limit and tonight was no exception.

"Did you think I wouldn't?"

"It's not like you call or text me just to see how I'm doing," I retorted. "For all I know, each time I see you could be the last."

"That's true, but not for the reason you think," he said.

"What do you mean?"

He glanced my way. "If I die, no one will show up on your doorstep to inform you of my untimely demise."

That shut me up. I hadn't considered that, or maybe I hadn't wanted to. I'd rather hate Devon for leaving me than consider the possibility that he could be dead.

"So where are you taking me?" I asked.

"Tonight to a hotel," he said, glancing in the rearview mirror and making an abrupt left turn. "And you can tell me what's happened, including the dismal extent to which the FBI agent failed to protect you."

"I didn't know it was his job to protect me," I retorted, stung at his insinuation. "I thought it was yours."

His gaze snapped to mine, but he didn't reply. I saw him glance at the bandage on my arm and his jaw tightened. I had the inkling that I was becoming a liability for Devon, and I didn't know how well he tolerated liabilities.

"I need my things from Scott's house," I said. "Take me there first."

I wondered if he'd know where Scott lived, and somehow I wasn't surprised to see that indeed, he did. He followed me to the door, and I didn't ask how he got the door unlocked, just stepped past him when it swung open.

It didn't take me long to pack and I hesitated when I saw the ten thousand dollars in the suitcase. Making a quick decision, I took out the money and left it sitting on the bedroom bureau. Scott's car was utterly wrecked. Leaving the money seemed the least I could do as an apology.

Only minutes after we got there, we were leaving, Devon hauling my suitcase to his car and stowing it in the trunk. Across town, he pulled in to a really nice hotel lot and handed his keys to the valet. Sliding an arm around my waist, he guided me inside and to the elevators.

"Don't you need to check in?" I asked, confused.

"I have a room," he clarified, punching the button to call the car.

I stared at him and felt my face grow pale. "For how long?" I asked. How long had he been staying just miles from me?

His gaze was unflinching when he looked at me. "A week."

I felt as though he'd slapped me. I was so stunned, I didn't move when the elevator doors opened. Placing his hand on the small of my back, Devon had to guide me inside. The door slid shut.

"You've been here a week and didn't tell me?" My voice sounded strangled.

"I've been working," he said. "And I came to see you when I could."

I didn't speak as the doors opened again, and he guided me out and down the hall to a room. He unlocked the door, and we stepped inside.

My mind was spinning, trying to figure out what I was going to do with this information. I was hurt that he'd been here and hadn't told me, hurt that he'd not been to see me more than the few hours he'd been in my bed the other night. And I didn't want to hurt, so I channeled it into anger.

"I'm so glad you could spare some time," I said, uncaring at the bitterness in my voice. "I'm sure it was hard to squeeze me in."

Devon pulled the drapes closed, then discarded his jacket on a nearby chair before replying. "I told you what you were getting when I agreed to continue our relationship," he said evenly. "I promised you nothing. You have no cause to be upset."

He was right, which hurt even more and just made me angrier. I hadn't counted on how his lack of emotional attachment to me was going to hurt. I'd been deluding myself into thinking that I was okay with just a physical relationship with Devon. Really, I'd been hoping if I waited it out, he'd grow to care more about me.

I'd been very, very wrong.

"Fine," I said, trying to take all the emotion out of my voice.

Devon was watching me, his hands in his pockets. His tie was still knotted and he hadn't yet removed his gun or holster.

"What happened?" he said. "The apartment is trashed."

"Clive happened," I replied, then I told him about Clive showing up in my car, how I'd been afraid to go home and called Scott instead.

"Why not Logan?" he interrupted. "Why call the FBI agent?"

"Logan and I aren't exactly speaking right now," I confessed. "Plus, I didn't want to put him in danger."

"You moved out and now he's not speaking to you?" Devon asked, his eyebrows climbing.

"Pretty much."

"What an arse," he groused. "Not that I'm surprised."

"I would've told you sooner, had you asked," I said.

Devon silently studied me and I wished more than anything that I could see inside his head, but his thoughts and emotions were an indiscernible puzzle to me.

"Then what happened?" he asked, drawing me back to my story.

I told him about returning to his apartment and finding it trashed, how Scott had taken me with him, and how I'd picked Clive from their photographs.

"But Clive found us," I said. "He caused Scott to wreck the car, then . . . he shot me."

Devon took a few steps toward where I sat on the bed until he stood in front of me. I tipped my head back to look at him. Reaching out, he gently brushed the back of his knuckles along my cheek.

"What's going to happen, Devon?" I asked. "I have nowhere to go and . . . I'm afraid."

A pained expression crossed his face before he replied. "You'll stay with me for now," he said. "Until I sort it."

I nodded. "Okay."

Leaning down, he pressed his lips to mine. "Don't be afraid," he murmured. "You're safe with me."

His touch was comforting, easing my tense muscles and relaxing my stiff posture. Devon would keep me safe, and I'd get to be with him. I shouldn't want to, not after realizing that this relationship with him wasn't good for me the way a normal, healthy relationship should be. But I couldn't help it. I was an addict and he was my drug of choice.

To my dismay, there was a knock on the door and Devon pulled away.

"Who could that be?" I asked.

"The good doctor, of course," he said, pulling open the door.

Doctor?

A man walked in who looked vaguely familiar. He was carrying a leather satchel.

"Ivy, this is Jensen," Devon said. The man nodded politely to me. "He's a doctor and I'd like him to take a look at your injury."

Jensen was about a foot shorter than Devon and older, perhaps mid-fifties. He had dark hair and eyes and an olive complexion. He was dressed in slacks and a plain white shirt.

"Um, okay," I said, unsure as to what else I could do.

"We're just going to take a look at this then," Jensen said, motioning for me to sit on the couch. He took the seat next to me and carefully rolled up my sleeve before removing the bandage.

It took me a few minutes before I realized where I'd seen him.

"I know you," I said suddenly. "You were there when I was sick. At Devon's." I remembered he'd had needles and had injected me with something.

Although I'd addressed Jensen, it was Devon who answered. "He gave you steroids and stimulants to try and help your body fight off the virus."

"How do you know each other?" I asked, turning back to Jensen. "Do you work for—"

"We met a while back," Devon interrupted. "Jensen helped me out and I did him a favor in return."

I'd been about to ask if Jensen worked for the Shadow, too, but caught the warning look Devon shot me, so I just nodded.

"The stitches look good," Jensen said, placing a new bandage on me. He dug in his bag and then gave me two bottles of pills. "This is for pain and discomfort, but you can switch to ibuprofen if the pain isn't too bad. This bottle is an antibiotic to ward off infection. Take it for ten days."

He smiled again before closing up his bag and retreating for the door. Devon followed him and they had a low conversation that I couldn't make out, then Jensen left.

Getting up from the couch, I went to the bed as Devon closed and locked the door.

"You need to get some rest," he said, turning away and unknotting his tie.

"Are you going to sleep, too?" I asked, scooting back on the bed.

"Eventually."

He wasn't looking at me and seemed to have dismissed me entirely as he removed his holster.

He cared enough to have a doctor come by a hotel, but didn't appear to want to coddle me. It was a little strange, the distance I felt him putting between us. I didn't know why, but I could guess well enough. My dreaded suspicions about what would happen if I became a tedious inconvenience to Devon—if my drawbacks outweighed my benefits—had come true. And there wasn't sex good enough to draw him back to me once he'd made up his mind.

Well then, so be it. It was what it was and nothing I said was going to change it. Besides, I had a little pride left—although that was one thing Devon could strip me of so easily. I wasn't going to beg again. I'd begged for this relationship, and look what it had gotten me.

I shucked my jeans but left on Scott's shirt, then climbed underneath the covers. By now, Devon had stripped down to his slacks. I rested my head on the pillow and admired the view of his naked back and chest, dotted with bullet wound scars and a couple of knife slices that were thin, white lines. His muscles were even more well defined than Scott's and the veins in his arms stood out in stark relief underneath his skin.

"No," he said. "Absolutely not."

I jerked my gaze from his washboard abs up to his face. He was staring at my chest.

"What?" I asked, glancing down. Did I have something on me?

"You're not wearing his clothes to bed with me," he said flatly. "Take it off."

I looked at him, my eyes narrowing. "No." Scott had been good to me. I felt safe with him. Wearing his shirt was almost like holding a teddy bear or something. It comforted me.

Devon stepped closer. "I said, take it off."

"What do you care if I wear his clothes?" I asked. "I don't have to do what you tell me to." My temper was flaring now and I glared at him.

The air between us fairly crackled with energy. Our eyes were locked together and I could tell by his tightly coiled muscles that he was angry. Not that I cared. He'd use and discard me, and then what would I have? Nothing and no one. Why should I let that happen?

"Oh yes, you do," he growled. He stood right next to the bed, almost close enough for me to touch.

I could smell him, his warm scent that was spice and musk and danger all rolled into one. In spite of myself, I could feel the flesh between my thighs begin to ache, pulsing with a familiar need.

"Make me."

He sprang before I could react, his hands catching hold of my waist and pushing me flat onto my back. He was on his knees, his body caging me from above. Before I could spit a retort at him, he was kissing me, and I forgot what I was going to say. His tongue pushed between my lips, demanding a response.

I hated and loved him in equal measure—I hated that he could bend me to his will, but I loved him for it, too. It confused me, so I shoved my emotions aside and turned off my brain.

I kissed him back with equal urgency, my fingers buried in his hair. He jerked the shirt open to bare my breasts, buttons flying off, then slid down to take a nipple in his mouth. I moaned in response, the wet heat of his tongue against my skin sending a bolt of pure pleasure through me, but then suddenly he pulled back.

Befuddled and aroused, I watched him push himself off the bed. His gaze was hungry and I felt it like an invisible touch on my skin, but then he abruptly turned away.

"What are you doing?" I asked. "Why'd you stop?"

"You've been hurt and terrorized," he said curtly. "You should be lobbing sharp objects at my head, not kissing me." He shoved a hand through his hair, then went to the table in the corner where a half-empty bottle of gin sat. He poured a healthy shot into a glass and tossed it back in one swallow.

I watched him. Devon ran so hot and cold on me from one minute to the next, though I didn't think it was a bad thing, not really. It might mean he was feeling more for me than responsibility and attraction. But a big part of our relationship was sex, and tonight I wanted that connection with him. I needed it.

After getting up, I crossed to him. He was unscrewing the gin bottle to pour himself another drink when I took it from him. Setting it back on the table, I said, "Well, I'm currently all out of sharp, pointy things."

His lips twitched and I took that as a good sign. Stepping close to him, I twined my arms around his waist, sighing contentedly at the feel of his skin against mine. It felt so right, even more so when his arms slid around me to pull me closer. His hand inched up underneath my hair to cup the back of my neck.

His heart beat strong in his chest, the dull thud reverberating into me. I tilted my head back to look at him. When our eyes met, I smiled. I couldn't help it. I was glad to see him in spite of our argument.

"Impossible, silly girl," he murmured, but his eyes were kind and his smile soft.

"Come back to bed," I implored. "I've missed you. I need you."

"Is that what you want?" he asked. "Even after Clive?"

"I don't give a damn about Clive," I said. "And I'm not about to let him ruin our time together. Now come. Make love to me. Don't make me ask again."

I took his hand and pulled him toward the bed, backing up as he followed me. He still seemed somewhat reluctant, but I saw his eyes tracing a path down my body and knew I'd won this round.

The backs of my knees hit the bed and I sat down, scooting backward as Devon climbed onto the mattress after me. His lips caught mine and I pulled him with me as I lay back against the soft pillows.

I wasn't wearing any panties, and eagerly spread my legs when his hand slipped down my stomach. If I wasn't beyond the point of embarrassment, I would have blushed at how wet I was. Instead, I just wanted him inside me. I gasped when his finger slid inside me, teasing my clit with gentle strokes as he pumped.

The restraint he'd shown earlier was gone as he kissed me with fierce abandon. I tore my mouth from his, sucking in air as his lips moved to my neck. Devon knew my body better than I did, bringing me to the edge and keeping me there. Keening sounds fell from my throat and I lifted my hips, seeking more friction, but he denied me.

"You were with the agent for two days," he whispered in my ear. "Did he touch you?" Two fingers filled me and I moaned, but it still wasn't enough.

"Tell me," he said.

"N-no," I gasped.

"Good," he said. "Then I won't have to kill him."

I clutched at his shoulders, the muscles hard underneath my fingers. "Yes, I'd rather you not kill him," I managed to say, trying to sound coherent even as his hand moved between my legs. "I like him."

He growled a curse against my neck. "If you're jealous, then you should have come back sooner," I said. "Now stop talking already and kiss me."

That achieved the desired result. In moments, he had shed his pants and was back. My eyes were glued to his cock, standing rigidly at attention. My mouth went dry at the sight. Devon was a large man, and his cock was proportionate. I thought he was probably larger than most men, not that I had a lot to compare it to. I'd only been with two men, if you didn't count Jace, and I never counted Jace.

Devon bent my knees, pushing them apart. He guided his cock and I felt the head at my entrance. I reached for him, but he remained sitting back on his haunches. Settling his hands on my hips, he pulled me toward him, burying his length inside me.

I made some kind of noise, though I know it wasn't actual words because I wasn't lucid enough for that. He stretched me, filled me, much better than his fingers had.

Prying open my eyes, I saw he was gazing down at where our bodies were joined, his expression rapt as he slid out of me and back in, a slow glide that made me feel every inch of him.

"Touch yourself," he ordered.

I hesitated, but desire and passion overcame my embarrassment at doing what he said and I reached down. My fingers slid between my folds and I found my clit, slick and plump. Stroking the bit of flesh, my eyes fluttered shut again as my thighs trembled.

"That's right, darling," he encouraged.

Devon's hands gripped my hips and he moved faster, his cock pumping hard into me. My hand moved faster, too, and I was splintering apart, crying out his name. Devon's body jerked into mine, his breathing hitched in gasps as he buried himself in me. I could feel the pulsing of his cock as he came and it prolonged my own orgasm.

Afterward, I was spent. My body felt boneless, but Devon wasn't through with me. After pulling out, he moved back on the bed and lowered his head between my legs. I jerked at the soft touch of his tongue, my body too sensitive, but he held my hips still.

"I can't," I said, still breathless.

"Yes, you can," he murmured. He licked me again, parting my folds with long sweeps of his tongue. My eyes slid shut.

Devon was very good at this, and soon my legs were trembling and I was clutching his head to me, moaning nonstop. I lifted my hips to his mouth as my body convulsed in an orgasm so powerful, tears came to my eyes.

If I'd been tired before, now I couldn't even summon the energy to move. Devon crawled up my body and kissed me. I could taste myself on his lips, and his tongue languidly stroked mine for a moment before he lay down beside me.

"You're beautiful. Sensual. I love watching you," he said, his lips brushing my ear. His voice was like smoke, drifting through the air and clinging to me.

His words made me blush. Devon had made sex an amazing experience for me. He'd turned it from something dirty and painful into something beautiful and filled with pleasure. I liked hearing him describe my body through his eyes, especially when being on the too-skinny side of thin made me all bones and pointy angles. I liked how I looked wearing the clothes I loved so dearly. With them off, not so much.

I tipped my head to look at him. His eyes were clear blue, intense as he studied me. The hard lines of his face were softened slightly with lovemaking.

"You're beautiful, too," I said softly.

His smile was faint, but there nonetheless. "No longer angry with me?" he asked.

I shrugged. Multiple orgasms had a way of softening my temper. "You're here now. Why waste time being mad? It is what it is. I can't change it."

He brushed my hair back, tucking it behind my ear. "And what would you change if you could?"

I sighed, turning to rest my head on him. I could feel the rise and fall of his chest as he breathed. I closed my eyes as I answered.

"There's no future for us," I said. "No matter how much I wish otherwise. Your job doesn't allow it, and you won't leave your job, even if you wanted a future with me, which I'm not sure you do. So . . . that's that."

Devon stroked my hair, his hand moving in gentle passes down the long locks splayed across my back.

"My job is the most important thing to me, yes," he said.

That hurt, no matter how much I'd already known it.

"But I wouldn't be here if you weren't important, too."

It was nice to hear that, the hurt easing inside. "I'm glad," I said, my voice quiet in the room.

We lay like that, him stroking my hair and me listening to his heart beating, for a long while.

"I should have foreseen this," he said at last, his voice a low murmur.

"Foreseen what?" I asked.

"Clive, coming after you. Perhaps I was too hopeful that he would go his own way. And now he's hurt you. Frightened you." His hand drifted down to touch the bandage on my arm ever so gently.

"He knows I'm carrying the vaccine," I said, then decided to come clean. "And now the FBI knows, too."

Devon's hand stilled. "You told the agent?"

"About the virus, yes. He overheard Clive talking about the vaccine."

"You said you hadn't told him anything," Devon reminded me.

I twisted to look up at him. "I lied. I'm sorry. I was afraid of what you'd do to him. Or me."

He frowned. "After all this, you still think I would hurt you?"

"I know where your loyalties lie." I wasn't trying to throw his words back in his face, but there it was.

His hand cupped my cheek. "My loyalties may lie with the Shadow, but you . . . you are dear to me."

My throat closed up at the unexpected confession. It wasn't love, but it was better than what I'd thought he felt. His eyes perhaps saw too deeply into me, but I couldn't look away.

"Which is why Clive will pay for hurting you," he added. "I'll see to that."

The thought of Devon and Clive going head-to-head again scared me. Clive had intimated months ago that he was afraid of Devon, but now it seemed he didn't care. Probably because he had nothing more to lose, I guessed.

"I know what we need to take your mind off things," he said, his lips curving into a tender smile.

"What's that?"

"Shopping, of course."

I hid a grin. "You think I can be placated with pretty clothes?" Then I quickly added, "And shoes?" Best not to forget the shoes.

"I know you can."

This time I laughed outright. When my chuckles had faded, Devon asked, "How's the arm? Are you in pain?"

I shook my head. I had a very high pain tolerance—courtesy of Jace—and while it was uncomfortable, it was bearable. "I'm fine."

"You should take a pain pill," he persisted, but I shook my head again.

"I don't want to. They knock me out."

"Yes, that is rather the point," he said dryly.

"I don't like that feeling," I said. "I'd rather put up with a little pain than feel like I can't stay awake." I hated that feeling of being out of control.

Devon's gaze was shrewd. "Yes, I believe I know exactly how you feel." Reaching over to the lamp, he switched it off, then lay back down with me. "Go to sleep, darling."

So I did.

❦

"That's an absolute yes."

I glanced uncertainly over my shoulder at Devon, who sat in an armchair outside the dressing room. "It costs way too much," I said, shaking my head.

"Of course it does, but you look stunning and I don't care."

I turned back to the three mirrors facing me to take another look at what was capping off an entire day of shopping.

The gown was by Elie Saab, black, floor-length, and made almost entirely of lace. The neckline plunged in a deep V and the sleeves were short. Swaths of silk served to cover areas of the body for modesty's sake, while the handmade lace billowed from the waist to my ankles. The way the dress was cut, it helped disguise my sad lack of cleavage. Black Christian Louboutin patent leather heels graced my feet, complete with bloodred soles. It was divine.

"If I could dress like this every day, I'd be a much more pleasant person," I mused to myself.

Devon's laugh startled me and I reflexively smiled at his amusement. "Darling, somehow I doubt you're a hardship to those around you," he teased.

He had been in a good mood all day, taking me tirelessly from store to store and insisting on buying me everything from lingerie, to shoes, to summer clothes, to designer jeans. Since what had been salvageable from his apartment hadn't been very much, the additions to my wardrobe were wholly appreciated. As for this dress, though, I had no idea when I'd ever have an occasion to wear it.

But it was still very, very pretty.

I was busy admiring the dress when he stood and came up behind me, resting his hands lightly on my waist.

"And there's no sense in owning a lovely dress if you have no occasion on which to wear it," he said. "Would you care to accompany me to a ball tonight?"

My eyebrows flew up. "A ball?"

"The symphony is holding their annual gala tonight," he explained, bending down to nuzzle my neck. His voice lowered, sending a shiver through me. "I'd like to take my lovely lady to an elegant dinner, then see how she sparkles under the chandeliers at Powell Hall." He pressed a light kiss underneath my jaw, the warmth of his breath tantalizing in my ear. "I want to memorize how beautiful you are while the melodies of masters wash over us, and spin a fantasy of forever in my mind."

Wow. It took me a second to overcome my surprise at this romantic side of him. "How could I possibly say no to that?" I asked with a smile.

"I might have overshot it a bit, just in case you were considering refusing," he said, making me smile wider. I loved this teasing side of him, so much lighter and carefree than when he was dogged by work.

But the dress and shoes weren't the only extravagances he bought for me. Tugging me into a jewelry shop, he insisted on buying a diamond and onyx necklace to go with the dress. A heavy, round pendant hung between my breasts on a long, white gold chain and the matching earrings adorned my lobes.

"Are you spoiling me out of guilt?" I asked him hours later as I sipped the red wine he'd ordered and we waited for our entrees. The restaurant was romantic, with dim lighting and the tables spaced far enough apart to convey some privacy. I knew it was the most exclusive and well-known restaurant in town, but had never been there.

Devon looked utterly at ease in this environment, his gaze not often straying from me. I hoped I'd done the dress justice by wearing dramatic smoky eye makeup with a touch of glitter, and pulling my hair back into a loose French braid. Tendrils escaped to frame my face and touch my neck.

"I'm spoiling you because I want to," he said simply. "It pleases me. If I felt guilty for something, I'd tell you so. And I wouldn't try something as pathetic as buying you gifts to attain your forgiveness."

Well, okay then.

He didn't seem offended that I'd asked, just matter-of-fact. And who was I to argue if he wanted to buy me the clothes that were my own personal version of crack?

Dinner was one of the best meals I'd ever had, barring Christmas dinner in Paris—which I *didn't* tell him—and by the time we entered Powell Hall, I felt like I was floating on air.

I'd never been to the symphony before and the gala ball had turned out the finest in St. Louis society. I wasn't the only woman in a designer dress with diamonds around her neck.

"Let's play a game," Devon said in my ear.

"What kind of game?"

"We should mingle, but the rules are we can't use our real names or jobs. So when we meet someone new, we'll take turns."

I looked questioningly at him, not quite following, but his lips twisted in a crooked, mischievous smile.

"I'll go first," he said.

Drawing my arm through his, he guided us over to where two couples were chatting. As we approached their small group, they turned and smiled politely.

"Hello," Devon said, only now he didn't have a British accent, but a Southern one. "I'm Travis, and this is Millicent. We're from Dallas here visiting family."

I struggled to keep the giggle that produced inside. Devon with a Southern accent just did not compute, though I couldn't fault his delivery.

Everyone kindly introduced themselves and we did a whole round of handshaking before the next question.

"What do you do, Travis?" one of the men asked. He was perhaps in his mid-fifties with salt-and-pepper hair and his wife had done a few too many rounds of Botox.

"My company works with oil and gas companies to obtain leasing permits from the government," Devon smoothly lied. "Millicent here is my secretary."

That shit. I choked back another laugh at his audacity. As if the name *Millicent* wasn't bad enough, he'd turned me into a cliché secretary dating her boss? My nails dug into his palm, but he just smiled blandly. I got him back once we'd moved on from that group to another.

"How do you do?" I asked, taking the hand of a woman who stood with two other ladies. They were all older, perhaps early sixties, and exuded class and wealth. This time, *I* adopted the accent—heavily French. "I am Vivienne. This is Marc." I indicated Devon.

"Pleased to meet you both," the woman said, introducing herself and her friends. "Is this your first time to the symphony?"

"Indeed," I said, laying it on thick. "I know no one in the States, so I hire a man to accompany me." I smiled as I saw all their eyes open wider. "He is very good, no?" Devon's hand tightened on my waist, but his face remained pleasant.

"Really?" one of them asked. "How interesting. And is he, perhaps, a . . . full-service escort?"

"Is there another kind?" I replied with a very French shrug.

Now they were all looking Devon over as if checking out the merchandise.

"Wherever did you find him, darling?" another woman asked, her gaze resting a tad longer than necessary on the bulge in Devon's trousers.

"How you say . . ." I pretended confusion. "Ah yes! The yellow pages."

"I do believe the performance is about to begin," Devon cut in. "A pleasant evening, ladies."

They all nodded as Devon herded me away.

"I do believe those pensioners are eyeing my arse," he complained in my ear. "And you certainly do not need any more encouragement on this game, I can see."

I laughed outright, unable to hold it in any longer, and we paused in an empty corner. The chandeliers twinkled above us as I gazed at Devon. He held my hands with each of his own, tugging me closer until he bent and brushed my lips in a sweet kiss.

"A gigolo, eh?" he murmured. I giggled again.

"Millicent the secretary?" I replied.

"Touché."

The symphony was a blur of happiness as we sat in a private box, my hand in Devon's. He ordered us champagne for intermission and told me how he'd played the violin for a short time, but had given it up because it never ceased sounding like writhing cats fighting.

I loved how he talked to me, just chatting, and he was constantly touching me—whether it was a hand on my knee, or a caress to my shoulder, or playing with my fingers. And since he was sharing stories with me, I told him of my one and only failed attempt to make the cheerleading squad—failed because of my inability to turn a proper cartwheel.

"But I could do the splits, which should have made up for it," I said. "But they still turned me down."

"I'm quite sure you would've been an excellent cheerleader," he teased. "Even without the cartwheels."

Chatting eventually led to more serious matters until Devon was telling me the story of his parents' deaths while we were driving back to the hotel.

"It was an IRA bomb," he said. "My parents had taken my younger sister with them into the city. The bomb went off while they were in the Tube. I was staying with a chum because I didn't want to go."

"I'm so sorry," I said. "That must've been horrible." My heart went out to him and I reached across the seat to take his hand. To my surprise, his grip was tight on mine.

"They said Shannon died instantly from the shrapnel," he continued. "And I remember feeling grateful because she hadn't bled to death like my parents had, waiting for help to arrive."

"They couldn't get to them in time?"

He shook his head, glancing at me before looking back at the road. "The damage and rubble were bad, which made getting to the survivors extremely difficult."

Good God, how awful. I didn't say anything after that, just held his hand as we drove. I couldn't begin to imagine the therapy he'd had to undergo to get past something like that. But then who was I kidding? *I* needed therapy, for crying out loud.

Devon made love to me as if it were our first time together, his touch gentle—almost reverent. I wanted so badly to tell him I loved him, but didn't know if he'd welcome the sentiment or not. I'd told him once, months ago, and hadn't repeated it. So instead, I tried to show him.

Afterward, we lay in bed, me cuddled into him again. If Devon had time to linger, I'd noticed he wasn't one of those men I'd always heard about that went right to sleep. He liked to hold me, oftentimes sipping from a shot of gin sitting on the table. It was a comfortable silence and my mind wandered. After tonight, I felt closer to him, and dared to ask the question that had lingered in the back of my mind for months.

"Why did you kill Jace?" I asked. We'd never talked about it. I'd just . . . known it had been him.

"How do you know I killed him?"

I twisted and looked up at him, but didn't speak. He must've been able to read my face because his lips twisted.

"All right then," he said softly.

"Why?" I repeated.

"He deserved to die," Devon replied, his shoulders lifting in a slight shrug. "I had the opportunity, motive, and capability. I believe that is all that's required."

"Motive?"

"He'd hurt you," he said simply. "I couldn't allow that to happen again."

I shuddered at the thought, remembering how Jace had attacked me in the parking lot of the bank.

It felt odd, and yet . . . "Thank you," I said. Was it right for me to be thanking the man who'd murdered my stepbrother? Probably not. But what Jace had done to me wasn't right either. It felt like justice.

"You're welcome."

"Did you think to maybe ask me first?" I asked.

"Now why would I do that?"

I shrugged. "I dunno. I just thought maybe . . . you should've, I guess. Maybe."

"And what would you have said?" he countered. "You would've told me not to because your conscience wouldn't have allowed you to sign his death warrant."

"He was an evil man," I said. "He deserved to die."

"I agree, but you wouldn't have been able to live with yourself," he said. "So I made the decision."

"What about *your* conscience?" I asked.

"That's simple, darling," he said. "I don't have one."

I didn't know if I could argue. I didn't know Devon very well, but I knew he could kill a man quicker than I could take a breath and not blink an eye afterward.

"Why are you so loyal to them?" I asked. I wanted to say "the Shadow," but I knew Devon didn't like me to talk about the secret spy organization he worked for.

"They gave my life meaning and purpose," he said.

"They?"

He hesitated. "Vega. Vega recruited me into the Shadow."

I remembered the older woman who'd shown up in the hospital when I'd been caught and beaten in an effort to get Devon to talk. She'd been anything but warm and fuzzy.

"She found you?" I repeated. "And then what?"

"She took me under her wing. Trained me. Helped me. Gave me a place, skills, and weapons to fight for my country. I could avenge my family."

It was hard for me to view the menacing woman who'd very nearly threatened me with the picture Devon painted of a nurturing type. It seemed incongruous with her character, but I'd been on pain medication at the time, so maybe she wasn't so bad.

"So are you loyal to the job?" I asked. "Or her?"

Before Devon could answer, I heard my phone buzz. Wondering if it was Scott or, God forbid, Clive, I stretched down to the floor and dug in my purse to unearth my cell. The number was blocked and my gut churned with renewed dread as I answered it. I hadn't thought about Clive all day.

"Ivy?"

My mouth dropped open in surprise. "Logan? Is that you?"

"Ivy, yeah, it's me. Please . . . help me."

CHAPTER FIVE

What is it? What's wrong?" The questions came tumbling out in a rush.

"I—" But he was cut off.

"Good evening, Ivy," Clive said. "I trust you're having a nice night?"

"Clive," I choked out. "Why is Logan with you?"

"I wanted to get to know more about you," he replied. "How better than to spend some quality time with your bestie?"

The phone was suddenly plucked from my hand.

"I believe I'm the one you're looking for, mate," Devon said, switching the phone to speaker-mode.

"Well, look who's come back to town!" Clive crowed. "You see, Ivy, I told you he'd come back for you. So predictable, aren't you, Clay?"

"If I was predictable, you would've found me by now," Devon retorted. "What do you want with Logan? I'm the one you're after."

"Yes, but it's been so much fun, tormenting your sweet Ivy, I decided to up the ante, so to speak."

"What are you talking about?"

"You always think you're so clever," Clive said. "Saint Devon, who can do no wrong. But your cleverness didn't help my Anna, did it? Instead, you saved your girl and let my wife die." Bitter accusation rang in his voice now. "Ivy should be dead. Not Anna."

"Clive, that's not what happened—"

"I don't care what you think happened," Clive cut him off. "Anna's dead and she's not coming back. Someone has to pay for that. I've decided it's you, Clay."

"Where's Logan?" Devon asked, apparently deciding it wasn't worth arguing with Clive any longer.

"He's someplace quite pure, and most likely will be there for an eternity, God rest his soul."

I gasped, covering my mouth with my hand.

"Can you be more specific?" Devon bit out.

"I'm afraid not. I'll give him back his phone, though, so he can be sure to say his final words. Ivy, dear, do be kind to him. You may be fucking Clay, but Logan's quite in love with you. Make his last moments on this earth mean something. See you around . . . Ivy."

My pulse was pounding, the bitter taste of fear in my mouth. I heard a scraping sound, like concrete against concrete, then silence.

"Logan?" I asked.

"Ives . . ." His voice echoed and I could tell the phone was on speaker-mode there, too.

"Logan, where are you?"

"I don't know," he said. "There's a blindfold. I-I think I'm in a coffin or something."

"Oh God," I breathed. "Can you get out?"

"My arms . . . they're tied with zip ties," he said. "I can't really move. He just tossed the phone in here and then I heard him shut the lid."

Devon was already up and out of the bed, yanking on his clothes.

I hurried to copy him. All I could think about was that Logan was somewhere enclosed, which meant he'd die of asphyxiation.

"Tell me everything you remember," Devon ordered. He was holstering his gun as I slipped on my shoes.

"I was heading home," Logan said. "This car pulled up next to me. I glanced over and the passenger window was down. Next thing I know, I'm out cold and waking up bound, blindfolded, and in this thing."

"Can you hear any sounds?" Devon asked, grabbing the phone and my hand before heading out the door.

"Not now. It . . . it's really quiet."

I could hear the fear in Logan's voice. He was keeping it controlled, but underneath the calm I could feel his panic lurking.

"Did you hear anything before?"

"I don't—wait, yeah, there was something, but . . ." He hesitated.

"What?" Devon prompted.

"It's weird, but I thought I heard . . . singing."

Devon was pulling open the car door, but paused just briefly, his face creasing in a frown.

"What kind of singing?"

"Like . . . lots of people. Nice music. But it was faint and far away."

"I need you to get your arms free," Devon said, starting the car. He stomped on the gas and the car shot down the street.

"I can't. They're zip tied. I told you that."

"If we can't find you, you'll run out of air in about an hour. It's already been almost ten minutes. Are your arms in front of you?"

"Yes."

"Then turn your elbows out and yank them apart. You're a strong man, Logan. You can do this."

Logan had less than an hour to live, the air he breathed becoming slowly poisoned by carbon dioxide as the oxygen depleted. My fingernails dug into the seat as I held on, my mind painting a picture of Logan alone, dying in the dark, and all because of me.

"I can't," Logan said.

"You can," Devon insisted, his voice loud and commanding. "Try again. This is your life we're talking about. Break the damn ties."

I heard a scuffing sound, then a couple of grunts, then a loud thump.

"I did it!" Logan sounded elated, but breathless.

"Good. Well done," Devon said, taking a corner at breakneck speed. I didn't even know where he was going, but he was going full tilt to get there. "Can you move the lid?"

I waited, praying. But after a moment Logan said, "No. I can't. It's . . . it's concrete."

The blood drained from my face. Logan was imprisoned in concrete. He couldn't move something like that.

"There's other stuff in here, but I can't tell what it is," he said. "I feel cloth . . . and sharp things, some are smooth." He paused. "I think they're bones."

Logan got very quiet as we all processed this information. I looked at Devon, but his jaw was locked tight and he was concentrating on driving, so I didn't say anything.

"Ives . . ."

"Yeah, Logan?"

"I-I miss you."

My heart nearly broke at those words, and tears leaked from my eyes. "I miss you, too," I said, "but you shouldn't talk. You-you're wasting your air."

"If I'm going to die, then I want to tell you," he said.

"Tell me what?"

"That I love you."

I sniffed, swiping at my cheeks. This couldn't be happening.

My best friend could not be minutes from dying a horrible death somewhere in the city. "I know you do," I replied. "I love you, too."

"No, not like that," Logan said. "I'm *in* love with you. I have been for . . . well, for forever, I guess."

I stared at the phone, unable to process this.

"I just thought, you know, that you should know," he said.

"Logan—" I didn't know what I was going to say, but it didn't matter because Devon cut me off.

"Save your breath," he said to Logan. "If you are where I think you are, we're almost there. It'd be a shame to miss being rescued within moments because you weren't conserving your oxygen." His tone was flat and he didn't look at me.

Logan didn't talk again, but I could hear him breathing. It was growing labored and raspy and I gripped the phone so hard that metal cut into my palm.

We pulled to a screeching halt and I looked out the window. We were in front of the Cathedral Basilica, one of the oldest churches in St. Louis. Devon vaulted out and I followed.

"Logan, hold on," I said, running after Devon.

I barely had time to take in the soaring ceiling and the mosaics covering the walls. The pews were empty as we raced by, me blindly following Devon to the back of the rectory then through a door and down a long, winding staircase. A heavy, wooden door blocked our path at the bottom, but Devon pushed it open. We emerged into a cold basement with portraits on the walls of people I didn't know—Catholic priests maybe, or past popes.

Devon had skidded to a halt, looking around.

"Now what?" I asked. "Is he here?" I couldn't keep the panic and fear out of my voice. What if Devon was wrong? What if this wasn't where Clive had taken Logan? We'd be too late to go anywhere else.

Devon didn't answer, but spied something. Another, smaller,

wooden door tucked around a corner. This one was locked and it took precious seconds to get it open.

"Logan? Are you still there?" I called into the phone, but there was no answer. "Oh God, oh God, oh God," I whispered, and maybe it was a prayer, too. We had to find him. I didn't know what I would do without Logan.

Devon flipped on a light switch, and a naked bulb dangling from the ceiling lit up. The room was large, the floor was packed earth, and it was at least thirty degrees cooler in there. I shivered, but it wasn't from the cold.

A dozen or more marble crypts filled the room, each one decorated in lavish fashion with a painting on the lid and sides.

"Is Logan in one of these?" I asked.

Devon nodded. "I think so."

But which one? Logan was no longer responding to try to help us, which meant time was almost out, if it wasn't gone altogether. I stared helplessly at the crypts, knowing we didn't have time to lift the lids on all of them.

Devon was studying the floor and I followed his gaze. There was a very slight impression of a shoe a few feet from the door. Devon cautiously followed it, until we ended up in front of a crypt nestled in the middle.

"Best guess, darling," Devon murmured to me, grabbing a crowbar that was leaning against the wall.

I watched, praying constantly, as it took what felt like forever for Devon to move the heavy lid. Logan had to be in there, he had to be alive, because the alternative was . . . unthinkable.

With a mighty heave, Devon finally moved the lid a few precious inches, then pushed again and the lid slid aside, falling to the floor with a resounding crash. I barely noticed, dropping the phone as I rushed forward.

"Logan!"

He was inside, but his eyes were closed and he didn't respond to his name.

Devon tapped hard on Logan's cheeks with the flat of his palm. "Come on, old boy, wake up," he said.

Tears were falling fast now, but my eyes were glued to Logan. I felt close to losing it. He had to wake up. He *had* to.

Suddenly, Logan sucked in a breath of air, his eyes popping open.

"There, that's better," Devon said, taking a step back.

I flew at Logan, who was struggling to sit up. Cupping his face in my hands, I made him look at me.

"Logan, are you all right?" I asked anxiously. "Please tell me you're all right."

He focused on me. "Yeah, yeah," he said. "I'm okay. Just help me get out of here."

Devon stepped forward and helped Logan out. Logan's shirt was torn and dirty from being inside the crypt. Glancing into the space, I saw the bones he'd felt in the dark. Someone else had been buried inside there, the tattered red velvet cloths now in disarray and the bones scattered. It had nearly become Logan's burying place, too. I shuddered.

Hands were on my shoulders, turning me around, then Logan was pulling me into his arms, wrapping me tightly against him. I started crying in earnest now, ugly sobs I couldn't control.

"Shh, Ives, I'm okay," he murmured.

I couldn't even answer him, I was crying too hard. I clung to him, relief so overwhelming coursing through me that it weakened my knees and I was glad Logan was holding me up or I would've fallen to the ground.

"We need to leave," Devon said.

Logan gently moved me to the side so he could walk, though I kept hold of him, my face buried against his chest. He maneuvered us up and out of the church. I couldn't let him go, and when we got back to Devon's car, I climbed into the backseat with him.

My sobbing had eased and now my head throbbed and my eyes were swollen. My arms were wrapped around his torso as I huddled close to his side. He had an arm around my shoulders, the other curved into my waist. I closed my eyes and concentrated on memorizing the feel of him, my best friend, who'd nearly died because of my obsession with Devon.

The car was moving, but I didn't care where we were going. I just knew I would not be separated from Logan, not for the moment anyway.

"How'd you know I was there?" Logan asked, his voice a rumble in his chest.

"Clive loves to play these kinds of games," Devon replied from the front seat. "He drops little clues. He called me *Saint Devon*, then he said you were somewhere *pure* for an *eternity*. You said you'd heard singing, and the only church around here that has evening services is the Basilica."

I'd heard Clive say all those things, too, but I still hadn't had a clue that Logan was in a church. I tightened my hold on Logan, who did the same to me.

"Where are you taking us?" Logan asked.

"We should discuss that," Devon said, parking the car. Curiosity made me glance up and I saw he'd picked the same all-night diner that he'd taken me to once before. "Let's have a cup of tea, shall we?"

Tea was the last thing I wanted—more like a stiff shot of Jack—but I didn't protest as we got out of the car. Logan took my hand and we followed Devon inside.

There were few patrons in the diner and a tired-looking waitress led us to a booth. I slid in next to Logan while Devon sat opposite us. She placed water and menus in front of us, then walked away.

Logan drank his water down immediately.

I inched closer to him, trying not to dwell on how close he'd come to dying tonight.

"I guess I should thank you," Logan said to Devon. "But seeing as how this wouldn't have happened to me if you weren't in Ivy's life, my gratitude is somewhat diminished. No offense."

"None taken," Devon replied easily. "And you're welcome."

The waitress came back and Devon ordered tea. Logan and I ordered coffee.

"So what now?" Logan asked, once she'd set our cups down and gone away. "Will that guy come back? Try to kill me again? Or Ivy?"

I didn't tell him that Clive had already tried to kill me.

"Yes, it is a bit of a problem," Devon admitted. "And I don't have the time right now to take care of it."

"What does that mean?" Logan asked, his eyes narrowing. "'Take care of it?'"

"It means I don't have time to hunt him down and kill him." Devon's bluntness made me wince. "I have to leave. But I obviously can't leave the two of you here."

Have to leave. The words made my heart sink into my stomach. I'd fallen a bit more in love with Devon today and he was leaving again.

"Yes, you can," Logan retorted. "We'll take a few days off. Go somewhere, maybe. Then you can let us know when you have taken care of it."

"You'll be dead within the day," Devon said flatly. "You do not have the skills to hide from someone like Clive."

"Then what do you suggest?" Logan shot back.

"Ivy should go home for a few days."

"I don't have a home," I said automatically. All my stuff, save for a small suitcase of possessions, was in Devon's destroyed apartment.

"I meant home to Kansas," Devon clarified.

I stared at him, then started shaking my head. "Uh-uh. No way. I'm not going back there."

"There's got to be another place we can go," Logan said.

Devon was studying me, his expression bemused, but I didn't want to clarify my antipathy for home.

"It's in the middle of nowhere and is a place you know well," Devon replied. "I think that's where you should go. Also, his next move when he can't find either of you will be to target Ivy's grandparents. It would be helpful if we were there first."

The thought of Clive getting to my grandparents shut down my protests.

"We'll go and I'll take care of him when he shows up," Devon continued.

"I thought you didn't have the time." Logan's voice was bitter.

"I don't have the time to hunt him," Devon said. "So we'll make him come to us. Much easier, and quicker."

I didn't know what to think about that. Clive was dangerous. By letting Devon lead him to my grandparents, I was putting them in danger, and I didn't know if I trusted Devon to keep them safe. But what choice did I have?

"It's Ivy's call," Logan said. Both men looked at me.

Logan's hand was still wrapped around mine underneath the table. He gave it a squeeze. He knew what it meant for me to go back home, what it would do to me, what it always did to me. But I nodded.

"Okay. If that's what we have to do to get rid of Clive, then okay."

Devon gave a curt nod and finished his tea. Logan and I hadn't even touched our coffee. Tossing some money on the table, Devon slid out of the booth. Logan and I followed him back to the car.

"We'll stay at the hotel tonight," Devon said, "and leave in the morning."

Neither Logan nor I was in a position to disagree.

At the hotel, things got awkward.

"I'll get a room for you," Devon said to Logan.

"He didn't take my wallet," Logan said stiffly. "I can get my own room."

"I'm quite sure you can," Devon replied. "But your credit card is likely being tracked, and rather than waiting for Clive to show up, I'd like to get some rest."

Logan's face flushed, but he didn't say anything. They faced off for a moment before Devon turned and headed for the registration desk. Logan turned to me.

"How much longer is this going to go on?" he asked. "You and him?"

"I don't know," I answered honestly. "Clive showed up, then Devon did, too."

"Who is this Clive? What does he want?"

"He wants to get back at Devon," I explained. "Something bad happened"—I really didn't want to go into Anna and the virus right now—"and he blames Devon."

"Should he?"

"No." My answer was unequivocal. Heinrich had killed Anna. Not Devon. Devon had tried to save her.

Logan digested this in silence as Devon returned.

"Lucky you," Devon said to Logan. "The room next to ours was vacant."

"Wonderful," Logan deadpanned.

"Come along, darling." Devon reached for me. I still had hold of Logan's hand and I had to make a split-second decision if I was going to let go or not. I hesitated, but before I could decide, Logan let go of me and Devon took my elbow.

When we reached our rooms, I gave Logan another long, hard hug.

"I love you," I said softly in his ear, then I released him and let Devon guide me into our room. I saw Logan staring at us from the hallway as the door swung shut.

I was exhausted, the emotional turmoil having taken a toll on me. Collapsing onto the bed, I heaved a sigh. Devon sat next to me.

"All right, darling?" he asked. Reaching out, he tucked a lock of my hair behind my ear.

"I'm all right," I said. "It's just . . . we were almost too late. Logan nearly died. A couple more minutes—"

"Don't think about it," he interrupted. "The *almost*s and *nearly*s will paralyze you with fear. Accept it and move on."

"I have to think about it," I said, stung. "Logan's my best friend. He means more to me than anyone in the whole world. And I could've lost him tonight. Forever. After my grandparents, he's all I have."

"That's not precisely true."

I looked at him, questioning.

"I'm here, am I not?" he asked. He said it lightly, but his expression was serious.

"Yes, but you said it yourself. We're temporary," I reminded him. "And apparently, you'd planned on leaving tomorrow."

"So why not be with Logan then?" he said, standing and walking to the closet. He discarded his holster and gun and began unbuttoning his shirt. "He loves you. You love him. It sounds like a match made in heaven."

I watched him, wondering if I was imagining the slightly bitter note in his voice. "I don't love him like that," I explained. "I don't . . . see him that way. Logan's like a big brother to me. I can't imagine being . . . sexual with him." I shied away from the very thought. It felt wrong to think of Logan in those terms.

"Well, he thinks of you that way," he said, shrugging off his shirt. "So perhaps you ought to tell the sorry bastard how you feel."

"I don't want to hurt him," I said.

"That's unavoidable. He's a grown man. He can take it."

Maybe Logan could, but it would forever change our relationship. Would he still want to be around me? What if he didn't? These last few months of hardly seeing him had been difficult. I knew I was being selfish and yet . . . I didn't want to lose him.

Devon shucked his pants and climbed onto the bed, reaching to pull my shirt over my head. He was completely comfortable being naked, which sometimes unnerved me.

"Aren't you tired?" I asked as he reached for the fastening of my jeans. His mouth settled over my breast.

"Never too tired for this," he murmured.

And that happened to be true.

⁓

We were ready to go as the sun was just peeking over the horizon in the morning. I was tired after only a few hours of sleep, but Devon gave every appearance of being utterly rested. I had no idea how he did what he did with as little sleep as he got.

Logan was awake, too, but his face was drawn and his smile forced when he saw me. Devon had lent him a fresh shirt to wear and we did a quick stop at his apartment on the way out of town for him to pack a bag. I was glad we were heading west, the rising sun at our backs, as I sipped a steaming cup of coffee.

Devon had situated me in the front passenger seat before I'd even really thought about it, and I wondered at his sudden possessiveness, if that's even what it was. Logan had taken the back without a word.

I'd left a message for my boss this morning, telling a white lie about my grandma being ill so I had to take off work for a few days.

It wasn't as though I could tell him the truth, and I hoped I'd have a job to come back to when this was all over.

We'd driven for almost thirty minutes when the silence started getting to me. It wasn't a comfortable silence, but rife with tension and unsaid things. Maybe Devon was right. Maybe I should've talked to Logan last night. He'd confessed something very personal, and I'd pretty much just ignored it. That had to hurt. But I also didn't think now was the right time to have that difficult conversation with him. It would have to wait.

"So how's work been?" I asked Logan, twisting in my seat so I could see him.

He shrugged. "It's all right. Supposedly, I'm on the short list for partner."

"That's great!" I enthused. "I know you've worked really hard for that."

"Thanks," he said. "Though after nearly dying last night, it doesn't seem quite as important in the big scheme of things."

"I'm glad you're okay," I said. "I don't know what I would have done if something had happened to you." When he didn't reply, I looked up again and our eyes met.

"But Logan survived and all is well," Devon interrupted. "Unless you're blaming Ivy. Are you, Logan?"

Logan's expression grew hard and his gaze swiveled to meet Devon's in the rearview mirror. "I think everyone knows it's your fault. Not hers," he retorted.

"Shite happens," Devon replied. "Consider it a temporary disruption to the dull monotony of your life."

I wanted to chastise Devon for baiting him, but Logan spoke first. "My life is dull only when Ivy's not in it. Can you say the same? Oh wait, she's a brief, fleeting thought in your mind as you pass through town. My mistake."

Well.

"I think you presume to know quite a lot about me," Devon said, his voice flat.

"I'm just saying what Ivy's thinking."

Devon glanced at me. "Is that true?"

I couldn't disagree, but I didn't want to start an argument either. Devon had promised me nothing. It wasn't his fault I was in love with him.

"It's fine," I said. "Logan's . . . overreacting."

"Really?" Logan said. "He tells you to jump and you say how high. How am I overreacting?"

"It's not really your business," I said, getting irritated and embarrassed. I'd just been wanting to have a bit of conversation to break the silence, not get in some pissing match with Logan. "It's my mistake to make, not yours—"

"You view me as a mistake?"

Devon's question cut me off and I glanced at him, surprised at the note of hurt in his voice.

"I . . . ah . . . of course not," I said, cheeks burning. "That came out wrong. That's all."

His blue eyes saw right through me until I had to look away. The car got quiet again after that, and this time I didn't bother trying to break the silence.

It took a little over eight hours to make it to Dodge City and I was more than ready to leave the car—as well as Devon and Logan—behind. When we finally pulled up in my grandparents' driveway, I was the first one out.

"You know, you can drop me off at my folks'," Logan said, climbing out. "There's no reason for me to stay here."

"Best if we're all together," Devon replied curtly, swinging his door shut. "I don't want to leave Ivy in possible danger because of having to go rescue you."

Logan stiffened and I braced myself for another argument

between them when the screen door on the porch swung open and Grams came out.

"Ivy? Logan? Is that you? Gracious, child! You didn't tell me you were comin'!" She hurried down the steps and I crossed the drive to meet her.

"It was kind of a last-minute trip," I said, hugging her. "Is that okay?"

"Of course it is! Your grandpa is going to be just beside himself to see you're here. You don't come to visit nearly as much as we'd like, you know that."

She smelled like homemade bread and fabric softener, giving me a hug that was longer and harder than usual. Guilt crept over me. She was right. I didn't come visit very often, and I had a good reason for that, but it wasn't anything I could tell her.

"And Logan," she said, finally releasing me. He picked her up off her feet in a big hug that made her laugh and blush.

"How you doing, Grams?" he asked, setting her back down. "Still breaking hearts all over Ford County?"

"Go on with you," she chastised him, but I could see her hiding a smile. She loved Logan and he always could charm her to get out of anything he'd done, including eating her freshly made strawberry preserves in the summer.

"Now who's this, Ivy?"

She was looking at Devon, her eyebrows raised as she took him in. Devon didn't look like he belonged on a farm in the middle of Nowhere, Kansas. The aura of danger that emanated from him couldn't be concealed and I saw Grams frown slightly. I hesitated, unsure how I should introduce him. Should I use his real name? Say he was my boyfriend? That felt odd.

"I'm Devon," he said, stepping forward to take her hand. Gallantly, he raised it to his lips and pressed a kiss lightly to the backs of her knuckles. "And you must be Ivy's sister."

Grams laughed outright at that, but her cheeks grew pinker. "Well aren't you the charmer," she teased. "I'm this young lady's grandmother, Ann. But you can call me Grams. Everyone does."

"Ann is a beautiful name," Devon said with a teasing smile. "Fitting for a lovely lady like yourself."

"And are you Logan's friend?" Grams asked. "Or—"

"Ivy has been kind enough to allow me to call on her," Devon said. "We've been seeing each other for a few months."

"Oh!" Grams said, noticeably brightening. Her smile was blinding. "You're her beau! That's wonderful! She's never brought home a beau before."

I wanted to groan, but kept quiet. At least she'd called him the old-fashioned "beau" rather than "boyfriend." That was something. Gave it a bit of class.

"Grams," I interrupted before she had us married off—I could almost see her eyes glaze over with wedding plan ideas. "We're just going to stay a few days. Is that all right?"

"Of course it is, honey," she said, waving off my concerns with a flick of her hand. "Your grandpa's out in the fields somewhere, checking the crops. We had some hail last night, but I think it wasn't too bad." She turned back to Logan and Devon. "Go on and get your things, bring them inside. Ivy and I will just whip up some lunch."

She slid her arm around my waist and I rested mine on her shoulders. A good foot shorter than me, she was plump and had hands that were work-roughened from many years of being a farmer's daughter, then a farmer's wife. We walked inside as she started chatting about the neighbors and the latest gossip from church. I didn't look back to see how Logan and Devon were faring.

Lunch turned out to be fried chicken, mashed potatoes, and gravy. I didn't complain because my grams made the best fried chicken on the planet and Logan could put away an entire chicken just on his own. By the time Grandpa got back inside, there was a heaping platter of chicken on the table, a mound of snow-white potatoes, and a bowl of gravy that had my mouth watering. I was just pulling the biscuits out of the oven when Logan walked up behind me.

"Just like old times," he said, snagging a biscuit off the sheet. And he was right. We'd spent many an afternoon at my grandparents', the smell of food wafting through the air and sunshine dappling the ancient linoleum kitchen floor.

"Yeah," I replied with a smile. "It is." I set the biscuits down and took the oven mitt off my hand.

"They melt in your mouth," Logan said. "Just like always." He held the biscuit up to my mouth. I automatically took a bite. No one's biscuits were as light and flaky as my grams's.

"Mmmm," was all I could manage with my mouth full.

Over Logan's shoulder, I saw Devon standing in the doorway of the old country kitchen, watching us. He did not look pleased. As a matter of fact, the glare he was sending Logan's way was intense enough that I took an instinctive step back to put some space between us.

"Is that my Ivy-girl?"

Logan stepped aside as my grandpa wrapped me in a hug. "Hi, Grandpa," I said, squeezing him back. He was dressed in a pair of faded, well-worn overalls and smelled like the earth and sunshine. His face was weathered from too many years in the sun, but his smile was as warm and kind as I remembered.

"I can hardly believe you've finally come home for a spell," he said once we parted. He moved past me and went to wash his hands in the sink. "Your grandmother's been missing you somethin' fierce."

"And you haven't?" I teased.

He laughed good-naturedly, drying his hands on a kitchen towel. "You know I always miss you. And I hear you brought home a special friend." He gave me a meaningful glance.

I shrugged. "Just a friend. Nothing serious," I lied.

"Well, you have the right of it, bringing him home to meet your grandmother. She can spot a bad apple at twenty yards."

I wondered what Grams thought of Devon. Remembering her enthusiasm at his greeting, I doubted she'd be able to see past his charm and easy smile.

Lunch was awkward for a few minutes, until the easy routine of gossip and chitchat while passing food around the table over-came my jitters at having Devon there. I caught his eye a few times and wondered what he thought of my country family and down-home cooking, especially considering all the places I was sure he'd traveled around the world.

"So. Devon, wasn't it?" Grandpa asked in his "old-school" voice, the kind that he used when teaching Sunday School and that was guaranteed to cow even the most unruly ten-year-old boy into obedience.

"Yes, sir," Devon replied.

"And what do you do for a living, young man?"

This should be interesting.

"I work for the government," Devon replied easily, helping himself to another serving of potatoes. "The British government."

Grandpa frowned. "So you're not American?" Devon's cultured accent was quite distinct from the sharp vowels and consonants of my grandpa's Midwestern accent, but I guess he'd just assumed Devon was American regardless of how he spoke.

"No, sir."

"Are you a Christian?"

"Protestant Church of England."

"Protestant. Well, that's all right then."

I hid a smile. Thank God he hadn't said he was Catholic.

"And what do you do for the government?" my grandpa continued.

"Grandpa, you don't have to quiz Devon like this," I interjected.

"Of course I do," Grandpa said. "Now hush and let me get to know your beau."

Oh, Lord. I wanted to slide from my chair and disappear under the table, but couldn't. If I didn't keep him in check, who knew if he'd be asking Devon about his "intentions" in the next few minutes? Which would just be mortifying.

"I work in foreign relations," Devon said, which I thought was a nice euphemism for "spy."

"That requires a lot of travel?" Grandpa asked.

"It does."

"Not real good for a family," Grandpa observed.

Devon hesitated, then gave a bland smile. "Perhaps not."

"Hmm." Grandpa was frowning and it seemed Grams sensed my dismay at the turn of the conversation, because she stood and started collecting empty plates.

"Ivy, you want to help me with these?"

I obeyed, jumping to my feet to help. I noticed Logan had a satisfied look on his face, so I stepped on his foot.

"Ow!"

I gave him a look. "You can help clean up, you know," I reminded him. He'd eaten enough meals here to no longer receive guest status. He grimaced at me, but started helping clear the table.

"I can help, too," Devon said quietly to me, getting to his feet. He'd discarded his jacket in the car, which was good because a full suit was way too overdressed for lunch at Gram's. But even so, his slacks, dress shirt, and leather shoes probably cost more than the table we'd eaten on. He looked very out of place, but seemed at ease. An odd dichotomy.

"It's okay," I said to him. "Grams won't approve of you clearing plates."

"Logan is helping." He sounded disgruntled as he cast a jaundiced glare at Logan's retreating back.

"Yes, but Logan's family. You're a guest and you're a man. No way will she let you help." Grams was old-fashioned like that. "Just wait for me. We won't be long."

Grandpa was already heading back into the fields and I heard the slam of the screen door. I guessed he was done quizzing Devon, for the moment, at least.

After doing dishes, I found Devon sitting on the front porch swing. I sat down next to him. His arm was stretched along the back, but he moved it to my shoulders, drawing me closer to his side.

"Where's Logan?" he asked.

"Grams has him cornered, giving him what-for about his love life and how he should settle down and stop being a tomcat."

Devon laughed lightly. His fingers traced circles on my shoulder, bared by the sleeveless summer dress he'd bought me. His touch made me shiver, which he felt, because he traced a light path down my arm and back up.

"Do you think Clive will come tonight?" I asked.

"No. Too soon. Tomorrow night, perhaps."

I nodded. Didn't speak. The late afternoon was beautiful, the sunshine bright and cheery. The weather neither too warm nor too cold. Bees buzzed and I could hear birds singing. It was the perfect country spring day. Devon gently pushed the swing, causing us to sway slowly back and forth.

"Why don't you come home?" he asked.

And suddenly, the day seemed a lot darker.

I swallowed before answering. "I don't like to talk about it."

"You've told me things before," he reminded me. I didn't answer. "Is it because of Jace?" he prodded.

"Shh!" I quickly glanced to make sure Grams wasn't around. "Don't talk about it," I told him in a low voice.

He frowned. "Why not?"

"Because they don't know."

Devon's eyebrows lifted in surprise. "You mean you've never told them what he did to you?"

I shook my head. "It was hard enough when my mom died. She was their only daughter. Then Jace and I came to live here, until he crashed his car and went to jail."

"I see."

And I knew he did. I'd been upfront with him about what Jace had done to me. Devon knew all my secrets. Almost. An image of the journal sheets with the vaccine formula flitted through my head. Why I was keeping them instead of destroying them, I wasn't sure. Maybe I didn't trust that Devon could keep me safe forever and someday, those sheets might be my only bargaining chip.

"Scott's been texting me," I confessed.

That got his attention. So much so that he stopped the swing.

"What has he been texting?"

"He wants to know where I am. Says the FBI is offering protective custody." I paused. "That I don't need you in order to be safe."

Devon snorted. "The protective custody of the FBI will be like having a spotlight on you. And they never offer something for nothing. Did he say what they want?"

"All that I know about the virus and vaccine."

I didn't tell him that Scott had sent personal notes as well, wanting to know if I was all right, telling me he'd come get me if I wanted out of Devon's shadow, that I should consider what Devon was getting from this and how I would be wise not to trust him. I hadn't replied to much, other than to tell him I was okay, but he persisted in texting every few hours. He'd also found the money I left, and though I told him it was for his car, he just said he'd keep it for me and I could have it when I came back. *If* I came back.

At least Scott was a realist, I supposed.

"Did you text him back?"

"A little," I admitted.

"You realize he's one of those men who want to save you," Devon said bluntly.

I looked up at him. "What do you mean?"

"Some men love to be the knight in shining armor and a tragic female is irresistible to them." He glanced at me. "One as beautiful as you, even more so."

I didn't answer. I'd already realized that what Scott felt for me was based on my unfortunate past and what he saw in my life now. And who was I kidding? My life was messed up. I had issues with a capital "I," not the least of which were my feelings for Devon. Was it any wonder that Scott and Logan were constantly trying to "save" me? Until now—until Devon had stepped into my life—I hadn't seen it.

"Is that why you like me?" I asked.

The corner of Devon's mouth lifted. "I don't see you as a tragic, fragile flower, darling. You're much more of a steel magnolia to me."

I liked that. I didn't *feel* tragic or fragile, though I'd been blinded to the extent of how dysfunctional my relationships were with men before I'd met Devon. He treated me the way I thought a man should treat a woman, and it had opened my eyes.

❧

To my relief, Devon seemed to be entirely at ease with my grandparents and being in a rambling farmhouse. Things didn't get awkward again until after dinner when Grams started sorting out the sleeping situation.

". . . and Logan, you can have Jace's old room. Ivy, you have your room. And Devon, I can fix up the couch in the den for you," she said, bustling around with an armful of sheets and blankets.

Wow. Okay, I really didn't want to have Devon sleep on a couch.

"Grams, Devon can share my room," I said, even though I felt my face get hot. Devon was indeed the first man I'd ever brought home, besides Logan. This was a new situation for me.

She gave me a look. "Oh, I'm sorry," she said. "Is there a ring on your finger that I missed? Honey, men don't buy the cow if the milk's for free. He'll sleep on the couch." She disappeared into the den.

Logan glanced at Devon. "I think Grams just cockblocked you . . . *mate*," he smirked.

"And I'm pretty sure she called me a cow," I mused.

Devon didn't have a chance to reply before Grams returned. His only response was a slight twitching of his lips as he assured her that the couch was fine and wished everyone a good evening.

"He sure has pretty manners," Grams said, staring at the closed door to the den.

"Manners are only skin-deep," Logan retorted with more force than necessary. Grams gave him a look and he flushed. "I'm going to bed, too," he said. "'Night."

"'Night, Logan," I replied. He hugged me and Grams, then headed upstairs.

"Your grandpa's already sawin' logs," Grams said with a sigh. "I'd better join him. You let me know if you need anything, you hear?" She kissed me on the cheek and bustled off to bed.

I turned off the remaining lights, delaying the inevitable. I didn't want to go upstairs, had avoided my room for the entire day. I debated sleeping on the couch in the TV room, but decided that then I'd have to answer uncomfortable questions from Grams, and I didn't want to do that.

I climbed the stairs slowly, each step feeling as though I was wading through quicksand. My room was at the far end of the hall, the closed door staring silently at me. I passed by Logan's room, noticing it was dark underneath his door. He must already be in bed asleep.

My door creaked ever so slightly when I opened it, and I shuddered. That sound had been a foreboding one when I'd heard it in the dead of night. I broke out in a cold sweat, hesitating on the threshold.

Gathering my courage, I took a deep breath. Jace was dead. He would never hurt me again. But that thought didn't ease the breakneck speed of my pulse. Stepping into the room, I let my eyes adjust to the darkness.

And saw a man sitting on the bed.

CHAPTER
SIX

I would have screamed, but in the next instant, a lamp flicked on and I saw it was Devon. I stood, staring at him in disbelief.

"How did you get in here?" I asked, my voice breathless. "You were just downstairs. I saw you go into the den."

"The window," he said, casually tipping his head toward the glass casement.

I stared. "You *climbed* up to my room?"

"How else was I to bypass Grams?"

Normally, I would have laughed, but my anxiety was still such that it was hard to clear my head. My eyes were drawn to the bed, then quickly skittered away. Avoiding it, I sat down at the small antique vanity my grandpa had painted white. The bench was padded pink velvet and I absently picked up the hairbrush. Drawing its bristles through my hair, I brushed the long strands until they gleamed.

I stopped thinking, instead becoming immersed in my nighttime ritual. I'd done the same things every night before bed when I'd lived here, until they were a compulsion. Opening my makeup case, I began doing my face, taking great care to get my eyeliner just right. The blush was a light dusting of pink on my cheeks, my eye shadow a blend of grays and deep blue. It wasn't until I was tracing my lips with liner that Devon spoke.

"What are you doing, darling?" he asked.

I started at the sound of his voice. I'd forgotten he was even there. He was watching me with a bemused expression.

"Putting on my makeup," I said. I thought it was pretty obvious what I was doing.

"Why? You're going to bed. You take *off* your makeup before going to bed, not put it on."

Our gazes met in the mirror's reflection. I gave a tentative shrug. "It's what I do."

"But why?"

I carefully used a brush to add lipstick to my lips. "It makes me feel better."

"You don't do this in St. Louis," he said.

"No."

"But you do here."

I didn't answer. I'd put a little too much on and now had to use a tissue to blot some of the color. There. Perfect. I turned around.

"How do I look?" I asked.

"Beautiful," he said. "But why don't you take the makeup off, darling, and come to bed with me."

I shook my head. "I like the makeup. It makes me feel clean and pretty. Nothing bad can happen to me if I'm wearing it."

Devon stood and walked to me, then crouched down so our faces were even.

"I understand," he said softly. "I really do. Come with me."

He took my hand and I got to my feet. Drawing me to the bed, he sat me down on the edge. I was jittery with nerves, though not because of him. I always felt this way in here. Devon removed my shoes and his, then folded back the covers. He lay down and pulled my stiff body into his before tugging the blankets over us. His arms surrounded me and I could smell the scent of his cologne. It was something new in the room and I took a deep whiff, the aroma easing the knot of lead in my stomach.

"I remember the first man I ever killed in cold blood," he said.

That got my attention. "Who was he?" I asked. Our voices were quiet in the room, the house still and silent around us.

"His name doesn't matter," he replied. "He had lied to me and betrayed my trust. Betrayed the trust of the woman I work for."

"Vega."

"Yes. He had sold us out for money. They came in the dead of night and took me. I endured three months of torture and beatings before I was able to escape. When I did, I went hunting for him. I found him at home in bed, a woman at his side. I didn't hesitate. One shot, center of the forehead. He was dead scarcely moments after he realized who I was."

Devon had been tortured for three months. Those words rang inside my head, making my chest ache. I held on to him a little tighter.

"Did you feel better?" I asked.

"Quite."

"What about the woman? Did you kill her, too?"

"No. She was just a prostitute."

I thought for a moment. "Three months is a long time," I said. "How did you survive?"

"I wanted revenge," he said simply. "I endured because I was not going to allow him to betray me and get away with it. If he'd tortured me himself, I would have had more respect for him. But he betrayed me. There is nothing worse." He paused. "Like how your stepbrother betrayed you. He was supposed to be your family, but at his hands you found only torture. I understand how you feel."

I was quiet, digesting this. Devon had gone out on a limb, telling me all that, just so he could share a bit of his pain with mine.

"You didn't undress," I said.

"No."

"And I'm still dressed, too."

"Yes."

"I don't want to be."

Turning his body, Devon braced himself above me, his gaze on mine. His hand found the hem of my dress and lifted it, his fingers skimming the tops of my thighs and sending a shiver through me. He didn't take his eyes off me, holding me in the present. I wanted to wash away the bad memories of this room and replace them with good ones.

The dress was drawn up and over my head, then tossed aside. The blankets fell back as Devon stripped off his clothes before removing my bra and panties. The light remained on and I think he understood I needed it to be that way.

His skin was warm against mine and I drew him to me with a sigh. This felt familiar. This felt right. He kissed me, a sweet brush of his lips against mine that said more than any words could that I was something special.

We didn't talk and he went slowly, until I forgot where we were and only saw him, only felt him. His mouth was between my legs, his tongue inside me, when I came. Cries and moans fell from my lips as my body shuddered.

"Do you want me, darling?" he asked, his mouth pressing light kisses to my abdomen.

It was sweet of him to ask and my eyes stung with tears. "Yes," I whispered.

"Good," he said.

I shifted my thighs wider to accommodate him as he moved back up my body. I felt the hard press of him at the entrance of my body and lifted my hips. We both sighed when he pushed inside me.

Devon and I'd had sex many, many times. We'd also fucked.

This was different. It felt more real, more giving, more sharing . . . less taking. Not that it had been bad before. Sex with Devon had always been amazing. But in this moment, he held me and kissed me, his body moving slowly above mine, and it felt more like becoming one than it ever had.

I was already in love with him, but tonight he stole my heart.

He took great care to push me to another peak, prolonging my pleasure as I came apart beneath him. My senses were acute. Our bodies were slick with sweat, my legs curved around his back to hold him close, and his breath was hot on my neck.

"Beautiful Ivy," he whispered by my ear. "You're turning me inside out."

I'd barely registered the words before he reached his own climax, his body jerking hard into mine. I memorized the feel of Devon losing control, the sound of his gasps and groans as he came, the tightly bunched muscles of his shoulders and arms as he held me tight to his chest.

Afterward, he went to the bathroom, returning with a warm, wet washcloth. Silently, he held me as he wiped off my makeup. I looked into his blue eyes as he worked assiduously, gently cleaning my face until my skin was bare.

"There. That's better," he said. "Pretty and clean without the makeup as well." He set aside the cloth and the meaning of what he'd done wasn't lost on me. We lay spoon-style, my back to his front, and he idly played with my hair.

"I love you, you know," I said. It was hard to confess the words, sure as I was that I'd be rejected.

His fingers paused. "I know," he said at last.

"Do you love me?" I held my breath, waiting for the answer, unable not to hope.

"I care about you a great deal," he said, his fingers resuming their path through my hair.

My heart sank and I said nothing.

"I'm incapable of loving anyone, sweet Ivy," he said, and his voice was resigned and a little sad. "I told you that. You're too sweet a soul to understand."

"I don't believe you," I whispered. "You love Vega."

"Not in the same way you're asking me to love you," he said. "She has my loyalty and yes, that's a form of love, I suppose."

We lay in silence while I tried to process this. I was bared to my soul and couldn't help the sharp stab of rejection I felt.

"Shall I stay in here with you tonight?" he asked, but I shook my head.

"No. I shudder to think of what Grams would do if she caught us."

"I would surmise I'd learn firsthand the true meaning of the phrase 'shotgun wedding,'" he teased.

I forced a smile, realizing he had no idea how much he'd just hurt me. "Thank you for being in here. For understanding." Because he *had* understood, and he'd helped me the way no one else had ever been able to.

He brushed a kiss to my forehead before getting out of bed. I watched him dress in silence, admiring the play of muscles underneath his skin. When he was done, he came back to the bed and pulled the covers tighter around me. My hair was splayed across the pillows and he carefully brushed it aside the way I always did before going to sleep. I hated the feeling of my hair tangled around my neck when I slept.

"I'll see you in the morning, sweet Ivy."

He left the light on for me.

I stared at the door once he'd gone, realizing with painful clarity how dependent I was on Devon, on our relationship. What would I do without him? He'd made me feel alive, had given me hope and life and love. I'd be lost without him.

And he'd never love me the way I did him.

I'd always felt I was dependent on Logan, but this was much more than my friendship with him had ever been. Would men always see me as Logan and Scott did? As someone tragic and sad, in need of a man to "save" me? It hurt to know Scott saw me that way, and that I'd been mostly blind to it. Devon had realized right away, of course.

I hated myself in that moment. Hated my past that had made me what I was. Hated Jace for hurting me in a way that had damaged me forever. Even hated Logan for how he'd lied to me, making me think I was strong when really he thought I was weak. And Devon earned some of my hatred as well, for making me love him and not loving me back.

I didn't want to be Devon's fuck buddy. I wanted him to love me. And since he'd declared he couldn't—wouldn't—love me, then there was no reason I should continue sleeping with him. He may not like it, but I had to start weaning myself off him, one step at a time until I could stand on my own.

~⌒~

Devon wasn't there when I got up the next morning. Grams casually informed me that he'd gone to town but had said he'd be back soon. I had no idea what he'd gone into town for, I was just glad that he'd be coming back.

"Did you sleep well?" Logan asked, taking a sip of coffee.

"Fine, I guess," I said. I'd been a little surprised Logan hadn't knocked on my door last night, knowing as he did my problems with coming home.

"It sounded like you didn't get a lot of sleep," he said, and I caught the meaning behind that and flushed. I guessed he'd heard Devon and me, which explained his absence last night.

There wasn't anything I could really say to that, so I didn't. Instead, I caught his sleeve as he went to pass me. "Hey, can we talk?" I asked.

"Ah, sure," he said, and I understood the reluctance in his voice. Was it ever a good thing when someone began a conversation that way? Not in my experience.

"Let's sit on the porch," I suggested, and he followed me outside. We sat in the same spot Devon and I had occupied last night.

"What did you want to talk about?" he asked.

"You. Me. Us," I said, looking down at my hands twisting nervously in my lap. "What you said the other night when you were trapped."

"That I'm in love with you."

His bald statement made me glance up at him. "Yes."

Logan looked away, his gaze resting on the fields surrounding the house. It was cloudy today and storms threatened. "I know you didn't want to hear it, and don't feel the same way."

"I do love you," I said. "You're my best friend, like a brother to me."

"A brother." His laugh was tinged with bitterness. "Permanently friend-zoned. I can't get you out of my head, and all I'll ever be is like a brother to you."

"I'm so sorry," I said. "I don't want to hurt you. More than anything, I don't want to hurt you. Please believe me." My throat was thick as I stared at my best friend since childhood. With all we'd been through together, he'd been my rock on countless occasions.

He looked at me. Pain etched his features, but his smile was soft. "Don't be sorry, Ives," he said. "You didn't do anything. It's all on me, isn't it?"

I didn't respond and we looked at each other. His face was a treasure to me and I reached out to cup his cheek.

"I wish I did feel like you do," I said softly. "I truly do."

His smile had faded and his gaze was intent. "You've never tried, Ives," he said. "You put me in a box a long time ago and never let me out. We have something between us—a history and life together. We could have more, you just don't see it. Or maybe you don't want to."

The accusation in his voice stung and I pulled my hand back. "That's not true."

"Isn't it?"

I remained stubbornly silent.

"If it's not true, then kiss me."

I gaped at him. "Kiss you? What are you talking about?"

"If there's nothing between us, then a kiss won't mean a thing," he said.

"I'm not going to try and prove something like that to you," I said, getting to my feet.

"Afraid, Ives?" he jeered, standing and blocking my way back into the house.

"Don't be ridiculous," I snapped, irritated with him.

"You'll let some stranger kiss you, touch you, make love to you, but the friend you've had the longest doesn't even get a kiss?"

His reference to Devon made me stop in my efforts to bypass him. "You want to bring Devon into this?" I asked. "Again? This isn't about Devon."

"No, it's about us and how you won't even give me a chance," he said.

Exasperated, I threw up my hands. "Fine," I said. "If a kiss is what it'll take to convince you there's nothing between us and never will be, then be my guest." I stood there, hands on hips, waiting.

Logan watched me, then took a step forward until our bodies were almost touching. I tipped my head back to look at him. His hands settled on my hips and he tugged me closer. I automatically rested my hands on his chest. Logan wasn't as big as Devon, but he was in very good shape and I could feel the muscles underneath the cotton of his T-shirt.

"I've waited a long time for this," he murmured. His head dropped slowly toward mine and my eyes drifted closed. I could feel the warmth of his breath as our lips were millimeters apart—

I jerked away at the sound of a car pulling up. Devon had returned.

I felt guilty, for no real reason. Devon and I weren't a permanent thing, what I did with Logan was my own business. If I wanted to kiss him, then I would, and Devon could just watch for all I cared.

Right.

He was eyeing us as he got out of the car, his mirrored sunglasses on despite the cloudiness of the day.

"His timing sucks," Logan muttered bitterly.

I gave him a quick glare, then turned back to where Devon was climbing the stairs to the porch. He was hooking his glasses on the front of the deep navy polo shirt he wore. Though he was dressed more casually in khaki pants and the polo, the short sleeves of the shirt still stretched to accommodate the girth of his biceps.

"Where did you go?" I asked, nervously shoving my hands into the back pockets of my jeans.

"Into town," Devon said, ignoring Logan completely.

"Why?"

"Had to pick up a few things."

And that seemed to be as much information as he was going to give me. I rolled my eyes. Fine. Whatever. I wasn't about to stand out there and play twenty questions with him.

"I'm going to help Grams," I said, before turning on my heel and walking away, leaving both men on the porch. They could bond. I snorted at the thought.

"Hey, honey," Grams said as I entered the kitchen. She was elbow-deep in flour.

"Need some help?" I asked. Grams was well aware that cooking wasn't a talent I possessed, but she'd never criticized me for it.

"You could peel those apples for me," she said, nodding to a bag of Granny Smiths. "Thought I'd make a pie today."

Grams's pies were legendary, and I was quick to obey, peeling and slicing the apples as we chatted. She made her own dough, of course, and I watched as she cut in the shortening before rolling it out.

"I like Devon," she said out of the blue. "And he seems to like you an awful lot, too."

She was still rolling out the crust. "We've been seeing each other for a while," I said, noncommittal.

"Well, if you brought him home, it must be serious," she replied. "He's certainly old enough to be wanting to get married and settle down."

Best nip that thought in the bud. "He travels a lot with his job," I said. "I'm not sure he's looking for a wife."

She glanced over at me. "Honey, that's what they all say."

I laughed at her dry observation. She was probably right. Grams usually was.

"He was a big help to your grandpa this morning," she said.

My ears perked up. "Really?"

She nodded. "A load of feed came in and he didn't wait to be asked, just rolled up his sleeves, set aside his coffee, and helped unload. Dirty, heavy work, but he didn't complain." She paused. "I believe your grandpa may have had a little chat with him while they worked."

Oh no. Lord only knew what my grandpa had said. I decided I didn't want to know.

"Do you love him?" she asked, setting the crust carefully in the pie dish.

I hesitated, but there was no sense lying to her. "Yeah. Yeah, I do. But . . . he doesn't love me." It pained me to say the words out loud, but sometimes the truth is hard to hear.

Grams just shook her head. "Ivy, I've been around a long time. I may not have lived in a big city or traveled the world, but people are the same everywhere. That man loves you, and don't you doubt it. He may not have said it, but he watches you like the rooster watches for the sunrise, as if his next breath depends on you being there."

Okay, *that* was an unexpected observation. "Really?" I asked, afraid to hope that maybe, just maybe, she might be right.

Turning fully to me, she smiled. "Really."

I couldn't help the wide smile that stretched across my face. She reached over and patted my hand. "Don't you worry, honey. Everything'll turn out all right. It usually does."

I hoped she was right, though deep down I had my doubts.

It was late afternoon and the rain had begun when Grams got the call.

"Honey," she said to me as I finished chopping the ingredients for a salad for dinner. I couldn't cook, but I could peel, chop, slice, and dice just fine. "Grandpa and I have to go help the Worells tonight." The Worell family had been friends of ours since Grams and Grandpa had gotten married.

"They're having trouble with their sump pump," she said. "Their basement is flooding."

I frowned. "Isn't Danny home?" Danny was their grown son and usually helped his dad with things like that.

"No, he went to Wichita this weekend," she replied. "I'm going to ride along so your grandpa doesn't have to drive over there by himself. We shouldn't be long. I'll call you."

"Okay." That would leave me alone with Devon and Logan, which sucked, but there was nothing I could do about it. I just hoped I wouldn't have to play referee for another one of their snide arguments.

"There's a chicken pot pie in the fridge for dinner," she said. "Just bake it at three-fifty for forty-five minutes. No longer."

"Got it."

I followed her to the door. Grandpa was already in the truck and Grams hurried through the rain to the passenger door.

"We'll be back later," Grandpa called to us. He pointed a crooked finger at Devon. "Remember what we talked about, son."

Devon just nodded at the warning and I watched the taillights disappear down the long gravel drive.

It was abnormally dark and I cast a practiced glance up at the foreboding sky. Clouds swirled in an angry turmoil above me. I was accustomed to spring storms. This was Kansas, after all. Tornados in the spring were as common as hay fever. But it hadn't been hot enough today to produce anything like that. Just a bad thunderstorm.

Back inside, I saw Devon had followed me into the kitchen. He'd made himself scarce today and I hadn't gone looking for him. Now, though, it was obvious what he'd been doing and why he'd gone into town.

There were two double-barrel shotguns and three handguns laid out on the kitchen table, along with their assorted ammunition.

"What's all this?" I asked, my eyes wide. Logan chose that moment to enter the kitchen as well.

"Preparation," Devon said. "Clive will likely come tonight. He might bring reinforcements. I would."

"But the weather—" I began.

"Will help him," Devon interrupted. "It'll be much harder to see or hear him coming." He turned to Logan. "Can you shoot a gun or rifle?"

Logan had grown up on a farm in Kansas. Guns were a staple. He nodded. "Yeah. Both."

Devon handed him one shotgun and one of the handguns. "Take

ammunition," he said. "Make sure they're both loaded and ready to go. You take the back of the house, top rear bedroom window."

I thought Logan might argue, but he didn't. Taking the weapons, he checked them both, loading two shells into the shotgun's barrel before locking it back into place with a loud click. The hairs on the back of my neck stood on end at the sound. He gave me a long look before heading upstairs.

"What if Grams and Grandpa come back?" I asked.

"They won't. Not until morning," Devon replied.

"How do you know that?"

He glanced at me. "Because I made sure of it. Sid at the gun shop was quite chatty about the people around here. Turns out the Worells have been having sump pump issues for a while. Good thing your grandpa's a longtime friend who'd help him out when a big storm rolls in and it breaks down completely."

My jaw was agape. "You broke the Worells' sump pump to get my grandparents out of here for the evening?"

"Did you have a better idea to keep them out of harm's way?" he asked.

Well . . . no.

"What am I supposed to do?" I asked.

"You're going in the storm cellar," Devon said. "It's the safest place for you until this is over."

I was already shaking my head. "No. You and Logan aren't going to be putting your lives on the line while I hide."

He didn't even bother looking at me as he filled his pockets with ammunition. "You don't have a choice," he said.

"I most certainly do. You can't force me, Devon. You won't like the results."

Now he looked at me. "You'll do as you're told," he said, his voice like steel. "Or would you rather be a distraction for me, or for Logan, that could get us killed?"

That shut me up. No, I didn't want to do anything that could distract them. "Can't I help in some way?" I asked. "Give you ammunition or something?" Our eyes met. "Please don't put me down there. Alone. Worrying about you."

Devon's jaw clenched tight. A beat passed.

"Fine," he said curtly. "But if I tell you to go hide, you must swear to me that you'll do it. No questions asked."

"I swear," I agreed quickly. I had to think my presence could help, not hurt, the two men I loved.

"Douse all the lights," he ordered, and I hurried to obey.

I saw Logan in the rear bedroom and he glanced up at me as I walked by. I didn't say anything.

Heading back downstairs, I saw that Devon had loaded his weapons as well and had taken a chair close to the open window. The curtains were blowing as the wind and rain came through.

"When will he come?" I asked.

"I don't know."

I made my way carefully through the darkened dining room and went to grab another chair, but Devon stopped me.

"No," he said. "The floor is safest."

I didn't complain, just sat on the floor at his feet.

My nerves were on a knife's edge as I wondered what the next few hours would bring. Would Devon be able to spot Clive and his team in time? Or would we be ambushed and overrun, all three of us killed in one night?

Devon must have sensed my anxiety. He reached for me, his hand settling on my shoulder. He was still watching out the window, the faint glow from the dusk-to-dawn light casting his face in stark shadows. I leaned toward him, resting my head against his thigh as he placed his hand on my head.

I knew I shouldn't talk, shouldn't distract him, so I stayed silent. Both of us waiting. Devon didn't seem tense, though. His body was taut and ready, but he breathed easily and his fingers trailed lightly through my hair, petting me.

It must have been nearly an hour before anything happened. Devon's hand suddenly stopped in its unceasing trips through the locks of my hair and he sat up straighter.

Then the lights outside went out.

"Stay down," he ordered.

I didn't argue, though it felt like I was going to throw up from the sudden rush of panic and fear in my gut. I watched him raise the handgun and sight it, waiting. Several long seconds later, it barked twice in rapid succession, then he was up and moving, shoving my head down so I was flat on the floor. The window exploded, glass flying everywhere and even more rain poured inside.

Devon ran to the window in the kitchen and I watched him through the breezeway. He stood to the side with his back to the wall, then took a deep breath and rotated so he faced out the window. He rapidly squeezed off more shots, then flung himself back as return fire ripped through the spot where he'd just been standing. Bullets embedded themselves in the door of the refrigerator.

I heard more gunshots from upstairs and knew Logan was firing at something. I was thankful that he'd been raised a hunter, so he'd know to find another spot once his shots gave away his location.

There was the sound of splintering wood from the back of the house and I jerked around to look at Devon.

"Stay here," he said, rushing past me.

Oh God. Someone had entered the house.

CHAPTER
SEVEN

I cowered under the dining room table, terrified of what was happening. I heard another few shots, then sounds of breaking glass and loud thumps, as though there was fighting. Devon's shotgun lay on the floor near his chair and I crawled to it. I'd just laid my hand on it when a foot came down on the barrel, holding it in place.

"You won't be needing that."

I flung myself onto my back, scurrying away from the man who'd quietly walked through the front door. The lock was gone and I realized he must've broken it while Devon was fighting in the back.

The new guy scrutinized me while I stared at him, eyes wide.

"Yep. You're the girl. Let's go," he said. Leaning down, he grabbed my arm and hauled me to my feet as easily as he'd pick up a sack of groceries.

I screamed and tried to pull my arm away. "Let me go! Devon!"

"None of that," he said before slamming a hard fist into my cheek. I reeled, my knees buckling, then found myself slung over his shoulder in a fireman's carry.

In seconds, we were out the door and rain immediately soaked me, which was a good thing because it woke me from the stupor I'd been in.

I thought hard and fast. Devon couldn't come. Maybe he was hurt. And now I saw I was being taken to an SUV. I was flung inside and I played unconscious. As soon as he slammed the door shut, I was up and over to the other side. Luck was with me and the door opened easily. I began to run.

"Sonofabitch," the man cursed. "Grab her!"

I hadn't seen them, but there were two more men outside, taking cover from the house behind my grandpa's field truck. Both of them began to run after me. I heard another gunshot and saw a flash from an upstairs window. Logan. One of the men following me fell and didn't get up.

The rain had turned the gravel driveway into a pebbly river, the grass into a field of mud. But I knew this farm like the back of my hand. The driver was chasing me now, too, but I kept going.

Rain filled my eyes and I brushed my hair out of the way so I could see. It was pitch black and I ran through the yard to where the cornfields began, hoping I could lose them inside the rows of stalks. I heard a gunshot, muffled in the pounding rain, and a split second later a searing pain pierced my leg. I'd been hit and it made me fall just as I entered the cornfield. I cried out, my hand going to my leg, but it wasn't a bad wound, having just nicked me, so I stumbled to my feet. They were closer, just yards away, and I dove into the stalks.

Mud coated my body from my fall and I slipped and slid my way through the field. Rushing through the rows, I turned, ran down between the lines of stalks, then made an abrupt right turn, ran twenty feet forward, then turned left. I slipped and fell two more times, tears mixing with water on my face as the pain in my leg made putting weight on it more and more difficult. Finally, I was limping and had to stop, my lungs heaving. I waited, listening for them, but heard nothing besides the pounding rain and thunder.

Lightning split the sky, another clap of thunder close on its heels, and I could see just for an instant.

Clive.

He was only feet from me, and he'd seen me.

I threw myself to my left as he lunged, pushing through the corn. The heavy, wet stalks clung to me as I ran through, like dead hands grabbing on to me. I didn't think about the pain in my leg—I just ran the best I could, limping with a weird gait.

I clutched at the wound in my thigh, feeling the heat of blood against the chilling cold of the rain-soaked denim. I lost track of time as my head started to get fuzzy. Growing dizzy, I knew I'd have to stop soon, but if I could just go a little bit farther . . .

The ground suddenly dropped beneath me and I fell hard. I scrabbled at the dirt, realizing I'd hit the embankment for the creek that ran through Grandpa's property. In the dark, I hadn't realized I'd been so close.

It was steep and I clawed at the ground, digging my hands into the mud. I halted my downward descent, feeling the squish of the rain-soaked earth between my fingers and underneath my nails. I could hear the sound of the water rushing, the creek swollen from the rain.

"Gotcha."

I cried out as Clive fisted a chunk of my hair and yanked. He was braced above me on the side, careful not to get too close to the edge.

"Climb out," he ordered. "If I have to come down there, you'll regret it."

My hair was slick with water and I jerked out of his grasp, the strands sliding free. I let go of the ground and slid down another foot. The water was only a couple of yards away. If I got caught up in the current in the dark, though it wasn't very deep, I could easily drown.

Clive ground out a curse. He grabbed on to a tree branch, using it to anchor himself as he stepped over the edge onto the mud-slickened slope. His arms were long and he grabbed for me again, this time latching on to my wrist and tugging.

"You are going to pay for this, you little bitch," he snarled.

There was a sudden loud bang and his hold on my wrist slackened. I blinked the rain out of my eyes as he toppled forward. Water splashed when he hit the creek.

Struggling to my feet, I fought the branches tearing at me. I had to get up the hill, but my body wouldn't obey. After only one step, my leg gave out and I collapsed on the ground with a grunt, the mud sucking at my hands and face.

On all fours, I tried to crawl up the slope. My leg had gone numb and I thought I was probably in shock, which I was glad of.

I didn't make it far. My arms were shaking with exhaustion and I was coated in mud. It was like the mud was a living thing, dragging me down with its weight until I was lying flat, unable to move an inch farther.

"Ivy!"

I heard my name and forced my body onto my back, my eyes slipping closed as the rain splattered against my face. Was that Devon? Or was this a trick? I couldn't tell from the voice—the rain was too loud.

"Ivy! Where are you?"

Again, I didn't answer, though I could hear the voice getting closer. Who was it?

"Darling, answer me."

My eyes popped open. Darling. Only one person had ever called me that.

"Here!" I called the best I could. My voice was mangled and hoarse. "I'm here. Please. Devon."

I needed to get up. He couldn't find me if I stayed lying on the ground. But my exhausted body wouldn't obey.

A figure loomed over me in the darkness, and I let out a sharp scream.

"Shh, darling. You're all right," Devon said, crouching down beside me. Rain dripped down his face as he cast a practiced eye over me before sliding his arms behind my back and knees. Standing, he lifted me from the mud.

"Hang on," he said, and I clung to his neck as he carried me through the back way into the house.

He brought me to my room then set me on the bed while he grabbed several towels.

Devon was soaked through, too, his hair dark and gleaming from the rain.

"What happened?" I asked.

"They sent two men in the back to distract me while the others came in the front for you," he said curtly.

"Where's Logan?" was my next question. "Is he okay?"

"He's fine. Just keeping watch on our prisoner."

"Prisoner?"

"Clive didn't arrive with the first group of men," Devon explained. "He came separately in an instance of particularly bad timing. I want to know who they were. But first, we need to stop the bleeding in your leg and patch you up." He reached for the fastening of my jeans, but I stopped him. I'd been the damsel in distress that had needed rescuing again, and my pride was hurting.

"I'll do it," I said, pushing his hands away. "Just help me into the bathroom."

"Don't be silly, darling," he said. "You're hurt and have lost blood. If I stand you up, you're likely to pass out."

"I'm fine," I insisted, pushing myself to a sitting position. The mud was starting to dry in places; it cracked when I moved. "I'm a mess. Just help me to the bath and I'll be okay." Not winning this argument wasn't an option. I was too vulnerable in a way that made me feel like I was exactly how people saw me—weak. Devon said he didn't see me that way, and I couldn't let that change.

To my relief, he stopped trying to take my clothes off and helped me the ten feet to the bathroom. But when he tried to come inside with me, I stopped him.

"I'll take it from here," I said.

Devon stared at me for a moment, his face going blank. "Is this my punishment for allowing you to be hurt?" he asked. "I'm not allowed to care for you because I didn't protect you?"

"Devon, that's not—" I began.

"Perhaps I should send Logan in to assist you," he cut me off. He smiled at me, but it was a humorless twist of his lips that was edged in bitterness. Then he was out the door and gone.

I bit back the stream of curses I wanted to let loose, starting with a rampage against him and his guilt. An emotional, guilt-ridden Devon was something I hadn't encountered before.

Shoving my frustration and confusion aside, I carefully stripped off my clothes while the water ran hot in the shower. Stepping under the spray, I nearly passed out again when the water hit my wounded thigh, but I made myself stand there, gritting my teeth.

It took a while and I had to sit on the edge of the tub a few times when I got lightheaded, but eventually, I was clean.

"Ives, you okay?" I heard the question and the knock at the door before it was pushed open.

"Yeah, I'm all right," I said, turning off the water. "Hand me a towel, would you?"

It was still storming outside, the rain pattering against the window, but the thunder and lightning had passed.

Logan passed me a towel and I wrapped it around me. My thigh had stopped bleeding and it wasn't a gunshot wound per se, but the bullet had skimmed my leg, taking a few layers of skin with it. It hurt like hell.

"Let me help you," Logan said as I pushed back the shower curtain. He didn't wait for me to agree, just wrapped an arm around my waist and lifted me out of the tub.

"What are you doing up here?" I asked. "I thought you were guarding one of the men."

"I was," he said. "But then Devon decided to interrogate him. I watched for a while, then . . . I . . . um . . ." He glanced away from me.

I waited. "Then what?"

His gaze met mine. "Devon's interrogation methods aren't for the faint of heart, Ives."

"What do you mean?"

"I mean he put a fucking sheet on the tile underneath the guy's chair," Logan said. "So cleaning up would be easier."

I stared wide-eyed at Logan, who seemed to have regretted his bluntness. He looked away again as he rubbed the back of his neck. "Let's not talk about it," he said. "You need a bandage on that."

He helped me hobble out of the bathroom and cleared away the ruined towels on my bed. I sat with a sigh. After grabbing the medicine kit he'd brought up, Logan returned and dumped out some antiseptic cream and bandages. I lay on my side and hiked up the towel enough for him to see the wound. Frowning, he set about putting on the medicine and a bandage.

A loud yell from downstairs made us both start in surprise. Instinctively looking at the door, neither of us spoke for a moment.

"Should we do something?" I asked, swallowing hard.

"Probably not," Logan replied. "If we did, who knows what Devon would do in turn? And while I don't want to watch, I'm not particularly attached to the guys who tried to kill us."

There was another yell, which was abruptly cut off.

After he'd bandaged me, Logan went to my suitcase and took out some clothes. "Here," he said, handing me a T-shirt and pair of shorts. I hurriedly pulled them on, carefully easing the shorts over the wound in my thigh.

"I want to see what's going on downstairs," I said, heading out the door. Logan grabbed my arm, halting me.

"Ivy, don't," he said.

"I'd think you'd want me to see," I countered, raising an eyebrow. "Or don't you think I should know what kind of man Devon is?"

Logan didn't reply to that, and I could see the indecision in his eyes. "Fine," he relented, releasing me. "You're right. You should know who you're sleeping with."

I walked down the stairs, pausing on the landing at the bottom. I could hear the man grunting and I took a deep breath.

"I would tell me what I want to know, if I were you," Devon said calmly. "My patience isn't going to last much longer."

Easing my head around the corner, I peeked into the kitchen. I couldn't see the man where he sat in a chair. His body was obscured by Devon, who stood in front of him. What I could see was the blood on the sheet protecting the floor.

"I don't know anyone named Clive," he spat. "We weren't hired by him."

"Then who hired you?"

"Orders came through London," the man said. He was gasping, as though in pain. "Come here. Get the girl alive, use any force necessary. Take her back."

My blood chilled at this. Someone had sent these men to take me away. If Devon hadn't been there, I'd be gone.

"Where were you supposed to take her once you got to London?"

"I don't know."

Devon did something—I couldn't see what—and the guy howled in pain.

"A woman! It was a woman, but I don't know her name. I swear!"

"You've been exceedingly helpful," Devon said. He got to his feet and now I could see the man. I covered my mouth with my hand at the sight of him.

It was the guy who'd grabbed me from the start. Blood dripped from his face as he cradled his hand. His sleeve was soaked red. I could barely recognize his face; it was swollen and matted with blood.

"So now what?" the man asked. "You going to let me go?"

"Please," Devon said. "You know how these things work. And . . . you hit my lady. I don't practice forgiveness, mate."

Before the man could utter another word, Devon raised his hand and fired his gun point-blank at the man's forehead. A hole erupted between his eyes and blood oozed. The back of his head had exploded from the exit wound. It seemed Devon had thought of that, too, because he'd turned him in such a way that not a drop of blood or brain matter had gotten anywhere except the sheet.

"Yeah, that's quite a guy, Ives," Logan hissed in my ear.

I ignored him. My mind was too busy processing what I'd seen. Devon, once again killing someone in cold blood. It had been easy to forget this side of him—a remorseless killer who didn't bat an eye at the death sentences he handed out.

"I'd give you a hand cleaning up, but I don't want to," Logan sneered at Devon as he stepped past me into the hallway. "You can bury your own bodies."

"These same men were trying to kill you," Devon said, not glancing at Logan as he pushed the dead body onto the floor and moved the chair out of the way. Absently, I noticed it was my grandpa's chair from the head of the table. "Perhaps you might consider not acting like a child who hasn't gotten their way and instead behave like the grown man you're supposed to be."

The chastisement made Logan's face flush and he didn't reply.

"Now grab his feet," Devon ordered. He'd wrapped the body in the stained sheet like a mummy and grasped the shoulders.

Logan hesitated, then bent and lifted the feet. Together, they hauled him out the front door. In a moment, they were back and I came out from hiding. Devon glanced at me, his eyes raking me from wet head to bare toes.

"You're just in time," he said, and I realized he didn't know I'd seen what had happened. "Logan's going to help me dispose of the bodies, but we'll be right back."

"Where are you going?" I asked, suddenly apprehensive.

"I'll drive the car into the woods and set it on fire. With all the rain, nothing nearby will catch, so it should be safe. Logan will follow me in the pickup, then drive us back."

"I don't want to be left alone," I said. "I'll come with you."

Devon might have argued, but then he looked into my eyes and gave a wordless nod.

I climbed into the pickup with Logan and we followed the dark SUV out through an empty field toward the woods that bordered the creek. When the SUV slowed, we stopped, and Devon drove a bit farther. Logan and I sat in silence as Devon got out of the car and did something with the engine. He dropped the hood and began walking toward us. When he was ten feet away, the SUV exploded.

I jumped, the sound and sudden light scaring me. Devon opened the passenger door and I scooted to the middle of the seat to make room for him.

"Not so fast." Logan leveled a gun at Devon, who froze. "This would be a perfect opportunity to dispose of you, too."

I stared in disbelief at the gun Logan held. I'd never seen him threaten anyone before.

"What the hell are you doing?" I squeaked in alarm. His arm was right in front of me as he pointed the weapon at Devon, but I was afraid to try to shove it aside. What if he pulled the trigger and Devon got hit?

"It's for your own good, Ives," Logan said. "This guy is a murderer and he's going to get you killed, too. He won't leave you alone. You won't tell him to leave you alone, so it's up to me."

Devon stood motionless in the rain, the steady downpour having lightened somewhat.

"This is what you want to do?" he asked Logan. "Kill your best friend's lover in cold blood? I can't imagine that would be helpful to you in the long run."

"Shut up," Logan spat. "None of this would've happened if not for you."

"Logan, please," I said. "Put down the gun." He sounded so angry.

"Now is the perfect time," he said to me. "No one will come looking for him here."

"You cannot do this," I said to him. "Please. Put down the gun and let's go back to the house. We'll talk, just you and me."

"I won't sit by and watch you get killed because of a man who isn't worth it."

His anger wasn't dissipating and I could see tears in his eyes as he stared in furious outrage at Devon. For his part, Devon seemed to be calculating, playing out in his mind the various scenarios of how this could go, and weighing his options. I didn't think he really had any, not if he didn't want to get shot, which motivated my actions.

"Logan," I said, moving very slowly and deliberately forward. "You can't do this. You won't."

He would have to bend his arm or he wouldn't be targeting Devon any longer. I was counting on him not wanting to let Devon out of range, and I was right. He bent his arm, which was perfect. I slid right between the gun and Devon, turning so the weapon now rested against my chest, rather than pointing at Devon.

"Are you going to shoot me, too?" I asked softly.

Logan stared at me, his face creased in lines of pain that tore me from the inside out.

"I love you," he said, the words barely audible.

I reached out and slid the gun from his unresisting grip, then handed it to Devon behind my back. I felt him take the weapon from me.

"And I love you," I said. "Thank you for taking care of me." Cradling his face in my palms, I leaned forward and pressed a kiss to his cheek. The truck bobbed a little as Devon climbed inside.

"Shall we?" Devon asked, as though he hadn't just been held at gunpoint.

I settled back between them in the seat and Logan didn't reply, just shifted the truck into drive and hit the gas. Minutes later, we were back at the house, the burning car a red glow in the distance.

Hurrying inside, I was glad not to be soaked through, like Devon and Logan were. I watched as Logan went upstairs and Devon disappeared into the bath on the first level to shower and change.

The need for something to steady my nerves had me heading for my grandpa's liquor cabinet. It was locked, like it always had been, but I opened the drawer in the end table next to the sofa and felt around in the back until the cold metal of the key touched my fingertips. After unlocking the cabinet, I pulled out a bottle of bourbon and poured myself a stiff shot. I tossed it back like the pro

I wasn't, then poured another. I sipped this one, settling myself on the couch and staring at nothing.

A while later, Devon appeared. He took in the scene at a glance, then headed over and poured himself a shot, too. I noticed it was about twice the amount I'd poured.

"Is this just another day at the office for you?" I asked, my gaze following him. He'd changed into dry, dark-washed jeans and a long-sleeved black Henley. The sleeves were pushed up and I watched the muscles flex in his arm as he raised the glass to his mouth.

"This one was a bit unusual," he admitted, taking another long drink. His throat moved as he swallowed.

"How so?"

His gaze met mine. "It's not often someone I'm protecting tries to kill me."

The curt indictment of Logan's actions stung, but there wasn't anything I could do about it. "He didn't, though," I said with a shrug. "So that's something."

Devon didn't reply as we stared at each other. After a moment, his lips twitched, and that was enough for a full-out smile from me.

"So are we safe now?" I asked.

Devon took the seat beside me, sitting down with a sigh that spoke of exhaustion. "Clive is dead," he said. "The other people were on a mission for you. So while I think Logan is safe, I think *you* are not."

I'd kind of been expecting that, but the words still provoked a twinge of fear.

"What do I do?" Once Devon left, how would I protect myself? Should I go on the run or something? How did somebody even do that?

"You come with me."

I twisted around so I could look at him. "Come with you?" I reiterated. "For how long?"

"Don't misunderstand," he interrupted. "It's not a permanent thing. But until I can find out who is hunting you and why, it might be our best course of action."

I was simultaneously glad and disappointed. Glad because we would have more time together, and disappointed because he'd already set a limit on it. It was disheartening and made my stomach feel as though I'd swallowed a ball of lead.

"What about Logan?" I asked. "You're sure he's safe?"

"Reasonably sure," he said. "Either way, he's not coming. He would slow us down."

"But—" I began.

"I saved his life because he meant something to you," he interrupted. "But make no mistake. If you think I won't sacrifice him—or anyone else, for that matter—to save your life, then you're quite wrong. I'll choose you, every time."

And in that moment, I believed him. I'd seen what Devon had done to the man they'd captured. There was a part of him capable of turning off his emotions completely. He'd have to in order to do all he'd done.

"Fine," I said, frustration overwhelming my other emotions. "I'll come with you. But you can't think I'll leave Logan behind and thank you for it."

"Perhaps you'll feel otherwise the next time I save your life," he replied.

"Or perhaps you're conveniently ignoring that my life wouldn't be in danger if it weren't for you. I've been shot—twice—and Logan nearly killed because of you and me being together."

That felt like hitting below the belt, though all of it was true. Perhaps he knew it as well because his eyes narrowed, but he didn't reply.

"Go pack," he said at last.

There was an overwhelming intensity coming off Devon. He'd been in a battle of life and death tonight, and it seemed he was still raw from the fight. His gaze dropped from my eyes to my mouth and I unconsciously licked my lips. The pulse underneath his jaw jumped at the sight and I saw his hands curl into fists. In that moment, I could understand the need to have sex after a battle. All that energy, aggression, and adrenaline was still unused and searching for an outlet.

Sidestepping him, I hurried down the hall and up the stairs, feeling his eyes burning a hole in my back as I left.

Packing didn't take long. I was leaving my bedroom when I ran into Logan.

"Where are you going?" he asked.

I took a breath. "With Devon," I said.

"But Clive is dead," he argued. "You don't need him anymore."

"He thinks I'm still in danger," I replied.

"Of course he does," Logan sneered. "He'll tell you anything so you'll go with him."

"He didn't make up those men," I said, pushing past him and starting down the stairs. Logan followed.

"Yes, but they're gone. He's just using the situation to take you away again. And you're letting him."

"I'll be back soon," I said, setting the suitcase down and turning toward him. "I promise."

"What am I supposed to tell Grams?"

Crap. I hadn't thought of that. "Tell her the truth," I said.

"The truth?"

"Sort of. Say that we were the victims of a . . . a home invasion or something," I said, thinking quickly. "But you and Devon fought them off, then Devon got called away for work and I went with him."

"And where are you going?" he asked.

I didn't know. Of course I didn't. It wasn't like Devon had told me, after all. "I'm not sure," I hedged, "but I'll call you."

"You're going to leave with just an 'I'll call you?'" Logan was incredulous. "Do you even give a shit that I'll be worried sick?"

"Don't worry," I pleaded with him. "I'm not doing this to hurt you."

"If you're going to walk out that door, then you're going to think about me while you're with him."

I opened my mouth to tell him that of course I'd think about him, but I didn't get the chance. Logan had me pressed against the wall in the span of a moment, his hands grasping my hips as his mouth came down on mine.

I immediately tried to push him away, but he wouldn't let me. His hands gripped my flesh and his chest pressed against mine, holding me in place.

He was kissing me, his lips coaxing me to respond, and I remembered that I'd promised him this. I'd promised him a kiss, and even though he was just taking it rather than asking me first, I stopped trying to get away. Logan wanted to prove a point? Fine. I'd let him. But he'd see that there was nothing between us, at least from my side. He was like a brother to me. That was all.

I felt nothing. Just the bland feel of a man's mouth on mine.

"Try, Ives," Logan breathed against my lips. "Please. For me. Just try."

I didn't know what else I could do, so I closed my eyes. It was nice, Logan kissing me. I opened beneath him and he deepened the kiss. His tongue slid alongside mine, tangling in a wet heat.

With my eyes closed, I could smell him better—the warm scent of Logan that had been a comfort to me for as long as I could remember. Tentatively, I lifted my arms and wrapped them around his neck. His hair was soft against my fingers.

At my touch, Logan groaned, deep in his throat. His teeth nipped at my lip, his tongue swiping gently to soothe the skin. He was a very good kisser. As good as Devon. But I didn't feel the fire and spark like when Devon kissed me.

"Don't let me interrupt."

I started in surprise at the sound of Devon's voice, jerking back and breaking our kiss, but Logan didn't move. His cheek brushed mine as he spoke.

"Then get lost," he growled.

"Ivy's coming with me, and I suggest you get your hands off her before I forget to be nice." The menace in those words was unmistakable.

"I've got to go," I said, squirming out from between the wall and Logan. He caught my hand.

"Stay," he said. "For me. You can't deny there's more between us. Not now."

And he was right. There could be more. Maybe. But the circumstances hadn't changed and I didn't want a man who loved me because he wanted to save me.

"I can't."

Logan's expression turned cold. "If you leave, then we're done, Ives. I don't want to see you again."

That stopped me in my tracks and I turned to stare at him in disbelief.

"I can't do this anymore," he said. "I can't watch you in this toxic relationship. And I won't be your second choice."

"Don't," I warned him. "Don't make me choose between the two of you."

"It's the way it is." His tone was implacable.

Time seemed to slow, in that way it does when something so awful is happening to you that every moment is drawn out in endless agony. The unthinkable was happening. Logan was ending our friendship. In all our years together, I'd never considered for one second that he would do such a thing.

My voice was a raspy whisper when I spoke. "Then I guess it's goodbye, Logan."

The shock across his face was brief, then hidden, and I realized he'd never expected me to choose Devon over him in such a stark way. But he'd given me an ultimatum, and even if Devon's threat wasn't there, I didn't do ultimatums.

Devon already had my suitcase in hand as I passed him on the way to the door. I heard him fall in step behind me, then we were outside and climbing into his car.

I glanced back at the house as Devon started the engine. Logan stood on the porch, staring after us. Then he blurred as I began to cry. I watched him as we headed down the drive until he was out of sight.

CHAPTER EIGHT

Dawn was breaking as we drove out of town, heading east. Devon hadn't said anything as I'd silently cried. I'd forced myself to stop and now stared blindly out the window.

I'd lost him. I'd lost my best friend.

My stomach ached and my head hurt. I was exhausted, heartbroken, hungry, and sore.

"Where are we going?" I asked.

"Kansas City," Devon replied.

"Why?"

"It's where I was heading in the first place," he said. "My mission is there."

I processed this. "If you're a spy for the British, why are you in America?"

"We go where the threat is," he replied. "It could be anywhere. Not every danger to British national security is on our soil."

I nodded, but didn't care if he saw me or not.

"I'm cold," I said, pulling my knees to my chest and resting my feet on the seat. I wrapped my arms around my legs. Devon reached for the heat, flipping the switch to a warmer setting.

"Other than that, how are you?" he asked.

"Awful. Miserable." Inside and out, but I didn't say that part.

Devon flicked a glance at me. "You'll feel better when we stop," he said. "Get some food and some rest."

"How do you keep going?" I asked. "Aren't you tired?"

"Maybe," he said. "But you have to do what needs to be done. Sometimes there's not enough time to eat or sleep. You train yourself—and they train you as well—to put the mission first, always."

"But you didn't," I said. "Otherwise you would have left Logan and me to fend for ourselves in St. Louis."

Devon didn't reply and I wished, not for the first time, that I could see inside his head.

"What did you mean?" I asked. "Earlier. When you said that you'd choose me, every time?"

"I thought the words were pretty self-explanatory," he said dryly.

"I know, but why?" I turned to look at him. "I'm nothing more than your fuck buddy, so why would—"

"My what?" he interrupted, turning sharply toward me. "What did you say?"

"Your . . . fuck buddy," I muttered, my face heating. "It-it's what Scott said, and pretty much how all my friends see our relationship. Even me."

"Scott doesn't know a bloody thing," Devon snapped, "and neither do your friends. Other than filling your head with a load of nonsense."

Relief at his obvious irritation eased the ache in my chest.

"What was I supposed to think?" I asked. "The only thing we've done until the last few days is have sex."

"Firstly, I would never use such a derogatory term in relation to you," he said. "Secondly, you have no idea the risks I took getting to you the few times I could. Any more or longer would have been dangerous for us both. And lastly," his cool blue gaze met mine, "just because we can't have more doesn't mean what we do have isn't worth something. At least, something more than what the term 'fuck buddy' encompasses."

One of those things stood out the most to me. "What do you mean by it being 'dangerous for us both'?" He'd put himself at risk just to come see me?

Devon turned back to the road, sliding his sunglasses on as the sun shone brightly above the horizon. "I told you what happened to Kira," he said. "If anyone sees me with you one too many times or gets an inkling of our relationship, they'll use it against me in a heartbeat. Clive is a perfect example of that."

"Anyone?" I asked, wondering if he meant just his enemies, though Vega's face floated through my mind.

"Anyone."

"So quit," I said. "Leave your job. Do something else. There's got to be other careers out there for you where we could be together." I held my breath, hoping his answer would be different. He cared for me. He'd nearly come out and said it, plain as could be.

"I won't quit my job," he said. "The only way I'll stop is when they carry me away in a body bag."

The absolute certainly in his voice made despair well inside me. Hearing Devon tell me how he cared for me—that I was "dear" to him—was wonderful . . . until he followed it up with the fact that he didn't care *enough*.

I turned away to stare out the window, leaning my head against the cool glass. I closed my eyes and tried not to think.

I woke when the car stopped. Sitting up from where I'd slumped against the door, I saw we were outside a hotel downtown.

"Wake up, darling," Devon said. "We're here."

A valet opened my door and I stepped out, rubbing my eyes and still trying to clear my head from the cloud of sleep. Devon took my elbow and steered me inside. I didn't say anything until he was telling the front desk the kind of room he wanted.

"I want a separate room," I interjected. I felt Devon's gaze on me, but I stared straight ahead at the man typing on his computer behind the desk.

"Two rooms, sir?" he asked Devon.

I looked down at the counter where my hands were tightly clasped.

"Yes, please," Devon replied. "Connecting, if you have it."

"Yes, sir."

They did have it and a few minutes later we were being shown into our connecting rooms. I noticed Devon took one of the two keys to my room, but I didn't object. He was paying, so he could do what he wanted, but having my own space would help in my resolve to put some distance between us and not sleep with him.

"I'll order some room service," he said. "Get some rest and I'll wake you when it comes."

I nodded, already toeing off my shoes and crawling underneath the covers of the king-size bed. I heard Devon go through the connecting door to his room, then I was out again.

∽

Devon must've thought I needed sleep more than food because he didn't wake me. I woke on my own when twilight was darkening the sky. The room was in deep shadows and I sighed. I didn't yet feel rested, but I felt a helluva lot better than I had earlier.

I got up to use the bathroom and splash water on my face, then dug in my suitcase for my toothbrush. When I was finished, I hesitantly approached the connecting door. It was open, but pulled nearly shut. I rapped lightly on the surface and waited. Nothing. I knocked again. Still nothing. Cautiously, in case Devon was sleeping, I eased the door open.

But the room was empty. Not only was it empty, it looked completely undisturbed. The sheets on the bed were pristine and there were no dirty dishes from the room service Devon had supposedly ordered. Not even a pillow was out of place.

It was odd that he wasn't there, and I paused for a moment, thinking. It made me a bit uneasy that he'd left me alone. Perhaps he'd been called to duty by Vega, I thought with more than a little bitterness. He'd already professed that his devotion to her superseded his feelings for me. So why was I still here? I could leave if I wanted to. I deserved more than what Devon was offering me, it had just taken a while for me to see it.

Was it wrong to love someone to the point of self-destruction? I'd been unable to help myself before—my need for Devon stronger than my sense of self-preservation—but hearing him so unequivocally state the boundaries of his affection left my love for him cold.

Decision made, I went back to my room and dug in my suitcase for a change of clothes. I'd have the hotel take me to a car rental place, and I'd drive back to St. Louis. As for the people supposedly after me . . .

One problem at a time.

I'd slipped on my shoes and was just wheeling my suitcase to the door when I heard the lock click. I froze in place as the door swung open and Devon walked in.

"Sorry, darling," Devon said. "Meant to be back earlier, but got held up." He said this as he unknotted his tie and I saw there was a tear in the sleeve of his jacket. His gaze was sharp as he took in the sight of me standing there fully dressed, suitcase in hand.

"Going somewhere?" he asked.

The note of warning in his voice gave me pause, but I lifted my chin and looked him in the eye.

"I've decided to leave," I said.

"I see. And why would you do that?" he asked. "I've told you there are people after you. It makes absolutely no sense for you to leave."

My temper sparked at the thinly veiled insult. "You've told me you'll never quit your job, that basically I'm not enough for you, then you want me to stick around just because some people are supposedly after me?" I shook my head. "Taking care of myself is something I need to work on, and now is as good a time to start as any."

I pushed past him, but he grabbed my arm.

"You're a bloody fool if you leave," he bit out.

"I'd be a bloody fool to stay," I retorted, jerking out of his grip. In another moment, I was out the door and heading for the elevator.

Tears stung my eyes, but I blinked them back. I could do this, and I would. It was my life, and I was going to live it on my terms, even if it meant it would be more dangerous for me.

I stood in front of the elevator, waiting for the car to arrive. I clutched the handle of my suitcase. I felt unbearably sad inside, but good, too. The chains of obsession for Devon were finally loosened, and I hadn't realized until now just how bound I'd been by them.

I heard a door open and close and I stiffened, seeing Devon approach in my peripheral vision. Staring resolutely ahead at the closed elevator doors, I said nothing. He walked toward me, not stopping until he was close at my side. He was looking at me, and I wondered if he'd try to make me stay through force.

But he didn't. Instead, he spoke, his voice a low rasp of sound.

"Don't go. Please."

"I know you're worried—"

"That's not why," he interrupted me. "Yes, I want to keep you safe. But it's you. I don't want to lose you, Ivy. Not like this."

"Because I'm leaving you for a change?" I asked. No sense sugarcoating it.

"Because I care about you, more than I've cared about anyone in a very long time. And I should have told you that. Weeks ago. But I didn't. And I hurt you."

My throat was thick with emotion at the stark vulnerability in his voice. "Yes, you did," I said simply.

His hand brushed my hair back from my cheek. "I am sorry, sweet Ivy."

The elevator doors opened.

"I want you in my life," he said. "Will you stay? Do you want me, too?"

I couldn't speak, could only nod. I hadn't meant to compel him to bare his feelings to me, but I was glad the threat of me walking away had caused him to tell me the truth.

He took my suitcase from me and grasped my hand, leading me back to the room.

"Where were you?" I asked.

"My mission," he reminded me. "Ran afoul of some characters, so I'll need to go back later." He discarded his jacket and I saw a bright-red stain on the pristine white of his shirt where the tear had been.

"You're hurt," I said, going to him.

"Just a scratch," he said, glancing at the wound. "One of the buggers had a knife." By now he'd finished unbuttoning his shirt and shrugged it off. "Be a darling," he said. "The bellman will be up shortly. Will you answer for me?"

"Um, yeah, sure," I said, hastily averting my gaze from his bare and well-muscled chest. My fingers itched to touch him, and it seemed to me he lingered longer than was necessary before heading into the bathroom.

It took me that long to figure out he was using my room instead of his, but unless I wanted to see him naked in the shower—which I really, really did—I'd just have to wait and deal with it when he came out.

The bellman did knock a few minutes later and when I answered the door, he gave me a garment bag. "These have been cleaned and pressed," he said, coming inside to hang them in the closet. He set a small leather bag on the bed, too, then waited.

"Oh, oh right," I said, scrambling for my purse and pulling out a tip for him.

"Thank you, miss."

He left and I took Devon's clothes and bag over to his room. I was staying, but I wasn't sure yet whether I was sleeping with him. He'd put himself out there, true, but so had I, multiple times.

I was sitting on the bed pretending to watch television when Devon emerged from the shower. He had a white towel slung low around his hips as he dried his hair with another. I watched from the corner of my eye as the muscles in his chest and arms flexed with his movements. His arm wasn't bleeding any longer, though I noticed a few additional bruises on his torso and the knuckles of his right hand.

"I was worried," I said. "I woke up and you were gone."

"You were sleeping so soundly, I didn't want to wake you when I left earlier," he said, tossing the towel aside. I averted my eyes in case he decided to drop the other towel, too. I only had so much willpower and a naked Devon was too hard to resist.

Devon picked up his discarded jacket and pulled something out of the pocket. "Here," he said, tossing it toward me. It landed with a soft thump by my knee.

I glanced down. It was a cell phone. "What is it?" I asked.

"It's a phone."

I rolled my eyes at his sarcasm. "Obviously. Why do I have one?"

"It's a burner phone. Untraceable," he replied. He moved to stand next to me and I tipped my head back to look at him. "It has one number programmed into it, and that's mine."

My eyes slipped shut and the barest hint of a smile crossed my lips. "I can call you," I said softly.

"You can call me," he echoed, his voice much closer. His lips brushed mine before he moved away.

I opened my eyes, my smile wide. This was a good thing, a positive development.

"Did the bellman come?" he asked.

"Yes," I said. "I put your things in your room."

The curve of his smile was faint. "Persisting in your self-imposed celibacy?" he asked, his tone sardonic.

"For now," I said. "I think it's best if we work on our relationship . . . outside of the bedroom. Surely you can see that."

"I see no reason to deprive either of us a few hours of pleasure. God knows it's in short supply considering all the other shite in life. So where does that leave us, sweet Ivy?"

"An impasse."

"For now," he said. "But, I think, not for long."

His knowing smile and the certainty in his gaze made my eyes narrow. Stubborn tenacity was a strength of mine. "We'll see," I said, wondering just what Devon would give to be allowed in my bed again.

Glancing at the waterproof watch on his wrist, he said, "Get dressed in dark clothes. You're coming with me." Then he was through the connecting door, leaving it open behind him.

I jumped up from the bed and peered into the room to see he'd discarded his towel. Devon's body was perfection. The muscles in his chest and back were as defined as his thighs and ass, which my eyes were currently glued to. He turned, and I'd be hard-pressed to say which was better—the front or the back—then he went still. His cock was heavy between his thighs, long and thick, and memories of what Devon could do with that particular asset made heat rush through my veins. As I watched, it twitched, hardening beneath my gaze.

Jerking my gaze up, I met his eyes watching me watch him. He raised an eyebrow and I quickly took a step back, closing the connecting door.

I hurriedly stripped off my skirt and T-shirt, then dug in my suitcase for dark jeans and a black shirt. All I had was a filmy one with elbow-length sleeves.

Black was one of my favorite colors to wear, making me feel more like the badass I wasn't. I loosely braided my hair on the side, letting the heavy mass fall over my shoulder. The blouse was see-through in the right light, so the black bra I wore underneath was clearly visible, which suited me fine. I slipped on a pair of black flats, got my purse, and sat on the bed to wait.

Devon came through the door a few minutes later. I stood, ready to go, and he gave me a once-over.

"Is this all right?" I asked. He was wearing black jeans and a long-sleeved black cotton shirt. The shirt fit him like a second skin.

"We're not going clubbing," he said, raising an eyebrow. "But it'll do."

I could tell by the darkening of his eyes that he liked the way I looked, which always pleased me. "You can buy me a cocktail on the way back," I sassed, passing by him on my way out the door. He stepped after me, closing the door behind him.

"I'll buy you a cocktail anytime you'd like, darling," he said. "Just say the word."

I paused. "Really?" Just relaxing in a bar, having a drink with Devon, sounded divine.

"Yes, really," he said, the corners of his lips tipping upward and his eyes softening.

I smiled, letting Devon have the last word, as he usually did, and headed for the elevator. A few minutes later, we were in his car and speeding down the road.

"Where are we going?" I asked. "And why am I coming?"

"I need to pick up someone," he said. "You might help them be a little more . . . cooperative about coming along."

"Me?"

"Yes, you."

I couldn't imagine what I could do to help and wondered if Devon was planning on kidnapping someone. I didn't think I wanted to be involved in something like that. But I didn't really have a choice in the matter, as we traveled from the nice, well-maintained part of town to an area where working streetlights were few and far between. Hardly any people were around and those that were, I didn't want to make eye contact with.

Finally, we stopped outside a tall, brick building, eight stories high. It was old—really old. The whole area was. Train tracks were only a street away and all the buildings seemed empty and lifeless, though their imposing structures loomed like haunted sentinels around us.

"Where are we?"

"The Bottoms."

Yeah, that fit.

"And the person you're picking up is here?" I asked, following his lead as he got out of the car.

"Yes. This way."

He led me behind the building, taking care with where he walked. At one point, he took my hand, keeping me closer as the shadows loomed. His weapon was at the small of his back and I was glad that he didn't think it dangerous enough to be holding it, even though it was creepy. The highway was above us, cars crossing on a bridge that spanned the area, the rush of traffic quieter at this hour than I imagined it would be during the day.

At the back of the building, Devon paused outside a door. "Reggie, it's me. Let me in." He was looking at the broken light hanging disconsolately from the dented gutter overhead. I opened my mouth to ask him who he was talking to, when there was a loud click and the door swung open.

"Come," he said quietly, tugging on my hand. I followed him through the doorway into a cavernous dark space. Glancing to my right, I let out a shriek of terror.

A man sat in a chair, an ax embedded in his chest. Blood had dripped down and puddled on the floor beneath him.

Devon's hand covered my mouth, stifling my scream, and he pulled me hard into him.

"Reggie, for fuck's sake," he called out, irritated. "I'm going to wallop you good for that one."

I was sucking in air behind Devon's hand, my eyes glued to the dead guy, when the lights came on.

"C'mon, man, just having a laugh."

I swiveled my gaze to see another guy walk in the room. He was skinny and tall, about my height, with brown hair that needed to be trimmed and the sallow, pale skin of one who avoided sunlight.

"You're lucky I'm not cranky," Devon chastised him. Turning his attention to me, he said, "You all right, darling?" He slowly removed his hand from my mouth.

Bewildered, I gazed at the two of them. They didn't seem to care that a dead man was feet away. I looked at the body again, then looked closer.

"It's not real," I said in confusion. "But it looked so real . . ."

"The Edge of Hell, my friend," the man said, going to the mannequin and tapping it fondly on the shoulder. "Their castoffs are the absolute best. Got this one for a steal."

"Meaning you did actually steal it," Devon said.

I figured out this must be Reggie, who just shrugged. "Whatever. It worked, didn't it?"

"Yes, you were quite successful in frightening the lady out of her wits, congratulations." Devon's dry reply made Reggie look my way for the first time. His eyes widened slightly.

"Oh, wow, yeah, hey, I'm sorry," he said, actually sounding somewhat contrite.

"The Edge of Hell?" I asked, rather than acknowledge his apology.

"It's the big haunted house down here," Reggie hastened to explain. "It's five stories tall and they run it every year. They're always upgrading their props and they sell the old stuff. I like to . . . pick up a few things to help keep people away."

"It's certainly realistic," I said, glancing back at the axed mannequin with a shudder.

"That's not even the best I have," Reggie boasted. "I have better stuff in this place."

"Are you ready to go?" Devon interrupted. "Our flight is in the morning."

Flight? What flight?

"Yeah, just need to grab my gear," Reggie said. "Be right back." He disappeared into the darkened hallway behind him.

"Where are you flying to?" I asked.

"Reggie's wanted in Amsterdam," he replied.

I couldn't imagine what kind of threat Reggie posed to national security, but before I could ask any more questions, we heard a yell from downstairs that was abruptly cut off. In a flash, Devon had his gun in his hand.

"Stay here," he ordered. "Keep out of sight." Then he was gone, following in the direction Reggie had walked.

Panic struck immediately and it was difficult to breathe. More danger. More unknown men seeking to do harm. My knees grew weak and I leaned against the wall, sinking down until my butt hit the floor. Spots danced in front of my eyes and I leaned over to put my head between my knees, making a conscious effort to breathe normally.

I could hear sounds from below, the popping of gunfire, and I started at each shot. Then I heard the back door creak open.

I was exposed here in the kitchen, with the lights on and nowhere to hide. On all fours, I crept backward into the shadows until I felt I was hidden enough that I could risk getting to my feet. My eyes on the kitchen, I stood and took another few steps back.

Something touched my shoulder.

CHAPTER NINE

It was only through the greatest effort at self-control that I did not scream. Whirling around, I saw a monster standing at least seven feet tall. It was covered in dank fur, its canine-like face contorted in a snarl. At my movement, it came to life. Its eyes glowed red and the arm that had dropped to my shoulder moved again. Though I knew it was fake, in that moment it was terrifying.

Turning, I scurried away into the darkness, and ran right through a spider web. I clawed at the sticky fibers, then saw the spiders on me. Frantically I brushed at them, strangled noises coming from my throat as I tried not to scream.

Stairs were on my right and I ran up them, my thoughts a tangled mass of black terror. A shadow moved in the hallway below—someone was following me from the kitchen. I hit the first landing and ducked down the hallway, trying the first door I came to. Locked.

A creak on the stairs. I jerked my head around, watching fearfully for the shadowy figure as I blindly reached for the second doorway's knob. It turned.

I flung myself into the room, shutting the door behind me as quietly as I could and locking it. I waited, casting a quick glance behind me at the room.

The moonlight filtered through the window and gauzy white drapes that moved, even though there was no breeze to stir them. The hair stood up on the back of my neck as my eyes were inexorably drawn to the sole occupant of the room—an old woman sitting in a rocking chair. As though feeling my gaze, the woman began to rock in the chair. Slowly at first, then faster, as the curtains billowed. I could hear her breathing, a deep rasping that seemed to echo in the room. With each rock of the chair, she came a tiny bit closer to me.

I was frozen in fear, my eyes wide as I stared. When she was only feet from me, the rocking suddenly stopped. I breathed a sigh of relief—

She stood in one quick, jerking movement, an arm raised above her head. She was holding a knife.

I screamed and screamed and screamed, instinctively raising my arms to protect myself.

The knob rattled behind me. He was trying to get in. My screams had led him right to me.

Caught between the man behind the door at my back and the old lady in front of me, I didn't know what to do.

Suddenly, she came rushing toward me. I screamed again, throwing myself to the floor as her arm came down, embedding the knife in the wooden door with a loud *thunk*. Scrambling to my feet, I lunged for the knife, knocking the lady out of the way. As soon as my body hit hers, I realized she was another automaton, strung up with pulleys and ropes. But the knife was very real, the hilt solid in my hand as I jerked it out of the wood just as the door was flung open.

"Ivy!" Devon said, raising his arms from where he'd had his gun pointed straight at me. "It's me."

"Oh, God," I breathed, the knife clattering to the floor from my nerveless fingers. Relief hit me so hard, my head swam. "I thought you were him," I said. "The other guy."

"The other guy is dead," Devon said flatly. In two strides, he was at my side. "And I see Reggie's amusements have been terrorizing you."

Reaching behind him, Devon flipped on the light, and I wanted to simultaneously laugh and cry at what I'd been so afraid of. The old woman looked ridiculously non-threatening in the harsh light, the chair and curtains obviously wired to produce the movement I'd seen.

But the man following me had been very real, and now I saw his body lying facedown in the hallway. He wasn't moving.

"Let's get you out of here," Devon murmured, his lips brushing my brow. I nodded, clinging to him like a vine.

Reggie was waiting for us downstairs, and if possible, he looked even paler than before. He didn't speak as we hurried by, but followed close on Devon's heels.

Outside was as eerie as before, only now even more menacing. I gazed into the shadows, wondering if more men were waiting to ambush us. But we met no one on the way back to the car.

I was still shaking like a leaf as Devon stashed me in the front passenger seat before getting behind the wheel. Reggie climbed in behind us and in moments, we were speeding down the street.

"Who were those men?" I asked Devon, once I felt I could speak without my voice quavering. I wasn't wholly successful.

"They were competitors, right, Reggie?"

I heard Reggie's gulp all the way from the front seat. "Y-yeah. I guess."

"It's not a guess!" Devon's voice was loud in the car and I jumped, startled. "You couldn't keep quiet, could you, Reggie? You had to brag."

Reggie said nothing to his accusation.

After a moment, I felt brave enough to venture another question. "Brag about what?"

"It's something I—"

"Do not say it," Devon sternly interrupted. "Have you learned nothing? The more people who know, the worse it is for you, Reggie. And dangerous for them. So keep your mouth shut."

That wasn't insulting or anything. "It's not like I'm going to tell anyone," I muttered.

Devon shot me a quick glance. "It's not about you," he said. "And there's no need for you to know."

After that, no one said anything all the way back to the hotel.

I was curious, but wasn't going to push my luck with Devon. He was angrier and tenser than I'd ever seen him.

With his hand on my elbow, Devon led us back to the rooms.

"You'll stay in there," Devon said to Reggie, pointing through the connecting door. "We'll be in here. Do not leave the room. Understood?"

Reggie nodded, looking ever so much like a chastised child rather than a grown man. He went through the door and Devon closed it behind him, but didn't lock it.

"We are not going to be in here," I said. "You can stay with Reggie. I'm not staying in the same room with you."

"I'll sleep on the couch," Devon said, discarding his gun onto the table.

"There isn't a couch!" I followed him, watching in dismay as he lay down on the bed with a sigh.

"I've killed two men tonight, plus the five last night," he said, "and slept a total of three hours in the last twenty-four. If you don't mind, I'd like to take a nap." He cracked open an eye. "Your virtue is safe with me."

His deadpan delivery, not to mention the facts he'd just reeled off about the last two days, made a blush stain my cheeks. I felt ridiculous.

He was already breathing deeply and steadily, perhaps asleep, and here I was thinking he was going to want to rip my clothes off and make love to me.

I guess he really did get tired like normal people sometimes.

Well, I wasn't tired. I'd slept enough that even though it was nearly midnight, I was wide awake. Curious about Reggie, I hesitantly tapped on the connecting door. No one answered, but I went ahead and opened it anyway.

Closing the door softly behind me, I glanced around the room and saw Reggie sitting in front of the television with headphones covering his ears. He looked up and saw me, quickly snatching off the headphones.

"Hey," he said, and I could tell he was nervous.

"Devon didn't introduce us," I said, walking over to him. I held out my hand. "I'm Ivy."

Reggie shook my hand. "Nice to meet you, Ivy," he said. His palm was very soft, which told me he probably didn't do a lot of hard labor.

"So what are you doing?" I asked, sitting next to him on the bed. I gestured to the TV. "Is that a game?"

"Yeah," he said. "World of Warcraft. It's an RPG."

"RPG?"

"Role-playing game," he clarified. "You wanna play?"

I glanced at the screen. "Um, no thanks. Maybe later."

We were both quiet for a moment in awkward silence. "So," I said with false cheer. "You know Devon."

He nodded, his eyes shifting away from mine. "Yeah, but I probably shouldn't talk about it. He always tells me I talk too much."

"So you see Devon often," I said.

"Um, yeah," Reggie said, fiddling with the game controller in his hands. "I mean, since like, last summer."

"That seems . . . odd," I said. "I mean, you and he aren't in the same business, right? What happened last summer?"

Reggie seemed uncomfortable with my fishing for information. "I should probably get back to this," he hedged. His gaze shifted to mine, then dropped to my breasts. I saw him swallow and quickly look away. His ears turned red.

"You know what," I said, "I changed my mind. Can you teach me how to play?"

"Sure, yeah, if you want," he said, sounding much more eager than I felt. He dug into his backpack and pulled out another game controller. Soon, he'd set me up and was teaching me what all the different buttons did.

I tried to follow, but it was a lot of information, and I wasn't really that interested anyway. But it was working. Reggie was a lot more relaxed after about a half hour of going through the game and showing me what to do.

"So you must spend a lot of time playing this," I said, wondering what in the world the British government wanted with a gamer like Reggie.

"Yeah, when I'm not working," he said, his eyes glued to the screen.

"What kind of work do you do?" I asked, keeping my tone carefully nonchalant.

"I write code," he said. "Operating systems, mainly."

"Operating systems?"

"Yeah. You know, it's the software that runs your computer, your iPad, your smartphone."

"And you write that?" I asked. "Don't, you know, corporations do that?"

"Well, yeah," he said, rapidly manipulating the buttons on his controller. "But they farm it out, too, ya know. Especially if they're under a time crunch. Investors and the market have deadlines and it's a competitive world. There's always someone else out there waiting to take a bigger slice of the pie."

"So you write code for computers?"

"Mainly smartphones," he said, reaching for the Red Bull on the table and taking a swig. "I wrote eighty percent of the software currently running on the world's most well-known smartphone." I could hear the pride in his voice. "Hey, watch it. That guy's about to take you out."

I looked back at the screen, but Reggie was already shooting over my avatar's head.

"Got him," he said.

"Thanks."

"No problem."

We played—or he did, I just pretended to—for a few more minutes as I thought this over. I wanted him to tell me what this was about without asking outright, which would probably make him clam up. Out of fear of Devon, if nothing else.

"That sounds really hard," I said. "You must be really good at it."

He shrugged. "It's one of those things, ya know? Some people are just born knowing how to do something. I was born knowing how to write code. It just made sense to me."

"It probably pays really well," I said.

"Yeah, but I don't handle the money. It gets sent to my bank and my bills are on auto pay. I don't like messing with money and accounting and shit like that." He immediately turned my way. "Oh, hey, sorry about that."

I smiled at his apology for cursing. "It's okay."

"And I heard you screaming," he said, "in my house. You were in the *Psycho* room, weren't you?"

"The *Psycho* room?"

"Yeah. Old lady in the chair, curtains, she had a knife."

Oh. "Yes, that sounds like the one."

Reggie cleared his throat. "Sorry you were in there," he said. "That room's kinda tripped out."

"So I noticed." My tone was dry, but I smiled and he smiled back. "You could make it up to me by telling me how you know Devon," I suggested.

He hesitated, glancing over my shoulder at the closed connecting door, then back to me. "Okay, but you have to swear to me you won't tell him I told you."

"I won't," I promised, scooting closer to him like two teenagers trading secrets. "Tell me."

"Okay, well, you see last summer, I was working on this OS," he began, his voice low like he was telling me a state secret. At my look, he clarified, "Operating system. Anyway, the company had very strict instructions about their biodetection software, which I thought was kind of strange. But I was being paid to do a job, so I did it. I coded my modules and sent them off. I asked them about it, but they told me it wasn't my area and thanks-but-get-lost, basically. Well, that pissed me off, so I decided to hack into their system and see what the code did when hooked into the other modules." He paused.

"What did it do?" I asked.

Reggie looked around again, as though afraid we were being overheard, then hissed in a low whisper, "It stole biomed data."

I stared at him, confused. "It did what?"

"You know those phones where you use your fingerprint?" he said. At my nod, he continued, "Well, it's supposed to just use that to unlock the phone and that's all. This phone took fingerprints and uploaded them in the background to the company's servers, creating an entire database of users, complete with their fingerprints. And that's not the worst. The front-facing camera was so good, it could take a retinal scan, too."

"That doesn't sound so awful," I said. "The police take your fingerprints—"

"That's the police and you have to be arrested for them to get your prints," he interrupted, and I could tell he'd forgotten all about Devon in his need for me to understand. "This is a *private company*. And you gotta realize where security is going—biomed. Think of it. One database, with millions and millions of users' data, including their biometric signature. It would be worth a fortune. And it could hold anyone's signature. CEO of some big corporation. The head of the IMF. Hell, even the president. What do you think someone would pay to get their hands on the president of the United States' fingerprints? Or his retinal scan?"

Okay, when he put it that way, I could see this could be very bad indeed. "But why are you here?" I asked. "What can you do about it? Shouldn't the authorities be notified?"

"The company is based in the Netherlands, which is notorious for its lack of privacy laws. It allows them to do this all legally."

"But just let people know," I persisted. "Social media will take care of it and no one will buy their phones."

"I haven't told you the worst part," he said.

"There's more?"

Reggie nodded glumly. "The code contains a provision that fuses the phone's components and, theoretically, turns it into an incendiary device."

I stared at him. "You mean a bomb."

"Yep."

"So people are walking around with smartphones that not only steal their privacy, but could kill them?"

"Yep."

It was hard to wrap my head around. "But why would anyone do that?" I asked.

"Theoretically, it was something tossed around a while back in black hat circles, but it was just considered vaporware." At my confused look, he elaborated. "Black hat—bad guys. In this case, black hat hackers. Vaporware is software that is supposedly in development, but never actually is released. So in theory, it was like this cool thing, but no one ever expected it to really happen."

"But someone did," I said, thinking Reggie's definition of "cool" and mine were vastly different.

He nodded. "It's an incredible feat, actually, and a perfect terrorist plan. You don't even have to deliver the bomb because everyone already has one. See, watch." He grabbed his tablet from his backpack and swiped a few times until a video began playing.

I watched as someone filmed a well-known smartphone sitting on a table. Nothing happened for about thirty seconds, then it suddenly blew up, with no warning whatsoever. Though the blast wasn't huge, if it had been in someone's pocket or God forbid at their ear, it would have killed them or at the very least, seriously injured them.

"I'd just discovered this and was trying to figure out what to do when Devon turned up," Reggie said. "He told me they knew about the code and that I had to find a way to disable it."

"How could you possibly do that?" I asked.

Reggie grinned. "The only thing easier than writing code," he said, "is breaking it. I wrote a hack that'll brick every one of those phones."

"Wow," I said, impressed.

Reggie's grin faded. "Yeah, the only bad part is that I can't do it through their servers. I need to get on-site to upload the hack so it gets pushed out to every phone as an automatic update."

"How will you do that?"

"That's where Devon comes in," Reggie said.

"So what were you 'bragging' about that got him so mad?" I asked.

Reggie's ears turned red again. "That I had stolen the rest of the retinal and fingerprint stealth scan software. Those guys who came . . . well, let's just say a lot of people would want to get their hands on that."

"Can't they just write their own?"

He shook his head. "It's not that simple to write a stealth program that'll do what you want without other code junkies figuring out what you're doing. It'd be just like you said, all over social media, the news, everywhere. The company would tank and then what's the point of having the software?"

"I see."

Reggie fiddled with the game controller, then turned back to the television and resumed his game.

"You didn't really want to learn how to play, did you?" he said.

I hesitated, not wanting to hurt his feelings. "I don't think I'm cut out for gaming," I hedged.

He glanced at me, a small grin playing at his lips. "If you're with Devon, I doubt he cares." Reggie gave me a quick once-over again. "You're beautiful," he blurted. "Devon's a lucky guy."

I forced a smile because it was a kind thing for him to say, though I wished it wasn't the first thing people saw about me, or the reason why he thought Devon was a "lucky guy." "Thank you."

Sitting back against the headboard, I watched Reggie play the game for a while, though I couldn't hear anything. He'd put his headphones back on and I thought about all he'd told me.

Devon really was working on a mission that could save millions of lives. Even after the virus Heinrich had tried to weaponize and had infected me with, it still seemed incredible to me.

"You know you can't trust them, right?" Reggie asked out of the blue.

I frowned, watching as he blew something up on the screen. "What do you mean? You trust him."

"Devon, yes, but not the people he works for," he clarified. "The stakes are too high for any one person to mean anything to them. So I have an insurance policy."

The idea of an "insurance policy" against the Shadow reminded me of my own—the pages of the diary I'd hidden.

"What is it?" I asked.

From in his pocket, he produced a tiny, silver flash drive and showed it to me. "The code I stole."

"The code that documents the biodata?"

He grinned. "Yep."

"Aren't you afraid they'd just take it from you?" I asked.

"It's encrypted," he explained. "If they try to crack the password, the data erases itself after three failed attempts." Reggie pushed the drive back into his pocket. "I figure, if it comes down to it and Devon isn't around or is unable to take my side, I at least have a bargaining chip."

"It's a smart idea," I said. He just shrugged modestly and continued playing his game.

"How old are you?" I asked after a few minutes. Reggie seemed barely out of his teens.

"Twenty-three," he said. "But I've been writing code since I was nine."

"Wow," I said, impressed. "That's really young."

"Yeah, I guess. I got bored with the kiddie stuff and started consulting when I was twelve. People said stuff like *kid genius* and *prodigy*. Shit like that. But I don't feel like a prodigy. I just do what comes natural to me."

"That's really cool," I said. "I don't really have anything that comes naturally to me. At least, nothing I could make a living from."

He glanced at me. "You're really nice," he blurted. "Most girls who look like you, they don't give me the time of day."

I felt my cheeks heat and I didn't really know what to say. "Thanks. I'm sorry that people treat you badly. That's not right."

He shrugged. "Whatever. People aren't always what they seem, I guess. You look at the outside and people judge, whether they think I'm some kind of socially inept loser or that you're a cold bitch." He seemed to catch himself at that. "Sorry," he said.

"It's fine," I replied. "Yes, a lot of people assume I'm not a very nice person based on how I look. I don't have a lot of friends."

"Me neither," he said.

"I'm your friend," I said, smiling. "Will you be my friend, too?"

He grinned. "Absolutely."

A sudden noise made me sit up in bed. I listened intently, then heard it again. A loud voice, almost like a cry, coming from my room.

I vaulted out of the bed and ran to the door. Flinging it open, I peered in confusion at my room. No one was there but Devon, asleep on the bed.

Okay, that was weird, I thought as I waved a goodnight to Reggie, who just shook his head at my antics and returned his attention to the flickering screen. Closing the door, I glanced back at the bed—

Devon cried out in his sleep, throwing his arms like he was hitting someone and grunting as though he was in pain.

I rushed to the bed, unsure what to do. He was flailing and I didn't want to get hit accidentally. I reached to turn on the lamp, but Devon knocked it to the floor.

"Ivy!"

I froze.

He'd called my name. In his sleep, Devon had called my name.

"Ivy!" he said again, his voice desperate. "Where are you?"

"I'm here," I answered, speaking loudly to try to break through his nightmare. "Devon, I'm here." Tentatively, I reached out and touched his shoulder. His hand snatched at mine.

"Ivy . . ." he breathed in relief, hauling me off my feet and into the bed.

Devon wasn't even awake. His eyes were still shut as he tucked me in beside him like a child with a teddy bear. An arm curved underneath my shoulders and another wrapped around my waist to hold me close. His face was buried in my neck, breathing in my scent.

He was murmuring something against my skin, but I couldn't tell what. He was falling back into a deeper sleep and his lips barely moved. It took a moment before I could make out what he was saying.

"Need you . . . need you . . ." Over and over and over until the words faded away to nothing and he was still, his chest steadily rising and falling with his breath.

I didn't know what to think. I was overwhelmed, stunned at what Devon's subconscious had shown me. I was wrapped so tightly in his arms, his bare legs entwined with mine, there was no way I was going anywhere in the foreseeable future.

Tears leaked from my eyes to trail down the sides of my face and into my hair. I wished Devon could tell me more about how he felt when he was awake. I wondered what prevented him from doing so . . . and if he'd ever overcome it.

We were a pair, he and I. Both damaged goods, but from the outside looking in we were perfect—our pretty façades hiding the broken and jagged parts of our souls. Perhaps that's why we fit so well together. The shattered pieces of our psyches were just enough to complete the other.

I loved him. I knew that, accepted it, despite realizing the chances of us being together were between slim and none. I thought, and tonight had given me hope, that Devon loved me, too. Even if he didn't want to admit it yet.

Hope was a dangerous thing. Hope could save me . . . but hope endlessly deferred would kill me by inches.

I woke slowly, my eyes fluttering open. The sky was just beginning to lighten outside.

Devon was kissing my neck, his lips trailing a warm path to my shoulder. He'd spooned me during the night, my back to his front, and his hand was palming my breast through the thin material of my blouse.

All the reasons I'd had for keeping him at arm's length had disintegrated in light of what had happened during his nightmare. I wanted him. He wanted me. This wasn't just about sex. That was now obvious.

It was a relief, giving in. My body craved his touch. To be so near and yet to be denied had been agony.

Closing my eyes again, I reached back, threading my fingers through his hair. At my touch, an obvious acquiescence, Devon groaned. His lips met mine in a hard kiss, his tongue stroking mine as his hands skated down my body.

He pushed my jeans and panties down my legs and off before pulling my shirt over my head, carelessly tossing away the blouse and my bra. I was just as eager, shoving at the boxer briefs hugging his hips. His erection sprang free into my hands.

Pushing against his chest, I was able to reverse our positions so he was on his back. I slid down his body and took him in my mouth.

The air left him in a sharp gasp, which was incredibly satisfying. He was thick and long and I had to wrap my hand around the base of his cock since I couldn't get all of it in my mouth.

My hair was in my way, so I flipped it up over my head with my hand. He tangled his fingers in the long blonde strands that trailed across his chest.

I lightly brushed the tip with my tongue, teasing him, circling the head before wrapping my lips around him again. I was no expert at deep-throating, but I did all right; at least by the noises he was making I was doing a fine job indeed.

Cupping his balls in my other hand, I gently squeezed. His hips thrust upward, pushing his cock into my mouth, sliding in and out at an ever-increasing pace. Seeing him lose control was an incredible turn-on, and I watched his face. His breathing was harsh and his face was creased in lines of pleasurable agony. The flesh between my legs began to throb with need.

When the steady rhythm of his thrusts began to change, I knew he was close. But before he came, he hauled me back up and flipped me onto my back.

"Want to be inside you, sweet Ivy," he rasped, spreading my thighs. His cock was still wet from my mouth and he slid right into me.

Our tongues tangled and I wrapped my legs around his waist, lifting my hips to meet his. He'd slowed, waiting for me to catch up, I expect. But I gripped the muscled globes of his ass, squeezing and urging him to move harder. Faster.

Devon groaned, deep in his throat, his hands biting into my hips hard enough to leave a mark. But I didn't care. If for now this was the only way he could show me how he really felt, I'd take it.

His orgasm overtook him, his body jerking hard into mine, and I could feel the pounding of his heart against my chest. The noises he made were more vocal than usual, the kisses afterward deeper and lingering. He petted my hair and pressed light kisses to my cheeks, my eyes, my jaw.

There was a sharp rap on the door, then Reggie walked in carrying his laptop. "Hey, guys—"

I shrieked and dove under the covers. Devon gave a heavy sigh.

"Dammit, Reggie," he said.

"Aw, shit, I'm sorry," I heard Reggie stammer.

"Do you mind?" Devon asked.

"Oh! Oh, yeah. Okay."

The door closed. I cautiously peeked out from under the covers. Reggie had retreated back to his room. I glanced at Devon and giggled at the ludicrousness of the situation, getting caught in bed like teenagers.

He cracked a smile, too, then rolled his eyes. "Reggie isn't the most socially aware person I know," he said dryly.

"I got that," I replied, still smiling. "He's nice, though. I like him. Obviously, he's a really smart guy."

"Too smart," Devon said. "The things he thinks about are on a whole other level than you and me. But that leaves him vulnerable because he just doesn't see the dangers around him or in what he does."

Glancing at the bedside clock, Devon swung his legs out of bed and stood. Sunshine flooded through the window and I didn't look away, staring unabashedly at his naked body as he walked to the desk and checked his phone.

"I need to go out," he said. "Can you watch him for me while I'm gone?"

"Yeah, sure," I said.

"I won't be gone long," he said. "Why don't you order us something to eat while I shower?"

That sounded good to me. I was starving.

When the food was delivered, Devon was still in the shower, so I knocked on Reggie's door. I'd thrown on one of the hotel's complimentary bathrobes.

"Are you hungry?" I asked once he'd called out for me to enter. "I ordered room service."

Reggie's face was beet red and he wouldn't look me in the eye as he stammered back, "Uh, no, I'm fine."

"Did you eat already?" I persisted.

He shook his head.

"Then come eat." I grabbed his elbow and tugged him into the room. His embarrassed shyness was sweet.

I made him a plate of eggs with bacon and sat down to eat with him. It took a little coaxing, but he relaxed once I got him talking about his gaming again. By the time Devon emerged, fully dressed in jeans and a black, fitted long-sleeved knit shirt, we were chatting away like old friends.

"You two all right to be left alone for a few hours?" Devon asked, grabbing a couple of strips of bacon from the tray.

"We'll be fine," I assured him, watching as he slipped his gun into the back of his jeans and shrugged on a leather jacket.

Devon cast a skeptical eye our way, but I just blew him a kiss and waved him off. After he'd gone, I turned back to Reggie.

"I think I'm going to take a shower," I said, "but I can come get you when I'm done. We can watch a movie or something."

"Okay, sure, no problem," he said, wiping his mouth with the napkin. "See you in a few."

He went back to his room and I was quick with my shower, slipping the robe back on as I combed out my wet hair. A noise from Reggie's room distracted me. Was that the sound of his door opening into the hallway?

Worried, I set down my brush and went to my door, peering through the peephole just in time to see Reggie creep stealthily by.

CHAPTER TEN

I wasted no time in yanking open the door.

"Reggie, where are you going?"

He spun around guiltily. "I, uh, um, I was, uh, just . . ." he stammered.

"Yeah," I said, sarcasm edging my voice. "You were just, uh, what? Leaving? After Devon told you to stay? He's here to help you, and this is how you're repaying him?"

Reggie hung his head. "I swear, I wasn't sneaking out," he said. "Well, I was, but not for the reason you think."

I crossed my arms over my chest. "Then why?"

"You'll think it's dumb," he muttered.

"Not any more dumb than sneaking out on Devon," I retorted.

"Fine," he huffed. "It's just that . . . there's this convention going on just a couple of blocks away, and I really wanted to go." He shrugged. "I didn't think Devon would miss me for a couple of hours. There'll be tons of people there and it's not far."

He looked so forlorn, like a kid desperate to go to the fair. "What kind of convention?" *Lord, please don't let it be one of those ones where people dress up—*

"Comic book," he said, confirming my fears.

I winced. "You're not going to dress up, are you?"

He looked so guilty, I knew I'd caught him.

I made a frustrated sound. I knew Devon had said to stay here, but the guy looked like I'd just drowned his cat. Surely it wouldn't hurt to pop over to whatever this thing was for a short time. "Okay, fine. We'll go, but just for a little while. Get in here so I can dry my hair."

He hustled past me into the room, and I made quick work of my hair and makeup. I threw on a pair of skinny khaki pants and a deep burgundy blouse, pulling on a pair of brown leather boots before grabbing my purse.

"Okay, let's go," I said. "But don't try to ditch me, got it?"

"Got it."

The convention really was only three blocks away and there were plenty of people in costume as we got closer. I tried not to stare but some of the costumes were downright risqué and chilly, I would think, for this time of year.

"You have to have tickets or something for this?" I asked.

He nodded. "Yeah, but don't worry. They know me so I can get you in. I wrote the software for their website's ticketing and ordering system."

Lovely.

The registration desk was being manned by two people who'd gone all-out on their costumes, complete with real leather and tattoos that I couldn't tell were temporary or permanent.

"Reggie! Hey, good to see you!" one of them said, smiling and shaking Reggie's hand. "We didn't know if you were gonna show or not. You missed opening ceremonies last night."

"Yeah, I was working. Kinda lost track of time," Reggie said. "I have a friend with me today, but she doesn't have a ticket. Is that going to be a problem?"

The man's eyes flicked over to me, widening slightly, then he shook his head. "Not for you, it's not. She's got a cool costume, though. Crossplay is so in right now. Have fun!"

Reggie snagged two badges, slipping one over his head and handing me the other as he pulled me away from the table.

I looked down at my clothes. "Reggie, what was he talking about?" I asked. "I'm not wearing a costume."

"Don't worry about it," he said, already hurrying ahead to where masses of people were clustering. I had no choice but to keep up with him.

We spent the next hour wandering through various booths selling everything you could possibly imagine, and some that I couldn't even tell what they were supposed to be. Reggie seemed to be having a ball, and I'd gotten a few more compliments on my non-costume. I'd just smiled and said thanks.

I was looking through a collection of famous sci-fi actors' autographs when I realized Reggie and I had gotten separated. Crap. That wouldn't do.

I'd last seen him by a display of samurai swords, so that's where I headed. To my relief, I spotted him talking to a couple of men and headed his way.

". . . figured you'd be all decked out, Reg," one of them was taunting as I approached. He was smiling at Reggie, but it was the kind of smile I'd seen a lot and usually directed at me. A sneering sort of smile that appeared friendly, but wasn't. Instantly, I was on alert.

"Yeah, well, I, ah, I'm not staying long," Reggie stammered a reply.

"Somebody's gotta play those video games, right?" the other guy jeered, not even pretending to be nice.

My eyes narrowed. What shits. Reggie had his hands shoved into his pockets and looked for all the world like he wanted the floor to open up and swallow him. While the two guys just looked like snakes, enjoying making him squirm.

Well. We'd see about that.

I tossed back my hair and put a model strut in my step as I walked up to Reggie. I slid my arm over his shoulders and put on my fake French accent.

"Reggie," I purred, "I could not find you. Why did you leave me?" I added a pout for effect.

Reggie seemed utterly taken aback, so I kept talking.

"I see something I want. Will you buy it for me? We can play with it later." I gave him a come-hither smile and leaned to put my lips by his ear. "Play along. I'm your girlfriend," I whispered.

To his credit, he caught on fast, slipping an arm around my waist. "Uh, yeah, absolutely. You bet."

Not exactly Lord Byron, but it would do. I glanced at the two men who stood staring at us, jaws agape.

"Who are you?" I asked, putting as much French haughtiness into the question as I could muster.

"We, uh, we're . . . friends of Reggie's," the first guy said. The second guy just swallowed, the Adam's apple in his throat bobbing up and down. "I'm Ryan, and this is Dale. And you are?"

"I am Ivy," I replied, raising an eyebrow as I turned to Reggie. "Is this true?" I asked him. "Are these two . . . men . . . friends of yours?"

"Um, yeah, I guess. Well, not really," he said.

"I did not think so." I put every ounce of disdain I had into my voice as I looked both men up and down before turning back to Reggie. I was pressed against his side with both arms wrapped around his neck. "Let's go," I pleaded. "I want to go back to the hotel and be with you."

One of the guys, maybe Dale, made a strangled sort of sound, but I ignored him.

"That sounds like a great idea," Reggie said, and his voice was much stronger now than it had been before. "Gotta go guys. Catch ya later."

We walked away and it wasn't until we were back on the street that Reggie let go of the death grip he had around my waist.

"Oh my God!" he said, bursting out laughing. "Did you see the look on their faces?"

"Yeah," I said, chuckling. "What a couple of jerks."

"Hey, Ivy, thanks," he said, stopping and facing me. "That was . . . that was awesome. Seriously."

I shrugged, my cheeks heating. "No problem. We're friends, right?"

"Absolutely," he said, grinning from ear to ear.

Our good moods lasted until we entered the hotel room. Devon was there, pacing, and when he saw us, the look on his face made me take an instinctive step back.

"I told you to wait here," he gritted out, pointing down at the floor. "Where the bloody hell have you been?" He was looking at me as he said this, not Reggie.

"Um, let me handle this," I said in an undertone to Reggie, pushing him through the connecting door into his room and closing it behind him. "I can explain," I said to Devon.

"You damn well better," he shot back. "After all my precautions, I thought they'd found you, taken you." Without any warning, he picked up a porcelain vase from the bureau and threw it. It hit the wall and shattered into a million pieces. I gasped in dismay, my hand flying up to cover my mouth.

Everything was quiet after that, only the sound of Devon's breathing audible in the room. I wasn't afraid, but this was the most emotion I'd ever seen from him and I wasn't sure how best to handle it. He was angry, yes. But he was angry because he'd been worried. Because he'd thought he'd failed.

I went to him, standing in front of him. He wasn't looking at me. He was looking at the floor and his hands were in fists at his sides.

"Devon," I said softly, covering his hands with mine. "I'm so sorry. I didn't mean for you to worry. I swear to you. Reggie just needed a little diversion for a while. If I'd known you'd get this worried and upset, I never would have gone."

Raising his eyes, his gaze met mine. We stood like that for a moment and I could almost feel the anger ebb from him. He was studying me intently, his forehead creased as his blue eyes gazed into mine. After a moment, he spoke. "When Kira was murdered, I was . . . devastated. I hadn't protected her. She'd died because of me. The pain and guilt were . . . overwhelming."

Devon unbuttoned his shirt a few buttons and pointed to a bullet wound scar on his chest. "This was the result."

I frowned in confusion.

"I was reckless. Too reckless. Perhaps I had a death wish, but was too much of a coward to do it myself. I felt I should pay, atone for what I'd done to her. And when it happened, when I was shot, I felt like pain was bleeding out of me."

"What happened?" I asked. "Obviously you survived."

"I had to decide I wanted to," he replied. Reaching up, he brushed my hair back, tucking it behind my ear. "But I've lived with the guilt of failing her. And I'm terrified of failing you."

I shook my head, my gaze dropping from his. Now I felt even worse for leaving the room. "You could never fail me, Devon," I said. His fingers brushed underneath my chin, tipping my head up until I looked at him again.

"Don't say that," he said. "Everyone fails everyone else. Always. It's the one constant that can be depended on."

It was a cynical thing to say, but then again, Devon lived in a world I'd only had the briefest exposure to. The guilt he carried from Kira's death had marked him as deeply as Jace's abuse had marked me.

"Our flight's in three hours," he said. "We need to pack up. Get your new best friend to pack up, too." I knew he was referring to Reggie, and by his tone I knew he'd forgiven us. I hurried to tell Reggie all was okay and that we were leaving.

Between last night and today, everything Devon had done and said had been so unexpected as to leave me reeling. I was over-whelmed with relief that things were changing between us, and suddenly, things didn't seem as horrible as they had yesterday.

I changed into a peach blouse that crossed over my torso and wrapped around my back. A tie held the filmy lengths of fabric together and, combined with my skinny jeans and nude heels that wrapped up around my ankles, I felt more put-together—inside and out—than I had in a long time.

As usual, Devon dressed in a suit. This one, a dark charcoal with tiny pinstripes. A stark white shirt and striped silk tie completed what I'd come to think of as his spy uniform. He finished the knot on his tie, then rapped on the door to Reggie's room.

Reggie was ready to go, so within our allotted hour, we were heading to the airport. As soon as we got to the ticket desk and Devon asked for three first-class tickets to Amsterdam, I knew we had a problem.

"I don't have my passport," I whispered to him as the agent tapped the keys on her keyboard.

"Don't be silly, darling," he replied, reaching inside his jacket. "What did you think I was doing this morning?" He handed the woman two passports. "Mr. and Mrs. Jared Ross, if you please."

My mouth dropped open, then I quickly closed it, averting my face so the agent wouldn't see my surprise. It was the name he'd given Logan last December when he'd crashed dinner.

Once Devon had handed over his credit card, the agent took our bags, handed us boarding passes, and told us which gate we were departing from. I'd heard the prices she'd said for the three last-minute tickets and had wanted to groan in dismay. The total cost more than some small cars. Reggie popped into a shop to get something to eat and Devon and I paused outside to wait for him.

"Mr. and Mrs. Jared Ross?" I asked.

"Easier this way," Devon said. "I'm Jared. You are—"

"Yes, do tell me my new name," I teased. "This should be good."

Devon faced me fully. "I would think it would be obvious," he said. "You're Rose, of course."

My teasing grin faded. His gaze roamed over my face and he lifted a hand to cup my cheek, his thumb brushing my skin. "I'd quote Shakespeare," he said, "if it wouldn't be so cliché."

I smiled, but was too caught up in how he was looking at me to reply. People passed us by but neither of us noticed. His hand drifted down my arm to my hand, slotting our fingers together.

"You sure you guys don't want anything? The cinnamon buns are awesome." Reggie was back and Devon glanced at him. He was chowing down on a pastry dripping with icing.

"Maybe later," Devon said with distaste. I huffed a laugh at the snooty Britishness he was displaying, but quickly smothered it when he slanted a glance my way.

Getting through security wasn't a problem, and soon we were ensconced in our first-class seats. Our flight went through Detroit and the entire trip took over twelve hours. I tried to sleep as much as possible, but was still exhausted when our plane landed early in the afternoon the next day in Amsterdam.

The lines at customs were long and I followed Devon as he led me to one. He handed me my passport.

"Just tell them you're here on holiday," he said in an undertone. "For a few weeks."

"A few weeks?" I repeated, thinking of how I'd only asked off work for a few days.

But Devon didn't respond because it was our turn. The agent took Devon's passport first and carefully studied the photo, then him. He asked a few questions and Devon answered, looking tired and bored.

"Enjoy your stay," the agent said, dismissing him and gesturing for me to step forward. I handed him my passport.

He looked me over even more carefully, then consulted his computer screen. My palms were sweating as I waited, then my worst fears came true as he said, "I'm afraid we need to ask you some additional questions." He motioned to a security guard.

"What? What does that mean?" I asked, trying not to panic.

"Miss, please come with me," the guard said. He was tall, and wide, and had a serious-looking gun attached to his hip.

"But I'm here on holiday," I said, echoing what Devon had told me to say. "I haven't done anything." Looking frantically past them for Devon, I saw he was trying to come back to me, but a guard was arguing with him.

"This way, miss," the guard said, taking a firm grip on my arm.

"I need my passport," I said, reaching out to take it from the customs agent, but he held it beyond my reach.

"You'll get your passport back shortly," he said.

The guard was already dragging me away and I looked to Devon. He'd stopped arguing with the agent and now stared after me, a grim look on his face. Reggie stood a few feet behind him, also watching me.

Then they were both lost to sight as we turned a corner and the guard punched in a code to unlock a door. After taking me through the door and down a sterile hallway, he unlocked another door in the same manner, but held it open for me to precede him. I did, then spun around in dismay when the door slammed shut behind me.

I ran forward and tried the knob, knowing even before I did that it was locked.

I stood for a moment, taking stock of my situation.

The room was small, maybe ten feet wide by ten feet long, and contained only one table and three metal folding chairs—two on one side, one on the other. The door was windowless, the walls thick and painted a gloomy shade of white.

What was happening? I hadn't done anything, hadn't even said anything, and they'd brought me here. Would Devon get me out? How could he possibly? I had no choice but to wait.

As I sat in one of the folding chairs, I realized that though my passport said Rose Ross, everything in my purse said Ivy Mason.

I leaned forward, elbows on the table, and covered my face with my hands. I didn't know what they'd do to me when they found out about the fake passport, but I knew it wouldn't be good.

My stomach was clenched in knots as I sat there imagining the horrible consequences. Prison in Amsterdam. Would I get a lawyer?

I looked at my watch a hundred times over the next hour, my anxiety only increasing with each passing minute. Was this how it was usually done? They had my passport. I didn't know how Devon had obtained it, but I doubted it would hold up to scrutiny.

The knob turned on the door and it swung open. I stared in stunned amazement at who entered the room.

"You're a slippery target," Vega said, her voice as smooth and as cold as I remembered it.

Since I wasn't drugged up on pain meds, I could take better stock of her now. She was the same height as me without my heels, and just as lean. She was incredibly well preserved, so much so that it was nearly impossible to determine her age. My best guess was late fifties, but ten years could have easily been added or subtracted from that. Her face was all planes and angles, her eyes and hair dark.

"What are you doing here?" I asked, watching suspiciously as she casually took a seat in a chair opposite me. She was wearing Chanel—I knew designer clothes when I saw them—and looked incredibly elegant and poised. Whereas I felt dirty after hours spent traveling, my clothes rumpled and yesterday's mascara staining the skin underneath my eyes.

"Ah, you remember me," she said, crossing one nylon-clad leg over the other. "You were a bit . . . under the weather the last time we spoke. I thought perhaps you might not recall our little chat."

"You're a difficult person to forget," I replied.

Her lips lifted ever so slightly at the corners.

"I'm a slippery target," I echoed her, realization hitting me. "It was you, wasn't it? You sent those men after me, sent them to my grandparents' home." Anger rose at what they'd put us through. "You fucking bitch."

Her cold, dark eyes narrowed. "What a perceptive little nuisance you are," she replied. "And you should keep in mind that I can walk out of here anytime I want. Whereas you . . ." She paused, glancing over me with mock pity. "You seem to be in a bit of a pinch. So I'd mind my manners, if I were you."

"Is that so?" I didn't want to give her the satisfaction of rattling me.

"Quite. Your passport is fraudulent, of course," she said with a careless wave of her hand. "We both know that you're not Rose Ross. But what I want to know is . . ." She leaned forward. "Why does Clay keep protecting you?"

I stared at her, frowning. "Why in the world are you asking me? Aren't you his boss? Ask him yourself." And I didn't care that I sounded like an insolent teenager.

Sitting slowly back in her chair, she considered me. "You're very beautiful, I'll give him that. But otherwise . . . you're just a little nobody. And even though he told me the diary was destroyed in Heinrich's lab, I can't help thinking that he's protecting you for a reason. What are you hiding, Ivy Mason? What did Heinrich tell you?"

Alarm shot through me. No one knew that I'd saved the encrypted pages from that diary, save Scott, and even he didn't know what those pages contained. "I don't know what you're talking about," I said, bluffing my way. "Heinrich did nothing but threaten me, not tell me state secrets. Devon and I just have a casual relationship. Friends with benefits, I'd guess you'd call it. There's no hidden agenda."

"You do know you're not the first woman to catch his interest for longer than a night," she said.

"I never said I was."

"Has he told you about her?" she asked. "I bet not."

Stung, I replied, "You might be surprised."

Vega raised an eyebrow as she said, "Clay's told you about his wife?"

The nonchalant way she said that contrasted sharply with the impact those words had as they hit me.

Devon was married?

"I can see that tidbit might have gone unmentioned," Vega said with satisfaction. "Clay's been lying all his life. It's what he's paid to do, amongst other things." She shrugged one slim shoulder. "His purpose in life—his absolute focus—is doing what I tell him to do. I'd keep that in mind, if I were you."

"What does this have to do with me?" I asked.

"I just wanted to see you again, have another little chat, face-to-face," Vega said. "You didn't think we'd just forget about you, did you? After Paris?" She leaned forward again, and menace replaced the false friendliness in her voice. "If you're hiding anything, I will eventually find out. Devon will probably tell me himself."

"I'm a bank teller," I said. "What could I possibly have to hide?"

"And yet, he keeps coming back," she mused.

"And with a wife, no less," I said bitterly. "However does he find the time?" How could Devon have not told me he was married? It was all I could do to keep a brave face in front of Vega, though my chest felt like a warm ball of wax someone was squeezing too hard.

"You should ask him about her," Vega said, getting up from her chair. She opened the door, but paused. "And you should remember—we're always watching. Don't forget that." Then she was gone.

My breath rushed out of me, the stiff spine I'd been maintaining went limp, and I folded over the table, resting my head on my arms. Devon had spoken in nearly reverent terms about how much he owed Vega for saving him. His loyalty to her was unquestionable. And it was obvious that went both ways since she knew he had a wife, and I—the woman he'd been having an affair with—didn't.

Plus, Vega suspected I was hiding something. She had the power to have me apprehended at customs heading into the Netherlands. She could send armed men anywhere in the world to hunt me down. No one could protect me from her. Not even Devon. And now I wondered—deep in my gut—if he would even attempt to do so, should Vega give him orders to the contrary.

The door reopened and I jerked upright, eyes wide at what might be in store for me now, but it was just the same guard who'd brought me in here almost two hours ago.

"Come with me. You're free to go," he said. He held out my passport.

It took me a moment to process this, then I jumped to my feet and hurried forward to claim the very important document certifying my false identity. I grabbed my purse and followed the guard a different way out. He eventually opened a door that dumped me near the terminal exit.

I looked around the masses of people moving past, but couldn't see Devon. Would he have waited? Or would he and Reggie have left so his mission wouldn't be compromised? As I stood there, searching in vain and increasing panic for his familiar face, it seemed my question had been answered.

"There you are."

A hand on my shoulder spun me around and I was face-to-face with Devon.

"Oh, thank God," I said, then promptly burst into tears.

"Shh, darling, it's all right," he comforted me, taking me in his arms.

But it wasn't all right. Vega had threatened me . . . and Devon was married. I wasn't sure which was worse at this point.

"Come, let's go," he said, pressing his pocket square into my hand. He took my elbow, leading me outside.

"Where's Reggie?" I asked, wiping the tear tracks from my face. I had to suck it up and get through this, and falling apart wouldn't help any.

"I sent him on to the hotel with strict instructions," Devon replied as he flagged down a cab. "Which means by now he's probably hacked into the Netherlands' seat of government." He sounded irritated and I guessed he'd dealt with Reggie and his spontaneous ways before.

A cab pulled over and Devon held the door while I climbed inside. All I could think about was Vega and what she'd said. Should I tell Devon about it? What would he do? What *could* he do? And did any of it even matter now that I knew he was married?

Devon had an entire life that I apparently knew even less about than what little he'd told me, whereas everything in my life was an open book to him. It wasn't hard to feel bitter about that.

After he'd given the driver our destination, he turned to me. "What happened in there?" he asked. Lifting his hand, he cupped my cheek, his fingers sliding into my hair. "I nearly had a heart attack when they took you."

It was nice to know he'd been worried. But now I had to make a decision. Come clean? Or lie? After all, he'd lied to *me*.

"It was a misunderstanding," I lied. "There's another Rose Ross on Interpol's list. Once they got the photos and compared them, they let me go. It just took forever."

Devon frowned slightly, his eyes studying me. I forced a small smile, feeling my gut sink that my instinct had been to lie. But I was nothing to him—a mere blip on the radar of his life—compared to what Vega was. And apparently another woman was even more than that.

I recognized the cold feeling inside for what it was—the acid burn of betrayal and bitterness, which was the real reason I'd lied. I wasn't ready to hear whatever excuse he might come up with to explain this.

"Where are we staying?" I asked, just to change the subject. Breaking our gaze, I glanced out the window at the passing scenery. Night was falling and the unfamiliar city felt strange and hostile to me. "Somewhere nice, I hope."

"Of course," he said, pulling his hand back. My skin felt cold in the absence of his touch. "Would I put you anywhere else?"

The teasing note in his voice made me turn back to him. Our eyes met. The lies between us were an invisible wall that only I could feel. I forced a smile I didn't feel.

The hotel was beautiful and I gasped when I saw it. Sitting on the edge of the water, it was lit up like a golden Christmas tree, and when we alighted from the cab, the doorman was wearing a three-piece suit complete with a top hat.

My eyes widened even further when I saw the inside of the hotel, the opulence of which rivaled the exterior. The entry had deep red carpet and walls, with two entire rows of chandeliers presiding over the seating along the hallway. The musical chords of a piano filtered through the room and I glimpsed a man seated at the instrument and playing on the far side.

"This way," Devon said, leading me to the elevator. A few minutes later, he was knocking on the door to a room. Reggie answered.

"Hey, glad they let you go," he said to me. "That was scary."

"Yes, I'm not quite sure what I would've done if they hadn't," I said.

Neither man replied to that and Reggie's gaze shifted nervously aside.

Well.

"Our key," Devon reminded him.

"Oh yeah, here you go," Reggie said, digging in his pocket and handing the key over to Devon.

"Stay out of trouble," Devon said, poking Reggie in the chest with his finger. "We have enough to worry about without you getting in dire straits."

Reggie just grinned, unabashed and unrepentant. Devon sighed.

We headed back to the elevator and went up another floor, where Devon let us into our room. As I'd known it would be, it was a suite that probably cost more a night than I made in a month. I was a girl who liked nice things—who didn't?—and the room definitely fell into that category.

The carpet and walls were the same deep red as the entry downstairs. The bed was huge and round, situated on a raised dais surrounded halfway in a curved wall, which shielded it from the deep soaking tub hidden behind another curved wall.

I'd never seen anything like it before. Everything in the room was round, no sharp edges anywhere. Even the table was rounded instead of square. The window was directly in front of the bed, a huge curved arch with a view of the water. Boats glided by, their lights twinkling in the night.

"This is amazing," I said, turning to Devon, who was watching me rather than the view outside. He still wore his suit and tie, and no wrinkles dared mar the perfection of the lines, regardless of how many hours we'd been traveling.

"I thought you'd like it," he said, tossing the key onto the table. "Hoped you would, anyway." He walked toward me and slid his arms around my waist and I had to make myself not cringe away from his touch. I felt his lips brush the top of my head. "Our last European adventure ended rather poorly."

Paris. Me betraying him, then believing he was going to kill me. Alone and afraid. Yes, *rather poorly* was one way to describe it—a very British understatement. *Utter disaster* was more apt.

And this one didn't look like it would end any better.

He'd lied to me. Was even now lying to me. Vega would kill me—or something very close to it—if our relationship continued much longer. And as before, I was thousands of miles from home in a strange country, at the whim of a man who couldn't be trusted.

Apparently, I hadn't learned a damn thing in Paris.

"I'm just going to take a shower," I said, easing out of his arms. Stepping from his embrace was an act of will. I liked being held by Devon. "Did they bring the luggage?"

"It's near the bath," he said.

I dug through my suitcase, pulling out pajamas and my brush, but Devon caught my arm as I made to pass by him.

"What's wrong?" he asked. "Did you think I'd left you there today?"

I looked at him and he saw the answer in my eyes.

He muttered a curse then palmed my cheek. "I won't leave you," he said.

And it was too much. Everything he'd said to me the past few days that had given me hope for us, and it had been lies. All of it. And I snapped.

"You won't leave me?" I echoed. "Really? Tell me, is that what you promise your wife?"

CHAPTER
ELEVEN

Everything went still.

"What did you say to me?" Devon asked at last, shock in his voice.

I decided to come clean and clear the air. I wanted no more lies between us. "I know you have a wife," I said. "I just don't understand why you didn't tell me you were married."

"Who told you I was married?"

I hesitated, unsure how he'd react when I told him his precious Vega had dropped this particular bombshell on me.

"Tell me," he ordered, squeezing my arm when I didn't immediately answer. "Who was it?"

"You're hurting me," I said. He immediately let go.

"It's important, Ivy," he said. "Tell me."

I took a deep breath, questioning the wisdom of my temper getting the best of me and admitting to him that I knew about his wife. But there was no backing out now. "Vega," I said. "It was Vega."

Devon looked as if I'd slapped him. "Vega. When could you possibly have spoken to Vega?"

"When she had me detained at customs."

Realization struck and his lips thinned as he pressed them tightly together.

"Tell me everything," he said.

"Why should I? You're *married*," I said. "And I had to hear it from her, rather than you."

I whirled around, but Devon jerked me back with a hard yank. He pulled me close until we were practically nose-to-nose.

"I am *not* married," he bit out.

My eyes narrowed. "Why would I believe you? She had no reason to lie to me, whereas you do." I tried to pull away, but didn't get anywhere.

"I'm not married now," he said. "I was once. A long time ago."

I stilled. "What happened? You got a divorce?"

"I've already told you what happened," he said. "It was Kira. My wife was murdered."

It was my turn to be shocked. A beat passed. "Why didn't you tell me from the start?" I asked. "Why hide it?"

"Because I didn't want you under the impression I'd make the same mistake twice."

"What mistake?"

His voice softened considerably as he said, "Marrying the woman I love."

Those words had the impact of a mortar blast inside my head. My eyes were wide as I processed this, and no sooner had I done so than they stung with tears.

"Do you mean that?" I whispered. "You love me?" I was afraid to ask, but more afraid not to.

Devon's hands cradled my face. "My sweet Ivy, do you really think I'd go to all this bother if I didn't?"

A short laugh escaped me even as the tears slipped down my cheeks.

Devon kissed me, his thumbs brushing away my tears. I could feel his smile against my lips and I laughed again in sheer delight.

"Why tell me now?" I asked, looking up into his eyes. "Why not back in Kansas when I first asked you?"

"I wasn't going to tell you at all," he admitted. "But I think you need to hear it more than I need to conceal it."

I wanted to ask why he needed to conceal it, but decided to let it go. That conversation sounded like it would lead nowhere happy and I wanted to enjoy the happiness I felt right now.

His hands moved to my blouse, slipping the buttons free of the silk, one by one, carefully undressing me. His lips trailed down my neck to the skin he revealed.

"How could I not fall in love with you?" he murmured. "We're alike, you and I. Pain turned us both into creatures with walls." He slid the blouse from my waistband and it fluttered to the floor. "You slipped past my walls the same way I've slipped past yours."

Devon was right, and it meant so much that he and I were at the same place in our relationship, at the same time. I'd never had that feeling before, of being utterly and completely in sync with someone.

He made love to me and it was the same . . . and completely different, knowing he loved me. The sex between us became an expression of that love, rather than how it had begun, as only a physical desire to be met.

Afterward, he hooked an arm around my waist and twisted to lie on his back on the bed, resting my body on top of his. He kissed me. My hair was a curtain around us and his hands moved to comb through the heavy mass, his palms cradling my face.

Eventually, he broke the kiss off, his lips gently releasing mine. I would have moved aside, but he held me there. The look in his eyes as he gazed at me was one I'd never seen on him before, and it took my breath away. His thumbs brushed my cheeks and it seemed as though he was memorizing my face.

"What is it?" I asked softly. "What's wrong?"

But he just gave a minute shake of his head. "Nothing is wrong. For once, everything is as perfect as it could possibly be." He paused. "It's terrifying, actually."

I frowned. The first part of that had sounded wonderful, but I didn't understand. "Why is it terrifying?"

"Because you and I weren't supposed to happen," he said. His voice was a low rasp. "And yet, here we are. And I don't want to feel this way about you, don't want to love you as much as I do, because people are fragile. You could be taken from me in an instant."

I closed my eyes, turning my face slightly so I could press a kiss to his palm, still resting against my cheek. When I reopened my eyes, my gaze settled on his. I had no reassurances for him, but I didn't think he was looking for any. Devon was no one's fool. He knew better than anyone the danger that surrounded his life like a shroud.

"Let's try out that tub," he suggested after a while, and I readily agreed. A hot bath sounded wonderful. Soon we were soaking together in the largest tub I'd ever been in. Steam from the water drifted through the air. Devon insisted on doing the washing, trailing the lathered sponge up my arms and down my stomach. I returned the favor, admiring his form and the lines of muscle as I always had.

I was leaning on the edge of the tub, my head resting on my arms, as he trailed water down my back. Then I felt his lips follow the curve of my spine and my eyes drifted closed. It was blissful. My body relaxed and my mind was at ease. My heart was light and a smile curved my lips.

He wrapped me in a towel and carried me to the bed, tucking me next to him. When we were warm in the cocoon of down and cotton, he turned on his side and propped himself on his elbow.

"Tell me the rest, darling," Devon coaxed. "What else did Vega say to you?"

My joy dimmed somewhat. What Vega had said wasn't something I wanted to discuss right now. Devon had finally, unbelievably, told me he loved me. I wanted to enjoy that for a while before I had to spoil everything.

"Can we talk about it in the morning?" I asked. "I'm so tired."

He appeared thoughtful as he gazed at me. "Yes, I suppose it can wait." Leaning forward, he pressed a kiss to my forehead. "Go to sleep. We'll deal with the real world in the morning."

He took me in his arms and before I knew it, I was sound asleep.

Chapter Twelve

A pounding on the door made me sit straight up in bed. It took me a minute to remember where I was, and by that time, Devon already had his gun in his hand and was standing to the side of the door.

"It's Reggie," a voice called from the other side. "Open up."

Devon pulled open the door and I made a grab for the sheets, holding them to my chest. Reggie hurried inside the room, his face turning red at the sight of Devon completely naked and me in the bed.

"Sorry to interrupt," he said, turning back to Devon, who was pulling on a pair of slacks. "But we have a problem."

"What is it?" Devon asked.

"The company's been sold."

"What do you mean, the company's been sold?" Devon asked.

"The parent company that holds the trigger code," Reggie explained, pacing the room. He looked like he hadn't slept at all. His T-shirt and jeans were wrinkled and his overly long hair was mussed. "The trigger that turns your smartphone into your own personal bomb. A hostile buyout has left the company in different hands."

That got a reaction.

"Who?" Devon asked, grabbing Reggie's arm and yanking him to an abrupt halt. "Who now owns that code?"

"Yeah, that's the really bad news, man," Reggie said. "It's some guy from Russia, with ties to terrorist groups. Dabbles in drugs, human trafficking, the usual shit."

"I need a name," Devon said.

"Levin, I think," Reggie said. "Do you know him?"

Devon nodded. "I know of him. How did you find out about this?"

"It was all over the news this morning," Reggie said. "The guy is flying in today to Amsterdam and meeting with the board of directors tomorrow morning. Once the paperwork's signed, he'll hold the keys to the kingdom."

"And there's only one reason why a man with ties to terrorists would want to buy a company like this," Devon said.

"He knows about the code," Reggie supplied. Devon looked grim.

Devon paced the room, thinking. Reggie and I watched him. After a moment, he stopped. "We have no choice," he said. "We need to get to the software first, upload Reggie's alterations, and send the updates to the phones ahead of the buy."

"We need to get to where their servers are," Reggie said. "But security at that facility is tighter than Fort Knox."

"I would think a potential buyer would want a tour of that facility, prior to the purchase," Devon said, his lips twisting. "Reggie, call them and tell them you're with Levin. Insist on a tour. You and I will go. Once we gain access, we'll do what needs to be done."

Reggie was nodding. "On it," he said, rushing back out the door.

I glanced at the clock and realized it was already late in the afternoon. We'd slept the morning away, courtesy of jet lag. And it seemed Devon and I wouldn't be getting much more time together if he and Reggie were going somewhere.

"Won't that be dangerous?" I asked.

Devon glanced up at me, a small smile playing about his mouth. "Did you forget what I do for a living?"

I felt my cheeks flush. "No, it's just that I worry, that's all. I don't want anything to happen to you any more than you want something bad to happen to me."

His smile faded and he approached the bed. I tipped my head back to look at him. Reaching out, he smoothed my hair from my face.

"I wish I could promise I'll always return to you," he murmured. "But I can't."

"Don't say that." After last night, I didn't want to think any further into the future than a few hours at a time. If I did, my happiness would surely drain away.

His lips twisted, the smile this time fake and barely there. "Hungry, darling? You must be. I'm starving."

He ordered room service, then showered while I picked at the food that was delivered on shining silver trays. I mulled over what Vega had said yesterday, how she'd threatened me. No way was I giving up on Devon, not now. Not when I knew he loved me. But I didn't want to tell Devon about the conversation. If he knew Vega was against our being together, who would he choose? Her or me? I was afraid of the answer to that, which was yet another reason to hold my silence.

"I take it Reggie spilled everything to you?" Devon asked as he buttoned his shirt.

I squirmed. "Not really his fault. I was . . . persuasive."

"Yes, you certainly can be."

He didn't sound angry, just resigned and perhaps a bit indulgent, so I felt better about coaxing the information out of Reggie.

We were both fully dressed by the time Reggie returned a couple of hours later.

"I set it up," he said. "But we have to move fast. If they get wind that you're not the real Levin, all hell's gonna break loose."

"Do we know where Levin will be tonight?" Devon asked.

"I hacked into the company he hires to drive him while he's in town," Reggie said. "He'll be at Club Elegance tonight. Apparently, he's a regular."

"Excellent," Devon replied. "Get into their system and reserve us a spot right next to his."

Reggie opened up his laptop and began typing.

I watched Devon prepare for the evening, checking his gun and ammunition clip. I looked over his shoulder as he opened a small case.

"What's that?" I asked, looking at the tiny electronic in his hand, no bigger than a postage stamp.

"A tracking device. I'm going to plant this on Levin so we can make sure he doesn't get anywhere near where I'll be impersonating him."

"How in the world are you going to plant it on him?" I asked. Reggie looked befuddled, too. "Just walk up to him?"

Devon stood, holstering his gun and tucking the tracker inside his jacket pocket. "It's my job," he said to me. "You know this. I'll figure it out."

"Dude, she'd have a way better chance of getting that on him at Club Elegance than you will," Reggie interjected.

"By posing as a prostitute, you mean?" I asked. I wasn't stupid.

Reggie looked embarrassed, but said frankly, "Yeah. It *is* Amsterdam, you know."

Devon glanced at me as I chimed in. "I can do that," I said, jumping at the chance to help Devon. "There will be lots of prostitutes there. I can get close enough to plant the transmitter, then slide out the back door."

He didn't say anything, so I added, "Please, Devon. Let me do something."

"You'll never get close enough, and she can," Reggie chimed in. "Plus, she's his type."

Devon glanced at Reggie, who was studying his laptop. "What do you mean?"

"I mean this guy has a thing for the blondes," Reggie said, turning his laptop around so we could see the screen. Sure enough, there were several pictures of a tall man with dark hair accompanied by beautiful women—all willowy blondes with hair nearly as light as mine.

"Ivy, a moment, please," Devon said, taking my hand. He drew me out of Reggie's earshot.

"What is it?" I asked.

"I want you to think very hard about what you're asking to do," Devon said. "You want to help and I understand that, but this will be an aggressive role using sex as currency. I don't think you've considered how that might . . . affect you."

Stiffening, I said, "Do you think I'm going to freak out or something?"

His gaze didn't falter. "Possibly."

I felt heat flood my cheeks. "I won't."

"You don't know that," he said. "I'm not in the habit of sugar-coating things, so I won't patronize you by doing so. Any kind of panic attack, flashback, or even faltering in who you're supposed to be and what you're doing could lead to very unpleasant consequences. For all of us."

"I said I'll be okay."

Devon looked in my eyes, measuring, it seemed. "Fine," he said curtly. "But we'll go together. You'll accompany me. We'll attract his interest and you can pop over for a hello, plant the transmitter, then we're out of there."

"Okay."

I hurried to my suitcase, rummaging through it and grabbing a few things. Hustling into the bathroom, I stripped off my clothes, and replaced them with matching pink lace bikini panties and bra.

I brushed my hair until it shone, then added a layer of deep crimson lipstick.

Outside the bathroom, I grabbed a suit jacket from Devon's luggage. I shrugged it on and found a wide belt to keep it closed, then I rolled up the sleeves and slipped on a pair of black heels that wrapped around my ankles.

"How do I look?" I asked the two men. The cut of Devon's coat was such that the deep V went nearly to my waist, exposing the lacy bra. "Do I look like a prostitute?"

"Now that's a question I wouldn't dream of actually answering," Devon replied. His levity made me smile and eased my nerves.

Reggie's eyes zeroed in on my cleavage, then dropped to my legs. I saw his Adam's apple bob as he swallowed.

"Your eyes look about to fall out of your head, mate," Devon teased him.

"You look amazing," Reggie blurted to me. Impulsively, I leaned down and gave him a hug. He turned beet red. "So what's my job?" he asked Devon, after clearing his throat slightly.

"You keep track of the transmitter and make sure it's working when we plant it," Devon said. "You'll be in the car."

Devon handed me the transmitter, which I slid into the inside pocket of the jacket I wore. "Plant this in a similar location," he said. "It doesn't have to be somewhere permanent, just on his person for a few hours."

"Understood."

"You have everything you need?" Devon asked Reggie, who nodded, slipping his laptop into his backpack.

"Ready."

Devon had a car waiting when we went downstairs and I assumed the hotel had arranged for it. He got behind the wheel and I slid into the passenger seat. Reggie got in back.

Club Elegance wasn't far from our hotel and we were pulling up sooner than I was prepared for, but I didn't let it show. Devon's words were echoing inside my head, but I was determined to not let him down.

Reggie replaced Devon behind the wheel after we got out about a block from the club.

"Stay close," Devon said to him before stepping away. He slid his arm around my waist and I clung to him the way I imagined a woman who knew he was her paycheck would . . . and that the amount of that paycheck depended on how well she pleased him.

Devon gave his fake name at the door and we were shown upstairs. It was a dark place, light filtering through the dim rooms and hallways from golden sconces on the walls. Upstairs was a big room with a stage in the middle. A barely clad woman danced to music I didn't recognize. Men milled in groups, both standing and sitting, as other nearly naked women draped themselves on their laps.

The VIP area seemed to be the couches edging the room, and that's where we were led. My nerves were jangling something fierce as I watched the prostitutes plying their wares. Some men obviously wanted to try the merchandise first, and I had to look away from where two men were fondling a woman's breasts. She didn't seem to mind, but I had a hard time wrapping my head around that.

Devon sat down on the cranberry velvet seat and I was going to sit next to him, but he pulled me down onto his lap instead. A server came by immediately, setting up bottles of liquor for us and pouring us both martinis.

Handing one to me, Devon said in an undertone, "All right, darling?"

I nodded, taking a large gulp of the drink, then set aside the glass. Leaning down, I kissed Devon's neck and whispered in his ear, "Is he here?"

"Right behind you."

I waited a moment, then casually turned and glanced over my shoulder. The man who'd been on Reggie's screen sat on the couch beside us. He was surrounded by several other men; a quick count turned up six.

Women had already latched on to their group and I noticed a brunette trying to get Levin's attention. He humored her, but didn't seem terribly interested.

"Can you work this?" Devon asked me, his arm tightening around my back. "If you can't, then I'll come up with another plan."

"I'm fine," I said, smothering my anxiety. "Trust me." Devon wouldn't have let me do this if he thought me incapable. And I knew how I looked. It had never taken much to get men's attention. Even with the competition here, I was confident I could make my way onto Levin's lap.

"Then let's be quick about it," Devon muttered.

I decided the jacket wasn't going to work, so I slipped my hand inside and grabbed the tracking device, moving it inside my bra. After shrugging off Devon's jacket, I took his empty glass and stood. I tossed my hair to the side, the long strands on full display for Levin to see, then leaned down to make Devon another drink.

My legs were long and the shoes showed them off well. I felt Devon's hands on my hips and ass as I poured the vodka. Turning, I handed him the drink, then smiled as I straddled his lap.

Devon made quick work of that drink and I flipped my hair to the other side so I could see Levin. From the corner of my eye, I could tell he was looking our way. Devon's hands skated up my thighs to rest on my waist, his lips tracing the curves of my cleavage. Sliding my fingers into his hair, I cut a sideways glance to Levin.

He was watching. Avidly. I sent him a coy smile and winked. He crooked his finger, beckoning me.

I felt a rush of adrenaline as I realized the ploy was working perfectly. I said to Devon, "He wants me to come over."

"Then go. I'll put up a bit of a fuss, then come get you. Put both hands in your hair when you're done."

With that last direction, I eased off his lap and strutted toward Levin. The brunette was still trying in vain to win his attention and she shot me a dirty look when I stopped in front of them.

"You can go," I told her, looking down my nose. "I'm here now."

Muttering angrily in another language, she stood and stalked off. I looked at Levin and raised an eyebrow.

"You wanted me?" I asked.

He looked me over from head to toe before giving me a satisfied smile. "Come sit down," he invited. There was a predatory gleam in his eyes that made me want to shudder, but I suppressed it. I was helping Devon. I could do this.

I went to sit sideways on his lap, but he stopped me. "No. Like how you were sitting with him," he said, gesturing toward Devon, who was watching us with an aggravated expression. The brunette had apparently decided to try her luck with him because she'd poured herself a drink and sat next to him, her scarlet-tipped fingers sliding up his thigh.

Jealousy spiked hard in me and I made myself tear my gaze away. It wasn't real, just like what I was doing with Levin wasn't real. I had to remember that.

I straddled Levin as I'd done to Devon, tamping down the squeamishness that surged inside. I didn't let men get this close to me, sexually, and never had. Until Devon. But I had a job to do, and Devon was counting on me.

"You're very beautiful," Levin said, his accent thick. He was a big guy, as big as Devon. He was older than Devon, I'd guess in his mid-fifties, and had a hard edge to him. You wouldn't want to meet Devon in a dark alley, but with this guy, you knew he wouldn't even need a dark alley to crush first and ask questions later. A jagged scar ran down his left cheek.

"Thank you," I said with as real a smile as I could muster. "What's your name?"

"André," he replied. "And yours?"

I decided to stick with the truth as much as possible, an adage my grams had taught me. "Ivy."

"A pleasure to meet you, Ivy," Levin said. His hands were on my waist and large enough to nearly span my body. If I wanted to get away, he'd have no problem subduing me and making me stay. I broke out in a cold sweat.

"Are you in town for business . . . or pleasure?" I asked, forcing my panic into submission. I crossed my arms over my chest and rested my hands on my shoulders, then slowly drew the straps of my bra down my arms. Teasing him, I let my palms drift down my chest to cover my breasts, palming the tracking device in the process.

"Business," Levin replied, his gaze avidly watching my movements. "But I think I can spare a few hours for pleasure." I felt his fingers at my back as he undid the clasp on my bra, the fabric falling from me.

I let the straps drop from my shoulders and slid my hands inside his jacket to circle his chest. Levin dipped his head, his mouth settling over my breast.

The cold sweat was back with a vengeance, as was a whisper of panic, but I didn't let it overtake me. I was almost done. I focused on breathing. I'd found the inside pocket of his jacket and dropped the tracking device inside. Relief flooded me. I'd done it. Now, to just get out of this.

Levin was caught up in things, I could tell, the hard press of his erection difficult to mask when I was sitting in this position. His mouth moved to my other breast as his hands tightened on my hips, pulling me down to grind against him.

Glancing up, I looked for Devon, and when I saw him, all the breath left my body.

He was staring at Levin with murder in his eyes.

Devon's icy blue gaze was unblinking as he watched Levin touch me, the hard set of his jaw clenched in anger. His hands were tightly fisted and it seemed he only held himself back by his own fragile restraint.

Raising my arms, I slid my fingers into my hair, pulling the long strands up. Levin took that as encouragement, his mouth moving up my neck as his hands covered my breasts.

"I'm afraid there's been a mistake." Devon's voice. I let out a slow breath of relief. "The lady is promised to me for the evening."

Levin didn't bother responding, he just snapped his fingers. One of the lackeys nearby jumped to his feet and approached Devon.

He didn't get far. Devon moved faster than I would've thought possible, smashing the heel of his hand against the guy's temple in a vicious jab. The guy dropped like a rock.

That got Levin's attention and he sat back in his chair, his steely gaze now resting on Devon.

"As I said, the lady is mine," Devon repeated.

"Listen, I don't want trouble—" I began, squirming to get off Levin's lap.

"Hush," he said to me, his grip tightening and holding me in place. "Whatever you were told, find two others here and I'll take care of the bill," he offered to Devon, then waved him away. His hands slid up my rib cage, flitting lightly across my breasts before resting on my shoulders.

"I'm afraid no one else will do," Devon said, his lips twisting in the semblance of a smile. In the next instant, he had his gun in his hand, the muzzle pointed directly at Levin's forehead.

I gasped, suddenly terrified. I was sure the men with Levin were armed. Devon was vastly outnumbered. And as I'd feared, the men with Levin all went for their guns.

"Stop!" Levin ordered, his voice commanding. His men immediately obeyed, all of them warily eyeing Devon.

Gesturing to me, Levin said, "No whore is worth this much trouble, my friend. You want her that badly, then take her."

My knees were shaking as Devon pulled me off Levin's lap. He didn't turn his back as we sidled away, and I grabbed the jacket I'd discarded earlier, pulling it on as we walked. When we were at the hallway, Devon holstered his gun and we moved at a faster clip. We didn't speak until we were outside and walking down the street to where our car stood idling, Reggie inside.

"I did it," I said quietly. "You know that, right? The tracker is on him."

Devon still looked pissed and I eyed him. He had a tight grip on my hand. He didn't respond at all to what I'd said.

"Devon?" I asked.

Looking left and right, Devon suddenly stopped and stepped into an empty alley, pulling me in with him.

"What are you—" But I didn't get to finish my sentence before he was kissing me.

His lips were firm against mine, his tongue hot and demanding. I was against the wall, his body pressing hard into me. It didn't occur to me to question or resist. I just kissed him back with equal urgency, reaching up to wind my arms around his neck.

The jacket fell open and Devon's hands were on me, erasing the feel of Levin's touch. Then his mouth was on my breast, his breath warm against my skin, and my pulse was racing. His mouth trailed up my neck to underneath my jaw.

"I *despise* seeing another man touch you," he hissed in my ear.

Ah. Now I understood. Devon's possessive streak was a mile wide, and even though tonight had been planned in advance, it seemed I hadn't been the only one struggling to keep reality and acting separate.

"Tell me you hated every moment," he said.

That wasn't a hardship. "I hated every moment," I repeated, my fingers sliding into his hair as his tongue dipped in my ear.

"Tell me you're mine."

"I'm yours," I breathed as his lips descended onto mine.

I knew we had no time for this, and yet, when would there be time? Devon's life was fraught with danger and I could understand why he'd taken a moment to exorcise the feelings of jealousy and anger that had dogged him inside the club. As for me, I took it all in, memorizing the feel of the brick against my back, the chill in the air, and the warm press of his hands on my flesh.

When we finally parted, his hand cupped my jaw as he gazed into my eyes.

"When this is over," he said, "I want us to go somewhere beautiful, and just . . . be . . . for a while. Will you do that for me?"

My smile was immediate. "I know I should play hard to get," I teased, "but I don't care. Yes, I'd like that very much." Time alone with Devon without the world at our backs and danger breathing down our necks? It sounded like heaven.

Taking my hand, he led me out of the alley and to the car, opening the back door for me to slide inside.

"Where'd you guys go?" Reggie asked. He sounded anxious. "I wasn't sure if I was supposed to wait or if I should hide."

"You did fine," Devon said, taking the driver's spot as Reggie slid over. "Let's finish this. Tonight."

The idea that Devon and I might be going somewhere as soon as tomorrow made me want to clap my hands. We just had to get through tonight.

Devon drove to the outskirts of the city. Reggie confirmed that the tracker was working on Levin, who was still at Club Elegance.

"Just watch this screen," Reggie said, pointing to the laptop he set beside me.

"If he should start heading this way, use the radio," Devon said, handing me a small walkie-talkie. He pointed to his ear. "I'll be listening."

"Okay," I said. I tried one more time. "Are you sure I can't come with you?" I'd asked on the drive and been told no. The look on Devon's face told me he hadn't changed his mind.

Devon laughed lightly at my expression. "Sweet Ivy," he said. "What a pretty pout you have." Leaning down, he brushed his lips against mine. "I'll be back as soon as I can," he whispered.

I wasn't about to let him go with that tiny kiss, so I grabbed his collar and pulled him back down. Heedless of Reggie standing a few feet away, I gave Devon the best kiss I was capable of, and it was several long moments before I let him go. His ice-blue eyes had darkened, and his gaze was hungry.

"I'll keep that in mind," he said.

I watched them walk across the dim parking lot toward a towering metal building. Many floors were lit, but I didn't think people were still working at this hour. The lot was deserted and Devon had parked the car in a shady corner beneath a tree, so even ambient light barely touched my location.

I watched the laptop for a few minutes, then decided to change into the extra clothes that I'd brought—jeans and a long-sleeved button-up shirt. After slipping off my heels, I put on a pair of flats instead. I glanced back at the laptop, noting that Devon and Reggie had been gone for nearly twenty minutes already. It felt like an hour.

The dot that showed Levin's location still glowed on the screen. It hadn't changed spots while I'd been watching, so it took me aback now to see that it had moved.

It was headed right for us.

CHAPTER
THIRTEEN

I grabbed the walkie-talkie and pressed the button. "Is anyone there?"

I released the button, but heard nothing but static. I tried again. "Hello. Can you hear me?"

Again, nothing.

I didn't know what to do. Devon had said to use the walkie-talkie, but hadn't said what to do if he couldn't be reached.

The cell phone he'd given me was in my pocket. Pulling it out, I dialed the programmed number. It went straight to voice mail.

"Damn it!" I stuffed the cell back in my jeans, watching the dot on the screen. It was heading our way very fast. They'd be here in minutes.

I glanced back at the building, then got out of the car. There didn't seem to be any other choice but to go after Devon. Maybe luck would be with me and I'd get inside and find him.

It sounded ridiculous, even to me, but . . . I had to try.

I ran toward the building's entrance, hesitating once I reached the doors. The lobby was fully lit inside, but I saw no one. Cautiously, I opened the door and stepped inside.

It was silent, the buzzing of the fluorescent lights overhead unnaturally loud. Heading for the elevators, I skidded to a halt when I glanced behind the front desk and saw two security guards lying on the floor.

Swallowing heavily, I punched the elevator button and rushed inside when the doors slid open. Then I thought twice and ran to the security guys, grabbing the identity card hooked to the lapel of the shirt on the guy closest to me. Running back to the elevator, I got there right before the doors closed, and squeezed inside.

Now where?

Figuring I'd want to go where only the security tag would take me, I hit the button next to the floor with the access slot. It was in the middle of the building, the tenth floor. I waited anxiously for the elevator, watching the floors go by, then the doors opened on the tenth floor.

A man was standing there.

We both stood, frozen in surprise. I recovered first and did the only thing I could think of. I launched myself at him.

He toppled backward and I fell on top of him. He had a gun attached to his hip and he reached for it as I scrambled to a sitting position on his chest. I grabbed his hair with both hands and slammed his head against the hard, tiled floor as he yanked at his gun. Once. Twice. The third time, his body went lax underneath mine.

I was breathing hard, my heart pounding so fast in my chest, it felt as though it would leap out. The combination of fear, adrenaline, and relief was overwhelming and I just sat there, on top of him, for a moment.

Then I thought, *What if he's dead?* Oh God, I didn't want to kill him. He was just doing his job. I felt underneath his jaw for a pulse, and breathed a sigh of relief when I felt one, strong and steady.

I felt the hands on my arms, lifting me to my feet, at the same time I heard the voice.

"What the bloody hell are you doing in here?"

Devon.

He turned me around and I wasted no time. "Levin's on his way," I said.

Reggie was right behind him, both of them looking at me.

"The radio wasn't working," I explained. "I came to warn you."

"We need more time," Reggie said.

Devon said nothing, just grabbed my arm and dragged me with them. We rushed down the hallway. He had a card identical to mine and used his to unlock the door at the far end. We hurried inside, and I stopped short as Devon let go of me to flip on the lights.

The room made my jaw drop. It looked like a war room, with screens lining an entire wall in front of three tiers of workstations. Reggie had gone to a desk at the back of the top row and had plopped himself in the chair, already typing like a demon on the keyboard there.

The screens in front of me changed and I could see what he was typing. It was all Greek to me, the lines scrolling by so fast it was hard to even tell what they said.

"How much longer?" Devon asked. He'd gone to the windows on the far wall that overlooked the parking lot.

"I'm going as fast as I can," Reggie muttered. His forehead was dotted with sweat.

Several minutes passed in a tense silence, broken only by the sound of Reggie's typing. Then, "They're here," Devon said.

The sound of him racking the slide on his gun made me jump.

"Just because he's here doesn't mean he'll come in *here*," I said hopefully. "Right?"

Devon glanced back at me, but it was Reggie who answered.

"Our tour guide managed to get a message to Levin before we shut him down."

There was a lot in that sentence I wanted to ask questions about, but I kept my silence.

"I just need five more minutes," Reggie said.

"Well you've got three," Devon said. "There's only one way out of this room and we're about to be blocked in."

"The code is in, but it has to upload to the servers before it automatically downloads onto the phones. Until it does that, Levin can still stop it."

I watched the screens. A map of the world was displayed, glowing lights in various cities. Beams of light were arching toward the cities, all from the central location of Amsterdam . . . headquarters sending the software to its remote servers around the world.

"Do you really think they'd just have one exit from this room?" Reggie scoffed. He hit a button and a panel in the far corner of the room slid back to reveal a darkness beyond.

"How long?" Devon asked, eyeing the screens.

"It has to download to every server," Reggie said, "or else they'll be able to designate a non-updated server as the master, and its copy will overwrite everything I've done."

"That doesn't tell me how long," Devon bit out, heading toward the door. He took up a position directly behind it, arm bent and gun pointed at the ceiling.

"I can lock out their cards," Reggie said, hitting more keys, and not a moment too soon.

I saw shadows outside the door and the lock beeped, but it didn't open. They tried it again. Nothing.

A gunshot sounded and I jumped. They were shooting at the lock on the door.

Devon retreated, grabbing my arm and running up the steps to Reggie. "We have to go," he said.

"I can't," Reggie insisted, pointing to the screens. "Four servers still haven't updated."

He was right. The longest arcs from Amsterdam weren't quite at their glowing destinations.

The shatter of glass and another gunshot startled a scream from me, and Devon shoved my head down as we hit the floor. He lifted his arm and fired two shots in return.

Cautiously raising my head, I saw that they'd shot through the glass . . . and hit Reggie.

"Oh my God," I breathed. Reggie had been knocked out of the chair. The bullet had gotten him in the abdomen and blood stained his shirt.

Reggie coughed as Devon scrambled over to him and tore his shirt open. The wound looked painful, and very bloody.

"How bad is it?" Reggie wheezed.

Devon's lips pressed into a grim line and he didn't reply, though it seemed Reggie didn't need an answer.

"That . . . really sucks," he managed.

More gunshots that went wide. Devon returned fire.

"Go," Reggie said, struggling to sit up. "I'll stay, make sure the software downloads."

"They're going to be in here any moment," Devon warned him.

"Then you'd better hurry."

Devon propped Reggie against the back of the desk, then handed him his gun. "Hold them off as long as you can," he said, then he took my hand and began pulling me away.

"We can't just leave him!" I protested, aghast.

"There's nothing we can do," Devon replied, drawing me inexorably toward the hidden doorway. "A belly wound like that is fatal without immediate treatment, which we can't get. He has minutes left."

I couldn't believe it, didn't want to believe it. Reggie was one of the good guys. He wasn't supposed to die because of this.

Reggie looked at me and our eyes locked. Weakly, he raised his hand and beckoned me. I struggled and broke away from Devon to run back to Reggie.

"Take this," he said, his voice barely audible. "You may need it."

I looked down and saw he held the flash drive he'd shown me back in Kansas City. Blood was smeared on the silver surface.

Taking it from him, I said, "But I don't know the password."

"It's . . ."

But I couldn't hear him. I leaned close, putting my ear by his lips as he tried again.

Hands landed heavily on my shoulders and nothing I did prevented Devon from grabbing me up bodily and hauling me with him through the hidden escape. I spared one last look for Reggie, who was watching us, and wanted to sob.

Devon slammed his hand on the interior button and the panel slid closed. Lights illuminated a small staircase made of concrete.

"Let's go," Devon said, propelling me along with his hand wrapped firmly around my arm.

He was moving fast, so fast I had a hard time keeping up. Fear was a bitter tang in my mouth. Reggie's death crystallized the reality that we might not escape from this.

I thought we'd go down, but instead we went up. We hit the top landing and headed for the door. Devon pulled me back behind him, carefully opening the door just a fraction and peering out before exiting the building onto the roof.

Suddenly, Devon tapped at his ear. "Confirm, secondary extraction point," he said.

Confused, I stared at him as we ran across the roof until a shout made me look back.

There was a whole group of men pouring from the staircase after us, weapons drawn.

They started firing immediately. I ducked as I ran and Devon pulled me in front of him. That's when I heard the sound of a helicopter.

Looking up, I saw the black outline of the chopper swirling above. Devon ran toward it as it dipped low.

It didn't even land, just hovered about six feet above the roof. Devon picked me up and hoisted me until I could grab hold of the open door, then he latched on as well. I was pulling myself up to the interior when it happened.

A bullet tore through Devon's back.

One of his hands lost its grip immediately and I grabbed his wrist. The chopper dipped lower and Devon struggled to get in. Blood seeped from the wound in his back, making him falter. Desperate, I grabbed his belt at the back of his pants and pulled. His legs still dangled off the side, but his torso was in and the man behind me finished pulling Devon in the rest of the way.

Devon's face was coated with sweat, a grimace of pain on his features. I didn't know what to do or how to help him.

"Agent down!" the man who'd helped pull us in called into the headset he wore. He flipped Devon over onto his stomach and the wound in his back made me gasp. Blood was everywhere and the man used a knife to cut off Devon's jacket.

The helicopter swooped and turned and I prayed we were heading for a hospital. Devon had passed out by now. I held one of his lax hands in mine, the roar of the motors and rush of air loud in my ears, my eyes on the blood still seeping from Devon's torn flesh.

It seemed an eternity but was in reality barely a couple of minutes before we were landing again. I could have cried in relief to see hospital personnel racing toward the landing pad. They took Devon off the plane, carefully loading him onto a gurney, then raced away.

I went to follow him, but the man in the chopper grabbed my arm, preventing me.

"Let me go," I demanded, pulling against him.

He ignored me, giving a hand signal to the pilot, then we were in the air again.

I watched in dismay as the roof of the hospital receded in the distance. What were these men going to do with me? Where were they taking me?

But it was pointless to ask. They couldn't hear me over the motors and there was nothing I could do about it anyway—save jumping from the chopper, which I didn't want to do.

Ten minutes later, we were landing again, this time at a small airport outside a hangar. The engine was cut and as the noise died down, the man with me motioned for me to get out.

I swung my legs out and climbed down from the chopper. Staying bent from the still slowly rotating blades, I hurried a few steps away. Glancing around, I saw a car waiting, its headlights pointed at me. As I watched, someone got out and began walking my way. It wasn't until they were close that I recognized the figure.

Vega.

"Ivy," she said, coming to a stop a few feet from me. "I must say, I'd much rather you had been shot than Devon."

Yeah, me, too, I thought but didn't say.

"Get in the car."

"What if I don't want to?" I asked.

"You don't have much of a choice, now, do you?" she replied, sounding almost bored.

I got in the car.

She got in the other side, sitting next to me in the backseat. Once she closed her door, the man began driving. I didn't ask where we were going, not that I thought she would have told me.

"How's Devon doing?" I asked. My gut was churning. All I could think about was how much blood there had been, how unresponsive he'd been, and the paleness of his face when they'd put him on the gurney.

"That's none of your business," she replied. "So tell me . . . what went wrong tonight?"

"Nothing went wrong," I said. "The plan worked. They just weren't supposed to show up."

"No, that's not what went wrong tonight," she said. "What went wrong was that you were with him. If Devon had not been trying to get *you* out of there, he wouldn't have been hurt."

I couldn't argue with that.

"So tell me why I shouldn't have you shot right now and dump your body in the canal."

I sucked in a breath at the coldness in her voice. She wasn't joking, and she wasn't bluffing. Even as I thought this, the car had drawn to a halt, the engine idling. Glancing out the window, I saw we were on a deserted bridge. Dark water streamed lazily below us.

When I looked back to Vega, the driver was pointing a gun at my head.

"Wait!" I cried, panic-stricken. "I-I have something."

Vega held up her hand and the driver remained motionless.

I reached in my pocket and pulled out the flash drive that Reggie had given me. "This."

"And what is that?" Vega asked.

"It's the biosecurity software," I said. "Reggie stole all of it and put it on this flash drive."

"And you're giving it to me?" Her tone was skeptical.

"I'm trading it to you," I clarified.

Her lips curved in a smile. "My dear, you aren't in any position to trade. I can just take it from you." Reaching out, she did just that.

"It's encrypted," I said. "The data will destroy itself if you try to crack the password." Vega's gaze met mine and her eyes narrowed. "Reggie wasn't stupid, and neither am I."

A beat. "So it would seem," she said. "All right then, what shall we trade?"

I swallowed. "First, I want to know Devon's status."

Vega reached into her pocket and produced a phone. She pressed a couple of buttons and held it to her ear.

"Yes, what's the status of Agent Clay?"

I tried to read her expression as she listened, but it remained unchanged.

"I see. Thank you." She ended the call and pocketed the phone again. "Devon did not survive."

I stared at her, and it took everything I had not to fall apart. "Are you sure?" I asked. My voice shook.

"Quite."

Vega showed absolutely zero emotion at Devon's death. It was as though she were telling me the weather forecast, which made me suspicious. She'd lied to me before, was she lying to me again?

I slowly shook my head. "No. I don't believe you." Devon couldn't die. He just . . . couldn't.

In an instant, she was in my face. "I don't give a damn what you believe," she hissed. "Because of you, one of my best agents is dead. That alone makes me want to shred you with my bare hands until I see your bones. The only thing preventing me from doing so is this." She held up the flash drive. "Now do tell me, Ivy," her voice dripping with bitter condescension, "what are the rest of your . . . demands?"

I was shaking from shock and fear in the face of her seething anger. I struggled to think, to pull myself together. Devon would have wanted me to get out of this alive, and the only way to do that was to be smarter than Vega.

"I want you to take me back to my hotel and I want my flight booked out of the country," I said. "I want to go home."

"Easy enough to accomplish," she said. "Done. Now what's the password?"

"You'll get the password once I'm in the air."

Vega considered this. "Done."

The driver put away his gun and began driving again.

"If the software on this drive isn't exactly what you say it is, you will pay the price," Vega said. She didn't say it in a threatening way, just matter-of-fact.

"I'll keep that in mind."

She didn't speak again until we were at the hotel. "Flight arrangements will be made. You'll be informed."

I didn't thank her; I just got out of the car. It was taking all I had not to think of Devon. She'd been convincing, but I knew her to be a liar. I'd have to see for myself that Devon was really dead before I believed it.

As I walked into the hotel—nearly deserted at this time of night—I wondered what I would have done if Reggie hadn't given me his "insurance." The only other card I had to play was the vaccine, and of the two evils—stealing people's biosignatures or giving someone the tools to unleash an incurable virus—I thought the former was a better option than the latter.

It wasn't until I was back in the room that I let myself think about Devon.

What if he *was* dead?

I gasped as a shaft of pain went through me, my steps faltering, then halting altogether. I spied the bed where we'd last made love. I hadn't known it would be for the last time.

I dropped to my knees on the floor, a sob building in my chest that I couldn't hold back, despite my desperation to try to keep it together. Not since my mother died had I felt such agony, but back then I'd bottled it up inside along with the guilt I'd felt for the sacrifice she'd made.

Now Devon had made a similar sacrifice. Vega had been right. If I hadn't been there, dragging him back and slowing him down, he'd have escaped. I was sure of it. If he'd climbed into the helicopter first rather than me . . .

I didn't recognize the sounds I was making. Harsh, ugly, pain-wracked sobs that tore from the depths of my being. Tears streaked my face as I bent over until my forehead rested on the carpet. I squeezed my arms tight around my middle, hugging myself as if that alone would stop me from breaking apart.

The sun was rising when I was finally spent. I had nothing left. My emotions felt raw, like naked wires, crackling and exposed. Devon might be gone, but I could make it on my own. I *would* make it on my own. I'd survive this. And I'd find out for sure if he was dead.

I showered and packed, carefully checking my purse to make sure the pages were still there. I didn't resist the impulse to take one of Devon's suits with me, carefully folding the expensive fabric and choosing my favorite of the ties he'd brought.

The hotel phone rang around mid-morning. When I answered, a disembodied voice said, "A car will pick you up at nineteen hundred hours and take you to your flight." Then they hung up.

Okay, then.

I was reasonably sure Vega would try to kill me once I gave her the password. I wasn't sure what I was going to do about that yet. But I had something more important on my mind.

Now that the sun was up, I felt safe enough to go back to the hospital. If Devon was alive, then we'd figure out what to do next.

If he wasn't, then this would be my chance to see him one more time, for closure and to say goodbye. Looking at a map of the city the concierge had helpfully provided, I found the hospital where they'd taken Devon last night. Grabbing my purse, I flagged down a taxi.

My hands were shaky as I paid the fare and walked into the hospital. If Devon was alive, chances were good there would be operatives from the Shadow here. I might be walking right into a trap.

"Excuse me," I said to the harried-looking woman behind the front desk. "Can you help me?" I was really hoping she spoke English.

"Yes, what can I do for you?" she asked, polite but to the point.

"I'm looking for a man who was admitted last night," I said. "He had a gunshot wound and he . . . he didn't make it." At that, her expression softened. "I'd like to see his body. I was a friend of his and I'd really like to say goodbye." My voice cracked on the last part and I flushed as I cleared my throat, blinking back tears.

"Let me see what I can do," she said. "What was his name?"

"Clay. Devon Clay. Though he might have been admitted as a John Doe." That last part had occurred to me once I realized how unlikely it was that Vega would tell them Devon's real name. "A helicopter dropped him off around one in the morning."

She typed on her computer for a moment. I looked around, taking in the usual sights and smells of a hospital. The lobby was nice and it was obvious they'd tried to make it more comfortable, but a hospital was still a hospital.

"I'm sorry, miss . . ." she said.

I glanced back at her. She was frowning as she studied her screen.

". . . there was a John Doe brought in last night, but he didn't die."

Hope flared inside like I'd swallowed a sparkler on the Fourth of July. "Are you sure it's the right man?"

"Gunshot wound to the back," she said. "Is that him?"

"Yes."

"Miss, he didn't die. Surgery removed the bullet and he was stabilized early this morning."

CHAPTER
FOURTEEN

I couldn't help the smile that was so wide it felt as though it was going to crack my face. Vega had lied to me. Big surprise. "So he's stabilized?" I repeated.

She nodded. "Looks like he's going to make a full recovery."

I had to see him. "Can you tell me his room number, please?" I asked.

Glancing back at her screen, she shook her head. "I'm sorry, but he was transferred to private care a short while ago."

My smile faded. "What does that mean?"

"It means he's no longer here."

"Where did he go?" Panic was rising in my chest.

"I'm sorry, but we weren't given that information."

"But . . . but I have to find him," I said, desperate now. "He means everything to me, and if he's still alive . . ."

"I'm very sorry," she said sympathetically. "But I can't help you."

I nodded. "It's okay. I understand," I said. Walking away, I tried to think.

Devon was alive.

But . . . where was he? Where had they taken him?

I stepped outside and warm air hit my face along with a rush of pure rage. She'd known Devon was alive, that he was going to make it, and she'd lied. Then she'd taken him away and hidden him from me.

The need for revenge burned like acid in my gut. I started walking, thinking. An idea, half-formed, occurred to me and I ducked into a store. After buying what I needed, I headed back to the hotel.

Several hours later, night had fallen and I used my cell to dial the number I'd memorized. A man answered.

"I'm the one you're supposed to be transporting," I said, watching the car from where I was sitting in an outdoor café a hundred yards away. I'd tipped the doorman to give a burner phone I'd picked up to whoever showed up for me. "But I'm not coming. Tell Vega the deal has changed. I know Devon's alive, and I'm not giving her the password until I see him. I'll call back in thirty minutes." I hung up.

I took a deep breath, wondering if this was the wisest course of action. Probably not. But I had to see Devon, had to see that he'd made it.

The next thirty minutes passed in slow motion. When I dialed again, Vega answered.

"You lied to me," were the first words I said.

"Exceedingly well, I might add."

My eyes narrowed. "I want to see Devon."

"And I want the password."

"Where is he?" I demanded.

"You're just too precious," she said. "This whole power play you're trying to do. I find it amusing."

I gritted my teeth. Never had I wanted to physically assault someone as much as I wanted to hurt her at this moment.

"This isn't a game," I retorted.

"Oh, but it is," she said. "And one you're really not equipped to play. Frankly, you're not worth my time. So I'm going to make a deal of my own."

"What do you want?"

"Sweetie, I hate to disappoint you, but you're not my partner in this." She paused. "You're my collateral."

Men surrounded me in the blink of an eye, all with very dangerous-looking muzzles pointed in my general direction. Carefully, I raised my hands in the universal signal of surrender.

Someone pushed through the line and André Levin appeared in front of me.

"Well, there you are, just as she said," he said, looking at me. "Bring her." He turned and walked away.

Two men grabbed me up, hauling me between them as they hustled me into the backseat of a running car. Levin got in after them and the car shot down the street.

"Well, well. I certainly hadn't expected to see you again," he said. Reaching out, he trailed the back of his hand down my cheek.

I jerked away. "Keep your hands off me," I snarled.

Levin got right up in my face. He was several inches taller than me, quite a bit wider, and outweighed me twice over. To say he was intimidating was putting it mildly.

"I'd suggest you take a sweeter tone. Your life is now in my hands, courtesy of the woman you've tried to fuck over." His voice was low and menacing and I swallowed hard. This wasn't going to end well for me, I was sure of it.

"I don't know what you're talking about," I said.

"I think you do," Levin said. "And you're going to tell me the password she wants from you."

"Why would I do that?"

He pushed a hand into my hair and grabbed a handful, jerking me toward him. I bit back a cry of pain.

"Because you're the one responsible for hacking my system," he hissed, "and costing me three hundred million dollars."

Vega had told him *I* was the hacker? Then she'd given me to him. Oh God . . .

Levin stared hard into my eyes for a long moment. I swallowed, squeezing my hands into fists so they wouldn't shake. Finally, he smiled and I breathed a sigh of relief as he turned away.

Without warning, he turned back and coldcocked me right in the jaw. Pain exploded in a blinding flash.

⸙

Ice-cold water splashed my face and I jerked awake with a startled gasp. I tried to sit up, but didn't get far.

Both my wrists were tied above my head and I was lying flat on something. My ankles were tied, too, one to each corner. I blinked the water out of my eyes, choking and coughing to get it out of my lungs.

"Now she's awake," I heard someone say.

Focusing my eyes, I saw Levin standing nearby while another man stood over me. He'd been the one with the water and the bucket still dangled from his fingers. Levin spoke.

"What's the password?" he asked.

I didn't answer, still trying to get my breath.

"Was that your boyfriend?" Levin asked me. "Our gallant and chivalrous mutual friend who fought for you at Club Elegance?"

I remained silent.

Levin sighed and glanced at the other man, then gave a curt nod.

I braced myself, but the blow still hurt, the flat of his palm stinging like fire against my cheek. Before I could take a breath, he'd hit me again and this time I tasted blood.

But it wasn't anything I hadn't gone through before, and I didn't make a sound.

"I said, what's the password," Levin repeated. At my continued silence, he said, "That password is worth three hundred million dollars."

He saw the look on my face and laughed. "Indeed. An exchange. I get the password out of you—by any means necessary, I might add—and I get my money back.

"It seems the British don't quite have . . . the stomach for the nasty business of making people talk. Too bad for you that we Russians have no such qualms."

I stared at the ceiling, my thoughts drifting away as I coaxed them down the tunnel inside my head. I didn't want to be around for whatever Levin had in store for me when he realized I wasn't going to talk. That password was my only leverage with Vega. I had no doubt she'd probably tell Devon I was dead, too, whenever he was well enough to ask about me.

The very thought of him made pain knife through me. I hoped he was okay, wherever she'd taken him. I prayed he'd think to try to find me, to not blindly accept what Vega said, as I had.

The last thought was instinctual. I knew I was in dire straits. Who knew how much time I had left before I wouldn't be able to survive Levin's attempt to get the password from me?

The man next to me used a knife and slit my shirt from hem to neckline. The cotton fell aside. I still stared at the ceiling. He began cutting, tracing a line in my stomach, but I didn't flinch.

"This one's accustomed to pain," Levin mused. "Perhaps her boyfriend likes it rough. Either way, this isn't going to work. Go get Izzy."

I heard the words as though from a long ways away. I was floating on a river, the water covering my ears, and staring up at a cloudless sky. I was alone. The blood on my abdomen tickled as it flowed in tiny rivulets, as though unseen fingers brushed my skin. Pain, flowing out of me.

A sharp cry penetrated my haze and I blinked twice, confused.

The man was no longer standing over me and I turned my head to see what was going on.

There was a little girl in the room, maybe seven or eight years old. She was tiny, with scrawny arms and legs and long, tangled brown hair. The man who'd been hitting me had her by the hair, his hand shoved up underneath the tattered dress she wore. Her eyes were wide and filled with terror. He jerked her hair and she screamed again, her eyes filling with tears.

"Stop that!" I pulled hard on my arms, but the bonds around my wrists held firm. "Leave her alone, asshole!"

"This is Izzy," Levin said, stepping forward from where he'd been silently observing me. "She's quite pretty, isn't she? You wouldn't believe how much she'd fetch on the open market. But there are always more where she came from."

The man produced a knife and held it so I could see.

"Shall she die today?" Levin asked me. "You can save her. Just tell me what I want to know."

The girl's panicked eyes swiveled between me and the blade. I couldn't tell if she understood English or not, but she knew well enough what the knife meant. She tried to squirm away, but the man switched his grip from her hair to her jaw, squeezing so tightly that she whimpered in pain.

"I'll give you the password," I said. "Now stop!" I had no choice. The girl . . . I couldn't let them hurt her.

"Excellent!" Levin cried, smiling. His teeth were very white. "We just needed the right persuasion, it seems."

I glared at him.

"What's her name? The woman who wants this password so badly?" he asked.

"Vega."

"Now, tell me *his* name. The boyfriend who helped you break my system."

His name. Even I knew that Devon's name was something that shouldn't be told under any circumstances. I hesitated.

"Ever seen a child sexually assaulted, Ivy?" Levin asked. "It's not pleasant, I can assure you." At my silence, he turned to the man with Izzy—

"Clay," I blurted. "Devon Clay." Tears burned my eyes but I blinked them back. "I'll tell you what you want, but you have to untie me and give me the girl." My eyes burned with hatred as I stared at him. A man who'd use a child in this way deserved the same fate as Jace.

Levin considered for a moment, then motioned to the man with Izzy. He stood, shoving her aside, and walked to the cot where I lay. Taking the knife, he cut the ropes holding my wrists, then cut the ones around my ankles.

In a flash, I was up and hurrying to the girl. She seemed to know I wanted to protect her, or maybe it was just the instinct of women trying to protect themselves from men, but either way she flung herself into my arms. I crouched down onto the floor, holding her close and shielding her with my body.

"Such a maternal instinct," Levin jeered. "I do hope you and Devon plan on having children someday. Now tell me: Who does Devon work for?"

"He works for Vega. They're called the Shadow," I said. "Devon is an agent."

Understanding dawned. "Ah. I see. And here I'd always thought those rumors were mere speculation and overwrought imaginations at work.

"Now the password, if you please."

"The edge of hell. No spaces."

I clutched Izzy to me, waiting for more, but Levin merely snapped his fingers and the other guy opened the door to the little room we were in. In a moment, they were gone. I breathed a sigh of relief.

Izzy didn't let go, so I kept holding her, my heart sick at the thought of what they'd done to her or would do. I didn't hold out a lot of hope that I'd be able to escape or that rescue was coming. The only one to rescue me was Devon, who may not be in any kind of condition to search for me. And while maybe I'd have a chance of escaping on my own, there was no way I'd leave the girl behind.

"Izzy," I said. "Is that your name?"

She shook her head, buried against my neck.

"What is it?" I asked.

"Ezabell."

"Hi, Ezabell," I said. "I'm Ivy. How old are you?"

"Eight."

She spoke English and had an accent. British or Irish or something like that. It was hard to tell, the way she was mumbling against my neck.

"How did you get here, Ezabell?"

"A man took me from the playground," she said. Her hands were fisted in my shirt. She began to cry. "I want my mom."

"Shh, sweetheart, I know you do," I tried to soothe her. It was one thing for me to get taken and locked up like this, and quite another to see them do it to an innocent little girl. I'd known the danger that surrounded Devon, though I hadn't counted on this happening. Ezabell was just an innocent bystander.

I studied the room we were in. There was a window above us, kind of on the smallish side, but I could see lights from the city outside. The only furniture was the cot I'd been tied to. The room itself was tiny, not even ten feet wide.

"Come with me," I said to Ezabell, disengaging her arms from around my waist and taking her by the hand. I tried the door, which of course was locked. Then I inspected the cot. If I set aside the paper-thin mattress on top, it was just a tough net strung up over metal bars.

I crouched down again, taking a closer look. I pried at the netting, which was knotted with a thin plastic-coated rope, and tied to the frame. But the knots could be pried off the netting, if your fingers were small and nimble enough.

Sitting back on on the floor, I began to work. If I could get the netting off the top bar, maybe I could take some of the bed apart, at least enough to give me a weapon I could swing at someone. The standoff I had with Levin wouldn't last long, I was sure of it.

I folded the mattress over on itself and patted it. "Come lie down," I encouraged Ezabell, but she just looked at me. Her eyes were haunted and looked too old for her. The same eyes I'd seen in the mirror a thousand times.

"I swear, no one is going to take you from me," I promised her. *At least, not while I am alive.* I'd die before I let anyone lay another hand on her.

Cautiously, she eased down onto the mattress, scooting it on the linoleum floor until it was closer to me. I smiled at her and went back to work.

I didn't have a watch, but saw the sky begin to lighten outside the window. Ezabell eventually fell asleep, curled in a little ball on the mattress. The knots were making my fingers bleed, but I was almost there. Three more and I'd be able to slip the metal frame off.

Then I heard steps outside the door.

"Wake up, Ezabell!" I hissed urgently. I grabbed her and scooted her off the mattress, throwing it over the top of the cot and pulling her into my arms as the door opened.

Ezabell was silent. I was sure she was confused since I'd jerked her awake from a dead sleep, but her gaze was on the man standing in the doorway. She shrank farther into my arms.

"What do you want?" I asked the man. It was a different guy than had been in here earlier.

"Boss is making me bring you both food," he said, "though I was against it." He smiled and it had a cruel edge to it. "I've found people tend to be more . . . agreeable when they're hungry."

I didn't reply and he tossed a plastic bag at me. I caught it, but kept my eye on him. I didn't like the way he was looking at Ezabell and my muscles tightened, ready to fight him if he came for her. But he left, the door closing and locking securely behind him.

From the bag, I pulled out a couple of shrink-wrapped sandwiches and gave one to Ezabell. She ate while I kept working on the cot. Finally, the last knot slipped free and I was able to get at the frame.

It was locked together, but if I used my feet against one side and pulled on the other, I had enough strength and leverage to pull the metal apart. It fell to the floor with a clatter. Afraid the noise would attract attention, I snatched up one of the rods and hurried to stand behind the door.

About three feet long, the rod was hollow, but sturdy, and I held it like I would a baseball bat. I waited a few minutes, but no one came. Lowering the rod, I breathed a sigh of relief.

Ezabell was watching me, her half-eaten sandwich held in her hand. Her eyes were wide and her face pale.

"Don't," she whispered. "They'll get mad."

I crouched down next to her. "That's probably true," I said. "But I have to try. If we want to get out of here, I'm going to need you to do what I tell you to. Can you do that?"

She nodded.

"Even if you're afraid, or I tell you to run, I need you to do it, okay?"

She nodded again.

"Okay then."

She looked scared, so I leaned forward and gave her a tight hug. "It's going to be okay," I said. "I'll get you back to your mother."

I stood behind the door and waited. The rod was tight in my grip as I tried to picture how it would happen. I only had one real chance to disable whoever came in. I hoped it was the same guy who'd delivered the food. He'd had a gun in the waistband of his jeans and that would go a long way to getting us out of here.

Each minute that passed felt like an eternity, my ears straining for the slightest sound from the hallway outside. It was full daylight out by the time I finally heard the scuff of a shoe.

I took a deep breath, casting a quick glance to Ezabell. I knew she understood. It was life and death for us. Children who went through things like this, they knew perhaps better than adults the stark reality of do or die.

The knob twisted and the door swung open. I was in luck. It was the same guy and he was looking at Ezabell, who'd begun to cry.

"I feel sick," she said, and I wanted to high-five her for her quick thinking. She'd immediately distracted him.

He took two steps toward her, by then realizing he didn't see me. He started to turn, but was too late. I was already swinging with every ounce of strength and desperation in me.

The rod hit him on the side of the head, right at the temple. His head snapped violently to the side. Then to my utter shock and relief, he crumpled to the ground and didn't move.

Both Ezabell and I stared for a moment, unable to believe our good fortune, then I sprang into action. I tossed the rod aside and grabbed the gun from his waistband. It was a large .38 and my fingers weren't strong enough to check the cartridge for how many rounds it had, so I just hoped it was loaded.

"Let's go," I said, grabbing her hand. We ran from the room, though I was careful to pull the door closed behind us. No sense making it easier for them to see we'd escaped.

I spent a precious few seconds orienting myself. We were in a long but narrow building. A quick glance out the window showed we were a few stories up, maybe three. Too high to jump onto the concrete below. We'd have to find stairs.

The hallway was dim despite the sunshine outside, and full of closed doors. I didn't want to open doorways if I didn't have to, so we ran down the hallway and again, were in luck. There were stairs in the very back. Narrow and wooden, they creaked as we walked down them and I cringed.

Ezabell's hand was small in my sweaty palm, our grip on each other tight to the point of pain. I could hear her breathing, sharp little gasps that spoke of her terror.

But it was too much to ask for our luck to hold. When we reached the bottom floor, the only exit was back into a hallway and not outside, as I'd hoped. And I could hear voices.

"Ezabell," I said. "Listen carefully. I'm going to try and clear a path, and I want you to head straight for the front door, okay? You run right outside and you find a woman, any woman, and tell her you're lost and need your mom." I knew that, statistically, a woman was more likely to help a child than a man. "Understand?"

"What about you?"

"Don't you worry about me," I said. "Remember our deal. You do as I say, okay? If I get out of this, I'll be at my hotel." Praying that was true, I gave her the address and room number, making her repeat them both until I was sure she had it. "Don't hesitate when the time comes, okay?"

She nodded, albeit reluctantly.

"Good." I took another breath and let go of her hand. "On the count of three. Ready? One . . . two . . . three."

I didn't throw open the door, but instead opened it normally, hoping to escape notice for as long as possible. We got ten feet before someone spotted us.

A man glanced up, saw us, and his eyes bugged out. He began yelling until I pointed the gun at him and pulled the trigger. Then he went down into the table behind him, both crashing to the ground.

"Run!" I yelled, and Ezabell took off. The front door was a shining white beacon at the end of the hallway.

Someone flung open a door and I aimed quickly, firing off another round, but it embedded itself in the wood.

I ran, too. Maybe I could make it out. Miracles did happen. Arms reached out and grabbed me. Blindly, I stuck the muzzle of my gun underneath my arm and pulled the trigger. The arms fell away.

Ezabell was nearly at the door when something hard hit me upside the head, knocking me into the wall. I lost my balance, and my grip on the gun, which went clattering to the floor. I dropped, scrabbling for it. My hand curved around the grip and I sat up, only to see everyone and everything had gone still.

Ezabell flung open the door and I felt a surge of triumph. But just as she stepped through, a man blocked her path. I gasped in dismay.

"Looks like your escape plan has gone awry."

Jerking around, I saw Levin standing in front of an archway that led to what looked to be the kitchen. He was furious, his eyes narrowed and his cheeks ruddy with rage. Five men stood in various positions in the hall, all of them with weapons pointed at me.

"You've killed two of my men," he said, pointing to the bodies on the floor. "The girl will pay for that." He snapped his fingers and the man at the door grabbed up Ezabell, who screamed.

I didn't hesitate, but lifted the gun I still held. The men watched, but I didn't point it at Levin or any of them.

I held the muzzle to my own temple.

CHAPTER FIFTEEN

Let the girl go," I said. "Or I'll pull the trigger."

Levin looked at me. "Why do you think I would care if you did that?"

"I'm not dumb," I said. "I know the real reason you're keeping me alive. You want me to give you what I gave to Vega. Software that'll turn all those cell phones into biodata-harvesting devices." I could tell by the surprised, then blank expression on Levin's face that I was right. He thought I was some genius hacker. No need to disillusion him just yet. Not if it could save my life.

"What do you want?" Levin asked.

"I want you to let the girl go," I said. "Or so help me, I'll blow my head off right now and you'll be left with nothing." I wasn't bluffing. It would be easier than Levin could possibly imagine to pull the trigger and end everything.

"You'll cooperate if I let her leave?" he asked.

I nodded. "I'll do whatever you say." It was a small price to pay. Ezabell was an innocent victim. She deserved her freedom.

A moment passed, tense and pregnant with anticipation as everyone waited to see what Levin would do. I watched him for the slightest sign that he'd try to double-cross me. If he so much as winked at one of the men, I'd pull the trigger. Part of me almost wanted him to.

"Agreed," he said at last. He looked to the door. "Put the girl down," he ordered. "Let her go."

I watched as Ezabell was set on her feet. Uncertain, she looked at me.

"Go," I said. "Run." I prayed she'd do as I'd told her, and in the next instant, she did. Springing for the open doorway, she was through it and gone. No one tried to follow her.

I breathed a sigh of relief as two men approached me. I made no move to fight them as they took away my gun and pulled me to my feet.

"I expect your full cooperation for that," Levin said. He was close enough for me to smell the scent of his cologne, overly sweet and heavy.

"I gave you my word," I replied. I was glad my hunch had been right, though a part of me longed to have escaped. I didn't know what Levin had in store for me, but I could well imagine it.

"Get her cleaned up," Levin said. "Make sure she doesn't escape again. We have business to attend to."

The two men shoved me down the hallway into another room that was much better than the first I'd been in. A huge bedroom complete with a bathroom that had every luxury you could imagine.

"Clothes are in the closet," one of the men said. The two exchanged glances, then one of them left. I looked at the remaining guard.

"Aren't you going to leave, too?"

He shook his head. "Eyes on you at all times," he said.

Nice. I knew what that meant. No privacy, period.

I tried to close the door when I went into the bathroom, but he stopped me. "Door stays open," he said.

He was a rough-looking guy with dark hair and eyes. Only a few inches taller than me, he still outweighed me by at least a hundred pounds. There would be no getting away from him, especially when his gaze followed my every movement.

I really had to use the bathroom, but didn't want him watching. I brushed my teeth instead, hoping he'd sit down or glance away or something. He didn't.

Bodily functions could only be denied for so long before there really wasn't a choice any more. My cheeks burning with embarrassment, I had to pee with him watching me. It was worse than I thought it'd be, more humiliating than some of what Jace had done to me.

The man's attention didn't waver as I washed my hands and face. My shirt had been shredded earlier and I kept it pulled closed, but hurried to rummage through the closet for something else to wear. There were no bandages for the cuts on my stomach, but they'd stopped bleeding. After I'd cleaned them, I found a pair of jeans that fit me, and a long-sleeved shirt. I tried to block out the weight of the guard's gaze on me, but it was hard.

Finally, I was as cleaned up as I was going to get while having someone watch me.

"What now?" I asked, careful to stay beyond the guard's reach.

"Now we wait."

Turning away, I paced the room, keeping the guard in my sight at all times. I didn't want him sneaking up on me. His khaki cargo pants didn't hide the erection he'd gotten while watching me dress and I was leery of what he might do. I was hungry, but my stomach was twisted into knots. Had Ezabell escaped all right? Maybe she'd gone for help? But the minutes crawled by with no change.

A knock on the door startled me and I stopped mid-step. The

knock was merely perfunctory, it seemed, because the door swung inward to reveal Levin.

"Time to pay the piper, my dear." He motioned to the guard, who got behind me and gave me a slight shove forward. I followed Levin back down the hallway to another room—a study or den maybe. The room contained a desk that held a computer, and various chairs scattered around; books with titles I couldn't read lined the walls.

A large television screen attached to the wall was tuned to CNN. A reporter was talking but the sound was muted, not that it mattered because everyone could see the headline blaring out the news:

Millions of Cell Phones Rendered Useless With Latest Software Update

My lips curved in the faintest of smiles. Reggie had done it. All the susceptible cell phones were "bricked," as he'd called it.

Levin watched the screen for a moment, and I could practically feel the anger radiating from him.

"Impressive work," he said to me. "It seems my investment has had a significant decrease in value over the past twenty-four hours."

I didn't reply.

"But you already knew that," he said. "Let's call our mutual friend, shall we?" He hit a button on his phone, the speaker came on, and he dialed.

I held my breath, waiting and praying that Devon would pick up. It rang twice. Then three times. On the fourth ring, someone answered.

"Yes." It was Vega.

"Vega, I presume," Levin said.

"I see she gave you my name," she said, sounding unperturbed. "What a surprise."

"So lucky for us that you don't like to get your hands dirty," Levin said, sinking into a leather chair and crossing his legs. "She was quite easy to break, once we found the right method."

"Excellent. Then you have a password for me?" Vega's voice was cold and clear.

"You owe me three hundred million dollars first," Levin said. "Or should I say, the Shadow does."

"We already discussed this," Vega said. "Password first, then you get your money. It's hardly my fault you didn't do your research properly on the viability of that software before buying."

"And the Shadow should learn to mind its own fucking business," Levin spat. "Now you're going to transfer that money for me or I don't give you squat. No password and I keep the girl."

"You can have her," Vega said. "I'll transfer half the money now, half the money after we've ensured she's given you the correct password."

"If she hasn't, then pretty little Ivy will pay a dear price."

"That's not my concern. Now what's the password."

"I'm awaiting confirmation of the transfer first."

A tense silence followed as Levin watched his computer screen. Finally, Vega said, "You should have it now."

"Confirmed," Levin replied. "The password is 'the edge of hell.'" He glanced at me. "No spaces."

"Excellent. Stand by."

We waited. I looked around as inconspicuously as I could. The nearest door was several feet away with two men between me and freedom. No way could I make it.

"Well, Levin, it looks like your methods need some improvement." Vega's voice was biting.

"What do you mean?" Levin asked.

"She tricked you. That password unlocked the drive, which has now unleashed a virus into our system."

Levin looked surprised, then recovered. "I think you're bluffing," he said. "I think you don't want to pay me the rest of my money." He signaled and the guard nearest me grabbed me by the elbow and dragged me over to where Levin stood. "Send me my money or I'll slit the girl's throat."

"You can slit her from neck to navel for all I care," Vega sneered. "Did you really think I'd give you something as valuable as the man who hacked your system? You're an idiot as well as a fool. She's just a piece of ass that somehow got taken along for the ride."

Levin's gaze swiveled to me and it didn't take a genius to see the fury in his eyes.

"Give her my best, won't you?" Vega added sweetly, then the line disconnected.

Levin had a knife in his hand and at my throat before I'd taken another breath.

"You lied to me, made a fool of me," he hissed. "You think you're smarter than me?"

The knife moved and I couldn't stop a whimper. I didn't dare so much as twitch a muscle, for fear the knife would slice me. The cold blade touched underneath my jaw, then brushed the lobe of my ear. Tears wet my lashes, but didn't fall.

"I'm just trying to survive," I rasped, doing my best not to move as I spoke. "You'd have done the same."

He looked at me, his face inches from mine. I held my breath, waiting. The knife was cold and sharp.

Levin stepped back and the tension broke. He handed the knife back to the guard and I finally took a deep breath. My knees were weak and I felt as though I was going to be sick.

"Your luck has held for a bit longer," he said to me. "Take her away until I decide what to do with her." He nodded to the guard, who dragged me away before I could say anything.

This time, he didn't take me to the nice bedroom, but to another cell-like room even more sparse than the one before. It didn't even have a bed. The guard gave me a hard push just to watch me stumble and fall, then he laughed. The door shut with the hard clang of metal on metal.

I sat on the floor for a long time, thinking. I was really hungry, my stomach cramping in pain, but I tried not to dwell on it. I was thirsty, too, but again was helpless to do anything about it. I'd already escaped once, or had nearly done so, and it seemed they were taking no chances this time. No windows, no cot, nothing I could even begin to think of using as a weapon.

I was glad what Reggie had whispered to me in his final moments had worked. He'd told me two passwords. One for if the drive fell into the wrong hands, and one if it didn't. I'd given the former to Levin, who'd in turn given it to Vega.

My stomach burned and my jaw ached. I lifted my shirt to look at the cuts on my skin. Angry red lines marred my abdomen. My face was bruised from where I'd been hit last night, and I was so tired, I felt I could curl up on the concrete floor and sleep. But I was too afraid of what might happen if I didn't remain on my guard, so I propped myself against the wall and waited.

Time crawled by, but I was grateful for each minute that someone didn't enter the room. I didn't want to think of what was going to happen to me now. I'd need to go along with whatever Levin did and hope for an opportunity to escape at some point . . . I just didn't know how long off that was.

When the door did finally open, it was to have someone toss me clothes.

"Put that on," the man said, then he set a shoebox on the floor. "These, too. You've got ten minutes."

"Or else what?" I called out as he was leaving.

"Or else you're no longer useful," he said. "And useless baggage is left outside with the garbage." The door clicked shut behind him.

Okay then.

I untangled the clothes, already knowing I wouldn't like what I was supposed to wear, and I was right. After stripping off my jeans and shirt, I hurried to pull on the skintight dress nearly the same shade as my hair, a light champagne. Straps went over my shoulders but it was sleeveless, the deep V in the front baring me nearly to my navel. It was made for a woman as thin as me, so it fit. The hem brushed mid-thigh, but a slit in the side went almost to my waist. The back was also nearly bare, the fabric dipping below my hips.

It wasn't Versace, that's for sure, and the shoes weren't Jimmy Choo. Strappy sandals with gold and rhinestones, they winked and twinkled merrily when I walked. I was immediately freezing cold, and aware I had no makeup on and my hair wasn't done up for wherever we were going.

No sooner had I tried a few steps in the heels, getting accustomed to their fit and height, than the door opened and Levin appeared. He smiled when he saw me, his gaze traveling from my face down to my feet and back up.

"I knew you'd look perfect in that," he said.

"Perfect for what?" I shot back. But he only smiled.

"Time to be useful in what I imagine is the only way you know how," he said.

The guard again herded me out, his meaty hand around my upper arm, and we were led outside. Night was falling as I was prodded into the back of a dark sedan. I could've made a break for it, but I wouldn't have gotten two steps in the shoes without being caught.

Levin was next to me, but didn't speak or look my way during the short ride that was a distance we could have easily walked. Not that I was complaining.

I shivered when we stepped out again, the cool evening air making goose bumps erupt on my skin. I had hopes that we were going someplace public. If so, I thought there was a decent chance I might get away, if I kept my wits about me and stayed sharp.

Two guards and I followed Levin down a long, narrow hallway, which opened to a large room. There was loud music playing, but the lyrics weren't in English, so I didn't know what they were about. Red lights were everywhere, throwing people and objects into weird shades of black and crimson. People crowded around a stage where a woman was dancing. She was really good. She was also really naked.

Averting my eyes, I tripped as I tried to follow Levin and knocked into someone.

"Sorry," I mumbled to the man who'd turned.

"Get moving," the guard behind me said, giving me a rough push.

"I'm going," I snapped, snatching my arm out of his grasp.

"Here we are," Levin said, stopping next to a couch that was roped off. A guard quickly moved the rope aside so Levin could sit down. Then he looked at me and patted his lap.

"What?" I asked, as if I couldn't read that signal loud and clear.

In answer, a guard shoved and I half stumbled, half fell into Levin's lap. I could tell right away that Levin was appreciative of my position and all the skin the dress revealed.

"I may have a use for you for a while," he said. "Before I slice you into tiny pieces." His fingers trailed from my collarbone, down between my breasts, and all the way to my navel. I shuddered, but didn't dare try to shove him away. The memory of the knife against my throat was too fresh, but that didn't stop me from mouthing off.

"I don't think I'm your type," I sneered. "To begin with, I'm conscious."

Levin backhanded me hard enough that I saw stars. I fell off his lap onto the floor and he shoved me with his foot.

"Make her work a window for a while," I heard him say. "That should teach her some respect."

I was yanked to my feet and borne away from Levin, which was good. Security was tightest around him. Anywhere else I went had to be better. Except I hadn't counted on where I was taken next.

It was an even darker room, the music throbbing through the walls like a living thing. I could see shabby curtains hiding little rooms. A woman and man stepped out of one and I saw him give her a kiss and hand her money before he left, then she disappeared behind the curtain again. A big guy was watching the curtains carefully, and I had the feeling he was keeping track of who was where and with whom.

"Lucas," the man with me said, and the guy turned around. "I've got a temp fill-in for you for the night. Needs to work off some debt. Got anything?"

Lucas nodded, giving me a careful once-over. "Last room on the right is vacant tonight. She can have that one for thirty percent."

"You're charging me thirty? You know we always do fifteen."

Lucas shrugged. "Last minute and she looks like a rookie. I don't need no drama bullshit. So I'll take thirty or you can find someplace else for her to work it off."

"Fine. Just make sure she gets at least six in. She'll do two at once, I know you got customers looking for that." The guard smiled at me—a sadistic smile that made my blood freeze.

"All right, let's go," Lucas said, taking my arm from the guard's hold and guiding me to the last room.

"There's been a mistake," I said. "I'm not a prostitute. They're holding me against my will. Please let me go." I pleaded with him, but Lucas seemed to have turned deaf. "Listen to me!" I cried, trying to get loose. "Let me go—"

Lucas had me by the throat and shoved me against the wall before I could finish my sentence.

"Listen, bitch," he growled. "I don't give a shit what sob story you have. I hear a hundred of 'em a week. You're here to earn me thirty percent, and that's what you're gonna do. It ain't hard. Dance in the window, invite them in. Fifty bucks for fifteen minutes, add twenty-five if they have a friend who wants to watch. A hundred for anything kinky, and twenty for a blow job only, got it? Cash up front. Even a stupid bitch like you should be able to figure that out, right?"

I couldn't breathe, his hand crushing my windpipe, and I nodded frantically. He let go. I gasped for air, coughing.

"That's better," he said. "I'd change clothes if I was you. Ain't nobody going to come in here with you wearing all that." Reaching out, he pulled at my dress and the fabric tore. I yelped and grabbed at the scraps, but it was too late.

"Maxine usually keeps some stuff in her room," he said, pushing me past the curtain. "Use that. You got tonight—I'd make the most of it if I were you. Or I'll take that thirty percent out of your sweet ass." The curtain dropped and he was gone.

I stood there, staring at the black curtain, dumbstruck as to what I was supposed to do. I clutched my torn dress to me and tried to make my brain function, to come up with some kind of plan.

Just then, a door in the paper-thin walls separating the rooms opened and a girl poked her head in.

"I thought I heard Lucas bring someone in," she said, her accent thick. Eastern European, I thought, but couldn't tell if it was Ukrainian, Russian, or any one of a dozen other languages I was only vaguely familiar with. "You are new?"

I nodded. "I'm supposed to work." I shrugged, utterly at loose ends. My mind wouldn't accept the position I now found myself in, so I just stood there.

The girl opened the door wider and came inside. She was wearing a G-string and knee-high leather boots. Long satin gloves adorned her arms, and that was all she had on.

"I am Angelina," she said.

"Ivy," I replied.

"This is your first time?" she asked. I nodded. "You must dress," she said, moving to a small vanity behind me and pulling open the top drawer. "If you do not pull in a customer, Lucas will beat you." She said it matter-of-factly as she returned with scraps of fabric. "Try this."

I let her help me out of the dress, a kind of numbness settling over me. This couldn't be happening. Not really. A prostitute was helping me put on underwear so I could pay off a non-existent debt by having sex for money. It was something out of a nightmare, not my reality.

When she was finished, she gave me a look up and down. "There," she said. "That is better."

I looked down at myself. I wore a filmy tank that was see-through, but it was dark enough to conceal the cuts on my skin. I had on the strappy heels instead of boots like her. I automatically raised my arms to cover my breasts, but she grimaced and pulled my arms down again.

"Modesty will win you no customers, Ivy," she said. "And Lucas enjoys his punishments. Do not give him a reason." She fluffed my hair to help cover the bruises on my face.

"But I'm not supposed to be here," I said.

Angelina just shook her head sadly. "None of us are."

Taking my hand she led me to the front of the room where another curtain hung. Pulling it aside a little, she motioned to the platform in front of the window. Red light filled the small space and I could hear the music from the club.

"What do I do?"

"You dance," she said. "The men will come inside if they want time with you. Open your mouth."

Obediently, I opened my mouth and she slipped some kind of pill onto my tongue. "This will make it easier," she said.

I swallowed the tiny pill even as fear made my limbs tremble. I wanted to run screaming from the room and only Angelina's tight grip on my arm kept me in place.

"Look at me, Ivy," she said, so I did.

She was pretty and young, very young, with too much makeup for her age. Petite with long brown hair and dark eyes, she had a lush figure that made me feel like a scrawny giraffe. A beat-up scrawny giraffe.

"It will be okay," she said. "Just give the drug a few minutes to work, and it will be easier for you."

I don't know how much time passed with me staring into her eyes, but gradually I began to relax. My thoughts grew lethargic, then melted away altogether, and there was only sensation. The too-warm heat of the room combined with the chill emanating from the window. Rancid odors of stale alcohol, sweat, and sex, overlaid with the sickly sweet smell of marijuana. The music pulsed in time with my heartbeat, pounding in my ears.

"There," Angelina said, giving my hand a squeeze. "Better for you." Stretching up, she kissed me on one cheek, then the other. "*Na vse dobre*, Ivy. Dance."

Before I could process her words or ask what she'd said, she was gone.

I stood, staring out the window. The platform looked inviting now, not nearly as terrifying as it had a few minutes ago, though it seemed to be moving. Knowing it wasn't, I climbed up onto it, the heels I wore making it awkward and more difficult, but I succeeded.

Faces loomed out of the darkness at me, their visages lit in the reflected red glow from the windows. Some were smiling. Some were not. All were watching me.

The music was loud like a living thing, twisting inside my head, demanding that I move. The eyes watching through the window were calculating and harsh. I closed my eyes to block them out.

It felt as though the platform was slowly turning, the music pushing my blood through my veins. *Dance*, Angelina had said. I started to move. Lifting my arms, I buried my fingers in my hair, combing the long strands as I bent and swayed. My skin was hypersensitive and I dragged my palms down my sides to my hips. That felt good, so I retraced the path up my abdomen to my breasts, then to my neck and throat, tipping my head back so the long strands of my hair brushed my lower back.

A persistent knock on the window made my eyes flutter open. I stared in confusion at the man gesturing to me. He was smiling and when he caught my eye, I saw him step away through a doorway.

I closed my eyes again. The music had changed, the pulsing more rhythmic, but I'd only just started moving again when I felt a rush of warm air.

"C'mon, doll. You have a customer."

The voice was male as was the hand that took mine. He wanted me to get out of the window, but I liked the music and tugged against him.

"What'll it be?" he asked. "Fifty? Nah, probably a hundred for you, right? Pricey, but totally worth it." He pulled harder and I had to step down or I'd fall. As it was, I lost my balance when the floor tilted and I fell against him. He didn't seem to mind, though, his arms catching me.

"Wow," he said, sounding awestruck. "You are really beautiful."

The room was spinning and it was hard to concentrate on what he was saying.

"Can you understand me?" he asked. "You know English, right?"

It was too much effort to speak—my tongue felt like lead—so I just nodded.

His hands drifted from my waist to my ass, skin against skin. Leaning down, his mouth skated down my neck.

"I'm guessing money first, right, sweetheart?"

Taking my hand, he pressed a folded bill into it. I didn't know what to do with it, so I just held it. From the way he was looking at me, it seemed like I should do something, but I had no clue what.

"I'm Rick. What's your name?" he asked.

His fingers threaded through my hair, which felt nice, and I closed my eyes. The room was tilting and spinning even harder now and I immediately forgot what question he'd asked me.

"I guess names aren't necessary," he muttered, then I felt his mouth on my breast. The G-string scraped the sides of my thighs as he pushed it down my legs to my ankles. "Keep the shoes on," he said. "Those are fuckin' hot."

I heard the sound of a zipper, then felt a prodding between my thighs. I frowned, mumbled something, and tried to step back. But his arm held me tight.

"Don't try to tell me I didn't pay enough," he said. "Because I know that's bullshit."

Forcing my eyes open, I saw someone looming behind the man who called himself Rick. Blue eyes glittered in the darkness. Then Rick was gone, crumpled at my feet.

I stared down at his body, shock echoing through me. Black liquid pooled underneath him, lapping at the toes of my shoes.

Rick was dead.

CHAPTER SIXTEEN

My mind was telling me things my body couldn't comprehend or react to. Such as who the man staring at me was. His face was a cold mask and his eyes burned with fury, menace rolling off him like oil from water. Danger whispered in my ear, but I wasn't afraid. A name slipped inside my head.

"Devon?"

He didn't answer. Glancing away from me, he tore a sheet from the makeshift bed and wrapped it around me. A moment later, he'd lifted me in his arms. My head lolled against his shoulder and I relaxed, watching in detachment as he stepped outside the room.

Lucas was lying on the floor, and he didn't move as we walked by. Instead of going out the back of the club, we went out the front to the street.

Catcalls and shouts followed us, but he didn't slow down. A car screeched to a stop and I was bundled inside the back. Devon climbed in behind me.

"Go," he ordered, and the car sped off.

I was pulled back onto his lap, my body lethargic and boneless. Lights went by the tinted window at a dizzying speed.

"Is she okay?" This came from the front seat and whoever was driving.

"Just drive," Devon said curtly.

Devon's hand cupped my cheek, turning my face toward him. "Ivy darling, talk to me. Are you hurt?"

My eyes drifted shut.

"Ivy, please . . ."

The note of desperation in his words made me go to the effort of opening and focusing my gaze on Devon.

The long lashes framing his ice-blue eyes were wet. I lifted my hand, which felt as though it were weighted down with stones, and touched his cheek. My fingers came away damp.

"I'm okay," I managed to say.

He turned his face into my hand and pressed his lips to the center of my palm.

Then I couldn't fight it any longer. The lethargy overcame me and I knew nothing.

A burning sensation on my stomach woke me and I tried to push it away.

"I know it hurts, darling, but I have to."

Opening my eyes, I saw Devon above me. Glancing down, I saw I was wearing a T-shirt that had been pushed up. He was rubbing some kind of ointment into the cuts on my stomach.

I was disoriented, my last memory one of hazy red lights, throbbing music, and swirling faces.

"Where am I?" I asked, my voice a hoarse croak.

"Safe," was his succinct response.

Looking around, I saw we were back at the hotel, back in our suite. I relaxed a little. I was safe, just like he'd said. My focus shifted to him, and memory returned.

"Oh my God, Devon . . . it's really you." I couldn't believe my eyes. I struggled to sit up.

"Take it easy," he said gently.

Then I was in his arms and I was crying and he was holding me tight enough to hurt, but I didn't care.

"They said you were dead, and then you weren't, and . . . oh God, I'd thought I'd lost you," I sobbed into his neck.

"Shh, I'm all right," he whispered in my ear.

I couldn't speak anything else. I was too overwhelmed with emotions, hardly able to believe he was really there.

I kissed his neck and his cheek, and then he was kissing me, his lips pressing hard against mine. We were overcome by desperation and longing and the feeling of disaster barely averted for both of us. It was only by sheer luck that we were both still alive.

Tearing his mouth from mine, he pulled me close, cradling my head between his neck and shoulder. "I was afraid to hope you might still be alive," he said.

"How did you find me?" I asked, breathless and sniffling.

"I'm not the only agent in Amsterdam keeping an eye on Levin. Other countries have an interest in him as well. I got lucky when they knew where he was tonight."

I leaned back so I could see him. "How did you know I'd be with him? Did Vega tell you?"

There was a tentative knock on the door, interrupting us, and Devon got up to answer it. When he opened the door, I glanced over.

Ezabell stood there. She gazed up at Devon, fear obvious on her face.

"Ezabell," I said. "What are you doing here, honey? Didn't you find anyone to help you?"

Both she and Devon looked over at me. Devon moved aside and she scampered past him to the bed, scrambling onto it with me.

"I was afraid," she said. "I didn't know what to do or where to go. So I came here and waited." She glanced sideways at Devon and sidled closer.

"He's okay," I told her with a weak smile. "He rescued me."

"He saved you? Like you saved me?"

I nodded.

I guess that was enough for her because she lay down next to me. I wrapped my arm around her and drew her closer.

Devon had his hands in his pockets as he stood, watching us. I gave him a smile.

"I'm so tired," I said. Now that the surge of emotion and adrenaline from seeing Devon had passed, I was even more exhausted than before.

"Then go to sleep," he said. "You're safe now."

So I did.

I stood in the bathroom, hours later, taking stock of my body in the mirror. I was famished, lightheaded from not eating. There was a livid bruise on my cheek, courtesy of Levin's temper the other night, and the knife marks on my stomach. They'd scabbed over to some extent and Devon cleaning them had helped.

Devon was waiting when I came out of the bathroom.

"How badly were you hurt?" I asked him. "I saw the wound . . ."

"They dug it out and patched me up," he said. "I didn't care about that. All I wanted was you. I could have sworn I'd gotten you into the helicopter, but you were gone."

I stared at him. "She didn't tell you anything, did she?" I could feel a sinking in my gut.

"Who? Vega? She said you disappeared at the hospital while I was in surgery." He shrugged, glancing away. "I assumed you were afraid, so you'd gone. But you weren't here when I returned. Your things were packed, but your luggage remained. I surmised you were still in town. When I informed Vega, she said she'd heard that Levin had you."

"She'd heard that Levin had me," I repeated, my hands clenching into fists at her incredible audacity. "Well, yes, I suppose she would've *heard* that, considering she's the one who gave me to him."

Devon went still. "What are you saying? What happened, exactly?"

"Ivy?"

I turned immediately at the sound of Ezabell's voice and hurried over to the bed. She'd woken and was sitting up, rubbing her eyes.

"Good morning," I said, smiling at her. "You must feel better after that long sleep."

She nodded. "I'm hungry."

"Me, too," I said. "We'll get something to eat right away." Glancing behind me, I saw Devon watching us. "This is my friend, Devon," I told her. "He's nice. He won't hurt you."

Ezabell looked over my shoulder, her expression sober as she took in Devon. "I have to go to the bathroom," she said.

"Of course. It's right in there." I showed her the small room and closed the door. My gaze met Devon's, who lifted an eyebrow in question.

"Levin had her," I said. "He used her to make me talk. I told him your name and about the Shadow." Shrugging, I said, "I'm sorry, Devon. I was able to keep quiet while they were hurting me, but I couldn't let them hurt her."

"You don't have to apologize," he said. "But what are we supposed to do with her?"

"I guess we should find her parents," I said. "Give her to the police?" My heart ached at that, and I knew I didn't want to leave Amsterdam until I had seen Ezabell safely returned to her mother. She'd been through enough.

"I can scan her prints and send them off to our database of missing persons," he offered. "That should speed things up a bit."

I nodded like that was a good thing, and it was. I just hated that I wouldn't be with her much longer. We had a bond, she and I, forged in a situation most women were lucky enough not to ever find themselves in.

"We need some clothes for her," I said.

"I can fix that. The concierge should be able to find something for her to wear." Devon slid his arm around my waist and pulled me close. I rested against him, and it took me a moment to realize how unusual this was for us—just hugging for the comfort of being together. There was nothing sexual about it. I couldn't stop touching him, and it seemed he felt the same way, for even when Ezabell came out of the bathroom, he still kept hold of my hand.

"Hello, Ezabell," Devon said, crouching down so he was on her level. "I'm going to get you and Ivy something to eat and some clean clothes, then we'll find your mum. Is that all right?"

Ezabell nodded very seriously. "Will there be crêpes?"

"Absolutely," Devon assured her. I smiled, my fingers combing through her tangles.

"May I see your hand?" Devon asked. "Just for a moment?"

Cautiously she gave him her hand and he pressed each finger firmly onto the face of his cell. I saw a laser scan her prints from inside the glass. It didn't look like any cell phone I'd ever seen before.

"There," Devon said. "That'll help us find your mum and dad."

Devon left the suite to get us something to eat and I bathed Ezabell. By the time he returned, I'd wrapped her in a much-too-big bathrobe and was carefully combing the tangles from her hair. I wanted to tell Devon what had happened after he'd been shot, but it would have to wait until later. I didn't want Ezabell traumatized any more than she already was.

"I got a bit of everything," Devon said as a waiter followed him into the room, rolling a laden cart. The smells wafting from the covered dishes made my mouth start watering immediately. As soon as the waiter had left, Ezabell was up inspecting all the food offerings before her.

"Thanks," Ezabell said around a mouthful of croissant.

Ravenous, we both dug in with equal gusto. Devon watched us as he ate, a smile on his lips.

The full tummy put Ezabell to sleep and I eyed her hair, knowing I'd have to comb it again. Not that I minded. My mother had combed my hair for me, a long time ago. It was a warm, pleasant memory, so different from what my childhood predominantly had been.

"What are you thinking?" Devon asked me. I was leaning back against him as we sat in the bed, Ezabell huddled asleep on the couch.

I shrugged. "Thinking of my mom, I guess. She had a hard life with my stepdad, but we had some good times, before he came along. And after, too, but those were fewer and fewer until she died."

"And Ezabell makes you think of your mother," he guessed.

"Perhaps myself at her age," I clarified. "I wonder sometimes who I would have been if my life had been different. Circumstances shaped my character and personality, my fears and weaknesses."

"But also your strengths," Devon said.

"I haven't felt strong lately," I confessed.

"You have strength of will, for one, or you would never have survived the past few days." Taking my hand, he pressed it between his own. "You have compassion. And empathy. Two qualities I lack, incidentally."

"That's not true," I said, turning to gaze up at him. "You stuck with me when it would have been easier to bail and find someone else."

His lips twisted. "Self-serving, I'm afraid. You're too beautiful by far. I believe a Brontë sister said that 'beauty is generally the most attractive to the worst kinds of men. Therefore, it is likely to entail a great deal of trouble on the possessor.'"

"She sounds wise beyond her years," I said dryly.

Devon laughed softly. "I cannot deny that I am one of those worst kinds of men, and I have brought nothing but trouble into your life. Which is why it's essential I send you back home as soon as possible."

Something in his voice alerted me that this wasn't a usual parting. "What do you mean?" I asked. "You need some time to finish this job? To finish Levin?"

"Amongst other things."

His phone buzzed, interrupting us. He pulled it out of his pocket and glanced at it, frowning.

"What is it?" I asked.

"It's Ezabell," he said, glancing to where she still slept on the couch. "They've found her parents, who'd filed a missing persons report for her three days ago."

I was glad for Ezabell and selfishly sad for myself that we'd found them so fast, though it was gratifying to see the joy light her face when I told her.

"I'm sure they'll be thrilled beyond words to have you back," I said to her.

The concierge had delivered new clothes for Ezabell and I dressed her, carefully brushing and braiding her long, dark hair before we left the hotel.

We walked hand in hand from the car into the police station where Devon took us. We'd stopped on the way and bought a phone like Devon had originally given me, only I'd programmed my number into it.

"Anytime you need me, you just call," I told Ezabell, crouching down next to her while Devon explained to the officer behind the desk why we were there.

"Thank you," she said to me. "You saved me from those bad men."

"I'm glad I could," I replied, hugging her again. Her little arms around my neck were tight.

"Ivy, this is Sheridan. She'll be able to help Ezabell." At Devon's words, I reluctantly let Ezabell go and stood.

"Hello, Ivy," the woman standing next to Devon said. "Hi, Ezabell. I'm Sheridan. I'm going to take you to your parents."

She seemed nice enough. Her English was accented, but I understood her easily. She was smiling and it wasn't her fault I disliked her on sight, which had a lot more to do with my losing Ezabell than with her.

I held back tears as I forced a smile for Ezabell, giving her another hug before watching her walk away with Sheridan. Devon reached for my hand and I gripped him tightly.

We didn't say much on the way back to the hotel. Once we were in our room, I sat on the bed, listlessly staring out the window. It had begun to rain.

"I don't want to leave you," I said. I could see him in the window's reflection. He was behind me, packing, but stopped and looked over at me.

"You don't have a choice." His words were flat, not to be argued with. "You have blinders on, Ivy," he said. "Tell me what Levin did to you."

"Why?" I countered, turning to face him. "So you can feel guilty for it?"

"So I can ensure his death is as painful as what you endured."

He was absolutely, deadly serious, and I knew he could make good on his threat.

"You're not why I fell into his hands," I said. "Vega is. She told me you were dead. If I hadn't had Reggie's flash drive—"

"His what?"

"Reggie's flash drive," I explained. "When I ran back to him, he gave it to me. He'd told me about it before, that it was his insurance policy because he didn't trust the Shadow. And he was right not to.

"If I hadn't had it, she would have had me killed," I said.

Devon frowned. "Vega is many things, and she can be ruthless, but she doesn't go about killing people just because the mood strikes her. And as far as she knows, you're just a civilian. Telling you I was dead would be standard procedure."

I stiffened at his defense of her. "So what would turning me over to Levin be then? Would that be *standard procedure*, too? And let's not forget that she knows I'm anything but 'just a civilian.' If she thought that, then why would she have detained me at customs, told me you were married, and wanted to know what I was hiding from her that has kept you so interested in me."

His gaze sharpened. "She said that?" he asked. "Said you were hiding something?"

"Yes. It's like she knew about the vaccine, or at least knew I had a secret. And the whole thing about telling me you were married . . . what was that about?"

He hesitated. "Yes, that . . . concerns me."

"She can't be trusted, Devon." Getting up from the chair, I approached him. "She gave me up to Levin and made it quite clear he could do whatever he wanted with me. I thought the Shadow was supposed to be in the business of *protecting* people. She bargained my life like it was nothing."

For the first time, it seemed like Devon was hearing me when it came to Vega.

"I know you're loyal to her," I said, "but I'm not sure how loyal she is to *you*."

"Does it matter?" he replied. "You and I can't continue. If nothing else, this last week has shown us that."

"I don't want to leave you." It seemed grossly unfair. Devon loved me. I loved him. That should have meant happiness for both of us.

He sighed, and it was a tired, resigned sort of sound. "Darling, it doesn't matter what we *want*. Our lives are incompatible. And the longer we drag this out, the higher your mortality rate climbs. The next time might very well be the *last* time."

It no doubt will be if Vega has anything to say about it, I thought but didn't say.

I was quiet for a moment. There was no counterargument to what he was saying, and it made me feel sick to my stomach.

"So is this the end of it then?" I asked. "You're going to put me on a plane back to America and we're done?"

"I don't see any other choice," Devon said. "Do you?"

I did, but if he was blind to it, then there wasn't a damn thing I could do about it. It obviously hadn't occurred to him to quit his job, or if it had, he'd discarded the idea.

"You said you loved me," I reminded him.

"I do," he said gently, cupping my cheek in his hand. "But that doesn't matter. The two of us don't matter, not in the larger scheme of things. The best thing for you is to go back to your life and forget all about me."

I searched his eyes. "That's what you want me to do?"

"It's what I need you to do."

Semantics. A nuanced difference, but the end result was the same.

"I'm not Kira," I said. "I've survived everything they've thrown at me so far. I can take it. I'm tougher than I look."

His palm was work-roughened rather than smooth, gently abrading my skin as he brushed a thumb along my cheekbone. "Indeed, you are," he said. "But I don't want to be the one responsible for breaking you beyond what you can endure."

"You said we'd go somewhere warm," I said to Devon. "When this was over, you said you'd take me somewhere warm. I want that. Before you end us, I want that." I wanted to be somewhere safe and beautiful. Somewhere far away from Amsterdam. "Will you do this one last thing for me?"

Devon's expression was unreadable. "It's the very least I owe you, is it not?" he asked rhetorically.

I stiffened, his lack of enthusiasm pricking my pride. "You don't *owe* me anything. I was hoping you still wanted some time together. It was *your* idea originally."

"It's not that I don't want to be with you—"

"Then what?" I snapped. "Both of us could have been killed in the past few days. It's only by sheer luck that I'm not still back in the red light district, drugged and turning tricks."

Devon's hands clenched into fists, and I had a fleeting moment of regret for telling him that part.

"So tell me," I said, pushing a hand through my hair in exasperation. "Because if you don't want to go—"

"It's because I want it too bloody much!"

His outburst shut me up and I stared at him in the charged silence.

Devon turned away, shoving his hands into his pockets. "Do you think I want to let you go?" he asked.

"I don't know what you want," I said honestly.

Devon paced a few steps, then turned to face me. "I never thought I'd feel this way again. Not after Kira. And yet . . . I can't stop. But I can't change anything either. Why prolong the inevitable for either of us?"

"If what we have is only temporary, then why rush to end it?" I countered.

"Self-preservation, I suppose," he said quietly.

"Let's go somewhere," I pleaded. "Please."

Devon's lips twisted. "How can I say no to that?"

CHAPTER SEVENTEEN

I stood on the beach, staring out over the water. The waves were rolling in and crashing against the sand. The early morning clouds threatened rain, but I knew it wouldn't rain for long. It had rained a bit each of the four days we'd been in Kapalua. Located on the northwestern shore of Maui, it was wet there, but I didn't complain. The result was a lush, tropical setting where our hotel was nestled, perched on top of a steep hill that led to the beach where I now stood.

Since Devon's part of the mission had been accomplished—the threat the phones had possessed now nullified—nothing prevented him from disappearing off the grid for a while, though I hadn't asked how long that would be. Levin remained, but was no longer a threat. For now.

The wind whipped my hair, freeing long strands from the braid I'd pulled it into. Devon slid his arms around my waist and pulled me back to rest against him.

"Tell me about your home," I said to him. "Your real one. You do have a home, don't you?"

There was a slight hesitation. "I do," he said. "Though I'm hardly there. It's in London. A three-bedroom flat with the usual amenities."

"Do you have friends?"

A longer hesitation this time. "No, not really. Not in the sense you mean. I have people I know—people in the business and from varying walks of life—who I consider acquaintances. I have perhaps two friends. People I trust implicitly, who would help me even if it meant putting themselves in danger."

Yes, I guess *friends* meant something very different in Devon's vocabulary than in mine.

"Do you ever get . . . lonely?"

"It's a lonely profession," he replied.

I took that as the closest he'd come to saying that yes, he did get lonely.

"How many times have you almost died?"

Devon sighed, his hold tightening on me. "Too many times for me to want to dwell on it."

"But you've saved people's lives, too," I said. "Right?"

"I like to think so."

"What about your family?" I asked. "Do you ever see them?"

"I've never met my extended family. I think I have a few cousins on my mother's side, but I've never met them."

"Why not?"

"They think I'm dead, for one. Informing them otherwise would be quite shocking, I'm afraid." His jesting tone made the comment sound light, though it was actually a sad thing—his family, the people who might love him, thought he was dead.

"I just thought maybe your family would know the truth," I said with a shrug.

"No one knows the truth," Devon said. "Just you."

Something warm unfurled inside me at that pronouncement. I'd been so vulnerable with Devon in so many ways. He knew all my deepest insecurities and secrets, the dark places in my psyche that I'd allowed no one else to know. It was good to realize he'd let me in, too, even if I hadn't understood it at the time.

The sun was starting to peek from behind the clouds. It would get up to the mid-eighties today and I was looking forward to another day lying by the pool and looking out over the ocean. I hadn't had a swimsuit when we'd come here, or any clothes appropriate to the tropical climate. Devon had taken me into the clothing stores at the hotel that stocked solely designer brands.

I'd tried on clothes and he approved or nixed each outfit, including several bikinis. I'd argued that I only needed one bathing suit, but his lips had lifted in a half-smile and he maintained he couldn't decide which he liked better, so I'd ended up buying five. I'd had to make a hurried appointment at the hotel spa for a wax just so I could wear them.

Today I wore a barely-there black crochet bikini that had Devon staring at me as I arranged myself on the chaise inside the cabana he'd reserved for us. Several days in the sun had bronzed my skin and lightened my hair.

Glancing at him, I winked and blew him a kiss as I slid my sunglasses on. His small smile widened.

Devon had told the hotel we were on our honeymoon, so the entire time we'd been there, they'd added romantic touches to everything we did. From rose petals on the bed at turndown service, to complimentary champagne at dinner. Today was no exception as a uniformed waiter stepped into our cabana, offering us chocolate-covered strawberries.

"You're spoiling me," I teased Devon. "Ruining me for regular vacations."

"And regular men, I hope," he said.

"You *want* to ruin me for other men?" I asked.

"Haven't I already?"

Yes, pretty much, but I didn't want to think about that.

A steady stream of mai tais and Devon taking his time rubbing sunscreen on my back and shoulders as he whispered teasing innuendos in my ear was my idea of a perfect day. The slow burn of sexual tension between us was a feeling I never wanted to end. Delayed gratification made it even sweeter when we finally went back to our room.

Devon was peeling off my suit before the door had even finished closing, his mouth coming down hard on mine. Our skin smelled of sun and coconut, and I knew I'd never smell that scent again and not think of Devon and this week.

We were walking hand in hand along the water's edge after dinner. The moon was full and bright, making the sand shine in the night. Devon carried my shoes, the dainty ankle straps dangling from his fingers.

"It's so peaceful here," I said with a sigh. "I don't want to leave."

"Well, we're not leaving yet," Devon said, which was true. In fact, he hadn't determined a day for us to leave and had left our reservation at the hotel open-ended.

"I know, but we can't hide here forever."

"Is that what it feels like we're doing?" he asked.

I paused, turning to face him. "Doesn't it to you?"

His lips twisted in a faint smile. "A bit. I prefer to think of it as a holiday. I rarely get those."

"Would you take them even if you could?" I asked. We'd carefully avoided discussion of his work since we'd arrived. Instead, we'd talked of everything and nothing, our conversations easy and light. These had been some of the best days we'd ever spent together.

He shrugged, his smile turning self-deprecating. "Probably not."

I thought for a moment. "Can I ask you something?"

"Always."

"Do you ever think about the future? Of what you want or where you'll be in ten years? Twenty?"

Devon was silent, studying me. "No."

I frowned. "Why not?"

"It's pointless," he said. "No one knows the future. Our car could crash on the way to the airport and both of us die. I live in the moment, in the now, which has enough trouble. The future will take care of itself."

I hoped he was right.

⌒⌒

That night I woke to Devon talking in his sleep. I heard my name and reached to rest a hand on his shoulder.

"Devon," I called. He didn't wake and I had to say it two more times before he sat straight up, his chest heaving and his hands clenched like he'd been fighting.

"Are you all right?" I asked. He glanced at me, his eyes feverishly bright in the moonlight streaming through the window. "You were having a nightmare, I think."

He didn't answer.

Throwing back the sheet, he stood and walked to the balcony. We'd left the doors open so we could hear the ocean and feel the breeze. The moon bathed his naked body with silvery light.

I tossed aside the blanket that had covered me and went to stand behind him. I slid my arms around his waist and leaned against him, resting my cheek against his back.

"Will you tell me about your nightmare?" I asked.

I didn't think he was going to answer me, but finally, he spoke.

"It was the night I found Kira," he said. "It was late, later than I'd told her I'd be back and I was afraid she'd be worried. Not that she didn't always worry, but I'd given her my word. I was . . . anxious to see her, needed to see she was okay. Marrying her had been against my better judgment, but I was young and stupid. Dangerously so.

"I'd reached our door and saw it wasn't locked. I'd told her time and again to make sure she locked the doors. She was artistic, a bit flighty, always looking for the sunshine and silver lining. It made me irritated because I couldn't count on her to watch out for herself. She'd never taken the danger we were in seriously. Then I felt guilty for being irritated with her. She was who she was."

He fell silent and I waited, picturing a younger Devon and the young, faceless woman who'd loved him.

"They'd . . . brutalized her," he choked out, his voice thick. "She was so delicate, fragile, and her blood was everywhere. I sat with her . . . I don't even know how long . . . before Vega found me. She was kind, comforting, yet unflinching in her assessment of how badly I'd handled the situation. Kira would still be alive if not for me. The moment I'd married her, I'd signed her death warrant."

Tears slid down my cheeks to wet his back. My arms tightened around him.

He was solid and strong, and it seemed impossible that anyone could control him, yet I knew his past still did, and so did Vega.

"Tonight, I dreamt of that night, but it was you lying in the bed. Not Kira."

My eyes slid shut at the agony in his voice, and I didn't know what to say. Several long moments passed before he spoke again.

"We should go," he said roughly. "Tomorrow, I think."

My heart sank, but I didn't argue. I knew his fears were justified—I had only to look at the scars on my stomach for proof.

His hands covered mine, slotting our fingers together. Lifting my left hand, he pressed his lips to my knuckles. I felt the warm brush of his breath against my skin. He turned and my arms lifted to rest on his shoulders. If it was my last night with Devon, then I wanted nothing between us. No lies or insecurities, pretenses or agendas.

His hands rested on my waist, drifting lightly to my hips, then farther down to cup my rear. "When did you become more than a beautiful woman to warm my bed?" he mused.

I didn't answer, instead transferring my focus to pressing my lips to his chest. My tongue tasted his skin, warm and solid. He didn't object and he didn't try to stop me.

"It kills me to think of you with another man," he said.

I paused, glancing up at him.

"Am I to pine away in celibate spinsterhood for you?" I asked mildly. "No one says you have to do this job until it kills you."

"Vega would disagree," he said dryly.

I stiffened at her name. "She seems to think she owns you," I said.

"In a way, she does."

The truth of it was a bitter taste in my mouth, but it wasn't a bond I could break for him. Devon had to want to be free of the Shadow—free of Vega—on his own.

"I don't want to talk about her anymore," I said, slipping my hand between us. He was hard and ready for me. "I want you to make love to me." I dropped to my knees.

I didn't want to think about the women that had come before me, or those who Devon would have after me. I just wanted to make sure he never forgot Ivy Mason.

His cock was jutting from his body, thick and long. I wrapped my hand around the base, leaning forward to lick the tip. Raising my eyes, I saw he was watching me. His gaze was molten, and our eyes locked.

Opening wide, I slid him into my mouth, memorizing his unique flavor. If someone had told me a year ago I'd willingly be in this position to perform this act on a man, I'd have thought they were insane. Only with Devon had I found the freedom to be sexual and find pleasure in it. Only with Devon had I found that love wasn't something that hurt me and stole my self-respect.

His body was beautiful. The scars that marked his skin only added to that dangerous edge that drew me in. His hands tangled in my long hair as I took him deeper in my mouth, his brow creasing in the pleasure and pain of holding back.

I wanted to be his. Marked by him. Owned by him. It would never change. No matter if this was our last night together. I'd be Devon's for always.

I moved my hands to cup his ass, an amazing part of his anatomy that I'd neglected, and squeezed, encouraging him to slide deeper. He groaned, his palms cupping the sides of my head.

I was mesmerized by his face as I moved, taking his shaft deep, then letting the length of him slide out until only the tip touched my lips. He refused to close his eyes. His blue gaze burned into mine as I performed this intimate act on him. For him. But he wouldn't let me continue for long before his hands were under my arms, pulling me to my feet.

He lifted me to wrap my legs around his waist, pushing inside me in a long, slow thrust. I clung to him as he kissed me, reveling in the feeling of being one with him, for the last time.

Devon kissed me, one arm wrapped around my back, the other sliding up the back of my neck. His fingers tangled in my hair as he kissed me with something more tonight, something tinged with a desperation that I felt, too.

He walked forward until we hit the bed, then braced his knees on the mattress and lowered me down, kissing me all the while. His hands moved down, the curve of my hips fitting in his palms. He made love to me slowly, languorously, as though he had all the time in the world to push me to the brink. Our skin became slick with a sheen of sweat, pleas and gasps falling from my lips. I urged him to move faster, harder, but he wouldn't give in, and I shattered around him. His mouth covered mine when I cried out his name, and only when I was coming down from my high did he speed up. His body covered mine completely, his cock growing harder and thicker inside me. The wet sounds of our bodies as they came together made an intimate chorus to the words he whispered in my ear. Words I'd never thought I'd hear him say.

"I love you," he said. "Never forget."

A promise and a goodbye, and as his body shuddered in my arms, tears dripped from my eyes to slide down my cheek and into my hair.

Afterward, he held me close and I staved off sleep as long as I could, listening to the steady sound of his heart and the deep evenness of his breath. Our legs were tangled together and his fingers made gentle patterns on the small of my back. But I couldn't stay awake forever, and as the hours passed, eventually my eyes grew too heavy, and sleep claimed me.

❧

Devon was already awake and dressed the next morning when I woke, and with his outer armor came his inner armor. I could tell immediately that he was putting distance between us, but it didn't make me angry. I understood. Self-preservation. An instinct he and I shared.

I showered in the tiny bathroom and dressed—a cap-sleeved wrap dress in a deep turquoise, the skirt hitting right above my knee. The fabric was soft and the neckline would have looked tacky on a woman with larger breasts, but on me it looked perfect. I could tell it was another designer creation made for the runway, and while I had no idea how he'd gotten hold of it, I knew it was a silent gift from him to me. Devon liked to dress me, perhaps only slightly less than undressing me, and he could afford to do so.

I French-braided my hair from one side of my head around to the other so the long tail draped over my shoulder. Wisps of hair escaped from the braid to dangle by my ear and neck. I took great care to look as good as I possibly could. If this was to be Devon's last glimpse of me, I wanted it to be a good memory.

"These are for you," he said when I came out of the bathroom, handing me a shoebox. He had a twinkle in his eye as I lifted the lid to see a pair of Jimmy Choo wedges. Again, I didn't know how he'd come by them, I was just glad he had.

I smiled, determined to keep our last few hours together light and not mar the time by crying. Of course, the shoes fit perfectly.

"How do I look?" I asked, doing a slow pirouette.

Devon didn't have to say anything; the slow burn in his eyes as he looked me down and back up told me exactly how I looked.

"Stunning," he said, and his voice was rougher than usual.

I felt the sting of tears and quickly looked away. "You're looking pretty dapper yourself," I said. And boy, did he ever.

No man I'd ever known could wear a suit like Devon. Custom-tailored, it fit perfectly, stretching across his wide shoulders and tapering to his lean hips. You couldn't tell he had a holster and weapon underneath his arm, and the deep gray he wore today made his eyes seem an even paler shade of blue than usual.

He'd once told me that he wore a suit to "blend in." I didn't understand then and I still didn't know how he could ever blend into a crowd. My eye was immediately drawn to him, the magnetism and charisma he exuded was something that couldn't be learned, but had been born in him. And beyond all of that was the edge of danger and menace emanating from him. The old phrase "not to be trifled with" came to mind, and it fit him perfectly.

"I have one more thing for you," he said, reaching inside his jacket and handing me a rectangular, blue Tiffany box.

I carefully lifted the lid, gasping in amazement when I saw what it contained.

A necklace, but unlike any I'd ever seen. The pendant was a yellow, pear-shaped diamond, so brilliant it looked as though the sun shone through it. Surrounding the diamond were small, round white diamonds.

"It's beautiful," I said as Devon lifted the jewelry from the box.

"Turn around," he said, and I complied.

He fastened the necklace for me, then gently turned me so he could see it.

"It doesn't do justice to your beauty," he said. "But it reminded me of you. Sunlight shining through something incredibly strong. That's what you are to me."

I was speechless, tears filling my eyes. Leaning down, Devon pressed a sweet, chaste kiss to my lips. When he lifted his head, our gazes locked together. For a moment, I could see in his eyes the pain echoing inside me, then there was a knock at the door and the moment was lost.

"Come in," Devon called, and the valet bustled inside to take our luggage.

The flight back stopped in L.A., where I would catch a flight to St. Louis and Devon would fly on to London.

It was chilly on the plane and there wasn't much to see out the window, not that I would have noticed. Devon and I had eyes only for each other. We didn't say much. We didn't need words. We both knew our time together was measured in hours now, rather than days. He held my hand and alternately kissed me and just touched me, his hand cradling my jaw.

Finally, the announcement that landing was imminent came over the sound system. We held hands as the plane landed, then joined the line of people waiting to deplane. Devon stood close behind me, his presence solid at my back. His hands slid softly up my arms to my shoulders, then back down to my elbows, a last touch of skin against skin. It made me want to cry, but I bit my lip until it hurt enough to chase the tears away.

My eyes were busy drinking in each movement Devon made. His arm was draped across my shoulders, holding me close to his side as we walked through the airport. He didn't look at me. His training was such that his eyes were always moving, always assessing possible threats, in a way that was as much a part of him as the way he walked.

When we came to the center of the terminals, he reached into his suit jacket and handed over two tickets for St. Louis. "This will get you home," he said.

"Wait," I asked, confused as I glanced at them. "Why two?"

"I thought you could use some company for the flight," he replied, nodding over my shoulder.

I turned around and my jaw fell open in shock.

Logan was standing a few yards away, watching us. He looked hesitant, his hands shoved into the pockets of his jeans. My vision blurred as tears came to my eyes and in the next moment we were walking toward each other, then I was caught up in his arms as he lifted me off the ground.

"Hey, Ives," he said softly in my ear.

"Logan," I choked out. "I can't believe you're here."

He squeezed me tight, then lowered me to my feet. "I was a complete and total dick," he said bluntly. "And I'm sorry."

I smiled through my tears. "Me, too."

"All is well between BFFs?" Devon said from behind me. I turned around, sadness striking once again.

"Yes. Thank you, Devon."

Logan gave him a curt nod. "Yeah. Thanks." And I was gratified, because he did sound grateful. The animosity that had marked his interaction with Devon previously was now gone.

"You just needed some time to figure out what an arse you were being," Devon chided him, his lips twitching in a half-smile.

Logan grimaced, then caught my eye. I raised an eyebrow and he gave me a sheepish smile. "True."

"My flight is departing shortly," Devon said to Logan. "If you wouldn't mind giving us a few moments?"

"Um, yeah, sure," Logan said, walking away a few paces and leaving Devon and me alone. An island of two in a sea of humanity.

We said nothing at first, our eyes locked together. It was only through sheer force of will that I kept the tears at bay. I didn't want our parting to be marked by sorrow any more than it already was.

His arms lifted and I went into them automatically.

Devon's lips met mine in a kiss that was bittersweet. I didn't want to cry so I pushed away the thought that it was our last. Instead, I tried to memorize the taste and texture of his lips as they moved over mine, the feel of his arms around me, the fingers of one hand sifting through my hair while the other curved around my hip.

It was several long moments before Devon slowly pulled back. Resting his forehead against mine, his voice was quiet as he said, "Remember. You're strong. Stronger than you realize. You've survived so much, and yet your soul is pure. Don't let the darkness consume you again. Do you hear me, sweet Ivy?"

I nodded, unable to speak past the lump in my throat.

"You're beautiful, inside and out. The past is gone forever. Tomorrow is never assured. There's only today. Live in today. Promise me."

"I promise." My voice was barely audible. I knew these were the last things he wanted to tell me, and I tried to memorize each word.

"I'll think of you," he said, and now his voice was even lower. "Quite often, I'm absolutely certain."

I wanted to ask again, to beg him to change his mind and choose a different path, one I could share with him, but I swallowed down the words. My asking would only taint the goodbye he was trying to make.

His smile was brief, as was the gentle swipe of his thumb across my lower lip. "Take care, sweet Ivy. Be well."

"You, too," I managed. "Be careful." I knew that the odds of me ever seeing him again were smaller only than my ever finding out if something happened to him.

We didn't say any "I love yous," and I was glad. I think that might have broken me. As it was, he wrapped his arms around me, squeezing me tight, then pressed a light kiss to my forehead. When he let me go, his fingers caught at mine, pressing once as he stepped away. In moments, he was lost in the crowd.

As I stared into the streams of passing people, unblinking, hoping for one more glimpse, a hand latched on to mine. Logan.

"I'm sorry, Ives," he said.

I looked up at him, tears on my lashes.

"I'm not so big of a jerk as to want you to lose the man you love," he said. Reaching out, he brushed a wet trail from my cheek and draped his arm over my shoulders. Drawing me close for a hug, I felt his lips brush my forehead. "I'm really sorry," he repeated.

The familiar feel of him was comforting and I was deeply glad he was there. "Thank you for coming," I said, clearing my throat and blinking rapidly to dispel the tears. "I don't deserve you."

"Bullshit," he retorted without heat. "You deserve better than

I treated you. Especially after all the shit that happened." Tugging on my hand, he said, "C'mon. Let's head to our gate."

We walked side by side to security, pulling out our passports and tickets to get through. I glanced at mine, getting another jolt when I saw Devon had again used the "Mrs. Rose Ross" name and passport for mine. Once through, we walked to our gate and sat down. The flight wasn't for another couple of hours. I wandered to the screens that showed departures, noting that Devon's flight to London left in mere minutes, though from a different terminal.

Strolling to the windows, I watched the planes take off, wondering which of them carried the man I'd fallen in love with . . . and lost.

I felt a presence behind me and saw Logan's reflection in the window.

"How are you doing?" he asked.

I thought about it before I answered. "I'm okay," I said. "It was never going to work, but it meant more—I meant more to him— than I thought." I turned to face him. "That's something, right?"

"Damn straight," he said with a small smile. "He'd have been a fool otherwise."

"I wish . . ." But my voice trailed off and I didn't finish the sentence.

"You wish what?"

I shrugged. "I wish he'd felt a bit more. Maybe then I could have competed with the loyalty he has for his job. But however much it was, it wasn't enough in the end."

Logan didn't say anything to that, not that I needed him to. It felt good to say it, though. Acknowledge the truth of it.

"Want to get something to eat before we take off?" he asked.

I was hungry, so that sounded good. "Yeah, let's."

We wandered to a small restaurant near our gate and ordered.

The service was quick and it wasn't long before we were finishing up. Logan and I had chatted while we ate, him catching me up on the white lies he'd told Grams and Grandpa about what had happened that night Devon and I had left.

"They actually believed you when you said lightning struck that SUV?" I asked, incredulous.

Logan grinned. "You know I can do no wrong in Grams's eyes," he teased.

"True." I laughed. "She likes you more than she likes me."

Silence fell for a moment, both of us lost in our thoughts, but it wasn't uncomfortable. It felt good to have my best friend back. A last gift from Devon.

"So," Logan began, and I could tell by his voice that he'd switched into serious mode. "How are you doing?"

"I'm all right," I said. "I am. It's sad and . . . I'm really going to miss him." I had to pause for a moment, a lump growing in my throat. I was hurting, deep inside, but I was dealing with it in a way I'd never been able to before. Devon was gone . . . and I would be okay.

Logan reached across the table and took my hand. "Good," he said. "I'm really glad."

"What about you?" I asked. "You said before I left that you didn't want to see me anymore."

But he was already shaking his head. "I was mad, and trying to force you into a decision. I guess I've accepted that things just aren't going to be what I always hoped they'd be."

His matter-of-factness didn't fool me. "I'm sorry, Logan."

His smile was a little forced this time. "No worries, Ives. We're friends. That's what counts."

I paused on our way back to the gate to use the restroom. "Go on ahead," I urged him. "I'll meet you at the gate."

"You sure?"

"Absolutely." I impulsively gave him another hug. I hadn't realized how much I'd counted on having Logan in my life until he hadn't been there anymore. "See you in a few."

In the bathroom, I fiddled with my hair and readjusted my dress, primping without really being conscious of the fact that I was doing so. It made me feel more normal, especially after all that had happened. This would be the first time I wouldn't be anticipating Devon's arrival since before Christmas.

It would take some getting used to.

CHAPTER EIGHTEEN

It was surreal, going back to work. I felt like I'd lived another life in the past three weeks. And if my boss, Mr. Malloy, didn't like me as much as he did, I might not have had a job to go back to after being gone that long.

Marcia wanted to hear all the details of my "exotic adventures," as she called them. She'd been so excited when I told her he'd taken me to Amsterdam and absolutely enthralled when I'd shown her the yellow diamond necklace Devon had given me.

"But it was a goodbye gift," I said.

She looked at me strangely. "A goodbye gift?" she echoed. "What does that mean?"

"It means we broke up," I said flatly. I refused to cry, no matter how badly I ached inside. The only time I allowed the tears to fall was at night when I was alone in my bed.

Marcia was shocked, staring at me wide-eyed. "Oh. Oh wow. I'm so sorry." She put her arms around me, but I didn't let her hug me for very long. I couldn't. Not if I wanted to keep it together.

"I thought you'd be glad," I said with a thin smile.

Her expression turned sympathetic. "I'm not that kind of friend, Ivy," she said. "If you're sad and unhappy, then so am I. No matter what I thought about your relationship, it was still *your* relationship."

That nearly broke the dam holding back the tears, but I took a deep, shaky breath and swallowed them down. I didn't trust my voice, so I just nodded.

"Let's go get a drink sometime this week after work and talk about it, okay?" she asked, rubbing a hand over my shoulder.

"Yeah," I managed. "Yeah. That'd be great." I smiled weakly at her, already knowing I wouldn't go. There was so much about my relationship with Devon that I couldn't tell her—that I could tell no one.

Except, maybe, one person.

As soon as I'd hit the mainland, my cell phone had started working again. I'd had over a dozen voice mails from Scott, each one more worried than the last.

I hadn't called him back yet and the guilt was weighing on me. But I didn't know what to tell him. I also didn't know if I wanted to drag him back into my life, though now there was no real reason why I shouldn't.

It wasn't like I would ever see Devon again.

The thought was another shaft of pain through me. Logically, I understood all the reasons why Devon had ended things between us. But my heart just wouldn't listen. I missed him. I missed everything about him.

He'd had a driver waiting for Logan and me at the airport when we'd landed, and he'd dropped me off at Devon's place. When I'd tried to argue, the driver had said that his instructions had been very clear, that I was to get out there.

Logan had followed me inside the building, both of us confused. The police tape was gone and the apartment was once again pristine. No sooner had I unlocked the door and stepped inside than Beau was poking his head out of his apartment across the hall.

"Hey! You're back!" he said.

"Hi, Beau." I smiled at him. "How're you?"

"I'm awesome," he replied with a huge grin. "The Cards are playing the Pirates Friday. You going to the game?"

"Um, probably not," I said.

"What about you?" he asked Logan.

"Yeah, season tickets," Logan said with a grin.

"Way to go, my man!"

They high-fived. I rolled my eyes as I pushed my suitcase into the apartment.

"Hey, wait, Ivy," Beau said, stopping me. "I've got something for you." He disappeared back into his apartment for a moment or two, then came back holding out an envelope for me. "Yeah, Devon sent this to me with a note that I should give it to you when I saw you."

I stared at the white envelope in his hand, almost afraid to take it. Logan solved my dilemma, reaching past me to take it from Beau.

"Thanks," he said.

"Sure, no problem." Beau's cell began vibrating and he gave us a wave before hitting the button on the Bluetooth earpiece he wore. The door to his apartment swung shut behind him.

Logan closed my door, then followed me to the couch, where my shaking legs had taken me.

"Do you want me to open it?" he asked.

I nodded.

Breaking the seal, he tore open the envelope and pulled out a sheaf of papers. Slowly flipping through them, he said, "It's about the apartment."

"It's what?"

"Here, this place," he clarified, glancing up at me. "It's in your name now."

"The lease?"

"No. The deed."

He handed me the papers and there it was, my name and the address of the apartment. It seemed Devon wasn't yet through with his parting gifts. Not that I was complaining. It was the first time in my life I'd ever had a place to call my own.

"That was . . . generous of him," Logan said.

I nodded, my throat thick. "Yeah, it was," I managed.

All my things had still been there, though Devon's clothes had been removed from the closet. He'd had no other personal things in the apartment, the décor and furniture all done by an interior decorating service.

I knew Devon had meant for me to move on, to close the chapter of my life that included him. I just wasn't sure I knew how. Devon and I had a connection. He'd understood me, understood how messed up I had been inside my head—probably because he was just as broken.

Although it was Friday night and I didn't know if he'd be home or if I'd be interrupting a date, I decided to call Scott back. Of course, once I'd decided, it still took me the better part of two hours to work up the guts. After all, the last time I'd seen him, my boyfriend had been pointing a gun at his head. He'd stopped texting once I'd stopped responding.

Not exactly the best of terms.

His cell rang three times and I thought I was going to get his voice mail, but he picked up on the fourth ring.

"Scott," I said, trying to hide my nervousness. "Hey, it's Ivy."

There was a pause, then, "Oh my God, Ivy? Is it really you?"

I smiled at the sound of his voice, gladder than I thought I would be to talk to him.

"Yeah, it's really me. I'm returning your call."

There was a long pause and when he spoke again, his voice was much more guarded. "I called you over a week ago, about a dozen times."

My smile faded. "I'm so sorry. I didn't get your messages. I-I was out of the country for a while and my phone didn't work."

"God, Ivy," he said, still sounding upset. "I thought you were dead."

"I'm sorry," I repeated. "And . . . I'm sorry about how I left, the way Devon behaved . . . and well, I'm just sorry."

"Stop apologizing," he said with a sigh. "It's not like it was your fault."

The words *I'm sorry* immediately sprang to my lips, but I bit them back.

"So where are you now?" he asked.

"Back at Dev—I mean my apartment." It was hard to think of Devon in past terms.

"Can I come see you?"

I couldn't say no, and wasn't sure I wanted to. I was hurting and any kind of distraction was better than nothing. It would be good to see him again. Scott was a really great guy, even if I was his rebound from his ex.

You realize he's one of those men who want to save you.

Devon's words flitted through my head, but I shoved them aside. I didn't need saving. Not anymore. "Yes. Yes, you can."

I brushed my hair again and checked my appearance in the mirror before he arrived. I wore jeans and a tank top that was comfortable enough for lounging around the house on a Friday night.

The knock came sooner than I'd thought and I checked the peephole before opening the door. As quick as I was, though, Beau had been quicker, already chatting with Scott.

". . . best from behind comeback ever," he enthused.

"Yeah, it was quite a game," Scott agreed, but he was looking at me, his gaze ranging from my head to my bare toes and back, seeming to drink me in.

"Okay, well, good talking to you, man," Beau said as Scott slipped inside my apartment. I finger-waved at Beau, who was surely the nosiest neighbor I'd ever known. He had to have ears like a hawk.

There was a moment of awkward silence, then we both spoke at once.

"Can I get—"

"You look—"

We both stopped. Laughed.

"You look amazing," he said. "Must have gone somewhere sunny, I guess."

"Um, yeah. For a little while," I hedged. "Can I get you something to drink?"

"Sure."

I'd said it automatically, then realized I didn't know if I really had anything here. It wasn't like I'd had time to go grocery shopping. But after a quick search, I found a bottle of wine in a cabinet.

"Red okay?" I asked.

"Sounds good."

Scott sat on the barstool while I opened the bottle of wine. Devon had a handy-dandy electric wine opener, which made it super easy.

I had an electric wine bottle opener, I mentally corrected myself.

As I was pouring the wine, Scott asked, "So you want to tell me what happened once he dragged you out of the hospital?"

Devon hadn't dragged me, but I didn't want to antagonize Scott, so I let it pass.

"The guy who was after me went after Logan instead," I said, shuddering as I remembered that night. "Devon got to Logan in time, thank God, and then the guy ended up tracking us to my grandparents' house." I took a hefty swallow of my wine as memories of running through that cornfield flashed through my mind.

"What happened there?"

"Devon killed him."

Scott frowned. "So if the guy was dead and there was no longer a threat to you, why didn't you come back?"

"We went to Amsterdam," I said, rounding the counter and taking the stool next to Scott's. I decided against telling Scott about the additional men that had been tracking me on Vega's orders.

Scott's eyebrows flew upward. "That sounds . . . nice," he said, his tone flat.

But I shook my head. "It wasn't. It was . . . pretty awful, actually." Absently, I rubbed my stomach where the cuts had healed but a couple of white scars had been left behind.

Scott reached out, stilling my hand. Cautiously, he lifted my shirt a few inches, as though fearing what he'd find. He sucked in a breath when he saw the scars.

"I'm okay," I assured him, covering his hand with mine and letting the fabric drop again.

Turning away, he drank the entire glass of wine. After setting the glass back on the counter, he rubbed a hand over his face.

"You're not, though," he said. "You're really, really not."

I stiffened. "What do you mean?"

His gaze met mine. "How many close calls were there this time, Ivy?" he asked. "How many wounds have healed? How many scars will he leave on you before you decide enough is enough?"

I looked away from his penetrating gaze. "Devon has a dangerous job," I said. "He's never hidden that from me. But it doesn't matter anyway because . . . we broke up."

Scott seemed utterly taken aback. "You broke up?"

I nodded. "He said it was too dangerous, us being together."

"You sound like you don't agree."

I shrugged. "He could've quit his job, just lived a normal life." My gaze lifted to Scott's. "But he didn't."

I could tell he'd understood what I couldn't say. "Aw, Ivy. Damn. I'm sorry," he said with a sigh. He wrapped an arm around my neck and drew me toward him for a hug.

"It's okay," I said. And it would be. Eventually.

Scott didn't stay much longer after that. Having assured himself that I was okay, and realizing that I needed time, he left after a while.

"Can I call you?" he asked as I walked him to the door. "Maybe we can get together. Have lunch or something."

I smiled, but hesitated.

"Just as friends," he assured me.

My smile widened and I relaxed. Friends were good. I needed them. And Scott had proven already to be a good friend, the kind even Devon would have given the appellation to.

"I'd like that," I said.

He'd nodded, given me one last hug, and disappeared down the hallway. For once, Beau didn't pop out of his apartment to check things out.

The days settled into the same routine after that, but my perspective had changed. What once I viewed as safe and normal now seemed tedious and dull. Whereas I'd been able to look forward to Devon's unexpected reappearances into my life—and my bed—now nothing loomed but day after day of unending sameness.

When I'd been unpacking, I'd come across the suit of his I'd stashed away what seemed like forever ago. I hadn't removed it from my luggage when we'd been in Amsterdam or on Maui, and now it was the sole reminder I had of Devon's presence. For a while, it smelled of his cologne, but the scent had faded to almost nothing now. It made me sad, so I no longer tried to smell the soft fabric.

I'd come across the phone Devon had given me, too. His number was still programmed in, but I didn't dial it. What was there to say that hadn't already been said? But I longed to hear his voice, hear him say my name, call me *sweet Ivy* again.

Perhaps he had already found another woman to "warm his bed," as he'd called it.

Tears dripped down my cheeks as I stared out the window at the dark sky. It was the middle of the night and I couldn't sleep. Insomnia had plagued me in the weeks since I'd been back, Levin invading my dreams with knives carving me to pieces until I woke up, screaming for Devon.

Beau had mentioned it once in passing, and I'd been mortified that I'd screamed loud enough for him to hear.

"Oh, just some nightmares," I'd said, blowing it off with a forced laugh. "Sorry to have disturbed you."

But he hadn't laughed. In fact, he'd looked downright serious when he'd said, "I know the name of a great psychiatrist. Talking about it can help."

I hadn't taken him up on it, but I had begun drinking more in the evenings. Wine helped me get to sleep and stay asleep.

I watched the news avidly, looking for any story that might give a clue as to Devon's whereabouts. But it was impossible to tell.

My friends had been wonderful, keeping me busy and trying to make sure I didn't dwell. Things had gone back to normal with Logan and me, which had been a relief. He hadn't been tomcatting like usual, but I didn't consider that a bad thing.

Scott and I had been spending a lot of time together, too, just as friends. I thought he might be interested in more, but I wasn't ready for that. So we just hung out. We went to a few ball games, had dinner, saw a couple of movies, but he hadn't tried to take things further.

It was the Friday before the Fourth of July and he'd convinced me to go to some play at the local university. It had been so awful, we'd left at intermission.

"I don't know what you thought was so bad," he teased as we'd strolled toward his car. "I find naked actors completely normal."

"Well, it was entertaining," I allowed, chuckling. "Just not exactly . . . my taste."

Scott laughed, too. "I'm sorry," he apologized. "I should've done more research on this one before bringing you here."

We'd reached his car and he opened the passenger door for me, as he always did. "It's not a problem," I said. "Certainly something I won't forget anytime soon. Unfortunately."

We shared a laugh and I turned to get in the car, then stopped, glancing behind Scott into the shadows that edged the lot.

"What is it?" he asked, turning to look as well.

I stared hard, but the movement I thought I'd seen didn't come again. I shook my head. "Nothing. Probably just a squirrel or something." I slid into the car.

"The evening is still early," he said. "Want to grab a bite to eat?"

"Yeah, sure."

We ended up at a cozy little restaurant that had outdoor seating, which was perfect for the weather. Summer was in full swing but the evenings could still have a chill to them. The light wrap I had was enough to keep my bare arms warm. I'd worn a cute little dress with strappy heels. Dressing up made me more cheerful, and I'd taken care with my hair and makeup.

Scott seemed to appreciate it, his gaze roving over me as we ate dinner. He kept refilling my glass of wine, telling me tales of when he'd gone into the FBI Academy after college. Some of his mishaps had me laughing until my stomach hurt.

"I can't believe they still let you be an agent," I teased him.

"Well, my aim has gotten a lot better since then," he said with a smile.

It was nice, being with him. Relaxing and easy. No drama, no angst, no bad guys wanting to use me as a punching bag.

It was something to think about.

I passed on dessert, though Scott ordered tiramisu. He insisted I have some.

"There's no way I can eat all this," he said. "C'mon, have a bite."

He scooped a bite and held it out to me. I eyed it, then gave in, leaning forward and letting him feed it to me.

"Mmmm." It was very good and he teased me as he scooped up a few more bites for me.

"I told you it was amazing," he said. His gaze dropped to my lips and a warning bell went off inside my head.

"No more, I'm so full!" I begged off, sitting back in my chair.

As I usually paid my share when we went out, I picked up my purse when the check came, but Scott waved me off.

"I got it," he said.

"Don't be silly. We always go Dutch."

"Not tonight," he said.

Something about the way he said that made me look more closely at him. "Why?" I asked. "Why not tonight?"

"I'm a cop, Ivy," he said with a grin. "Did you think I wouldn't know it's your birthday?"

My cheeks grew warm. "I didn't really tell anyone," I said. Logan was out of town on business and had made me promise I'd go to dinner with him when he got back.

"So you're going to let me buy you dinner," he said. "It's kind of a present for myself as well."

"What do you mean?"

"If I pay, then it's a date. And I'd really like to think of tonight as a date." He shrugged, looking somewhat abashed.

It was sweet, and unexpected, and it caught me off guard. I suddenly realized Scott had dressed nicer than usual. Not that he didn't always look good, but tonight he'd worn a sport coat with jeans, his shoes gleaming from a fresh shine, and he'd shaved, his jaw bereft of any five-o'clock shadow.

"I really appreciate it, thank you," I said as the server retrieved the check and money Scott had put down.

He stood, setting aside his linen napkin and taking my hand as I got to my feet. "I've had a good time tonight," he said. "And I'm really glad I got to spend your birthday with you. So I'll buy, and you can sing instead of me."

I laughed. "Oh no. I promise that you do *not* want to hear me sing."

He grimaced. "That bad?"

"I make yowling cats sound like a symphony of angels."

Scott laughed, slotting our fingers together as we walked to the car. "Well, you couldn't be perfect," he said. "There had to be something wrong with you."

I shook my head. "I'm far from perfect, but even I know that singing is not a talent I possess."

We'd reached the car and he paused in front of me, his expression turning serious. "I think you're about as perfect as it gets," he said.

He was so sincere, my smile faded, too. I was touched that he'd think that of me. I certainly wasn't worthy of being put on a pedestal, but the way he was looking at me made me feel like I was.

As he stepped closer, Scott's hands moved to settle on my waist and it felt like the most natural thing to rest my hands on his shoulders.

"Thanks for my birthday dinner," I said.

"I didn't get you a gift," he said. "Except maybe . . ." He gave me plenty of time to move away, but I didn't. Lowering his head, he kissed me.

It was a good kiss. I was attracted to Scott and we'd become good friends the past few months. His tongue lightly brushed mine, tentative at first, then more sure when I didn't pull away. He moved closer, his hands tightening as his body pressed mine against the car.

Unbidden, Devon flitted through my mind, and a shaft of bitter sorrow hit my gut. And I couldn't be in the moment with Scott when all I was thinking about was Devon.

I pushed gently and Scott lifted his head, breaking off the kiss. He lifted his hand to cup my jaw, his thumb brushing my cheek.

"Sorry," I said.

Scott laughed lightly. "You apologize too much," he said.

"I don't want you to think—"

"Shh," he said. "Don't overthink it. I know it's soon. That's fine. I'm not going anywhere, and there's no rush."

His eyes were warm in the darkness, his touch soft, and I felt safe. I wondered if he still saw me as the damsel in distress, though now there was nothing to save me from. I hoped not. I hoped what he saw when he looked at me was just a normal girl who'd had it rough for a while but was living her life like anybody else.

Scott drove me home and walked me to my door. He didn't try to kiss me again and I told him I'd make him a cake for dessert after our next dinner out.

"It'll be out of a box and the icing from a jar, but hey, it's cake," I said.

"I'd like that," he said, giving my hand a squeeze.

He pressed a kiss to my cheek and was the perfect gentleman. I lingered outside my door and watched him head down the hallway.

He glanced back when he got to the stairs, giving me a crooked smile, then he was gone.

Beau had his door open in a flash.

"So I see we've moved the FBI agent out of the Friend Zone," he said with a knowing smile, crossing his arms as he leaned against the doorjamb.

I laughed. "Beau, do you mind everyone else's business but your own?"

"Hey, I'm just looking out for you," he said.

"I bet."

"You don't want him around anymore for any reason, just let me know. I'll take care of it."

I gave him a weird look. That seemed a strange thing for him to say. "Really, it's okay. But I'll keep that in mind." I stepped back into my apartment. "Good night, Beau."

"'Night, Ivy."

I closed and locked the door behind me, setting aside my purse. The phone with Devon's number sat inside and my fingers itched to touch it.

I hesitated, then grabbed my purse, digging the phone out. I kept it charged at all times, but it had never rung. It just sat there, a constant reminder that Devon *wasn't* calling me, and that I shouldn't call him.

But it was my birthday, so . . .

Before I could change my mind, I punched the buttons to dial the one pre-programmed number. Barely breathing, I waited, wondering if the number still worked and if it did, if Devon would answer.

It rang in my ear . . . then it rang in my apartment.

I nearly screamed, flinging myself backward against the door in a panic and dropping the phone.

Devon stepped out of the shadows.

"You rang?" he asked.

I stared in stunned amazement, speechless.

"Wh-what are you doing here?" I stammered, unable to believe my eyes.

"I'm afraid I left something behind," he said, walking toward me.

My heart had leapt when I'd seen him. Now, it sank.

"You're here because you *left* something? Are you kidding me?"

The half-smile on his face faded away at my furious words.

The sound of my palm striking his face made a loud *crack* in the silent apartment.

I'd hit him as hard as I could, without even thinking about it first. It had just been my immediate reaction. My hand stung something fierce.

Neither of us spoke and he was slow to turn back to me, his icy blue eyes meeting mine.

I was shaking with rage. "How dare you?" I spat at him. "I'm not enough for you. You end us. Then you show up here, months later, because you *forgot* something?"

Devon raised a hand to his jaw, rubbing it slightly.

"I was referring to you," he said. "I came for you. I was . . . quite wrong."

"About what?" I was afraid to hope. He'd disappointed me before.

"About whether or not I want to live without you."

My eyes filled and he blurred in my vision. "What changed your mind?" I asked.

"A particularly lethal knife fight. And as it happens, your face was the one that came to mind. The one I wanted to see one more time. Nothing quite puts things in proper perspective than a brush with death."

"But you said you've nearly died lots of times," I said. "What made this time any different?"

"You made this time different." Devon took my face in his hands.

"I love you, my sweet Ivy. And I'll do whatever I need to do in order to keep you in my life."

"Is this real?" I whispered.

"It's very, very real."

It felt almost like slow motion when he kissed me; the contours of his lips and the touch of his skin against mine felt like coming home.

"I can smell his cologne on you," Devon murmured, his lips moving against mine.

I pulled back slightly. "What?"

"Tonight. The date with the FBI agent. I was watching. I thought I was going to have to kill the bastard if he managed to get an invitation inside for a nightcap."

"Scott is a good friend of mine," I said. "He's . . . helped me."

"I'll bet he has."

I could hear the resentful anger in Devon's voice and it made me step back, out of his embrace.

"I don't know, Devon," I said. "How do I know you won't change your mind again? You were so sure before, and now you've done a one-eighty. What else has changed? Is it safe now?"

"It will be," he said. "I'm putting plans in motion now so we'll not be watching our backs for the rest of our lives."

"What about the rest?" I asked, still worried. I was afraid. It couldn't be as easy as he was making it sound.

"Trust me," he said. "You were right. I've given enough, especially to Vega."

It wasn't just the words, but the way he said them—as though Vega was no longer held in his highest esteem—that convinced me.

"Okay," I said, finally allowing myself to believe. Maybe a happily-ever-after was in the cards for us after all. "Okay, so what's next?"

"I can't stay, darling," he said. "I have to leave, right away, but I'll be back. I'll be back and we'll go away together. A new start on a new life. Together."

He kissed me again, before I could respond, overwhelming me in every way. The heat of his mouth, the firm hold he had on either side of my head, his body hard against mine.

I was breathless when he finally let me go.

"I'll be back tomorrow night," he whispered. "Wait up for me."

And then he was gone. I was left staring at the door, wondering if I'd just imagined all that. Had Devon really come back, told me he loved me, and that he wanted to be with me?

It was amazing. Unbelievable.

Joy spread through me like warm rays of sunshine. I wanted to dance around the apartment, but instead I headed to my bedroom to pack.

I wished Devon could have stayed, but I wasn't about to begrudge him needing to leave tonight. I wanted so badly to call someone and share my happiness, but I knew none of my friends would be glad of Devon's reappearance in my life.

Especially Scott.

I felt a twinge of guilt at that, but what was I to do?

Sleep was difficult, and I found myself awakening again in the middle of the night, my mind spinning.

What would happen when Devon came back? He'd said we'd be leaving. Where would we go? What would we do? What kind of job would he get if he quit working for the Shadow?

These questions and dozens more ran through my head until finally, I got up and went to the kitchen for something to drink. Maybe a glass of wine would help me sleep.

I was reaching for the cupboard when I heard something strange.

I paused, frowning as I listened. I heard it again. The rustle of cloth and the slight tread of a shoe against the hardwood floor in the hallway.

Someone was in the apartment.

CHAPTER
NINETEEN

I moved silently, reaching for the butcher block on the counter and sliding a knife from one of the slots. If I could make it to the door, I could get out and run for help.

Fear was a sharp tang in my mouth and adrenaline poured ice in my veins. I didn't move for a moment, listening. The darkness intensified my other senses, but I heard nothing further.

Sliding along the edge of the counter, I crept toward the hallway. If whoever had broken in had already passed the kitchen entrance, I'd be behind them and could scurry down the hall and out the door.

I stood with my back to the wall, breathing as quietly as I could and listening. My pulse was thundering in my ears as I took a deep breath, readying myself. Deciding it was now or never, I stepped into the hallway . . . and right into the path of the intruder.

"Hello, Ivy. Miss me?"

I stared in stunned horror at Clive.

"No," I said, shaking my head in denial. "No, no. That's impossible. You're dead."

"I'm afraid I'm very much alive," he said, taking a step toward me. I took a jerky step back. "No thanks to you and Devon, of course. Lucky for me, Kansas farmers are so helpful to an injured hunter. It's taken me weeks to recuperate, but I'm ever so glad I didn't kill you before, because I need you now."

Confusion warred with panic. "I don't know what you mean."

"Of course you don't," he said. "But it doesn't matter. You're coming with me."

"The hell I am," I snapped, tightening my grip on the knife in my hand. I lunged, my only advantage that of surprise.

But he was fast, faster than I'd thought he'd be. I sliced him across the chest, but not deep enough to do damage. Then he had my wrist and twisted it in such a way that I had no choice but to release the knife with a pained cry.

"Look at you, drawing blood," Clive bit out.

"Anna would have fought you, too," I retorted. At the mention of his dead wife, Clive flinched. "She would have hated what you've become, what you're doing to me."

His hesitation gave me another instant and I brought my knee up hard, getting him right in the crotch.

Clive let go of me instantly as he dropped to the floor. His body blocked the hallway. I wasted no time scrambling over him. The door was open and it loomed like a beacon for me.

I'd made it two steps when Clive grabbed my ankle and gave it a vicious yank. I fell hard and kicked backward, trying to get away. I made contact with something, because I heard a crunch and a grunt, but he wouldn't let me go. He was pulling me backward, climbing on top of me as I clawed at the carpet, desperate to get away.

Opening my mouth, I drew in a ragged breath and let loose a scream. Surely someone would hear and call the police. I prayed Beau would come out of his door the way he had so many times before. But his door remained firmly closed.

"Fucking bitch," I heard Clive mutter. I heard something clatter to the floor, then felt a sharp prick in the back of my neck.

⁓

Bright lights. That was the first thing I saw when I woke.

I stared at the ceiling, slowly blinking. The thought that being knocked unconscious and waking in an unfamiliar location was becoming a commonplace event in my life flitted briefly through my mind.

Fluorescent lights, the kind you find in a hospital, adorned the ceiling of flat, white tiles. A persistent, steady beeping sound was emanating from something close to me.

Turning my head was more painful than it should have been, and I winced, but I saw what was making the noise. A heart monitor and blood pressure cuff were attached to my left arm.

I tried lifting my arm and realized I was strapped down. My breath caught and I turned to my right, only to see that arm was likewise restrained. In trying to move my legs, I found my ankles held immobile, too.

I was able to lift my head and look around, hoping I was in a hospital. Maybe someone had heard me scream and come to help. Maybe they'd chased Clive off.

But I wasn't in a hospital. And I wasn't alone.

A man in scrubs and a white lab coat stood in the corner, his back to me, messing with something on the counter.

"Hey," I called to him. "Hey, where am I?"

He glanced back at me, but didn't answer. After a moment, he went back to what he was doing.

"Hey, I'm talking to you," I tried again. "Where am I?"

The man walked toward me and I thought for a moment he was going to release me, then I saw the needle and vials in his hands.

"Who are you? What are you doing?" I asked, panic edging into my voice as he swabbed my right arm and I smelled the sharp, antiseptic odor of alcohol.

Again, there was no answer. He tied a rubber tourniquet around my arm and readied the needle.

"Stop! Let me go!" I cried, struggling to get loose. Alarm and panic flooded me as he continued to ignore me.

"Will you be still?"

The stern voice made me whip my head around and my stomach sank when I saw who'd entered the room.

Vega.

Fear morphed into fury. "I should have known," I said, struggling to stay calm. Nothing would be achieved by me losing my cool. Right now, I had to focus on trying to get out of this, preferably alive.

A pinch in my arm made me twist again to see the man was drawing blood from my vein, filling one of the vials he held.

"Your obsession with me is reaching the level of paranoia," I said to Vega. "My blood? Really? You could have just asked."

"And deprive Clive of his opportunity at redemption?" she asked. "I wouldn't think of it."

"*You* sent him after me?" I asked, confused now. "He tried to kill Devon."

"I know," she said with a sigh. "I'm not very pleased with him for that. Devon is far more useful to me than is Clive, which is too bad. He used to be one of my best agents. Then he met that woman, and it spelled the end of him and his usefulness."

"You mean Anna," I said.

Vega shrugged, glancing at the vials the man was filling, one after the other. "Was that her name?" she mused.

I studied her. "You know it was her name. You know Clive fell in love with her."

"A stipulation of all my agents is the lack of familial ties," Vega said. "Did you know that? Clive was the only child of a single father who was killed in a car wreck when he was ten. No siblings. No extended family."

"No one to compete with his loyalty to you when you swooped in to rescue him," I guessed.

A smile played about her thin lips and her gaze returned to mine. "You're an astute woman, Ivy. Ties of loyalty and brotherhood link men in the armed forces. A soldier will put his life on the line for the soldier at his side. But in my business, agents are solitary. Loyalty to queen and country is ephemeral and mercurial, subject to change. But loyalty to a person—especially one to whom they feel indebted—that is concrete and not easily dissuaded."

"You've brainwashed them," I said.

"I saved them," she retorted. "I gave them a purpose and a focus for their lives."

The man interrupted our conversation by removing the needle from my arm and undoing the restraint. Reaching over me, he removed the monitor and restraint on my left arm, too. I rubbed my wrists where the bands had left marks against my skin as he removed the ankle bands, too.

"Why the blood?" I asked, sitting up on the gurney. I was glad that the restraints were gone, but it also made me uneasy. Was Vega just going to let me go?

"When agents cease being useful," Vega said, ignoring my question, "they must be eliminated. Clive was no longer useful—indeed he'd become a dangerous nuisance, targeting another agent as he did, and involving civilians."

"So you're the one who put the hit out on Clive?" I asked, incredulous. "You'd murder the man you said you 'saved'?"

"You say *murder*, I say *terminate his employment*."

"That's just semantics."

Vega turned around and the guy in the lab coat walked out, vials of my blood in his hands. She didn't do anything to stop me, so I slid off the gurney. I had to wait a moment as lightheadedness struck, but then it passed.

"Come with me," she said. "I want to show you something."

I followed her out of the room and into a long, generic-looking hallway. A guard waiting outside the door followed us.

We walked past a couple of closed doors, then Vega opened a third door. Entering behind her, I saw it was empty, save for one wall with a huge window into the adjacent room.

I was surprised to see Clive in the other room. He was pacing, and I could tell he couldn't see us in the window. Was it just one-way, then?

Another man stood in the room with Clive, and he reminded me of a soldier or a guard. He didn't interact with Clive, but merely stared straight ahead, his face expressionless.

"I warned Clive," Vega said. "Warned him that Anna wasn't good for him, that he needed to keep his mind focused on the work and put aside the childish delusions of love and marriage."

"You can't just tell people to turn their feelings off," I said. "It doesn't work like that."

"Doesn't it?" Vega replied, her gaze still on Clive. She sighed. "I suppose you're right. Sometimes drastic measures need to be taken. Clive was suspicious of me, I think, and hid himself and Anna from me." She flashed me a cool smile. "Fortunately, Devon is exceedingly good at finding people."

Looking at her, a sudden thought came to me. "Heinrich poisoned Anna, infected her with that virus. But he knew where to find her because *you* told him."

"Let's just say, I made a strategic move," Vega said. "Heinrich rid me of a problem, and we also got to see firsthand the effects of his virus."

A cold chill crept up my spine. Vega showed absolutely no humanity, no remorse for having served up an innocent woman to a horrible death.

"Does Clive know what you did?" I asked. Somehow I doubted he'd have been so adamant on meting out his revenge if he'd known who exactly was behind Anna's death.

"Of course, if I'd known how completely useless Clive would become, I wouldn't have bothered," she said, ignoring my question. "Now, watch and learn." She brushed past me and exited the room. The guard who'd followed us stepped inside, taking up a post similar to that of the one watching Clive.

It seemed I was supposed to stay here.

Through the window, I saw Vega enter the room with Clive. I drifted back toward the glass to watch.

Clive looked at Vega and straightened. "I was wondering exactly how long I was supposed to remain here."

His voice was tinny, coming through speakers that I hadn't seen somewhere in the room.

"I had business to attend to," Vega replied.

"So do we have a deal?" Clive asked. "I brought you the girl, told you what her blood contained, just as I said I would."

"You've done very well," Vega said.

The relief Clive expressed was nearly palpable to me.

"Brilliant," he said. "Then I can go my own way, and the Shadow, theirs."

He headed for the door, but his way was blocked by the guard.

"It's not that simple, Clive," Vega said.

Clive spun to face her and I saw the fear he was trying to hide.

"I've done everything you asked of me," he said. "All I want is to be left alone to live my life. I'm not going to say anything to anyone or write some tell-all novel."

"Clive, you know I can't just let you walk out of here, knowing what you know," Vega replied, her voice as calm and reasonable as if she were discussing dinner plans.

"What are you going to do?" Clive asked in exasperation. "Kill me? I've proven my loyalty to you and the Shadow over and over again."

"You have indeed," Vega said. "And we are grateful for your service."

Clive stared hard at her, his lips pressed in a thin line, and when she didn't say anything further, he gave her a curt nod. Turning for the door, he saw what I'd seen a moment ago.

The guard had a gun in his hand, pointed right at Clive.

Clive had no chance to react in any way before he was shot. The single bullet was centered in Clive's forehead.

His body crumpled to the floor and I was left staring at Vega, who wasn't even bothering to look at Clive. No . . . she was looking straight through the window at me.

My hands were shaking and I bit my lip to keep from screaming. They'd just killed him in cold blood, for no reason. Even now, Vega was casually stepping over Clive's body as she slipped out the door, careful to not get any blood on the nude pumps she wore.

"Clean this up," she said over her shoulder to the guard, who hastened to obey. A moment later, Vega was back in the room with me.

"Were you watching?" she asked. At my silence, she smiled. "Of course you were. It's a valuable lesson and I hope you learned it well."

"I don't need any lessons," I gritted out, determined not to show my fear to her.

"Oh, you do, actually," Vega said. "Because this was a lesson in what will happen to Devon . . . if you succeed in persuading him to continue this relationship with you."

My blood ran cold. "You don't mean that."

She actually laughed. "After my demonstration, you really think I wouldn't do the same thing to Devon? He's spouting stories of quitting his job, as if he's love-struck and determined to pursue a happily-ever-after."

"But . . . Devon is devoted to you," I said. Her threat to Devon was real and I believed every word. I was desperate to make her not question Devon's loyalty.

"Of course he is," Vega said. "And I want to make sure he always will be. Which is where you come in."

"What do you want?"

"What I *want* is for you to be dead, but my scientists tell me we need to keep you alive—for a while, at least—because your blood is valuable and contains the only vaccine for that virus. And they need access to that vaccine to properly formulate an antidote."

I swallowed. My hands clenched into fists at my sides to stop them from shaking.

"So what I want *you* to do," she continued, "is to break it off with Devon. Say whatever you need to in order to convince him, beyond a doubt, that it's over. You don't want him, you don't need him, and above all, you don't love him. Understood?"

"And if I don't . . ."

"If you don't, then I'll be forced to wonder to whom Devon's loyalty truly lies," she said. "And in my business, there's no room for maybes . . . or quitters."

It couldn't have been plainer if she'd spoken it aloud. If I didn't break it off with Devon—permanently—Vega would kill him.

"So," she said, smiling again as though we were the best of friends, "are we in agreement? And you must be sure to not speak a word of this to Devon."

"Why?" I asked. "Are you afraid he wouldn't be so easy to kill if he knew you for what you really are?"

In an instant, her smile was gone and she was in my space. I was tall, but with her heels on, she had a couple of inches on me. When she spoke, her voice was quiet, as if meant for my ears alone, which made it even more menacing.

"If Devon should come to know what happened here today, then not only will he die, but I will *personally* see that the remainder of your days—numbered though they be—are filled with the kind of pain that will leach your beauty until you're left with looks that make small children run screaming in terror."

Our eyes were locked and I didn't dare look away or show weakness. After a tense moment, she turned and walked away.

I remained where I was, taking a minute to suck in a deep breath to steady my nerves.

"Until we meet again, Ivy," I heard her call to me.

I had only a moment to see her disappearing into an elevator at the end of the hallway before a hood was yanked over my head. Hands grabbed me from behind as I instinctively screamed. There was a sharp prick in my arm and the burn of whatever it was shot into me. A lethargy overtook me, despite the panic and terror pounding in my veins, and I couldn't fight back when I was picked up. I was thrown over a man's shoulder in a fireman's carry, and my eyes slid shut.

When I woke, I was lying on my couch and the sun was streaming through the window.

I would have thought that perhaps it had all been a particularly realistic nightmare, if not for the needle tracks in my arm.

My movements were automatic as I got up, showered, and dressed. It was Saturday and Devon had said he'd be back tonight.

I thought about it all day, but knew there was no way out of the corner Vega had backed me into. The image of her standing impassively by as Clive was shot dead kept going through my mind, only it was Devon instead of Clive.

Part of me was angry with Devon, for choosing this path in the first place. I knew it was irrational, but I couldn't help wondering how he'd thought this would end with Vega and the Shadow. Had he considered that at any point? Or had he assumed he'd be killed in the line of duty so it wouldn't really matter?

And what about me? Vega had made it perfectly clear that she was going to kill me . . . eventually. There was nowhere to go, nowhere to hide from her reach. I had no means of fighting back. I couldn't even use the pages from the journal because no way could Vega be allowed to get her hands on that vaccine formula. Considering how easily Clive had broken into my apartment, I was glad I'd had the foresight to hide the journal pages at Scott's. I should've probably found a way to get them back and hide them somewhere safer.

The idea that Vega would kill me right out from under Devon, just as she had to Clive and Anna, made me shudder. Devon had already gone through losing Kira. How much more damaged would he be if I was killed, too? But if we were no longer together, perhaps he wouldn't even hear of my death.

I didn't cry. I was too stunned, too horrified by the choice I'd been given, which was no choice at all, not really. I'd rather break Devon's heart and see him live than watch him die the way Clive had died.

But what to say to him? I didn't know of anything I could say that he'd believe. I'd wanted this—wanted him—too much for him to think I'd just change my mind.

I was no closer to figuring out what I was going to do when evening fell. I stood in front of my closet, clad only in a matching panty and bra set of nude-colored lace and satin. I surveyed my clothes, wanting to wear something nice, something appropriate for the last time Devon and I would see each other.

The doorbell rang, which I thought was odd. Devon usually let himself in.

I grabbed a robe and threw it on, belting it as I hurried to the door. But when I opened it, Scott was there, not Devon.

"I guess you're not ready yet?" he asked, looking me over with his eyebrows climbing.

And I remembered. "Oh! Yes, we're supposed to go to the fair tonight, and fireworks." We'd planned weeks ago to attend the Veiled Prophet Fair, especially since the headliner for tonight's grandstand was one of my favorite bands.

"How could you forget?" he teased. "And I promise there won't be naked people. Probably."

"Of course I didn't forget," I said, forcing a smile. "Come in."

Scott moved past me into the hallway and I closed the door behind him.

"I was just . . . getting dressed," I said. "Would you like a glass of wine?"

"Sounds great," he said, following me into the kitchen. I poured two glasses and handed one to Scott.

"Cheers," I said, clinking my glass against his before taking a drink. I drank nearly the entire glass before setting down the goblet.

Scott eyed me. "Is everything okay?"

I smiled brightly. "Everything's fine. Great, actually." I took a deep breath. "Scott . . . Devon came back . . . and Clive . . . Clive did, too."

In as succinct a way as possible, I told him everything that had happened last night. From Clive kidnapping me and taking me to Vega, to her harvesting my blood and murdering Clive. And finally, her threat to Devon if he tried to leave the Shadow.

"I don't know what to do," I said. "I have to somehow convince Devon I don't love him when he's going to be here any minute."

"She took your blood?" he asked, making me pause. Of all the things I'd told him, that was the least of my concerns.

"Yeah, but I'm more concerned about how to protect Devon right now."

"I know, but just hold on," he said. "You're saying that Vega—the Shadow—could right now be formulating the only known vaccine for a deadly, airborne virus that they also have?"

"I-I guess," I stammered, suddenly worried at the intense look on his face. He didn't respond, seeming to be lost in thought, so I tried again. "Can you help me? I thought, maybe, if Devon came and found us . . . together . . . I'd be able to convince him to go."

He stared blankly at me for a minute. "Yeah," he said at last. "Yeah, sure. I can do that. So you're not going to tell him about Vega?"

"It could get him killed," I said. "You didn't see her, Scott. She was . . . ruthless. Utterly without emotion or remorse." I shuddered, remembering.

"So how do you want to play this?" he asked.

I shrugged, my face getting hot. "Um, I guess if he found us in bed together, that would help."

"Yeah, that oughta do the trick," he said dryly. "I know it would for me. I just need to make a phone call first, okay?"

I nodded, finishing my wine in one swallow while I waited as Scott slipped outside into the hallway to make his call. When he came back, I led him uneasily down the hallway to my bedroom. We didn't speak as I dropped my robe and climbed under the bed-covers in my bra and panties. Scott removed his shirt and shoes, but left his jeans on. I didn't object.

Scott pulled me into his arms and I didn't resist. "Did they hurt you?" he asked.

I shook my head, his skin warm against my cheek. "No. Clive was a little rough, but all they did was drug me up and take my blood."

"So you didn't see where they took you."

"No."

His arms tightened around me. "I'm glad you're okay."

"Yeah. Me, too."

I tried to keep my eyes open, but found them drooping. I must have fallen asleep, because the next thing I knew, Scott was kissing me. Too groggy and surprised to do anything, I was frozen, his body on top of mine. Then I realized Devon was there and that was why Scott had taken the initiative so abruptly.

He hauled Scott up from the bed and I watched in horror as Devon smashed his fist into Scott's jaw. Scott was unprepared and went careening into the wall. He was up in an instant and tackled Devon, slamming him against the closet door.

"No! Stop!" I clambered out of the bed and ran forward, which was a colossally stupid thing to do when two huge men were trying to kill each other in a small space.

A flying fist hit me almost immediately, making me cry out in pain as I was knocked into a table and fell to the floor. I clutched my side; the corner had dug hard into my ribs, and I tasted blood. My teeth had cut the inside of my mouth.

The men stopped fighting instantly and I felt someone's hands on my back. I was face-first on the carpet, my knees drawn up toward my chest as I sucked in air. I'd known something like this would happen, the two men fighting, it was just very real all of the sudden. As were the things I knew I had to say and do.

"Ivy . . . God . . . are you all right? Let me help you," Scott said.

"Get out of the way, you bloody bastard," Devon snarled. "Don't touch her."

"She's hurt because of you, you sonofabitch," Scott retorted.

I pushed myself painfully up off the floor, grabbing my robe and pulling it hastily on. When I was on my feet, I pushed my hair out of my face and turned toward the two men watching me.

"Shit. You're bleeding," Scott said, but Devon was already there with his pocket square, dabbing at the corner of my mouth.

I took the fabric from him, my thoughts spinning frantically.

"You want to tell me what's going on?" Devon asked me, his voice like cold steel.

Raising my gaze, I met his eyes. "I don't want to go with you."

Nothing changed on his face, not even a flicker of emotion. After a moment, he said, "Because of this?" He motioned to my face.

"Because of . . . a lot of things," I said, improvising on the spot.

"You seemed of a different mind last night."

"Last night?" Scott interrupted. "What's he talking about, Ivy? You were with me, then him?"

I could tell by the look in Devon's eyes that he thought I'd slept with Scott, which was exactly what I wanted.

"You've been gone for months," I said, injecting some anger into my voice. "Then you just show up and tell me you've changed your mind? It's too late, Devon."

"I see," he said, and I could hear anger creeping into his tone as well. "Is that what you call love then? I wasn't aware your feelings were so ephemeral."

"It was exciting, being with you," I said stiffly. "How many women can say they've slept with a spy?"

"More than you'd think," he retorted.

I couldn't help flinching at that.

"Ivy, what's this about?" Scott said. I glanced over to where he stood. "I thought you and Devon were through."

"She's leaving with me," Devon replied, his eyes still on me.

"No, I'm not," I said, panic flitting through me. I had to make him believe it was over. His life depended on it. Even now, I wondered if Vega was somehow listening or watching.

Scott was watching me and I was glad he could improvise so well, but I was at a loss now.

"She's not going anywhere with you," he said to Devon. "Especially if she doesn't want to." He turned back to me. "I'll give you a few minutes to finish this, but don't worry. He won't take you with him if you don't want to go." With one last warning look at Devon, he left the room.

"This is certainly not what I was expecting," Devon said.

"I'm with Scott now. You and I are over, Devon." Afraid he'd see the truth in my eyes, I turned away, searching for more to say that would drive him away. "I think I got the better end of the deal. A new apartment, new clothes, jewelry. Don't you agree?"

"You do like your luxuries."

"Which aren't cheap," I reminded him. I walked to the vanity and sat on the little stool, automatically reaching for my makeup. After flipping open my powder, I brushed a light dusting across my nose.

"You should go," I said. "There's nothing more to say." Eye shadow was next and I chose a color, applying to one eye, then the other. I saw in the mirror as Devon approached me from behind.

There was a tense silence for a moment and I reached for lipstick.

"After all we've been through, all you've told me . . ." He stopped, his lips pressing together in a tight line. "I said I'd change things, try to make a life with you. And now you're saying you don't want this? You don't want us?"

The gritted anger in his voice, the betrayal in his eyes, made me want to cry. Instead, I swallowed my tears and forced myself to keep going.

"I'm sorry, Devon."

"You're sorry."

The lipstick was a deep red slash on my too-white face.

My composure broke. "I said, I'm done!" I cried, slamming my palms flat on the vanity. He had to leave. Now. I couldn't keep this up, couldn't keep hurting him. "Do you want me to show you the scars on my stomach, the one on my back? What more do you want from me?"

"I don't want anything from you. Not anymore." And he was gone.

I felt like a knife had been embedded in my chest. This was really it. I would never see Devon again, would never know if he lived or died. He was entirely in Vega's clutches and there wasn't a thing I could do about it.

I couldn't breathe, couldn't believe the last few minutes had happened.

I'd driven him away, permanently breaking off our relationship and any future with him. Just as Vega had told me to do. I'd brought Devon back into Vega's good graces . . . and safety.

At the cost of the man I loved and everything I'd ever wanted.

Thunder echoed outside as the sky opened up. Rain splattered hard against the window and lightning split the sky.

Devon was gone and this time . . . he wasn't coming back.

Scott suddenly appeared in my doorway. Quickly, I wiped the tears from my cheeks.

"Thanks," I said. "He, um, yeah, he bought it."

Sympathy was etched on Scott's face as he approached me and crouched down. "I'm really sorry, Ivy," he said.

I forced a weak smile. "It's okay. Sometimes you have to do what you have to do, right?"

Now he looked even sadder. "Right. Which is why I hope you'll understand."

I frowned, confused, then saw two other men step into my bedroom. I gripped Scott's arm, afraid.

"Who are you? What do you want?" I asked. Had Vega sent

them? Would they kill me and Scott? His death would be on my hands. He wouldn't even be here if it wasn't for me.

"They're here to take you into protective custody," Scott said.

My gaze whipped to his. "What do you mean?"

"Ivy, you said yourself that this Vega person—her organization—not only has a deadly virus, but now the only known vaccine." He paused. "Except for you."

I stared at him, horrified.

You can't just have the vaccine up and walking about now, can you.

Heinrich's words seemed prophetic, though it wasn't the Shadow taking me—it was my own government. And under the guise of "protecting" me.

"How could you do this to me?" I asked Scott, my voice a painful whisper.

"I'm sorry," he said. "I really am, but it's like you said, sometimes you have to do what you have to do." His expression was pained but resolute. Turning to the men, he nodded and they moved to flank me as he stepped away.

I shot to my feet, but they each gripped an arm. "Scott, no, please, don't let them take me!" I struggled against them, but it was no use. Their hold was too tight.

Scott appeared in front of me again, only this time he held a needle.

"This will make things easier," he said. "Don't fight it, okay? We'll protect you. I promise."

I drew breath to scream, but a hand was clapped over my mouth and I could only watch, immobilized, as Scott pressed the needle into my flesh. His face swam in my vision and his words sounded like they were spoken underwater.

"I'm sorry, Ivy . . ."

EPILOGUE

Devon stood in the hallway, still stunned at all Ivy had said to him. The rage that had flooded him when he'd walked in and seen the FBI agent on top of her—kissing her, touching her—still sizzled in his veins. His hands curled into fists.

His gaze settled on the door across the hallway, and he didn't bother knocking as he went into the apartment.

Beau glanced up and got to his feet. "Hey, man—"

Devon grabbed him by the collar of his shirt and slammed him against the wall. "Why the *bloody* hell didn't you tell me she was fucking the FBI agent?"

Beau moved fast, pushing his hands between Devon's arms and shoving outward, breaking Devon's hold. In another second, he'd slipped from his position against the wall and stood behind Devon.

"What the hell, man?"

Devon had already spun around, but didn't lunge for him again. "Ivy just told me to sod off," he ground out.

Beau seemed stunned. "No way. Are you shitting me?"

Throwing up his hands, Devon turned and paced a few steps away. "I walked in on her and . . . the agent." He had a name but Devon didn't bother trying to remember what it was.

"That's not possible," Beau said, shaking his head. "He just escaped the Friend Zone last night. No way has she been sleeping with him. I'd know."

"What happened last night?"

"He kissed her *cheek*, man, that's it. First time I've seen them kiss at all."

"Where were you? I stopped by when I left her apartment and you were gone."

"Had a job," Beau said, heading into the kitchen and grabbing a bottle of beer from the fridge. He popped off the tab and handed it to Devon before taking another for himself. "Flight just got back a couple of hours ago."

"The CIA working you too hard?" Devon mocked.

"Damn sight less boring than watching your lady, which you owe me for. Don't think I won't collect."

"Then explain to me why she just kicked me out."

"Did she really?"

Devon nodded, taking a long swig of the beer before replying. "Said she was over it. Over me." Saying the words caused an actual physical pain inside his gut. Beau's gaze was piercing, so he looked away.

"That doesn't jive," Beau said, shaking his head. "She's been moping for weeks. When she has nightmares, she screams for you, not the FBI agent, and not the BFF."

"Nightmares?" Devon asked, frowning.

"Yeah, man. She's been having them less than at first, but still at least once a week."

"Did she have one last night?" Maybe that's what changed. Maybe she'd gotten scared and decided she'd had enough.

"I don't know," Beau said. "I haven't checked the tapes." He headed into one of the bedrooms he'd converted into an office and Devon followed.

Four screens were set up, all with various views from cameras placed strategically around the building. After Beau fiddled with the computer for a few moments, recorded images time-stamped from the previous night scrolled across the screens.

Both Devon and Beau watched the footage speed by, the camera view on the third screen of particular note, since it was a view of the hallway inside Ivy's apartment.

"Wait, pause it," Devon said, but Beau was already reaching for the mouse, having seen what Devon had.

"Who the hell is that?" Beau asked, advancing the screen frame-by-frame. A man had entered the apartment in the dead of night.

The way he moved down the hallway, right to the room where Devon knew Ivy had been sleeping, sent a chill down his spine.

He didn't reply to Beau and they both watched in stiff silence as the man passed the kitchen, then as Ivy peeked from the kitchen, only to be attacked by the man. The fight was silent on the screen and it was only when Ivy was unconscious and slung over the man's shoulder did Devon get a clear view of his face.

Clive.

"He's supposed to be dead," Devon said. "I killed him."

"You *thought* you killed him."

Guilt burned like acid in Devon's stomach. Ivy had been attacked in her own home, a place where she was supposed to be safe. And he couldn't blame Beau. It was *his* responsibility to keep Ivy safe, not his friend's.

"How did she get back?" he asked.

Beau sped up the footage until another man appeared a couple of hours later, also carrying an unconscious Ivy. It wasn't Clive.

"Recognize him?" Beau asked, pausing the video.

Devon looked closely. The face did look familiar, but he couldn't place it. "Print out a copy," he said.

Beau clicked a few times, zooming in on his face, and the printer spit out the grainy black-and-white image.

"I'm sorry, man," Beau said, scrubbing a hand over his face. "Of all the nights for me to be gone."

"It's not your fault," Devon said. Cold terror gripped him at the thought of what could have happened to her. Images of Kira's broken and bloody body flitted through his mind. Last night, that could have been Ivy.

"That explains her sudden change of heart," Beau said. "Wonder where they took her."

"And why Clive didn't kill her," Devon added, thinking aloud.

"Yeah, not to be morbid, but if they got in to grab her, there's no purpose to keep her alive, is there," Beau said, and there was a very good reason why that wasn't a question. He was right. Ivy had no purpose, especially if she was no longer seeing Devon. So why keep her alive?

But even as Devon thought it, the answer came to him.

"No. He didn't. He wouldn't," he murmured aloud. But he already knew the truth.

"What?"

Devon glanced at Beau. "He used her. Clive was using her as a bargaining chip for his own life."

"Why her? What use is she?"

"Her blood," Devon said grimly. "The antibodies in her blood. That's what he needed, and that's why she's still alive." Devon trusted fewer people than fingers on his right hand, but Beau was one of them. He'd kept a close eye on Ivy for months, ever since Clive had shown his face again. It had been pure bad luck that he'd been gone last night.

"Which means your secret is out," Beau replied. "Someone else knows about her."

Their eyes met in mutual understanding.

"What're you going to do?" Beau asked.

"I need to find Clive and see who he told. He was the only other person who knew."

"What about Ivy?"

"Get a security system installed, send me the bill," Devon said. "Have the feed sent here, and accessible to me remotely."

"Consider it done."

"The FBI agent," Devon mused. "He could be useful. He did an adequate job before, protecting her. At least he'd be a trained and armed escort." Jealousy bit deep at the thought of Ivy being in close company with the man.

"That sucks, man," Beau said, shaking his head. He took another pull of his beer.

Devon ruthlessly kept his emotions from his face and voice when he replied. "It's nothing that can be helped. I have to find out who knows, and plug the leak." A euphemism, but one they both understood.

"So you're just going to let some other guy move in on your lady? I thought you were quitting this oh-so-glamorous lifestyle and settling down." Beau's sarcasm was thick. Both of them knew this line of work sucked and had an expiration date.

"Considering what she's been through because of me, I think her tossing me out was one of the smartest things she could've done." The video of Ivy struggling in vain to fight off Clive would remain with Devon for a long time.

"Don't give me that bullshit British martyr crap," Beau scoffed. "She loves you. You love her. Get your shit together and go live happily-fucking-ever-after."

Devon's lips twisted. "If she doesn't fall in love with the agent first," he said. "Speaking of which, she used him to push me away tonight, so some repair needs to be done there." He'd been a bloody idiot, falling for it. Now that he was looking at it outside the prism of emotion, he remembered seeing dots of sweat on her brow when he'd walked in. Her body had been stiff, and not in a way that said she'd been enjoying the agent's attention.

Then after her big speech, what had she done? She'd put on her makeup, just like she had back home in Kansas. Her automatic defense mechanism. All of it, right under his nose as plain as day, and he'd been too blinded by rage and jealousy to see it.

"Now I'm a fucking love doctor? Jesus Christ."

Beau's exasperation was a complete put-on and Devon knew it. Beau loved nothing more than sticking his nose into other people's business. His curiosity and inability to leave things alone were just a few of the reasons they'd met in the first place, and why he was an excellent intelligence agent.

Devon drank the last of his beer, then tossed the empty bottle in the trash can nearby. "I've got work to do," he said. "Keep me informed." He cast one last look at the live feed from inside Ivy's apartment. He'd been tempted to wire the whole place, but had resisted the urge, not wanting to completely invade her privacy.

He wanted to go back to her, tell her he'd seen what happened, ask her why she hadn't told him the truth—yet another mystery. Was she trying to protect him somehow? Or perhaps she really thought all this would stop if she ended their relationship.

"Hold on, what's this?"

He'd just caught sight of two men going into her apartment. Another two waited outside in the corridor.

"What the hell—" Beau had seen it, too.

They watched in silence as the men walked toward her bedroom. A few moments later, they came out, one of them with Ivy slung over his shoulder. The agent brought up the rear, looking completely unfazed by this turn of events.

Devon's gun was out of its holster and in his hand before he'd even thought about the action. Beau's hand locked around his wrist.

"Hold on, man, be cool," he said. "You can't go out there shooting at these guys."

"Why the bloody hell not?" Devon retorted. "They've got Ivy." He yanked his arm free, but Beau scrambled to block his path.

"Because there's five of them and two of us," Beau said urgently.

"Not a problem. Out of my way."

"And Ivy might get hurt if we go out there guns blazing! Look," he grabbed Devon's arm again, "one of them has a badge on his belt. FBI." He pointed to the screen. "They'll all be armed. You getting killed won't help Ivy, and neither will you offing a bunch of FBI agents."

"The agent betrayed her," Devon said bitterly. "I'll kill him for that."

"Agreed, and I'll help, but we gotta know more first. Like why they want her. Is it because of you?"

Devon had a sinking feeling he knew why. Ivy had trusted the agent, had told him about the virus and the vaccine in her blood, and now they were kidnapping her. It didn't take a genius to put two and two together.

"I'll be in touch," he said to Beau. Minutes later, he was in his car and heading toward the one person who might know where Ivy had been taken. The only problem was that Devon no longer trusted her.

Vega.

Acknowledgments

Thank you to Kele Moon for being an awesome sounding board for me.

Thank you to Nicole for crashing through this manuscript, twice, and being able to put into words what I really needed to hear.

Thank you to Shannon for being honest and willing to drop your entire TBR list when I needed you.

Thank you to Melody Guy, for being so Type A it hurts (in a good way).

Thank you to my BFFs, Nicole and Leslie, for always being available and willing to read, and reread, and reread again.

Thanks, as always, to my wonderful family who didn't commit me to the loony bin as I was stressing writing this book.

Thank you to Kendra Elliot for making sure everything passed the bullshit test.

Thank you to Melinda Leigh for listening to me whine and moan.

Thank you to my amazing editor, Maria Gomez, for her endless cheer and encouragement, her extremely deft handling of sensitive issues, and most of all for her unwavering belief in me and my writing.

And thank you to the team of awesome people at Montlake Romance. You all are a true pleasure to work with.

About the Author

Photo © 2014 Karen Lynn

Tiffany Snow has been reading romance novels since she was too young to read romance novels. After a career working in the information technology field, Tiffany now has her dream job of writing full time.

Tiffany makes her home in the Midwest with her husband and two daughters. She can be reached at Tiffany@TiffanyASnow.com. Visit her on her website, www.Tiffany-Snow.com, to keep up with her latest projects.